AGAINST THE SHADOWEN

Even with the silver dust exploding all through them, the Shadowen came on. Despairing, Cogline used the last of his power, igniting a wall of flame that brought a temporary halt to their advance. Swiftly he darted inside and snatched the Druid history from its place. *Now we'll see!*

He barely made the door again before the Shadowen were through the wall and on him. He heard Rimmer Dall screaming at them. There was nowhere to run and no point in trying, so he simply stood his ground, clutching the book to his chest, a scarecrow in tattered robes before a whirlwind. His attackers came on.

When they were on him, as his body was about to be ripped apart, he felt the rune marking on the book flare to life. Brilliant fire burst forth. Everything within fifty feet was consumed. *It remains for you now, Walker Boh,* was Cogline's last thought.

He disappeared in the flames.

By Terry Brooks

The Magic Kingdom of Landover
MAGIC KINGDOM FOR SALE—SOLD!
THE BLACK UNICORN
WIZARD AT LARGE
THE TANGLE BOX
WITCHES' BREW
A PRINCESS OF LANDOVER

Shannara
FIRST KING OF SHANNARA
THE SWORD OF SHANNARA
THE ELFSTONES OF SHANNARA
THE WISHSONG OF SHANNARA

The Heritage of Shannara
THE SCIONS OF SHANNARA
THE DRUID OF SHANNARA
THE ELF QUEEN OF SHANNARA
THE TALISMANS OF SHANNARA

The Voyage of the *Jerle Shannara*
ILSE WITCH
ANTRAX
MORGAWR

High Druid of Shannara
JARKA RUUS
TANEQUIL
STRAKEN

The Genesis of Shannara
ARMAGEDDON'S CHILDREN
THE ELVES OF CINTRA
THE GYPSY MORPH

Legends of Shannara
BEARERS OF THE BLACK STAFF

THE WORLD OF SHANNARA

Word and Void
RUNNING WITH THE DEMON
A KNIGHT OF THE WORD
ANGEL FIRE EAST

SOMETIMES THE MAGIC WORKS:
LESSONS FROM A WRITING LIFE

STAR WARS®:
EPISODE I THE PHANTOM MENACE™

Books published by The Random House Publishing Group are available at quantity discounts on bulk purchases for premium, educational, fund-raising, and special sales use. For details, please call 1-800-733-3000.

THE DRUID OF SHANNARA

Book Two of
The Heritage of Shannara

Terry Brooks

A Del Rey® Book
BALLANTINE BOOKS • NEW YORK

FIC
BRO   — Fantasy
V.5

Sale of this book without a front cover may be unauthorized. If this book is coverless, it may have been reported to the publisher as "unsold or destroyed" and neither the author nor the publisher may have received payment for it.

A Del Rey® Book
Published by The Random House Publishing Group
Copyright © 1991 by Terry Brooks

All rights reserved.

Published in the United States by Del Rey Books, an imprint of The Random House Publishing Group, a division of Random House, Inc., New York, and simultaneously in Canada by Random House of Canada Limited, Toronto.

Del Rey is a registered trademark and the Del Rey colophon is a trademark of Random House, Inc.

www.delreybooks.com

Cover art by Keith Parkinson

Map by Shelly Shapiro

Library of Congress Catalog Card Number: 90-42424

ISBN 0-345-37559-9

Manufactured in the United States of America

First Hardcover Edition: March 1991
First Mass Market Edition: March 1992

OPM 29 28 27 26 25

To Laurie and Peter,
for their love, support, and encouragement
in all things

I

The King of the Silver River stood at the edge of the Gardens that had been his domain since the dawn of the age of faerie and looked out over the world of mortal men. What he saw left him sad and discouraged. Everywhere the land sickened and died, rich black earth turning to dust, grassy plains withering, forests becoming huge stands of deadwood, and lakes and rivers either stagnating or drying away. Everywhere the creatures who lived upon the land sickened and died as well, unable to sustain themselves as the nourishment they relied upon grew poisoned. Even the air had begun to turn foul.

And all the while, the King of the Silver River thought, *the Shadowen grow stronger.*

His fingers reached out to brush the crimson petals of the cyclamen that grew thick about his feet. Forsythia clustered just beyond, dogwood and cherry farther back, fuchsia and hibiscus, rhododendrons and dahlias, beds of iris, azaleas, daffodils, roses, and a hundred other varieties of flowers and flowering plants that were always in bloom, a profusion of colors that stretched away into the distance until lost from sight. There were animals to be seen as well, both large and small, creatures whose evolution could be traced back to that distant time when all things lived in harmony and peace.

In the present world, the world of the Four Lands and the Races that had evolved out of the chaos and destruction of the Great Wars, that time was all but forgotten. The King of the Silver River was its sole remnant. He had been alive when the world was new and its first creatures were just being born. He had been young then, and there had been many like him. Now he was old and he was the last of his kind. Everything that had been, save for the Gardens in which he lived, had passed away. The Gardens alone survived, changeless, sustained by the magic of faerie. The Word had given the Gardens to the King of the Silver River and told him to tend them, to keep them as a reminder of what had once been and what might one day be again. The world without would evolve as it must, but the Gardens would remain forever the same.

Even so, they were shrinking. It was not so much physical as spiritual. The boundaries of the Gardens were fixed and unalterable, for the Gardens existed in a plane of being unaffected by changes in the world of mortal men. The Gardens were a presence rather than a place. Yet that presence was diminished by the sickening of the world to which it was tied, for the work of the Gardens and their tender was to keep that world strong. As the Four Lands grew poisoned, the work became harder, the effects of that work grew shorter, and the boundaries of human belief and trust in its existence—always somewhat marginal— began to fail altogether.

The King of the Silver River grieved that this should be. He did not grieve for himself; he was beyond that. He grieved for the people of the Four Lands, the mortal men and women for whom the magic of faerie was in danger of being lost forever. The Gardens had been their haven in the land of the Silver River for centuries, and he had been the spirit friend who protected its people. He had watched over them, had given them a sense of peace and well-being that transcended physical boundaries, and gave promise that benevolence and goodwill were still accessible in some corners of the world to all. Now that was ended. Now he could protect no one. The evil of the Shadowen, the poison they had inflicted upon the Four Lands, had eroded his own strength until he was virtually sealed within his Gardens, powerless to go to the aid of those he had worked so long to protect.

He stared out into the ruin of the world for a time as his despair worked its relentless will on him. Memories played hide-and-seek in his mind. The Druids had protected the Four Lands once. But the Druids were gone. A handful of descendents of the Elven house of Shannara had been champions of the Races for generations, wielding the remnants of the magic of faerie. But they were all dead.

He forced his despair away, replacing it with hope. The Druids could come again. And there were new generations of the old house of Shannara. The King of the Silver River knew most of what was happening in the Four Lands even if he could not go out into them. Allanon's shade had summoned a scattering of Shannara children to recover the lost magic, and perhaps they yet would if they could survive long enough to find a means to do so. But all of them had been placed in extreme peril. All were in danger of dying, threatened in the east, south, and west by the Shadowen and in the north by Uhl Belk, the Stone King.

The old eyes closed momentarily. He knew what was needed to save the Shannara children—an act of magic, one so powerful and intricate that nothing could prevent it from succeeding, one that would transcend the barriers that their enemies had created, that would break past the screen of deceit and lies that hid everything from the four on whom so much depended.

Yes, *four*, not three. Even Allanon did not understand the whole of what was meant to be.

He turned and made his way back toward the center of his refuge. He let the songs of the birds, the fragrances of the flowers, and the warmth of the air soothe him as he walked and he drew in through his senses the color and taste and feel of all that lay about him. There was virtually nothing that he could not do within his Gardens. Yet his magic was needed without. He knew what was required. In preparation he took the form of the old man that showed himself occasionally to the world beyond. His gait became an unsteady shamble, his breathing wheezed, his eyes dimmed, and his body ached with the feelings of life fading. The birdsong stopped, and the small animals that had crowded close edged quickly away. He forced himself to separate from everything he had evolved into, receding into what he might have been, needing momentarily to feel human mortality in order to know better how to give that part of himself that was needed.

When he reached the heart of his domain, he stopped. There was a pond of clearest water fed by a small stream. A unicorn drank from it. The earth that cradled the pond was dark and rich. Tiny, delicate flowers that had no name grew at the water's edge; they were the color of new snow. A small, intricately formed tree lifted out of a scattering of violet grasses at the pond's far end, its delicate green leaves laced with red. From a pair of massive rocks, streaks of colored ore shimmered brightly in the sunshine.

The King of the Silver River stood without moving in the presence of the life that surrounded him and willed himself to become one with it. When he had done so, when everything had threaded itself through the human form he had taken as if joined by bits and pieces of invisible lacing, he reached out to gather it all in. His hands, wrinkled human skin and brittle bones, lifted and summoned his magic, and the feelings of age and time that were the reminders of mortal existence disappeared.

The little tree came to him first, uprooted, transported, and set down before him, the framework of bones on which he would build. Slowly it bent to take the shape he desired, leaves folding close against the branches, wrapping and sealing away. The earth came next, handfuls lifted by invisible scoops to place against the tree, padding and defining. Then came the ores for muscle, the waters for fluids, and the petals of the tiny flowers for skin. He gathered silk from the unicorn's mane for hair and black pearls for eyes. The magic twisted and wove, and slowly his creation took form.

When he was finished, the girl who stood before him was perfect in every way but one. She was not yet alive.

He cast about momentarily, then selected the dove. He took it out of the air and placed it still living inside the girl's breast where it became her heart. Quickly he moved forward to embrace her and breathed his own life into her. Then he stepped back to wait.

The girl's breast rose and fell, and her limbs twitched. Her eyes fluttered open, coal black as they peered out from her delicate white features. She was small boned and finely wrought like a piece of paper art smoothed and shaped so that the edges and corners were replaced by curves. Her hair was so white it seemed silver; there was a glitter to it that suggested the presence of that precious metal.

"Who am I?" she asked in a soft, lilting voice that whispered of tiny streams and small night sounds.

"You are my daughter," the King of the Silver River answered, discovering within himself the stirring of feelings he had thought long since lost.

He did not bother telling her that she was an elemental, an earth child created of his magic. She could sense what she was from the instincts with which he had endowed her. No other explanation was needed.

She took a tentative step forward, then another. Finding that she could walk, she began to move more quickly, testing her abilities in various ways as she circled her father, glancing cautiously, shyly at the old man as she went. She looked around curiously, taking in the sights, smells, sounds, and tastes of the

Gardens, discovering in them a kinship that she could not immediately explain.

"Are these Gardens my mother?" she asked suddenly, and he told her they were. "Am I a part of you both?" she asked, and he told her yes.

"Come with me," he said gently.

Together, they walked through the Gardens, exploring in the manner of a parent and child, looking into flowers, watching for the quick movement of birds and animals, studying the vast, intricate designs of the tangled undergrowth, the complex layers of rock and earth, and the patterns woven by the threads of the Gardens' existence. She was bright and quick, interested in everything, respectful of life, caring. He was pleased with what he saw; he found that he had made her well.

After a time, he began to show her something of the magic. He demonstrated his own first, only the smallest bits and pieces of it so as not to overwhelm her. Then he let her test her own against it. She was surprised to learn that she possessed it, even more surprised to discover what it could do. But she was not hesitant about using it. She was eager.

"You have a name," he told her. "Would you like to know what it is?"

"Yes," she answered, and stood looking at him alertly.

"Your name is Quickening." He paused. "Do you understand why?"

She thought a moment. "Yes," she answered again.

He led her to an ancient hickory whose bark peeled back in great, shaggy strips from its trunk. The breezes cooled there, smelling of jasmine and begonia, and the grass was soft as they sat together. A griffin wandered over through the tall grasses and nuzzled the girl's hand.

"Quickening," the King of the Silver River said. "There is something you must do."

Slowly, carefully he explained to her that she must leave the Gardens and go out into the world of men. He told her where it was that she must go and what it was that she must do. He talked of the Dark Uncle, the Highlander, and the nameless other, of the Shadowen, of Uhl Belk and Eldwist, and of the Black Elfstone. As he spoke to her, revealing the truth behind who and what she was, he experienced an aching within his breast that was decidedly human, part of himself that had been submerged for many centuries. The ache brought a sadness that threatened to cause his voice to break and his eyes to tear. He stopped once in surprise to fight back against it. It required some effort to resume speaking. The girl watched him without comment— intense, introspective, expectant. She did not argue with what he told her and she did not question it. She simply listened and accepted.

When he was done, she stood up. "I understand what is expected of me. I am ready."

But the King of the Silver River shook his head. "No, child, you are not. You will discover that when you leave here. Despite who you are and what you can do, you are vulnerable nevertheless to things against which I cannot protect you. Be careful then to protect yourself. Be on guard against what you do not understand."

"I will," she replied.

He walked with her to the edge of the Gardens, to where the world of men began, and together they stared out at the encroaching ruin. They stood without speaking for a very long time before she said, "I can tell that I am needed there."

He nodded bleakly, feeling the loss of her already though she had not yet departed. *She is only an elemental,* he thought and knew immediately that he was wrong. She was a great deal more. As much as if he had given birth to her, she was a part of him.

"Goodbye, Father," she said suddenly and left his side.

She walked out of the Gardens and disappeared into the world beyond. She did not kiss him or touch him in parting. She simply left, because that was all she knew to do.

The King of the Silver River turned away. His efforts had wearied him, had drained him of his magic. He needed time to rest. Quickly he shed his human image, stripping away the false covering of skin and bones, washing himself clean of its memories and sensations, and reverting to the faerie creature he was.

Even so, what he felt for Quickening, his daughter, the child of his making, stayed with him.

II

Walker Boh came awake with a shudder.

Dark Uncle.

The whisper of a voice in his mind jerked him back from the edge of the black pool into which he was sliding, pulled him from the inky dark into the gray fringes of the light, and he started so violently that the muscles of his legs cramped. His head snapped up from the pillow of his arm, his eyes slipped open, and he stared blankly ahead. There was pain all through his body, endless waves of it. The pain wracked him as if he had been touched by a hot iron, and he curled tightly into himself in a futile effort to ease it. Only his right arm remained outstretched, a heavy and cumbersome thing that no longer belonged to him, fastened forever to the floor of the cavern on which he lay, turned to stone to the elbow.

The source of the pain was there.

He closed his eyes against it, willing it to disperse, to disappear. But he lacked the strength to command it, his magic almost gone, dissipated by his struggle to resist the advancing poison of the Asphinx. It was seven days now since he had come into the Hall of Kings in search of the Black Elfstone, seven days since he had found instead the deadly creature that had been placed there to snare him.

Oh, yes, he thought feverishly. Definitely to snare him.

But by whom? By the Shadowen or by someone else? Who now had possession of the Black Elfstone?

He recalled in despair the events that had brought him to this end. There had been the summons from the shade of Allanon, dead three hundred years, to the heirs of the Shannara magic: his nephew Par Ohmsford, his cousin Wren Ohmsford, and himself. They had received the summons and a visit from the once-

Druid Cogline urging them to heed it. They had done so, assembling at the Hadeshorn, ancient resting place of the Druids, where Allanon had appeared to them and charged them with separate undertakings that were meant to combat the dark work of the Shadowen who were using magic of their own to steal away the life of the Four Lands. Walker had been charged with recovering Paranor, the disappeared home of the Druids, and with bringing back the Druids themselves. He had resisted this charge until Cogline had come to him again, this time bearing a volume of the Druid Histories which told of a Black Elfstone which had the power to retrieve Paranor. That in turn had led him to the Grimpond, seer of the earth's and mortal men's secrets.

He searched the gloom of the cavern about him, the doors to the tombs of the Kings of the Four Lands dead all these centuries, the wealth piled before the crypts in which they lay, and the stone sentinels that kept watch over their remains. Stone eyes stared out of blank faces, unseeing, unheeding. He was alone with their ghosts.

He was dying.

Tears filled his eyes, blinding him as he fought to hold them back. He was such a fool!

Dark Uncle. The words echoed soundlessly, a memory that taunted and teased. The voice was the Grimpond's, that wretched, insidious spirit responsible for what had befallen him. It was the Grimpond's riddles that had led him to the Hall of Kings in search of the Black Elfstone. The Grimpond must have known what awaited him, that there would be no Elfstone but the Asphinx instead, a deadly trap that would destroy him.

And why had he thought it would be otherwise? Walker asked himself bleakly. Didn't the Grimpond hate him above all others? Hadn't it boasted to Walker that it was sending him to his doom by giving him what he asked for? Walker had simply gone out of his way to accommodate the spirit, anxiously rushing off to greet the death that he had been promised, blithely believing that he could protect himself against whatever evil he might encounter. Remember? he chided himself. Remember how confident you were?

He convulsed as the poison burned into him. Well and good. But where was his confidence now?

He forced himself to his knees and bent down over the opening in the cavern floor where his hand was pinned to the stone. He could just make out the remains of the Asphinx, the snake's stone body coiled about his own stone arm, the two of them forever joined, fastened to the rock of the mountain. He tightened his mouth and pulled up the sleeve of his cloak. His arm was hard and unyielding, gray to the elbow, and streaks of gray worked their way upward toward his shoulder. The process was slow, but steady. His entire body was turning to stone.

Not that it mattered if it did, he thought, because he would starve to death long before that happened. Or die of thirst. Or of the poison.

He let the sleeve fall back into place, covering the horror of what he had become. Seven days gone. What little food he'd brought with him had been consumed almost immediately, and he'd drunk the last of his water two days ago. His strength was failing rapidly now. He was feverish most of the time, his lucid periods growing shorter. He had struggled against what was happening at first, trying to use his magic to banish the poison from his body, to restore his hand and arm to flesh and blood. But his magic had failed him completely. He had worked at freeing his arm from the stone flooring, thinking that it might be pried loose in some way. But he was held fast, a condemned man with no hope of release. Eventually his exhaustion had forced him to sleep, and as the days passed he had slept more often, slipping further and further away from wanting to come awake.

Now, as he knelt in a huddle of darkness and pain, salvaged momentarily from the wreckage of his dying by the voice of the Grimpond, he realized with terrifying certainty that if he went to sleep again it would be for good. He breathed in and out rapidly, choking back his fear. He must not let that happen. He must not give up.

He forced himself to think. As long as he could think, he reasoned, he would not fall asleep. He retraced in his mind his conversation with the Grimpond, hearing again the spirit's words, trying anew to decipher their meaning. The Grimpond had not named the Hall of Kings in describing where the Black Elfstone could be found. Had Walker simply jumped to the wrong conclusion? Had he been deliberately misled? Was there any truth in what he had been told?

Walker's thoughts scattered in confusion, and his mind refused to respond to the demands he placed on it. He closed his eyes in despair, and it was with great difficulty that he forced them open again. His clothes were chill and damp with his own sweat, and his body shivered within them. His breathing was

ragged, his vision blurred, and it was growing increasingly difficult to swallow. So many distractions—how could he think?
He wanted simply to lie down and . . .

He panicked, feeling the urgency of his need threaten to swallow him up. He shifted his body, forcing his knees to scrape
against the stone until they bled. A little more pain might help
keep me awake, he thought. Yet he could barely feel it.

He forced his thoughts back to the Grimpond. He envisioned
the wraith laughing at his plight, taking pleasure at it. He heard
the taunting voice calling out to him. Anger gave him a measure
of strength. There was something that he needed to recall, he
thought desperately. There was something that the Grimpond
had told him that he must remember.

Please, don't let me fall asleep!

The Hall of Kings did not respond to the urgency of his plea;
the statues remained silent, disinterested, and oblivious. The
mountain waited.

I have to break free! he howled wordlessly.

And then he remembered the visions, or more specifically
the first of the three that the Grimpond had shown him, the one
in which he had stood on a cloud above the others of the little
company that had gathered at the Hadeshorn in answer to the
summons of the shade of Allanon, the one in which he had said
that he would sooner cut off his hand than bring back the Druids
and then lifted his arm to show that he had done exactly that.

He remembered the vision and recognized its truth.

He banished the reaction it provoked in horrified disbelief
and let his head droop until it was resting on the cavern stone.
He cried, feeling the tears run down his cheeks, the sides of his
face, stinging his eyes as they mingled with his sweat. His body
twisted with the agony of his choices.

No! No, he would not!

Yet he knew he must.

His crying turned to laughter, chilling in its madness as it
rolled out of him into the emptiness of the tomb. He waited until
it expended itself, the echoes fading into silence, then looked
up again. His possibilities had exhausted themselves; his fate
was sealed. If he did not break free now, he knew he never
would.

And there was only one way to do so.

He hardened himself to the fact of it, walling himself away
from his emotions, drawing from some final reserve the last of
his strength. He cast about the cavern floor until he found what

he needed. It was a rock that was approximately the size and shape of an axe-blade, jagged on one side, hard enough to have survived intact its fall from the chamber ceiling where it had been loosened by the battle four centuries earlier between Allanon and the serpent Valg. The rock lay twenty feet away, clearly beyond reach of any ordinary man. But not him. He summoned a fragment of the magic that remained to him, forcing himself to remain steady during its use. The rock inched forward, scraping as it moved, a slow scratching in the cavern's silence. Walker grew light-headed from the strain, the fever burning through him, leaving him nauseated. Yet he kept the rock moving closer.

At last it was within reach of his free hand. He let the magic slip away, taking long moments to gather himself. Then he stretched out his arm to the rock, and his fingers closed tightly about it. Slowly he gathered it in, finding it impossibly heavy, so heavy in fact that he was not certain he could manage to lift it let alone . . .

He could not finish the thought. He could not dwell on what he was about to do. He dragged the rock over until it was next to him, braced himself firmly with his knees, took a deep breath, raised the rock overhead, hesitated for just an instant, then in a rush of fear and anguish brought it down. It smashed into the stone of his arm between elbow and wrist, hammering it with such force that it jarred his entire body. The resulting pain was so agonizing that it threatened to render him unconscious. He screamed as waves of it washed through him; he felt as if he were being torn apart from the inside out. He fell forward, gasping for breath, and the axe-blade rock dropped from his nerveless fingers.

Then he realized that something had changed.

He pushed himself upright and looked down at his arm. The blow had shattered the stone limb at the point of impact. His wrist and hand remained fastened to the Asphinx in the gloom of the hidden compartment of the cavern floor. But the rest of him was free.

He knelt in stunned disbelief for a long time, staring down at the ruin of his arm, at the gray-streaked flesh above the elbow and the jagged stone capping below. His arm felt leaden and stiff. The poison already within it continued to work its damage. There were jolts of pain all through him.

But he was free! Shades, he was free!

Suddenly there was a stirring in the chamber beyond, a faint

and distant rustling like something had come awake. Walker
Boh went cold in the pit of his stomach as he realized what had
happened. His scream had given him away. The chamber beyond was the Assembly, and it was in the Assembly that the
serpent Valg, guardian of the dead, had once lived.

And might live still.

Walker came to his feet, sudden dizziness washing through
him. He ignored it, ignored the pain and weariness as well, and
stumbled toward the heavy, ironbound entry doors that had
brought him in. He shut away the sounds of everything about
him, everything within, concentrating the whole of his effort on
making his way across the cavern floor to the passageway that
lay beyond. If the serpent was alive and found him now, he knew
he was finished.

Luck was with him. The serpent did not emerge. Nothing
appeared. Walker reached the doors leading from the tomb and
pushed his way through into the darkness beyond.

What happened then was never clear afterward in his mind.
Somehow he managed to work his way back through the Hall
of Kings, past the Banshees whose howl could drive men mad,
and past the Sphinxes whose gaze could turn men to stone. He
heard the Banshees wail, felt the gaze of the Sphinxes burning
down, and experienced the terror of the mountain's ancient
magic as it sought to trap him, to make him another of its victims. Yet he escaped, some final shield of determination pre-
serving him as he made his way clear, an iron will combining
with weariness and pain and near madness to encase and preserve him. Perhaps his magic came to aid him as well; he thought
it possible. The magic, after all, was unpredictable, a constant
mystery. He pushed and trudged through near darkness and
phantasmagoric images, past walls of rock that threatened to
close about him, down tunnels of sight and sound in which he
could neither see nor hear, and finally he was free.

He emerged into the outside world at daybreak, the sun's light
chill and faint as it shone out of a sky thick with clouds and rain
that lingered from the previous night's storm. With his arm
tucked beneath his cloak like a wounded child, he made his way
down the mountain trail toward the plains south. He never looked
back. He could just manage to look ahead. He was on his feet
only because he refused to give in. He could barely feel himself
anymore, even the pain of his poisoning. He walked as if jerked
along by strings attached to his limbs. His black hair blew wildly
in the wind, whipping about his pale face, lashing it until his

eyes blurred with tears. He was a scarecrow figure of madness as he wandered out of the mist and gray.

Dark Uncle, the Grimpond's voice whispered in his mind and laughed in glee.

He lost track of time completely. The sun's weak light failed to disperse the stormclouds and the day remained washed of color and friendless. Trails came and went, an endless procession of rocks, defiles, canyons, and drops. Walker remained oblivious to all of it. He knew only that he was descending, working his way downward out of the rock, back toward the world he had so foolishly left behind. He knew that he was trying to save his life.

It was midday when he emerged at last from the high peaks into the Valley of Shale, a tattered and aimless bit of human wreckage so badly fevered and weakened that he stumbled halfway across the crushed, glistening black rock of the valley floor before realizing where he was. When he finally saw, his strength gave out. He collapsed in the tangle of his cloak, feeling the sharp edges of the rock cutting into the skin of his hands and face, heedless of its sting as he lay facedown in exhaustion. After a time, he began to crawl toward the placid waters of the lake, inching his way painfully ahead, dragging his stone-tipped arm beneath him. It seemed logical to him in his delirium that if he could reach the Hadeshorn's edge he might submerge his ruined arm and the lethal waters would counteract the poison that was killing him. It was nonsensical, but for Walker Boh madness had become the measure of his life.

He failed even in this small endeavor. Too weak to go more than a few yards, he lapsed into unconsciousness. The last thing he remembered was how dark it was in the middle of the day, the world a place of shadows.

He slept, and in his sleep he dreamed that the shade of Allanon came to him. The shade rose out of the churning, boiling waters of the Hadeshorn, dark and mystical as it materialized from the netherworld of afterlife to which it had been consigned. It reached out to Walker, lifted him to his feet, flooded him with new strength, and gave clarity once more to his thoughts and vision. Spectral, translucent, it hung above the dark, greenish waters—yet its touch felt curiously human.

—Dark Uncle—

When the shade spoke the words, they were not taunting and hateful as they had been when spoken by the Grimpond. They were simply a designation of who and what Walker was.

—Why will you not accept the charge I have given you—

Walker struggled angrily to reply but could not seem to find the words.

—The need for you is great, Walker. Not my need, but the need of the Lands and their people, the Races of the new world. If you do not accept my charge, there is no hope for them—

Walker's rage was boundless. Bring back the Druids, who were no more, and disappeared Paranor? Surely, thought Walker in response. Surely, shade of Allanon. I shall take my ruined body in search of what you seek, my poisoned limb, though I be dying and cannot hope to help anyone, still I . . .

—Accept, Walker. You do not accept. Acknowledge the truth of yourself and your own destiny—

Walker didn't understand.

—Kinship with those who have gone before you, those who understood the meaning of acceptance. That is what you lack—

Walker shuddered, disrupting the vision of his dream. His strength left him. He collapsed at the Hadeshorn's edge, blanketed in confusion and fear, feeling so lost that it seemed to him impossible that he could ever again be found.

Help me, Allanon, he begged in despair.

The shade hung motionless in the air before him, ethereal against a backdrop of wintry skies and barren peaks, rising up like death's specter come to retrieve a fresh victim. It seemed suddenly to Walker that dying was all that was left to him.

Do you wish me to die? he asked in disbelief. *Is this what you demand of me?*

The shade said nothing.

Did you know that this would happen to me? He held forth his arm, jagged stone stump, poison-streaked flesh.

The shade remained silent.

Why won't you help me? Walker howled.

—Why won't you help me—

The words echoed sharply in his mind, urgent and filled with a sense of dark purpose. But he did not speak them. Allanon did.

Then abruptly the shade shimmered in the air before him and faded away. The waters of the Hadeshorn steamed and hissed, roiled in fury, and went still once more. All about the air was misted and dark, filled with ghosts and wild imaginings, a place where life and death met at a crossroads of unanswered questions and unresolved puzzles.

Walker Boh saw them for only a moment, aware that he was

seeing them not in sleep but in waking, realizing suddenly that his vision might not have been a dream at all.

Then everything was gone, and he fell away into blackness.

When he came awake again there was someone bending over him. Walker saw the other through a haze of fever and pain, a thin, sticklike figure in gray robes with a narrow face, a wispy beard and hair, and a hawk nose, crouched close like something that meant to suck away what life remained to him.

"Walker?" the figure whispered gently.

It was Cogline. Walker swallowed against the dryness in his throat and struggled to raise himself. The weight of his arm dragged against him, pulling him back, forcing him down. The old man's hands groped beneath the concealing cloak and found the leaden stump. Walker heard the sharp intake of his breath.

"How did you . . . find me?" he managed.

"Allanon," Cogline answered. His voice was rough and laced with anger.

Walker sighed. "How long have I . . . ?"

"Three days. I don't know why you're still alive. You haven't any right to be."

"None," Walker agreed and reached out impulsively to hug the other man close. The familiar feel and smell of the old man's body brought tears to his eyes. "I don't think . . . I'm meant to die . . . just yet."

Cogline hugged Walker back. He said, "No, Walker. Not yet."

Then the old man was lifting him to his feet, hauling him up with strength Walker hadn't known he possessed, holding him upright as he pointed them both toward the south end of the valley. It was dawn again, the sunrise unclouded and brilliant gold against the eastern horizon, the air still and expectant with the promise of its coming.

"Hold on to me," Cogline urged, walking him along the crushed black rock. "There are horses waiting and help to be had. Hold tight, Walker."

Walker Boh held on for dear life.

III

Cogline took Walker Boh to Storlock. Even on horseback with Walker lashed in place, it took until nightfall to complete the journey. They came down out of the Dragon's Teeth into a day filled with sunshine and warmth, turned east across the Rabb Plains, and made their way into the Eastland forests of the Central Anar to the legendary village of the Stors. Wracked with pain and consumed with thoughts of dying, Walker remained awake almost the entire time. Yet he was never certain where he was or what was happening about him, conscious only of the swaying of his horse and Cogline's constant reassurance that all would be well.

He did not believe that Cogline was telling him the truth.

Storlock was silent, cool and dry in the shadow of the trees, a haven from the swelter and dust of the plains. Hands reached up to take Walker from the saddle, from the smell of sweat and the rocking motion, and from the feeling that he must at any moment give in to the death that was waiting to claim him. He did not know why he was alive. He could give himself no reason. White-robed figures gathered all around, supporting him, easing him down—Stors, the Gnome Healers of the Village. Everyone knew of the Stors. Theirs was the most advanced source of healing in the Four Lands. Wil Ohmsford had studied with them once and become a healer, the only Southlander ever to do so. Shea Ohmsford had been healed after an attack in the Wolfsktaag. Earlier, Par had been brought to them as well, infected by the poison of the Werebeasts in Olden Moor. Walker had brought him. Now it was Walker's turn to be saved. But Walker did not think that would happen.

A cup was raised to his lips, and a strange liquid trickled down his throat. Almost immediately the pain eased, and he felt

16

himself grow drowsy. Sleep would be good for him, he decided suddenly, surprisingly. Sleep would be welcome. He was carried into the Center House, the main care lodge, and placed in a bed in one of the back rooms where the forest could be seen through the weave of the curtains, a wall of dark trunks set at watch. He was stripped of his clothes, wrapped in blankets, given something further to drink, a bitter, hot liquid, and left to fall asleep.

He did so almost at once.

As he slept, the fever dissipated, and the weariness faded away. The pain lingered, but it was distant somehow and not a part of him. He sank down into the warmth and comfort of his bedding, and even dreams could not penetrate the shield of his rest. There were no visions to distress him, no dark thoughts to bring him awake. Allanon and Cogline were forgotten. His anguish at the loss of his limb, his struggle to escape the Asphinx and the Hall of Kings, and his terrifying sense of no longer being in command of his own destiny—all were forgotten. He was at peace.

He did not know how long he slept, for he was not conscious of time passing, of the sweep of the sun across the sky, or of the change from night to day and back again. When he began to come awake once more, floating out of the darkness of his rest through a world of half-sleep, memories of his boyhood stirred unexpectedly, small snatches of his life in the days when he was first learning to cope with the frustration and wonder of discovering who and what he was.

The memories were sharp and clear.

He was still a child when he first learned he had magic. He didn't call it magic then; he didn't call it anything. He believed such power common; he thought that he was like everyone else. He lived then with his father Kenner and mother Risse at Hearthstone in Darklin Reach, and there were no other children to whom he might compare himself. That came later. It was his mother who told him that what he could do was unusual, that it made him different from other children. He could still see her face as she tried to explain, her small features intense, her white skin striking against coal black hair that was always braided and laced with flowers. He could still hear her low and compelling voice. Risse. He had loved his mother deeply. She had not had magic of her own; she was a Boh and the magic came from his father's side, from the Ohmsfords. She told him that, sitting him down before her on a brilliant autumn day when the smell of dying leaves and burning wood filled the air, smiling and reassuring as she spoke, trying unsuccessfully to hide from him the uneasiness she felt.

That was one of the things the magic let him do. It let him see sometimes what others were feeling—not with everyone, but almost always with his mother.

"Walker, the magic makes you special," she said. "It is a gift that you must care for and cherish. I know that someday you are going to do something wonderful with it."

She died a year later after falling ill to a fever for which even her formidable healing skills could not find a cure.

He lived alone with his father then, and the "gift" with which she had believed him blessed developed rapidly. The magic was an enabler; it gave him insight. He discovered that frequently he could sense things in people without being told—changes in their mood and character, emotions they thought to keep secret, their opinions and ideas, their needs and hopes, even the reasons behind what they did. There were always visitors at Hearthstone—travelers passing through, peddlers, tradesmen, woodsmen, hunters, trappers, even Trackers—and Walker would know all about them without their having to say a word. He would tell them so. He would reveal what he knew. It was a game that he loved to play. It frightened some of them, and his father ordered him to stop. Walker did as he was asked. By then he had discovered a new and more interesting ability. He discovered that he could communicate with the animals of the forest, with birds and fish, even with plants. He could sense what they were thinking and feeling just as he could with humans, even though their thoughts and feelings were more rudimentary and limited. He would disappear for hours on excursions of learning, on makebelieve adventures, on journeys of testing and seeking out. He designated himself early as an explorer of life.

As time passed, it became apparent that Walker's special insight was to help him with his schooling as well. He began reading from his father's library almost as soon as he learned how the letters of the alphabet formed words on the fraying pages of his father's books. He mastered mathematics effortlessly. He understood sciences intuitively. Barely anything had to be explained. Somehow he just seemed to understand how it all worked. History became his special passion; his memory of things, of places and events and people, was prodigious. He began to keep notes of his own, to write down everything he learned, to compile teachings that he would someday impart to others.

The older he grew, the more his father's attitude toward him seemed to change. He dismissed his suspicions at first, certain that he was mistaken. But the feeling persisted. Finally he asked his father about it, and Kenner—a tall, lean, quick-moving man with wide, intelligent eyes, a stammer he had worked hard to overcome, and a gift for crafting—admitted it was true. Kenner did not have magic of his own. He had evidenced traces of it when he was young, but it had disappeared shortly after he had passed out of boyhood. It had been like that with his father and his father's father before that and every Ohmsford he knew about all the way back to Brin. But it did not appear to be that way with Walker. Walker's magic just seemed to grow stronger. Kenner told him that he was afraid that his son's abilities would eventually overwhelm him, that they would develop to a point where he could no longer anticipate or control their effects. But he said as well, just as Risse had said, that they should not be suppressed, that magic was a gift that always had some special purpose in being.

Shortly after, he told Walker of the history behind the Ohmsford magic, of the Druid Allanon and the Valegirl Brin, and of the mysterious trust that the former in dying had bequeathed to the latter. Walker had been twelve when he heard the tale. He had wanted to know what the trust was supposed to be. His father hadn't been able to tell him. He had only been able to relate the history of its passage through the Ohmsford bloodline.

"It manifests itself in you, Walker," he said. "You in turn will pass it on to your children, and they to theirs, until one day there is need for it. That is the legacy you have inherited."

"But what good is a legacy that serves no purpose?" Walker had demanded.

And Kenner had repeated, "There is always purpose in magic—even when we don't understand what it is."

Barely a year later, as Walker was entering his youth and leaving his childhood behind, the magic revealed that it possessed another, darker side. Walker found out that it could be destructive. Sometimes, most often when he was angry, his emotions transformed themselves into energy. When that happened, he could move things away and break them apart without touching them. Sometimes he could summon a form of fire. It wasn't ordinary fire; it didn't burn like ordinary fire and it was different in color, a sort of cobalt. It wouldn't do much of what he tried to make it do; it did pretty much what it wished. It took him weeks to learn to control it. He tried to keep his discovery a secret from his father, but his father learned of it anyway, just as he eventually learned of everything about his son. Though he said little, Walker felt the distance between them widen.

Walker was nearing manhood when his father made the decision to take him out of Hearthstone. Kenner Ohmsford's health had been failing steadily for several years, his once strong body afflicted by a wasting sickness. Closing down the cottage that had been Walker's home since birth, he took the boy to Shady Vale to live with another family of Ohmsfords, Jaralan and Mirianna and their sons Par and Coll.

The move became for Walker Boh the worst thing that had ever happened to him. Shady Vale, though little more than a hamlet community, nevertheless seemed constricting after Hearthstone. Freedom there had been boundless; here, there were boundaries that he could not escape. Walker was not used to being around so many people and he could not seem to make himself fit in. He was required to attend school, but there was nothing for him to learn. His master and the other children disliked and mistrusted him; he was an outsider, he behaved differently than they, he knew entirely too much, and they quickly decided that they wanted nothing to do with him. His magic became a snare he could not escape. It manifested itself in everything he did, and by the time he realized he should have hidden it away it was too late to do so. He was beaten a number of times because he wouldn't defend himself. He was terrified of what would happen if he let the fire escape.

He was in the village less than a year when his father died. Walker had wished that he could die, too.

He continued to live with Jaralan and Mirianna Ohmsford, who were good to him and who sympathized with the difficulties he was encountering because their own son Par was just beginning to exhibit signs of having magic of his own. Par was a descendent of Jair Ohmsford, Brin's brother. Both sides of the family had passed the magic of their ancestors down through the bloodline in the years since Allanon's death, so the appearance of Par's magic was not entirely unexpected. Par's was a less unpredictable and complicated form of magic, manifesting itself principally in the boy's ability to create lifelike images with his voice. Par was still little then, just five or six, and he barely understood what was happening to him. Coll was not yet strong enough to protect his brother, so Walker ended up taking the boy under his wing. It seemed natural enough to do so. After all, only Walker understood what Par was experiencing.

His relationship with Par changed everything. It gave him something to focus on, a purpose beyond worrying about his own survival. He spent time with Par helping him adjust to the presence of the magic in his body. He counseled him in its use, advised him in the cautions that were necessary, the protective devices he must learn to employ. He tried to teach him how to deal with the fear and dislike of people who would choose not to understand. He became Par's mentor.

The people of Shady Vale began calling him "Dark Uncle." It began with the children. He wasn't Par's uncle, of course; he wasn't anybody's uncle. But he hadn't a firm blood tie in the eyes of the villagers; no one really understood the relationship he bore to Jaralan and Mirianna, so there were no constrictions on how they might refer to him. "Dark Uncle" became the appellation that stuck. Walker was tall by then, pale skinned and black haired like his mother, apparently immune to the browning effect of the sun. He looked ghostly. It seemed to the Vale children as if he were a night thing that never saw the light of day, and his relationship toward the boy Par appeared mysterious to them. Thus he became "Dark Uncle," the counselor of magic, the strange, awkward, withdrawn young man whose insights and comprehensions set him apart from everyone.

Nevertheless, the name "Dark Uncle" notwithstanding, Walker's attitude improved. He began to learn how to deal with the suspicion and mistrust. He was no longer attacked. He found that he could turn aside these assaults with not much more than a glance or even the set of his body. He could use the magic to shield himself. He found he could project wariness and caution into others and prevent them from following through on their violent intentions. He even became rather good at stopping fights among others. Unfortunately, all this did was distance him further. The adults and older youths left him alone altogether; only the younger children turned cautiously friendly.

Walker was never happy in Shady Vale. The mistrust and the fear remained, concealed just beneath the forced smiles, the perfunctory nods, and the civilities of the villagers that allowed him to exist among them but never gain acceptance. Walker knew that the magic was the cause of his problem. His mother and father might have thought of it as a gift, but he didn't. And he never would again. It was a curse that he felt certain would haunt him to the grave.

By the time he reached manhood, Walker had resolved to return to Hearthstone, to the home he remembered so fondly, away from the people of the Vale, from their mistrust and suspicion, from the strangeness they caused him to feel. The boy Par had adjusted well enough that Walker no longer felt concerned about him. To begin with, Par was a native of the Vale and accepted in a way that Walker never could be. Moreover, his attitude toward using magic was far different than Walker's. Par was never hesitant; he wanted to know everything the magic could do. What others thought did not concern him. He could get away with that; Walker never could. The two had begun to grow apart as they grew older. Walker knew it was inevitable. It was time for him to go. Jaralan and Mirianna urged him to stay, but understood at the same time that he could not.

Seven years after his arrival, Walker Boh departed Shady Vale. He had taken his mother's name by then, disdaining further use of Ohmsford because it linked him so closely with the legacy of magic he now despised. He went back into Darklin Reach, back to Hearthstone, feeling as if he were a caged wild animal that had been set free. He severed his ties with the life he had left behind him. He resolved that he would never again use the magic. He promised himself that he would keep apart from the world of men for the rest of his life.

For almost a year he did exactly as he said he would do. And then Cogline appeared and everything changed . . .

Half-sleep turned abruptly to waking, and Walker's memories faded away. He stirred in the warmth of his bed, and his eyes blinked open. For a moment he could not decide where he was. The room in which he lay was bright with daylight despite the brooding presence of a cluster of forest trees directly outside his curtained window. The room was small, clean, almost bare of furniture. There were a sitting chair and a small table next to his bed, the bed, and nothing else. A vase of flowers, a basin of water, and some cloths sat on the table. The single door leading into the room stood closed.

Storlock. That was where he was, where Cogline had brought him.

He remembered then what had happened to bring him here.

Cautiously, he brought his ruined arm out from beneath the bedding. There was little pain now, but the heaviness of the stone persisted and there was no feeling. He bit his lip in anger and frustration as his arm worked free. Nothing had changed beyond the lessening of the pain. The stone tip where the lower arm had shattered was still there. The streaks of gray where the poison worked its way upward toward his shoulder were there as well.

He slipped his arm from view again. The Stors had been unable to cure him. Whatever the nature of the poison that the Asphinx had injected into him, the Stors could not treat it. And if the Stors could not treat it—the Stors, who were the best of the Four Lands' Healers . . .

He could not finish the thought. He shoved it away, closed his eyes, tried to go back to sleep, and failed. All he could see was his arm shattering under the impact of the stone wedge.

Despair washed over him and he wept.

An hour had passed when the door opened and Cogline entered the room, an intrusive presence that made the silence seem even more uncomfortable.

"Walker," he greeted quietly.

"They cannot save me, can they?" Walker asked bluntly, the despair pushing everything else aside.

The old man became a statue at his bedside. "You're alive, aren't you?" he replied.

"Don't play word games with me. Whatever's been done, it hasn't driven out the poison. I can feel it. I may be alive, but only for the moment. Tell me if I'm wrong."

Cogline paused. "You're not wrong. The poison is still in you. Even the Stors haven't the means to remove it or to stop its spread. But they have slowed the process, lessened the pain, and given you time. That is more than I would have expected given the nature and extent of the injury. How do you feel?"

Walker's smile was slow and bitter. "Like I am dying, naturally. But in a comfortable fashion."

They regarded each other without speaking for a moment. Then Cogline moved over to the sitting chair and eased himself into it, a bundle of old bones and aching joints, of wrinkled brown skin. "Tell me what happened to you, Walker," he said.

Walker did. He told of reading the ancient, leatherbound Druid History that Cogline had brought to him and learning of the Black Elfstone, of deciding to seek the counsel of the Grimpond, of hearing its riddles and witnessing its visions, of determining that he must go to the Hall of Kings, of finding the secret compartment marked with runes in the floor of the Tomb, and finally of being bitten and poisoned by the Asphinx left there to snare him.

"To snare someone at least, perhaps anyone," Cogline observed.

Walker looked at him sharply, anger and mistrust flaring in his dark eyes. "What do you know of this, Cogline? Do you play the same games as the Druids now? And what of Allanon? Did Allanon know . . ."

"Allanon knew nothing," Cogline interrupted, brushing aside the accusation before it could be completed. The old eyes glittered beneath narrowed brows. "You undertook to solve the Grimpond's riddles on your own—a foolish decision on your part. I warned you repeatedly that the wraith would find a way to undo you. How could Allanon know of your predicament? You attribute far too much to a man three-hundred-years dead. Even if he were still alive, his magic could never penetrate that which shrouds the Hall of Kings. Once you were within, you were lost to him. And to me. It wasn't until you emerged again and collapsed at the Hadeshorn that he was able to discover what happened and summon me to help you. I came as quickly as I could and even so it took me three days."

One hand lifted, a sticklike finger jabbing. "Have you bothered to question why it is that you aren't dead? It is because Allanon found a way to keep you alive, first until I arrived and second until the Stors could treat you! Think on that a bit before you start casting blame about so freely!"

He glared, and Walker glared back at him. It was Walker who looked away first, too sick at heart to continue the confrontation. "I have trouble believing anyone just at the moment," he offered lamely.

"You have trouble believing anyone at any time," Cogline snapped, unappeased. "You cast your heart in iron long ago, Walker. You stopped believing in anything. I remember when that wasn't so."

He trailed off, and the room went silent. Walker found himself thinking momentarily of the time the old man referred to, the time when he had first come to Walker and offered to show him the ways in which the magic could be used. Cogline was right. He hadn't been so bitter then; he'd been full of hope.

He almost laughed. That was such a long time ago.

"Perhaps I can use my own magic to dispel the poison from my body," he ventured quietly. "Once I return to Hearthstone, once I'm fully rested. Brin Ohmsford had such power once."

Cogline dropped his eyes and looked thoughtful. His gnarled

hands clasped loosely in the folds of his robe. It appeared as if he were trying to decide something.

Walker waited a moment, then asked, "What has become of the others—of Par and Coll and Wren?"

Cogline kept his gaze lowered. "Par has gone in search of the Sword, young Coll with him. The Rover girl seeks the Elves. They've accepted the charges Allanon gave to them." He looked up again. "Have you, Walker?"

Walker stared at him, finding the question both absurd and troubling, torn between conflicting feelings of disbelief and uncertainty. Once he would not have hesitated to give his answer. He thought again of what Allanon had asked him to do: Bring back disappeared Paranor and restore the Druids. A ridiculous, impossible undertaking, he had thought at the time. Game playing, he had decried. He would not be a part of such foolishness, he had announced to Par, Coll, Wren, and the others of the little company that had come with him to the Valley of Shale. He despised the Druids for their manipulation of the Ohmsfords. He would not be made their puppet. So bold he had been, so certain. He would sooner cut off his hand than see the Druids come again, he had declared.

And the loss of his hand was the price that had been exacted, it seemed.

Yet had that loss truly put an end to any possibility of the return of Paranor and the Druids? More to the point, was that what he now intended?

He was conscious of Cogline watching him, impatient as he waited for Walker Boh's answer to his question. Walker kept his eyes fixed on the old man without seeing him. He was thinking suddenly of the Druid History and its tale of the Black Elfstone. If he had not gone in search of the Elfstone, he would not have lost his arm. Why had he gone? Curiosity, he had thought. But that was a simplistic answer and he knew it was given too easily. In any case, didn't the very fact of his going indicate that despite any protestations to the contrary he indeed had accepted Allanon's charge?

If not, what was it that he was doing?

He focused again on the old man. "Tell me something, Cogline. Where did you get that book of the Druid Histories? How did you find it? You said when you brought it to me that you got it out of Paranor. Surely not."

Cogline's smile was faint and ironic. "Why 'surely not,' Walker?"

"Because Paranor was sent out of the world of men by Allanon three hundred years ago. It doesn't exist anymore."

Cogline's face crinkled like crushed parchment. "Doesn't exist? Oh, but it does, Walker. And you're wrong. Anyone can reach it if they have the right magic to help them. Even you."

Walker hesitated, suddenly uncertain.

"Allanon sent Paranor out of the world of the men, but it still exists," Cogline said softly. "It needs only the magic of the Black Elfstone to summon it back again. Until then, it remains lost to the Four Lands. But it can still be entered by those who have the means to do so and the courage to try. It does require courage, Walker. Shall I tell you why? Would you like to hear the story behind my journey into Paranor?"

Walker hesitated again, wondering if he wanted to hear anything ever again about the Druids and their magic. Then he nodded slowly. "Yes."

"But you are prepared to disbelieve what I am going to tell you, aren't you?"

"Yes."

The old man leaned forward. "Tell you what. I'll let you judge for yourself."

He paused, gathering his thoughts. Daylight framed him in brightness, exposing the flaws of old age that etched his thin frame in lines and hollows, that left his hair and beard wispy and thin, and that gave his hands a tremulous appearance as he clasped them tightly before him.

"It was after your meeting with Allanon. He sensed, and I as well, that you would not accept the charge you had been given, that you would resist any sort of involvement without further evidence of the possibility that you might succeed. And that there was reason to want to. You differ in your attitude from the others—you doubt everything that you are told. You came to Allanon already planning to reject what you would hear."

Walker started to protest, but Cogline held up his hands quickly and shook his head. "No, Walker. Don't argue. I know you better than you know yourself. Just listen to me for now. I went north on Allanon's summons, seeming to disappear, leaving you to debate among yourselves what course of action you would follow. Your decision in the matter was a foregone conclusion. You would not do as you had been asked. Since that was so, I resolved to try to change your mind. You see, Walker, I believe in the dreams; I see the truth in them that you as yet do not. I would not be a messenger for Allanon if there were any way to avoid it. My time as a Druid passed away long ago, and I do not seek to return to what was. But I am all there is and since that is so I will do what I think necessary. Dissuading you from refusing to involve yourself in the matter at hand is something I deem vital.''

He was shaking with the conviction of his words and the look he extended Walker was one that sought to convey truths that the old man could not speak.

''I went north, Walker, as I said. I traveled out of the Valley of Shale and across the Dragon's Teeth to the valley of the Druid's Keep. Nothing remains of Paranor but a few crumbling outbuildings on a barren height. The forests still surround the spot on which it once stood, but nothing will grow upon the earth, not even the smallest blade of grass. The wall of thorns that once protected the Keep is gone. Everything has disappeared— as if some giant reached down and snatched it all away.

''I stood there, near twilight, looking at the emptiness, envisioning what had once been. I could sense the presence of the Keep. I could almost see it looming out of the shadows, rising up against the darkening eastern skies. I could almost define the shape of its stone towers and parapets. I waited, for Allanon knew what was needed and would tell me when it was time.''

The old eyes gazed off into space. ''I slept when I grew tired, and Allanon came to me in my dreams as he now does with all of us. He told me that Paranor was indeed still there, cast away by magic into a different place and time, yet there nevertheless. He asked me if I would enter and bring out from it a certain volume of the Druid Histories which would describe the means by which Paranor could be restored to the Four Lands. He asked if I would take that book to you.'' He hesitated, poised to reveal something more, then simply said, ''I agreed.

''He reached out to me then and took my hand. He lifted me away from myself, my spirit out of my body. He cloaked me in his magic. I became momentarily something other than the man I am—but I don't know even now what that something was. He told me what I must do. I walked alone then to where the walls of the Keep had once stood, closed my eyes so that they would not deceive me, and reached out into worlds that lie beyond our own for the shape of what had once been. I found that I could do that. Imagine my astonishment when Paranor's walls materialized suddenly beneath my fingers. I risked taking a quick look at them, but when I did so there was nothing to see. I was forced to begin again. Even as a spirit I could not penetrate the magic if I violated its rules. I kept my eyes closed tightly this time, searched out the walls anew, discovered the hidden trapdoor concealed in the base of the Keep, pushed the catch that would release the locks, and entered.''

Cogline's mouth tightened. "I was allowed to open my eyes then and look around. Walker, it was the Paranor of old, a great sprawling castle with towers that rose into clouds of ancient brume and battlements that stretched away forever. It seemed endless to me as I climbed its stairs and wandered its halls; I was like a rat in a maze. The castle was filled with the smell and taste of death. The air had a strange greenish cast; everything was swathed in it. Had I attempted to enter in my flesh-and-blood body, I would have been destroyed instantly; I could sense the magic still at work, scouring the rock corridors for any signs of life. The furnaces that had once been fueled by the fire at the earth's core were still, and Paranor was cold and lifeless. When I gained the upper halls I found piles of bones, grotesque and misshapen, the remains of the Mord Wraiths and Gnomes that Allanon had trapped there when he had summoned the magic to destroy Paranor. Nothing was alive in the Druid's Keep save myself.''

He was silent for a moment as if remembering. "I sought out the vault in which the Druid Histories were concealed. I had a sense of where it was, quickened in part by the days in which I studied at Paranor, in part by Allanon's magic. I searched out the library through which the vault could be entered, finding as I did so that I could touch things as if I were still a creature of substance and not of spirit. I felt along the dusty, worn edges of the bookshelves until I found the catches that released the doors leading in. They swung wide, and the magic gave way before me. I entered, discovered the Druid Histories revealed, and took from its resting place the one that was needed.''

Cogline's eyes strayed off across the sunlit room, seeking visions that were hidden from Walker. "I left then. I went back the same way as I had come, a ghost out of the past as much as those who had died there, feeling the chill of their deaths and the immediacy of my own. I passed down the stairwells and corridors in a half-sleep that let me feel as well as see the horror of what now held sway in the castle of the Druids. Such power, Walker! The magic that Allanon summoned was frightening even yet. I fled from it as I departed—not on foot, you understand, but in my mind. I was terrified!''

The eyes swung back. "So I escaped. And when I woke, I

had in my possession the book that I had been sent to recover and I took it then to you."

He went silent, waiting patiently as Walker considered his story. Walker's eyes were distant. "It can be done then? Paranor can be entered even though it no longer exists in the Four Lands?"

Cogline shook his head slowly. "Not by ordinary men." His brow furrowed. "Perhaps by you, though. With the magic of the Black Elfstone to help you."

"Perhaps," Walker agreed dully. "What magic does the Elfstone possess?"

"I know nothing more of it than you," Cogline answered quietly.

"Not even where it can be found? Or who has it?"

Cogline shook his head. "Nothing."

"Nothing." Walker's voice was edged with bitterness. He let his eyes close momentarily against what he was feeling. When they opened, they were resigned. "This is my perception of things. You expect me to accept Allanon's charge to recover disappeared Paranor and restore the Druids. I can only do this by first recovering the Black Elfstone. But neither you nor I know where the Elfstone is or who has it. And I am infected with the poison of the Asphinx; I am being turned slowly to stone. I am dying! Even if I were persuaded to . . ." His voice caught, and he shook his head. "Don't you see? There isn't enough time!"

Cogline looked out the window, hunching down into his robes. "And if there were?"

Walker's laugh was hollow, his voice weary. "Cogline, I don't know."

The old man rose. He looked down at Walker for a long time without speaking. Then he said, "Yes, you do." His hands clasped tightly before him. "Walker, you persist in your refusal to accept the truth of what is meant to be. You recognize that truth deep in your heart, but you will not heed it. Why is that?"

Walker stared back at him wordlessly.

Cogline shrugged. "I have nothing more to say. Rest, Walker. You will be well enough in a day or two to leave. The Stors have done all they can; your healing, if it is to be, must come from another source. I will take you back to Hearthstone."

"I will heal myself," Walker whispered. His voice was suddenly urgent, rife with both desperation and anger.

Cogline did not respond. He simply gathered up his robes and walked from the room. The door closed quietly behind him.

"I will," Walker Boh swore.

IV

It took Morgan Leah the better part of three days after parting with Padishar Creel and the survivors of the Movement to travel south from the empty stretches of the Dragon's Teeth to the forest-sheltered Dwarf community of Culhaven. Storms swept the mountains during the first day, washing the ridgelines and slopes with torrents of rain, leaving the trailways sodden and slick with the damp, and wrapping the whole of the land in gray clouds and mist. By the second day the storms had passed away, and sunshine had begun to break through the clouds and the earth to dry out again. The third day brought a return of summer, the air warm and fragrant with the smell of flowers and grasses, the countryside bright with colors beneath a clear, windswept sky, the slow, lazy sounds of the wild things rising up from the pockets of shelter where they made their home.

Morgan's mood improved with the weather. He had been disheartened when he had set out. Steff was dead, killed in the catacombs of the Jut, and Morgan was burdened with a lingering sense of guilt rooted in his unfounded but persistent belief that he could have done something to prevent it. He didn't know what, of course. It was Teel who had killed Steff, who had almost killed him as well. Neither Steff nor he had known until the very last that Teel was something other than what she appeared, that she was not the girl the Dwarf had fallen in love with but a Shadowen whose sole purpose in coming with them into the mountains was to see them destroyed. Morgan had suspected what she was, yet lacked any real proof that his suspicions were correct until the moment she had revealed herself and by then it was too late. His friends the Valemen, Par and Coll Ohmsford, had disappeared after escaping the horrors of the Pit in Tyrsis and not been seen since. The Jut, the stronghold of the members of the Movement, had fallen to the armies of the Federation, and Padishar Creel and his outlaws had been chased north into the mountains. The Sword of Shannara, which was what all of them had come looking for in the first place, was still missing. Weeks of seeking out the talisman, of scrambling to unlock the puzzle of its hiding place, of hair-raising confrontations with and escapes from the Federation and the Shadowen, and of repeated frustration and disappointment, had come to nothing.

But Morgan Leah was resilient and after a day or so of brooding about what was past and could not be changed his spirits began to lift once more. After all, he was something of a veteran now in the struggle against the oppressors of his homeland. Before, he had been little more than an irritant to that handful of Federation officials who governed the affairs of the Highlands, and in truth he had never done anything that affected the outcome of larger events in the Four Lands. His risk had been minimal and the results of his endeavors equally so. But that had all changed. In the past few weeks he had journeyed to the Hadeshorn to meet with the shade of Allanon, he had joined in the quest for the missing Sword of Shannara, he had battled both Shadowen and Federation, and he had saved the lives of Padishar Creel and his outlaws by warning them of Teel before she could betray them one final time. He knew he had done something at last that had value and meaning.

And he was about to do something more.

He had made Steff a promise. As his friend lay dying, Morgan had sworn that he would go to Culhaven to the orphanage where Steff had been raised and warn Granny Elise and Auntie Jilt that they were in danger. Granny Elise and Auntie Jilt—the only parents Steff had ever known, the only kindred he was leaving—were not to be abandoned. If Teel had betrayed Steff, she would have betrayed them as well. Morgan was to help them get safely away.

It gave the Highlander a renewed sense of purpose, and that as much as anything helped bring him out of his depression. He had begun his journey disenchanted. He had lagged in his travel, bogged down by the weather and his mood. By the third day he had shaken the effects of both. His resolution buoyed him. He would spirit Granny Elise and Auntie Jilt out of Culhaven to somewhere safe. He would return to Tyrsis and find the Valemen. He would continue to search for the missing Sword of Shannara. He would find a way to rid Leah and the whole of the Four Lands of both Shadowen and Federation. He was alive and everything was possible. He whistled and hummed as he walked, let the sun's rays warm his face, and banished self-doubt and discouragement. It was time to get on with things.

Now and again as he walked his thoughts strayed to the lost magic of the Sword of Leah. He still wore the remains of the shattered blade strapped to his waist, cradled in the makeshift sheath he had constructed for it. He thought of the power it had given him and the way the absence of that power made him feel—as if he could never be whole again without it. Yet some small part of the magic still lingered in the weapon; he had managed to call it to life in the catacombs of the Jut when he destroyed Teel. There had been just enough left to save his life.

Deep inside, where he could hide it and not be forced to admit the implausibility of it, he harbored a belief that one day the magic of the Sword of Leah would be his again.

It was late afternoon on that third day of travel when he emerged from the forests of the Anar into Culhaven. The Dwarf village was shabby and worn where he walked, the refuge of those now too old and as yet too young who had not been taken by the Federation authorities to the mines or sold as slaves in the market. Once among the most meticulously maintained of communities, Culhaven was now a dilapidated collection of buildings and people that evidenced little of care or love. The forest grew right up against the outermost buildings, weeds intruding into yards and gardens, roadways rutted and choked with scrub. Wooden walls warped under peeling paint, tiles and shingles cracked and splintered, and trim about doorways and windows drooped away. Eyes peered out through the shadows, following after the Highlander as he made his way in; he could sense the people staring from behind windows and doors. The few Dwarves he encountered would not meet his gaze, turning quickly away. He walked on without slowing, his anger rekindled anew at the thought of what had been done to these people. Everything had been taken from them but their lives, and their lives had been brought to nothing.

He pondered anew, as Par Ohmsford had done when last they were there, at the purpose of it.

He kept clear of the main roads, staying on the side paths,

not anxious to draw attention to himself. He was a Southlander and therefore free to come and go in the Eastland as he pleased, but he did not identify in any way with its Federation occupiers and preferred to stay clear of them altogether. Even if none of what had happened to the Dwarves was his doing, what he saw of Culhaven made him ashamed all over again of who and what he was. A Federation patrol passed him and the soldiers nodded cordially. It was all he could do to make himself nod back.

As he drew nearer to the orphanage, his anticipation of what he would find heightened perceptibly. Anxiety warred with confidence. What if he were too late? He brushed the possibility away. There was no reason to think that he was. Teel would not have risked jeopardizing her disguise by acting precipitately. She would have waited until she was certain it would not have mattered.

Shadows began to lengthen as the sun disappeared into the trees west. The air cooled and the sweat on Morgan's back dried beneath his tunic. The day's sounds began to fade away into an expectant hush. Morgan looked down at his hands, fixing his gaze on the irregular patchwork of white scars that crisscrossed the brown skin. Battle wounds were all over his body since Tyrsis and the Jut. He tightened the muscles of his jaw. Small things, he thought. The ones inside him were deeper.

He caught sight of a Dwarf child looking at him from behind a low stone wall with intense black eyes. He couldn't tell if it was a girl or a boy. The child was very thin and ragged. The eyes followed him a moment, then disappeared.

Morgan moved ahead hurriedly, anxious once more. He caught sight of the roof of the orphanage, the first of its walls, a window high up, a gable. He rounded a bend in the roadway and slowed. He knew instantly that something was wrong. The yard of the orphanage was empty. The grass was untended. There were no toys, no children. He fought back against the panic that rose suddenly within him. The windows of the old building were dark. There was no sign of anyone.

He came up to the gate at the front of the yard and paused. Everything was still.

He had assumed wrong. He was too late after all.

He started forward, then stopped. His eyes swept the darkness of the old house, wondering if he might be walking into some sort of trap. He stood there a long time, watching. But there was no sign of anyone. And no reason for anyone to be waiting here for him, he decided.

He pushed through the gate, walked up on the porch, and pushed open the front door. It was dark inside, and he took a moment to let his eyes adjust. When they had done so, he entered. He passed slowly through the building, searched each of its rooms in turn, and came back out again. There was dust on everything. It had been some time since anyone had lived there. Certainly no one was living there now.

So what had become of the two old Dwarf ladies?

He sat down on the porch steps and let his tall form slump back against the railing. The Federation had them. There wasn't any other explanation. Granny Elise and Auntie Jilt would never leave their home unless they were forced to. And they would never abandon the children they cared for. Besides, all of their clothes were still in the chests and closets, the children's toys, the bedding, everything. He had seen it in his search. The house wasn't closed up properly. Too much was in disarray. Nothing was as it would have been if the old ladies had been given a choice.

Bitterness flooded through him. Steff had depended on him; he couldn't quit now. He had to find Granny and Auntie. But where? And who in Culhaven would tell him what he needed to know? No one who knew anything, he suspected. The Dwarves surely wouldn't trust him—not a Southlander. He could ask until the sun rose in the west and set in the east.

He sat there thinking a long time, the daylight fading into dusk. After a while, he became aware of a small child looking at him through the front gate—the same child who had been watching him up the road. A boy, he decided this time. He let the boy watch him until they were comfortable with each other, then said, "Can you tell me what happened to the ladies who lived here?"

The boy disappeared instantly. He was gone so fast that it seemed as if the earth must have swallowed him up. Morgan sighed. He should have expected as much. He straightened his legs. He would have to devise a way to extract the information he needed from the Federation authorities. That would be dangerous, especially if Teel had told them about him as well as Granny and Auntie—and there was no reason now to believe that she hadn't. She must have given the old ladies up even before the company began its journey north to Darklin Reach. The Federation must have come for Granny and Auntie the moment Teel was safely beyond the village. Teel hadn't worried that Steff or Morgan or the Valemen would find out; after all, they would all be dead before it mattered.

Morgan wanted to hit something or someone. Teel had betrayed them all. Par and Coll were lost. Steff was dead. And now these two old ladies who had never hurt anyone . . .

"Hey, mister," a voice called.

He looked up sharply. The boy was back at the gate. An older boy stood next to him. It was the second boy who spoke, a hefty fellow with a shock of spiked red hair. "Federation soldiers took the old ladies away to the workhouses several weeks ago. No one lives here now."

Then they were gone, disappeared as completely as before. Morgan stared after them. Was the boy telling him the truth? The Highlander decided he was. Well and good. Now he had a little something to work with. He had a place to start looking.

He came to his feet, went back down the pathway, and out the gate. He followed the rutted road as it wound through the twilight toward the center of the village. Houses began to give way to shops and markets, and the road broadened and split in several directions. Morgan skirted the hub of the business district, watching as the light faded from the sky and the stars appeared. Torchlight brightened the main thoroughfare but was absent from the roads and paths he followed. Voices whispered in the stillness, vague sounds that lacked meaning and definition, hushed as if the speakers feared being understood. The houses changed character, becoming well tended and neat, the yards trimmed and nourished. Federation houses, Morgan thought—stolen from Dwarves—tended by the victims. He kept his bitterness at bay, concentrating on the task ahead. He knew where the workhouses were and what they were intended to accomplish. The women sent there were too old to be sold as personal slaves, yet strong enough to do menial work such as washing and sewing and the like. The women were assigned to the Federation barracks at large and made to serve the needs of the garrison. If that boy had been telling the truth, that was what Granny Elise and Auntie Jilt would be doing.

Morgan reached the workhouses several minutes later. There were five of them, a series of long, low buildings that ran parallel to each other with windows on both sides and doors at both ends. The women who worked them lived in them as well. Pallets, blankets, washbasins, and chamber pots were provided and pulled out from under the workbenches at night. Steff had taken

Morgan up to a window once to let him peer inside. Once had been quite enough.

Morgan stood in the shadows of a storage shed across the way for long moments, thinking through what he would do. Guards stood at all the entrances and patroled the roadways and lanes. The women in the workhouses were prisoners. They were not permitted to leave their buildings for any reason short of sickness or death or some more benevolent form of release—and the latter almost never occurred. They were permitted visitors infrequently and then closely watched. Morgan couldn't remember when it was that visits were permitted. Besides, it didn't matter. It infuriated him to think of Granny Elise and Auntie Jilt being kept in such a place. Steff would not have waited to free them, and neither would he.

But how was he going to get in? And how was he going to get Granny and Auntie out once he did?

The problem defeated him. There was no way to approach the workhouses without being seen and no way to know in which of the five workhouses the old ladies were being kept in any case. He needed to know a great deal more than he did now before he could even think of attempting any rescue. Not for the first time since he had left the Dragon's Teeth, he wished Steff were there to advise him.

At last he gave it up. He walked down into the center of the village, took a room at one of the inns that catered to Southland traders and businessmen, took a bath to wash off the grime, washed his clothes as well, and went off to bed. He lay awake thinking about Granny Elise and Auntie Jilt until sleep finally overcame him.

When he awoke the following morning he knew what he needed to do to rescue them.

He dressed, ate breakfast in the inn dining room, and set out. What he was planning was risky, but there was no help for it. After making a few inquiries, he discovered the names of the taverns most frequented by Federation soldiers. There were three of them, and all were situated on the same street close to the city markets. He walked until he found them, picked the most likely—a dimly lit hall called the High Boot—entered, found a table close to the serving bar, ordered a glass of ale, and waited. Although the day was still young there were soldiers drifting in already, men from the night shift not yet ready for bed. They were quick to talk about garrison life and not much concerned with who might be listening. Morgan listened closely. From time to time he looked up long enough to ask a friendly question. Occasionally he commented. Once in a while he bought a glass for someone. Mostly he waited.

Much of the talk revolved around a girl who was rumored to be the daughter of the King of the Silver River. She had appeared rather mysteriously out of the Silver River country south and west below the Rainbow Lake and was making her way east. Wherever she went, in whatever villages and towns she passed through, she performed miracles. There had never been such magic, it was said. She was on her way now to Culhaven.

The balance of the tavern's chatter revolved around complaints about the way the Federation army was run by its officers. Since it was the common soldiers who were doing the complaining, the nature of the talk was hardly surprising. This was the part that Morgan was interested in hearing. The day passed away in lazy fashion, sultry and still within the confines of the hall with only the cold glasses of ale and the talk to relieve the heat and boredom. Federation soldiers came and went, but Morgan remained where he was, an almost invisible presence as he sipped and watched. He had thought earlier to circulate from one tavern to the next, but it quickly became apparent that he would learn everything he needed to know by remaining at the first.

By midafternoon he had the information he needed. It was time to act on it. He roused himself from his seat and walked across the roadway to the second of the taverns, the Frog Pond, an aptly named establishment if ever there was one. Seating himself near the back at a green cloth table that sat amid the shadows like a lily pad in a dark pool, he began looking for his victim. He found him almost immediately, a man close to his own size, a common soldier of no significant rank, drinking alone, lost in some private musing that carried his head so far downward it was almost touching the serving bar. An hour passed, then two. Morgan waited patiently as the soldier finished his final glass, straightened, pushed away from the bar, lurched out through the entry doors. Then he followed.

The day was mostly gone, the sun already slipping into the trees of the surrounding forests, the daylight turning gray with the approach of evening. The soldier shuffled unsteadily down the road through knots of fellow soldiers and visiting tradesmen, making his way back to the barracks. Morgan knew where he was going and slipped ahead to cut him off. He intercepted him as he came around a corner by a blacksmith's shop, seeming to bump into him by accident but in fact striking him so hard that the man was unconscious before he touched the ground. Morgan let him fall, muttered in mock exasperation, then picked the fellow up, hoisting him over one shoulder. The blacksmith and his workers glanced over together with a few passersby, and Morgan announced rather irritably that he supposed he would have to carry the fellow back to his quarters. Then off he marched in mock disgust.

He carried the unconscious soldier to a feed barn a few doors down and slipped inside. No one saw them enter. There, in near darkness, he stripped the man of his uniform, tied and gagged him securely, and shoved him back behind a pile of oat sacks. He donned the discarded uniform, brushed it out and straightened its creases, stuffed his own clothes in a sack he had brought, strapped on his weapons, and emerged once more into the light.

He moved quickly after that. Timing was everything in his plan; he had to reach the administration center of the workhouses just after the shift change came on at dusk. His day at the taverns had told him everything he needed to know about people, places, and procedures; he need only put the information to use. Already the twilight shadows were spreading across the forestland, swallowing up the few remaining pools of sunlight. The streets were starting to empty as soldier, trader, and citizen alike made their way homeward for the evening meal. Morgan kept to himself, careful to acknowledge senior officers in passing, doing what he could to avoid drawing attention to himself. He assumed a deliberate look and stance designed to keep others at bay. He became a rather hard-looking Federation soldier about his business—no one to approach without a reason, certainly no one to anger. It seemed to work; he was left alone.

The workhouses were lighted when he reached them, the day's activities grinding to a close. Dinner in the form of soup and bread was being carried in by the guards. The food smells wafted through the air, somewhat less than appetizing. Morgan crossed the roadway to the storage sheds and pretended to be checking on something. The minutes slipped past, and darkness approached.

At precisely sunset the shift change occurred. New guards replaced the old on the streets and at the doors of the workhouses. Morgan kept his eyes fixed on the administration center. The officer of the day relinquished his duty to his nighttime counterpart. An aide took up a position at a reception desk. Two men on duty—that was all. Morgan gave everyone a few minutes to settle in, then took a deep breath and strode out from the shadows.

He went straight to the center, pushed through the doors, and confronted the aide at the reception desk. "I'm back," he announced.

The aide looked at him blankly.

"For the old ladies," Morgan added, allowing a hint of irritation to creep into his voice. He paused. "Weren't you told?"

The aide shook his head. "I just came on . . ."

"Yes, but there should be a requisition order still on your desk from no more than an hour ago," Morgan snapped. "Isn't it there?"

"Well, I don't . . ." The aide cast about the desktop in confusion, moving stacks of papers aside.

"Signed by Major Assomal."

The aide froze. He knew who Major Assomal was. There wasn't a Federation soldier garrisoned at Culhaven who didn't. Morgan had found out about the major in the tavern. Assomal was the most feared and disliked Federation officer in the occupying army. No one wanted anything to do with him if they could help it.

The aide rose quickly. "Let me get the watch captain," he muttered.

He disappeared into the back office and emerged moments later with his superior in tow. The captain was clearly agitated. Morgan saluted the senior officer with just the right touch of disdain.

"What's this all about?" the captain demanded, but the question came out sounding more like a plea than a demand.

Morgan clasped his hands behind his back and straightened. His heart was pounding. "Major Assomal requires the services of two of the Dwarf women presently confined to the workhouses. I selected them personally earlier in the day at his request. I left so that the paperwork could be completed and now I am back. It seems, however, that the paperwork was never done."

The watch captain was a sallow-skinned, round-faced man who appeared to have seen most of his service behind a desk. "I don't know anything about that," he snapped peevishly.

Morgan shrugged. "Very well. Shall I take that message back to Major Assomal, Captain?"

The other man went pale. "No, no, I didn't mean that. It's

just that I don't . . ." He exhaled sharply. "This is very annoying."

"Especially since Major Assomal will be expecting me back
momentarily." Morgan paused. "With the Dwarves."

The watch captain threw up his hands. "All right! What difference does it make! I'll sign them out to you myself! Let's
have them brought up and be done with it!"

He opened the registry of names and with Morgan looking
on determined that Granny Elise and Auntie Jilt were housed in
building four. Hurriedly he scribbled out a release order for the
workhouse guards. When he tried to dispatch the aide to collect
the old ladies, Morgan insisted that he go as well.

"Just to make certain there are no further mix-ups, Captain,"
he explained. "After all, I have to answer to Major Assomal as
well."

The watch captain didn't argue, obviously anxious to be shed
of the matter as quickly as possible, and Morgan went out the
door with the aide. The night was still and pleasantly warm.
Morgan felt almost jaunty. His plan, risky or not, was going to
work. They crossed the compound to building four, presented
the release order to the guards stationed at the front doors, and
waited while they perused it. Then the guards unfastened the
locks and beckoned for them to proceed. Morgan and the aide
pushed through the heavy wooden doors and stepped inside.

The workhouse was crammed with workbenches and bodies
and smelled of stale air and sweat. Dust lay over everything,
and the lamplight shone dully against walls that were dingy and
unwashed. The Dwarf women were huddled on the floor with
cups of soup and plates of bread in hand, finishing their dinner.
Heads and eyes turned hurriedly as the two Federation soldiers
entered, then turned just as quickly away again. Morgan caught
the unmistakable look of fear and loathing.

"Call their names," he ordered the aide.

The aide did so, his voice echoing in the cavernous room and
near the back two hunched forms came slowly to their feet.

"Now wait outside for me," Morgan said.

The aide hesitated, then disappeared back through the doors.

Morgan waited anxiously as Granny Elise and Auntie Jilt
made their way gingerly through the clutter of bodies, benches,
and pallets to where he stood. He barely recognized them. Their
clothes were in tatters. Granny Elise's fine gray hair was unkempt, as if it were fraying all around the edges; Auntie Jilt's
sharp, birdlike face was pinched and harsh. They were bent over

with more than age, moving so slowly that it appeared it hurt them even to walk.

They came up to him with their eyes downcast and stopped.

"Granny," he said softly. "Auntie Jilt."

They looked up slowly and their eyes widened. Auntie Jilt caught her breath. "Morgan!" Granny Elise whispered in wonder. "Child, it's really you!"

He bent down quickly then and took them in his arms, hugging them close. They collapsed into him, rag dolls lacking strength of their own, and he could hear them both begin to cry. Behind them, the other Dwarf women were staring in confusion.

Morgan eased the two old ladies gently away. "Listen now," he said softly. "We haven't much time. I've tricked the watch captain into releasing you into my custody, but he's liable to catch on if we give him the chance so we have to hurry. Do you have somewhere that you can go to hide, someplace you won't be found?"

Auntie Jilt nodded, her narrow face a mask of determination. "The Resistance will hide us. We still have friends."

"Morgan, where's Steff?" Granny Elise interrupted.

The Highlander forced himself to meet her urgent gaze. "I'm sorry, Granny. Steff is dead. He was killed fighting against the Federation in the Dragon's Teeth." He saw the pain that filled her eyes. "Teel is dead, too. She was the one who killed Steff. She wasn't what any of us thought, I'm afraid. She was a creature called a Shadowen, a thing of dark magic linked to the Federation. She betrayed you as well."

"Oh, Steff," Granny Elise whispered absently. She was crying again.

"The soldiers came for us right after you left," Auntie Jilt said angrily. "They took the children away and put us in this cage. I knew something had gone wrong. I thought you might have been taken as well. Drat it, Morgan, that girl was like our own!"

"I know, Auntie," he answered, remembering how it had been. "It has become difficult to know who to trust. What about the Dwarves you plan to hide with? Can they be trusted? Are you sure you will be safe?"

"Safe enough," Auntie replied. "Stop your crying, Elise," she said and patted the other woman's hand gently. "We have to do as Morgan says and get out of here while we have the chance."

Granny Elise nodded, brushing away her tears. Morgan stood

up again. He stroked each gray head in turn. "Remember, you don't know me, you're just my charges until we get clear of this place. And if something goes wrong, if we get separated, go where you'll be safe. I made a promise to Steff that I would see to it that you did. So you make certain I don't break that promise, all right?"

"All right, Morgan," Granny Elise said.

They went out the door then, Morgan leading, the two old ladies shuffling along behind with their heads bowed. The aide was standing rigidly to one side by himself; the guards looked bored. With the Dwarf ladies in tow, Morgan and the aide returned to the administration center. The watch captain was waiting impatiently, the promised release papers clutched in his hand. He passed them across the reception desk to Morgan for his signature, then shoved them at the aide and stalked back into his office. The aide looked at Morgan uncomfortably.

Inwardly congratulating himself on his success, Morgan said, "Major Assomal will be waiting."

He turned and was in the process of ushering Granny Elise and Auntie Jilt outside when the door opened in front of them and a new Federation officer appeared, this one bearing the crossed bars of a divisional commander.

"Commander Soldt!" The aide leaped to his feet and saluted smartly.

Morgan froze. Commander Soldt was the officer in charge of supervising the confinement of the Dwarves, the ranking officer off the field for the entire garrison. What he was doing at the center at this hour was anybody's guess, but it was certainly not going to do anything to help further Morgan's plans.

The Highlander saluted.

"What's this all about?" Soldt asked, glancing at Granny Elise and Auntie Jilt. "What are they doing out of their quarters?"

"Just a requisition, Commander," replied the aide. "From Major Assomal."

"Assomal?" Soldt frowned. "He's in the field. What would he want with Dwarves . . ." He glanced again at Morgan. "I don't know you, soldier. Let me see your papers."

Morgan hit him as hard as he could. Soldt fell to the floor and lay unmoving. Instantly Morgan went after the aide, who backed away shrieking in terror. Morgan caught him and slammed his head against the desk. The watch captain emerged just in time to catch several quick blows to the face. He staggered back into his office and went down.

"Out the door!" Morgan whispered to Granny Elise and Auntie Jilt.

They rushed from the administration center into the night. Morgan glanced about hurriedly and breathed out sharply in relief. The sentries were still at their posts. No one had heard the struggle. He guided the old ladies quickly along the street, away from the workhouses. A patrol appeared ahead. Morgan slowed, moving ahead of his charges, assuming a posture of command. The patrol turned off before it reached them, disappearing into the dark.

Then someone behind them was shouting, calling for help. Morgan pulled the old ladies into an alleyway and hastened them toward its far end. The shouts were multiplying now, and there was the sound of running feet. Whistles blew and an assembly horn blared.

"They'll be all over us now," Morgan muttered to himself.

They reached the next street over and turned onto it. The shouts were all around them. He pulled the ladies into a shadowed doorway and waited. Soldiers appeared at both ends of the street, searching. Morgan's rescue plans were collapsing about him. His hands tightened into fists. Whatever happened, he couldn't allow the Federation to recapture Granny and Auntie.

He bent to them. "I'll have to draw them away," he whispered urgently. "Stay here until they come after me, then run. Once you're hidden, stay that way—no matter what."

"Morgan, what about you?" Granny Elise seized his arm.

"Don't worry about me. Just do as I say. Don't come looking for me. I'll find you when this whole business is over. Goodbye, Granny. Goodbye, Auntie Jilt."

Ignoring their pleas to remain, he kissed and hugged them hurriedly, and darted into the street. He ran until he caught sight of the first band of searchers and yelled to them, "They're over here!"

The soldiers came running as he turned down an alleyway, leading them away from Granny Elise and Auntie Jilt. He wrenched the broadsword he wore strapped to his back from its scabbard. Breaking free of the alleyway, he caught sight of another band and called them after him as well, gesturing vaguely ahead. To them he was just another soldier—for the moment, at least. If he could just maneuver them ahead of him, he might be able to escape as well.

"That barn, ahead of us," he shouted as the first bunch caught up with him. "They're in there!"

The soldiers charged past, one knot, then the second. Morgan turned and darted off in the opposite direction. As he came around the corner of a feed building, he ran right up against a third unit.

"They've gone into . . ."

He stopped short. The watch captain stood before him, howling in recognition.

Morgan tried to break free, but the soldiers were on him in an instant. He fought back valiantly, but there was no room to maneuver. His attackers closed and forced him to the ground. Blows rained down on him.

This isn't working out the way I expected, he thought bleakly and then everything went black.

V

Three days later she who was said to be the daughter of the King of the Silver River arrived in Culhaven. The news of her coming preceded her by half a day and by the time she reached the outskirts of the village the roadway leading in was lined with people for more than a mile. They had come from everywhere—from the village itself, from the surrounding communities of both the Southland and the Eastland, from the farms and cottages of the plains and deep forests, even the mountains north. There were Dwarves and Men and a handful of Gnomes of both sexes and all ages. They were ragged and poor and until now without hope. They jammed the roadside expectantly, some come simply out of a sense of curiosity, most come out of their need to find something to believe in again.

The stories of the girl were wondrous. She had appeared in

the heart of the Silver River country close by the Rainbow Lake, a magical being sprung full-blown from the earth. She stopped at each village and town, farm and cottage, and performed miracles. It was said that she healed the land. She turned blackened, withered stalks to fresh, green shoots. She brought flowers to bloom, fruit to bear, and crops to harvest with the smallest of touches. She gave life back to the earth out of death. Even where the sickness was most severe, she prevailed. She bore some special affinity to the land, a kinship that sprang directly from her father's hands, from the legendary stewardship of the King of the Silver River. For years it had been believed that the spirit lord had died with the passing of the age of magic. Now it was known he had not; as proof he had sent his daughter to them. The people of the Silver River country were to be given back their old life. So the stories proclaimed.

No one was more anxious to discover the truth of the matter than Pe Ell.

It was midday, and he had been waiting for the girl within the shade of the towering old shagbark hickory on a rise at the very edge of town since just after sunrise when word had reached him that today was the day she would appear. He was very good at waiting, very patient, and so the time had gone quickly for him as he stood with the others of the growing crowd and watched the sun lift slowly into the summer sky and felt the heat of the day settle in. Conversation around him had been plentiful and unguarded, and he listened attentively. There were stories of what the girl had done and what it was believed she would do. There were speculations and judgments. The Dwarves were the most vehement in their beliefs—or lack thereof. Some said she was the savior of their people; some said she was nothing more than a Southland puppet. Voices raised in shouts, quarreled, and died away. Arguments wafted through the still, humid air like small explosions of steam out of a fiery earth. Tempers flared and cooled. Pe Ell listened and said nothing.

"She comes to drive out the Federation soldiers and restore our land to us, land that the King of the Silver River treasures! She comes to set us free!"

"Bah, old woman, you speak nonsense! There is nothing to say she is who she claims to be. What do you know of what she can or cannot do?"

"I know what I know. I sense what will be."

"Ha! That's the ache of your joints you feel, nothing more! You believe what you want to believe, not what is. The truth is that we have no more sense of who this girl is than we do of what tomorrow will bring. It is pointless to get our hopes up!''

''It is more pointless to keep them down!''

And so on, back and forth, an endless succession of arguments and counterarguments that accomplished nothing except to help pass the time. Pe Ell had sighed inwardly. He seldom argued. He seldom had cause to.

When at last she was said to approach, the arguments and conversation faded to mutterings and whispers. When she actually appeared, even the mutterings and whispers died away. A strange hush settled over those who lined the roadway suggesting that either the girl was not at all what they had expected or, perhaps, that she was something more.

She came up the center of the roadway surrounded by the would-be followers who had flocked to her during her journey east, a mostly bedraggled lot with tattered clothes and exhilarated faces. Her own garb was rough and poorly sewn, yet she evinced a radiance that was palpable. She was small and slight, but so exquisitely shaped as to seem not quite real. Her hair was long and silver, shining as water would when it shimmered in the moonlight. Her features were perfectly formed. She walked alone in a rush of bodies that crowded and stumbled about her yet could not bear to approach. She seemed to float among them. Voices called out anxiously to her, but she seemed unaware that anyone was there.

And then she passed by Pe Ell and turned deliberately to look at him. Pe Ell shuddered in surprise. The weight of that look— or perhaps simply the experience of it—was enough to stagger him. Almost immediately her strange black eyes shifted away again, and she was moving on, a sliver of brilliant sunlight that had momentarily left him blind. Pe Ell stared after her, not knowing what she had done to him, what it was that had occurred in that brief moment when their eyes met. It was as if she had looked into his heart and mind and read them quite clearly. It was as if with that single glance she had discovered everything there was to know about him.

He found her to be the most beautiful creature he had ever seen in his life.

She turned down the roadway into the village proper, the crowd trailing after, and Pe Ell followed. He was a tall, lean man, so thin that he appeared gaunt. His bones were prominent, and the muscles and skin of his body were molded tightly against them so as to suggest he might easily break. Nothing could have been further from the truth. He was as hard as iron. He had a long, narrow face with a hawk nose and a wide forehead with eyebrows set high above hazel eyes that were disarmingly frank to look upon. When he smiled, which was often, his mouth had a slightly lopsided appearance to it. His hair was brown and cropped close, rather spiky and uncontrolled. He slouched a bit when he walked and might have been either a gangly boy or a stalking cat. His hands were slim and delicate. He wore common forest clothing made of rough cloth dyed various shades of green and taupe, boots of worn leather laced back and across, and a short cloak with pockets.

He carried no visible weapon. The Stiehl was strapped to his thigh just below his right hip. The knife rode beneath his loose-fitting pants where it could not be seen but where it could be reached easily through a slit cut into a deep forward pocket.

He could feel the blade's magic warm him.

As he moved to keep up with the girl, people stepped aside—whether from what they saw in his face or the way he moved or the intangible wall they sensed surrounded him. He did not like to be touched, and everyone seemed instinctively to know it. As always, they shied away. He passed through them as a shadow chasing after the light, keeping the girl in sight as he did so, wondering. She had looked at him for a reason, and that intrigued him. He hadn't been certain what she would be like, how she would make him feel when he saw her for the first time—but he hadn't thought it would be anything like this. It surprised him, pleased him, and at the same time left him vaguely worried. He didn't like things that he couldn't control and he suspected that it would be difficult for anyone to exercise control over her.

Of course, he wasn't just anyone.

The crowd was singing now, an old song that told of the earth being reborn with the harvesting of new crops, the bearing of food from the fields to the tables of the people who had worked to gather it. There was praise for the seasons, for rain and sun, for the giving of life. Chants rose for the King of the Silver River; the voices grew steadily louder and more insistent. The girl seemed not to hear. She walked through the singing and the cries without responding, making her way first past the houses that lay at the edge of the village, then the larger shops that formed the core of the business center. Federation soldiers began to appear and tried to police the traffic as it surged ahead. They were too few and too ill-prepared, thought Pe Ell. Appar-

ently they had misjudged badly the extent of the community's
response to the coming of the girl.

The Dwarves were feverish in their adoration. It was as
if they had been given back the lives that had been stolen
from them. A broken, subjugated people for so many years,
there had been little enough to happen to give them hope.
But this girl seemed to be what they had been waiting for. It
was more than the stories, more than the claims of who she
was and what she could do. It was the look and feel of her.
Pe Ell could sense it as readily as the people who rallied
about her. He could feel something of it in himself. She was
different from anyone he had ever seen. She had come here
for a reason. She was going to *do* something.

Business ground to a halt in Culhaven as the whole of the
village, oppressed and oppressors alike, turned out to discover
what was happening and became a part of it. Pe Ell had the
sense of a wave gathering force out in the ocean, growing in
size until it dwarfed the vast body of water that had given life to
it. It was so with this girl. There was a sense of all other events
beyond this one ceasing to exist. Everything but what she was
faded away and lost meaning. Pe Ell smiled. It was the most
wonderful feeling.

The wave swept on through the village, past the shops and
businesses, the slave markets, the workhouses, the compounds
and soldiers' quarters, the shabby homes of the Dwarves and
the well-kept houses of the Federation officials, down the main
thoroughfare, and out again. No one seemed able to guess where
it was going. No one but the girl, for she led even at the center
of the maelstrom of bodies, guiding somehow the edges of the
wave, directing it as she wished. The cries and singing and
chants continued unabated, exhilarated, rapturous. Pe Ell marveled.

And then the girl stopped. The crowd slowed, swirled about
her, and grew still. She stood at the foot of the blackened slopes
that had once been the Meade Gardens. She lifted her face to
the stark line of the hill's barren crest much as if she might have
been looking beyond it to a place that no one else could see.
Few in the crowd looked where she was looking; they simply
stared at her. There were hundreds of them now, and all of them
waited to see what she would do.

Then slowly, deliberately she moved onto the slope. The
crowd did not follow, sensing perhaps that it was not meant to,
divining from some small movement or look that it was meant

to wait. It parted for her, a sea of faces rapt with expectation. A few hands stretched out in an attempt to touch her, but none succeeded.

Pe Ell eased his way through the crowd until he stood at its foremost edge less than ten yards from the girl. Although he was purposeful in his advance, he did not yet know what he meant to do.

A knot of soldiers intercepted the girl, led by an officer bearing the crossed shoulder bars of a Federation commander. The girl waited for them. An unpleasant murmur rose from the crowd.

"You are not allowed here," announced the commander, his voice steady and clear. "No one is. You must go back down."

The girl looked at him, waiting.

"This is forbidden ground, young lady," the other continued, an officer addressing an inferior in a manner intended to demonstrate authority. "No one is permitted to walk upon this earth. A proclamation of the Coalition Council of the Federation government, which I have the honor to serve, forbids it. Do you understand?"

The girl did not answer.

"If you do not turn around and leave willingly, I shall be forced to escort you."

A scattering of angry cries sounded.

The girl came forward a step.

"If you do not leave *at once*, I shall have to . . ."

The girl gestured and instantly the man's legs were entwined in ground roots an inch thick. The soldiers who had accompanied him fell back with gasps of dismay as the pikes they were holding turned to gnarled staffs of deadwood that crumbled in their hands. The girl walked past them, unseeing. The blustering voice of the commander turned to a whisper of fear and then disappeared in the shocked murmur of the crowd.

Pe Ell smiled fiercely. Magic! The girl possessed real magic! The stories were true. It was more than he could have hoped for. Was she really the daughter of the King of the Silver River? he wondered.

The soldiers kept away from her now, unwilling to challenge the kind of power she obviously wielded. There were a few attempts at issuing orders by lesser officers, but no one was sure what to do after what had happened to the commander. Pe Ell glanced swiftly about. Apparently there were no Seekers in the village. In the absence of Seekers, no one would act.

The girl proceeded up the empty, burned surface of the slope toward its summit, and her passing barely stirred the dry earth on which she walked. The sun beat down fiercely out of the midday sky, turning the empty stretch of ground into a furnace. The girl seemed not to notice, her face calm as she passed through the swelter.

As he stared at her, Pe Ell felt himself drawn to the rim of a vast chasm, knowing that beyond was something so impossible that he could not imagine it.

What will she do?

She came to the summit of the slope and stopped, a slim, ethereal form outlined against the sky. She paused for a moment, as if searching for something in the air around her, an invisible presence that would speak to her. Then she knelt. She dropped down to the charred earth of the hillside and buried her hands within it. Her head lowered and her hair fell about her in a veil of silver light.

The world about her went absolutely still.

Then the earth beneath began to tremble and shake, and a rumbling sound rose out of its depths. The crowd gasped and fell back. Men steadied themselves, women snatched up children, and cries and shouts began to sound. Pe Ell came forward a step, his hazel eyes intense. He was not frightened. This was what he had been waiting for, and nothing could have chased him away.

Light seemed to flare from the hillside then, a glow that dwarfed even the sunlight's brilliance. Geysers exploded from the earth, small eruptions that burst skyward, showering Pe Ell and the foremost members of the crowd with dirt and silt. There was a heaving as if some giant buried beneath was rising from his sleep, and huge boulders began to jut from the ground like the bones of the giant's hunched shoulders. The burned surface of the hillside began to turn itself over and disappear. Fresh earth rose up to cover it, rich and glistening, filling the air with a pungent smell. Massive roots lifted out like snakes, twisting and writhing in response to the rumblings. Green shoots began to unfold.

In the midst of it all, the girl knelt. Her body was rigid beneath the loose covering of her clothes, and her arms were buried in the earth up to her elbows. Her face was hidden.

Many in the crowd were kneeling now, some praying to the forces of magic once believed to have controlled the destiny of men, some simply steadying themselves against tremors which had grown so violent that even the most sturdy trees were being shaken. Excitement rushed through Pe Ell and left him flushed. He wanted to run to the girl, to embrace her, to feel what was happening within her, and to share in the power.

Boulders grated and boomed as they rearranged themselves, changing the shape of the hillside. Terraced walls formed out of the rock. Moss and ivy filled the gaps. Trails wound down from one level to the next in gentle descent. Trees appeared, roots become small saplings, the saplings in turn thickening and branching out, compressing dozens of seasons of growth into scant minutes. Leaves budded and spread as if desperate to reach the sunlight. Grasses and brush spread out across the empty earth, turning the blackened surface a vibrant green. And flowers! Pe Ell cried out in the silence of his mind. There were flowers everywhere, springing forth in a profusion of bright colors that threatened to blind him. Blues, reds, yellows, violets—the rainbow's vast spectrum of shades and tones blanketed the earth.

Then the rumbling ceased and the silence that followed was broken by the singing of birds. Pe Ell glanced at the crowd behind him. Most were on their knees still, their eyes wide, their faces rapt with wonder. Many were crying.

He turned back to the girl. In a span of no more than a few minutes she had transformed the entire hillside. She had erased a hundred years of devastation and neglect, of deliberate razing, of purposeful burning off and leveling out, and restored to the Dwarves of Culhaven the symbol of who and what they were. She had given them back the Meade Gardens.

She was still on her knees, her head lowered. When she came back to her feet she could barely stand. All of her strength had been expended in her effort to restore the Gardens; she seemed to have nothing left to give. She swayed weakly, her arms hanging limply at her sides, her beautiful, perfect face drawn and lined, her silver hair damp and tangled. Pe Ell felt her eyes fix upon him once more and this time he did not hesitate. He went up the hillside swiftly, bounding over rocks and brush, skipping past the trails as if they were hindrances. He felt the crowd surging after him, heard their voices crying out, but they were nothing to him and he did not look back. He reached the girl as she was falling and caught her in his arms. Gently he cradled her, holding her as he might a captured wild creature, protectively and possessively at once.

Her eyes stared into his, he saw the intensity and brilliance of them, the depth of feeling they held, and in that moment he was bound to her in a way that he could not describe. "Take me to where I can rest," she whispered to him.

The crowd was all about them now, their anxious voices a babble he could not lock out. A sea of faces pressed close. He said something to those closest to reassure them that she was only tired and heard his words pass from mouth to mouth. He caught a glimpse of Federation soldiers at the fringes of the crowd, but they were wisely choosing to keep their distance. He began moving away, carrying the girl, amazed at how little she weighed. There was nothing to her, he thought. And everything.

A handful of Dwarves intercepted him, asking him to follow them, to bring the daughter of the King of the Silver River to their home, to let her rest with them. Pe Ell let himself be guided by them. One home was as good as another for now. The eyes of the crowd followed after, but already it was dispersing at its fringes, straying off into the paradise of the Gardens, discovering for themselves the beauty that it held. There was singing again, softer now, songs of praise and thanksgiving for the girl, lyrical and sweet.

Pe Ell descended the hillside and passed out of the Meade Gardens and back into the village of Culhaven with the girl asleep in his arms. She had given herself into his keeping. She had placed herself under his protection. He found it ironic.

After all, he had been sent there to kill her.

VI

Pe Ell carried the daughter of the King of the Silver River to the home of the Dwarves who had offered to keep her, a family that consisted of a man, his wife, their widowed daughter, and two small grandchildren. Their home was a stone cottage at the east end of the village sheltered by white oak and red elm and set back against the wall of the forest close by the channel of the river. It was quiet there, isolated from the village proper, and by the time they reached it most of the following crowd had turned back. A handful chose to stay and set up camp at the edge of the property, most of them those who had followed the girl up from the country south, zealots who were determined that she would be their savior.

But she wasn't for them, Pe Ell knew. She belonged now to him.

With the help of the family he placed the girl in a bed in a tiny back room where the man and woman slept. The husband and his wife and widowed daughter went out again to prepare something to eat for those who had chosen to keep vigil over the girl, but Pe Ell remained. He sat in a chair next to the bed and watched her sleep. For a time the children remained, curious to see what would happen, but eventually they lost interest, and he was left alone. The daylight faded into darkness and still he sat, waiting patiently for her to wake. He studied the line of her body as she lay sleeping, the curve of her hip and shoulder, the soft rounding of her back. She was such a tiny thing, just a little bit of flesh and bone beneath the coverings, the smallest spark of life. He marveled at the texture of her skin, at the coloring, at the absence of flaws. She might have been molded by some great artist whose reflection and skill had created a once-and-only masterpiece.

Fires were lit without, and the sound of voices drifted in through the curtained window. The sounds of night filled the silence between exchanges, the songs of birds and the buzzing of insects rising up against the faint rush of the river's waters. Pe Ell was not tired and had no need to sleep.

Instead, he used the time to think.

A week earlier he had been summoned to Southwatch and a meeting with Rimmer Dall. He had gone because it pleased him and not because it was necessary. He was bored and he was hopeful that the First Seeker would give him something interesting to do, that he would provide him with a challenge. To Pe Ell's way of thinking, that was all that mattered about Rimmer Dall. The rest of what the First Seeker did with his life and the lives of others was of no interest to him. He had no illusions, of course. He knew what Rimmer Dall was. He simply didn't care.

It took him two days to make the journey. He traveled north on horseback out of the rugged hill country below the Battle-

mound where he made his home and arrived at Southwatch at
sunset on the second day. He dismounted while still out of sight
of the sentries and made his approach by foot. He need not have
bothered; he could have come all the way in and gained immediate admittance. But he liked the idea of being able to come
and go as he chose. He liked demonstrating his talent.

Especially to the Shadowen.

Pe Ell was as they were as he came into the black monolith,
seemingly through the creases in the stone, a wraith out of darkness. He went past the sentries unseen and unheard, as invisible
to them as the air they breathed. Southwatch was silent and dark,
its walls polished and smooth, its corridors empty. It had the
feel and look of a well-preserved crypt. Only the dead belonged
here, or those who trafficked in death. He worked his way
through its catacombs, feeling the pulse of the magic imprisoned
in the earth beneath, hearing the whisper of it as it sought to
break free. A sleeping giant that Rimmer Dall and his Shadowen
thought they would tame, Pe Ell knew. They kept their secret
well, but there was no secret that could be kept from him.

When he was almost to the high tower where Rimmer Dall
waited, he killed one of those who kept watch, a Shadowen, but
it made no difference. He did so because he could and because
he felt like it. He melted into the black stone wall and waited
until the creature came past him, drawn by a faint noise that he
had caused, then drew the Stiehl from its sheath within his pants
and cut the life out of his victim with a single, soundless twist.
The sentry died in his arms, its shade rising up before him like
black smoke, the body crumbling into ash. Pe Ell watched the
astonished eyes go flat. He left the empty uniform where it could
be found.

He smiled as he floated through the shadows. He had been
killing for a long time now and he was very good at it. He had
discovered his talent early in life, his ability to seek out and
destroy even the most guarded of victims, his sense of how their
protection could be broken down. Death frightened most people, but not Pe Ell. Pe Ell was drawn to it. Death was the twin
brother of life and the more interesting of the two. It was secretive, unknown, mysterious. It was inevitable and forever when
it came. It was a dark, infinitely chambered fortress waiting to
be explored. Most entered only once and then only because they
had no choice. Pe Ell wanted to enter at every opportunity and
the chance to do so was offered through those he killed. Each

time he watched someone die he would discover another room, glimpse another part of the secret. He would be reborn.

High within the tower, he encountered a pair of sentries posted before a locked door. They failed to see him as he eased close. Pe Ell listened. He could hear nothing, but he could sense that someone was imprisoned within the room beyond. He debated momentarily whether he should discover who it was. But that would mean asking, which he would never do, or killing the sentries, which he did not care to do. He passed on.

Pe Ell ascended a darkened flight of stairs to the apex of Southwatch and entered a room of irregular chambers that connected together like corridors in a maze. There were no doors, only entryways. There were no sentries. Pe Ell slipped inside, a soundless bit of night. It was dark without now, the blackness complete as clouds blanketed the skies and turned the world beneath opaque. Pe Ell moved through several of the chambers, listening, waiting.

Then abruptly he stopped, straightened, and turned.

Rimmer Dall stepped out of the blackness of which he was a part. Pe Ell smiled. Rimmer Dall was good at making himself invisible, too.

"How many did you kill?" the First Seeker asked in his hushed, whispery voice.

"One," Pe Ell said. His smile tugged at the corners of his mouth. "Perhaps I will kill another on the way out."

Dall's eyes shone a peculiar red. "One day you will play this game too often. One day you will brush up against death by mistake and she will snatch *you* up instead of your victim."

Pe Ell shrugged. His own dying did not trouble him. He knew it would come. When it did, it would be a familiar face, one he had seen all his life. For most, there was the past, the present, and the future. Not for Pe Ell. The past was nothing more than memories, and memories were stale reminders of what had been lost. The future was a vague promise—dreams and puffs of smoke. He had no use for either. Only the present mattered, because the present was the here and now of what you were, the happening of life, the immediacy of death, and it could be controlled as neither past nor future could. Pe Ell believed in control. The present was an ever-evolving chain of moments that living and dying forged, and you were always there to see it come.

A window opened on the night across a table and two chairs, and Pe Ell moved to seat himself. Rimmer Dall joined him.

They sat in silence for a time, each looking at the other, but seeing something more. They had known each other for more than twenty years. Their meeting had been an accident. Rimmer Dall was a junior member of a policing committee of the Coalition Council, already deeply enmeshed in the poisonous politics of the Federation. He was ruthless and determined, barely out of boyhood, and already someone to be feared. He was a Shadowen, of course, but few knew it. Pe Ell, almost the same age, was an assassin with more than twenty kills behind him. They had met in the sleeping quarters of a man Rimmer Dall had come to dispatch, a man whose position in the Southland government he coveted and whose interference he had tolerated long enough. Pe Ell had gotten there first, sent by another of the man's enemies. They had faced each other in silence across the man's lifeless body, the night's shadows cloaking them both in the same blackness that mirrored their lives, and they had sensed a kinship. Both had use of the magic. Neither was what he seemed. Both were relentlessly amoral. Neither was afraid of the other. Without, the Southland city of Wayford buzzed and clanked and hissed with the intrigues of men whose ambitions were as great as their own but whose abilities were far less. They looked into each other's eyes and saw the possibilities.

They formed an irrevocable partnership. Pe Ell became the weapon, Rimmer Dall the hand that wielded it. Each served the other at his own pleasure; there were no constraints, no bonds. Each took what was needed and gave back what was required—yet neither really identified with nor understood what the other was about. Rimmer Dall was the Shadowen leader whose plans were an inviolate secret. Pe Ell was the killer whose occupation remained his peculiar passion. Rimmer Dall invited Pe Ell to eliminate those he believed particularly dangerous. Pe Ell accepted the invitation when the challenge was sufficiently intriguing. They nourished themselves comfortably on the deaths of others.

"Who is it that you keep imprisoned in the room below?" Pe Ell asked suddenly, breaking the silence, ending the flow of recollections.

Rimmer Dall's head inclined slightly, a mask of bones that gave his face the look of a fleshless skull. "A Southlander, a Valeman. One of two brothers named Ohmsford. The other brother believes he has killed this one. I arranged for him to think so. I planned it that way." The big man seemed pleased with himself. "When it is time, I will let them find each other again."

"A game of your own, it seems."

"A game with very high stakes, stakes that involve magic of unimaginable proportions—magic greater than either yours or mine or anyone else's. Unbounded power."

Pe Ell did not respond. He felt the weight of the Stiehl against his thigh, the warmth of its magic. It was difficult for him to imagine a magic more powerful—impossible to envision one more useful. The Stiehl was the perfect weapon, a blade that could cut through anything. Nothing could withstand it. Iron, stone, the most impenetrable of defenses—all were useless against it. No one was safe. Even the Shadowen were vulnerable; even they could be destroyed. He had discovered as much some years back when one had tried to kill him, sneaking into his bedchamber like a stalking cat. It had thought to catch him sleeping; but Pe Ell was always awake. He had killed the black thing easily.

Afterward it had occurred to him that the Shadowen might have been sent by Rimmer Dall to test him. He hadn't chosen to dwell on the possibility. It didn't matter. The Stiehl made him invincible.

Fate had given him the weapon, he believed. He did not know who had made the Stiehl, but it had been intended for him. He was twelve years old when he found it, traveling with a man who claimed to be his uncle—a harsh, embittered drunkard with a penchant for beating anything smaller and weaker than himself—on a journey north through the Battlemound to yet another in an endless succession of towns and villages they frequented so that the uncle might sell his stolen goods. They were camped in a ravine in a desolate, empty stretch of scrub country at the edge of the Black Oaks, fence-sitting between the Sirens and the forest wolves, and the uncle had beaten him again for some imagined wrong and fallen asleep with his bottle tucked close. Pe Ell didn't mind the beatings anymore; he had been receiving them since he was orphaned at four and his uncle had taken him in. He hardly remembered what it was like not to be abused. What he minded was the way his uncle went about it these days—as if each beating was being undertaken to discover the limits of what the boy could stand. Pe Ell was beginning to suspect he had reached those limits.

He went off into the failing light to be alone, winding down the empty ravines, trudging over the desolate rises, scuffing his booted feet, and waiting for the pain of his cuts and bruises to ease. The hollow was close, no more than several hundred yards away, and the cave at its bottom drew him as a magnet might iron. He sensed its presence in a way he could not explain, even afterward. Hidden by the scrub, half-buried in loose rock, it was a dark and ominous maw opening down into the earth. Pe Ell entered without hesitation. Few things frightened him even then. His eyesight had always been extraordinary, and even the faintest light was enough to let him find his way.

He followed the cave back to where the bones were gathered—human bones, centuries old, scattered about randomly as if kicked apart. The Stiehl lay among them, the blade gleaming silver in the dark, pulsing with life, its name carved on its handle. Pe Ell picked it up and felt its warmth. A talisman from another age, a weapon of great power—he knew at once that it was magic and that nothing could withstand it.

He did not hesitate. He departed the cave, returned to the camp, and cut his uncle's throat. He woke the man first to make certain that he knew who had done it. His uncle was the first man he killed.

It had all happened a long time ago.

"There is a girl," Rimmer Dall said suddenly and paused.

Pe Ell's gaze shifted back to the other's raw-boned face, silhouetted against the night. He could see the crimson eyes glitter.

The First Seeker's breath hissed from between his lips. "They say that she possesses magic, that she can change the character of the land simply by touching it, and that she can dispatch blight and disease and cause flowers to spring full grown from the foulest soil. They say that she is the daughter of the King of the Silver River."

Pe Ell smiled. "Is she?"

Rimmer Dall nodded. "Yes. She is who and what the stories claim. I do not know what she has been sent to do. She travels east toward Culhaven and the Dwarves. It appears that she has something specific in mind. I want you to find out what it is and then kill her."

Pe Ell stretched comfortably, his response unhurried. "Kill her yourself, why don't you?"

Rimmer Dall shook his head. "No. The daughter of the King of the Silver River is anathema to us. Besides, she would recognize a Shadowen instantly. Faerie creatures share a kinship that prohibits disguise. It must be someone other than one of us, someone who can get close enough, someone she will not suspect.''

"Someone." Pe Ell's crooked smile tightened. "There are lots of someones, Rimmer. Send another. You have entire armies of blindly loyal cutthroats who will be more than happy to dispatch a girl foolish enough to reveal that she possesses magic. This business doesn't interest me.''

"Are you certain, Pe Ell?"

Pe Ell sighed wearily. Now the bargaining begins, he thought. He stood up, his lean frame whiplike as he bent across the table so that he could see clearly the other's face. "I have listened to you tell me often enough how like the Shadowen you perceive me to be. We are much the same, you tell me. We wield magic against which there is no defense. We possess insight into the purpose of life which others lack. We share common instincts and skills. We smell, taste, sound, and feel the same. We are two sides of one coin. You go on and on. Well then, Rimmer Dall, unless you are lying I would be discovered by this girl as quickly as you, wouldn't I? Therefore, there is no point in sending me.''

"It must be you."

"Must it, now?"

"Your magic is not innate. It is separate and apart from who and what you are. Even if the girl senses it, she will still not know who you are. She will not be warned of the danger you pose to her. You will be able to do what is needed.''

Pe Ell shrugged. "As I said, this business doesn't interest me.''

"Because you think there is no challenge in it?"

Pe Ell paused, then slowly sat down again. "Yes. Because there is no challenge.''

Rimmer Dall leaned back in his chair and his face disappeared into shadow. "This girl is no simple flesh-and-blood creature; she will not be easily overcome. She has great magic, and her magic will protect her. It will take stronger magic still to kill her. Ordinary men with ordinary weapons haven't a chance. My legions of cutthroats, as you so disdainfully describe them, are worthless. Federation soldiers can get close to her, but cannot harm her. Shadowen cannot even get close. Even if they could, I am not certain it would make any difference. Do you understand me, Pe Ell?''

Pe Ell did not respond. He closed his eyes. He could feel Rimmer Dall watching him.

"This girl is dangerous, Pe Ell, the more so because she has obviously been sent to accomplish something of importance and I do not know what that something is. I have to find out and I have to put a stop to it. It will not be easy to do either. It may be too much even for you."

Pe Ell cocked his head thoughtfully. "Is that what you think?"

"Possibly."

Pe Ell was out of his chair with the swiftness of thought, the Stiehl snatched from its sheath and in his hand. The tip of the blade swept upward and stopped not an inch from Rimmer Dall's nose. Pe Ell's smile was frightening. "Really?"

Rimmer Dall did not flinch, did not even blink. "Do as I ask, Pe Ell. Go to Culhaven. Meet this girl. Find out what she plans to do. Then kill her."

Pe Ell was wondering if he should kill Rimmer Dall. He had thought about it before, contemplated it quite seriously. Lately the idea had begun to take on a certain fascination for him. He felt no loyalty to the man, cared nothing for him one way or the other beyond a vague appreciation of the opportunities he offered and even those were no longer as rewarding as they had once been. He was tired of the other's constant attempts to manipulate him. He no longer felt comfortable with their arrangement. Why not put an end to him?

The Stiehl wavered. The trouble was, of course, that there was no real point to it. Killing Rimmer Dall accomplished nothing, unless, of course, he was ready to discover what secrets might reveal themselves at the moment of the First Seeker's dying. That could prove interesting. On the other hand, why rush things? It was better to savor the prospect for a time. It was better to wait.

He sheathed the Stiehl with a quicksilver movement and backed away from Rimmer Dall. For just an instant he had a sense of missed opportunity, as if such a chance might never come again. But that was foolish. Rimmer Dall could not keep him away. The First Seeker's life was his to take when he chose.

He looked at Rimmer Dall for a moment, then spread his hands agreeably. "I'll do it."

He wheeled and started away. Rimmer Dall called after him. "Be warned, Pe Ell. This girl is more than a match for you. Do not play games with her. Once you have discovered her purpose, kill her quickly."

Pe Ell did not respond. He slipped from the room and melted back into the shadows of the keep, uninterested in anything

Rimmer Dall thought or wished. It was enough that he had agreed to do what the Shadowen had asked. How he accomplished it was his own business.

He departed Southwatch for Culhaven. He did not kill any of the sentries on his way out. He decided it wasn't worth the effort.

Midnight approached. He grew tired of thinking and dozed in his chair as the hours slipped away. It was only several hours from dawn when the girl awoke. The cottage was silent, the Dwarf family asleep. The fires of those camped without had burned to coals and ash, and the last whispers of conversation had died away. Pe Ell came awake instantly as the girl stirred. Her eyes blinked open and fixed on him. She stared at him without speaking for a very long time and then slowly sat up.

"I am called Quickening," she said.

"I am Pe Ell," he replied.

She reached for his hand and took it in her own. Her fingers were as light as feathers as they traced his skin. Then she shivered and drew back.

"I am the daughter of the King of the Silver River," she said. She swung her legs off the bed and faced him. She smoothed back her tangled silver hair. Pe Ell was transfixed by her beauty, but she seemed completely unaware of it. "I need your help," she said. "I have come out of the Gardens of my father and into the world of men in search of a talisman. Will you journey with me to find it?"

The plea was so unexpected that for a moment Pe Ell did not respond but simply continued staring at the girl. "Why do you choose me?" he asked finally, confused.

And she said at once, "Because you are special."

It was exactly the right answer, and Pe Ell was astonished that she should know enough to give it, that she could sense what he wanted to hear. Then he remembered Rimmer Dall's warning and hardened himself. "What sort of talisman is it that we search for?"

She kept her eyes fastened on him. "One of magic, one with power enough to withstand even that of the Shadowen."

Pe Ell blinked. Quickening was so beautiful, but her beauty was a mask that distracted and confused. He felt suddenly stripped of his defenses, bared to his deepest corners, the light thrown on all his secrets. She knew him for what he was, he sensed. She could see everything.

In that instant, he almost killed her. What stopped him was

how truly vulnerable she was. Despite her magic, formidable indeed, magic that could transform a barren, empty stretch of hillside back into what was surely no more than a memory in the minds of even the most elderly of the Dwarves, she lacked any form of defense against a killing weapon like the Stiehl. He could sense that it was so. She was helpless should he choose to kill her.

Knowing that, he decided not to. Not yet.

"Shadowen," he echoed softly.

"Are you frightened of them?" she asked him.

"No."

"Of magic?"

Pe Ell breathed in slowly. His narrow features twisted in upon themselves as he bent toward her. "What do you know of me?" he asked, his eyes searching her own.

She did not look away. "I know that I need you. That you will not be afraid to do what is necessary."

It seemed to Pe Ell that her words held more than one meaning, but he was unable to decide.

"Will you come?" she asked again.

Kill her quickly, Rimmer Dall had said. Find out her purpose and kill her. Pe Ell looked away, staring out the cottage window into the night, listening to the rushing sound of the river and the wind, soft and distant. He had never much bothered with the advice of others. Most of it was self-serving, useless to a man whose life depended on his ability to exercise his own judgment. Besides, there was a great deal more to this business than what Rimmer Dall had revealed. There were secrets waiting to be discovered. It might be that the talisman the girl searched for was something that even the First Seeker feared. Pe Ell smiled. What if the talisman happened to fall into his hands? Wouldn't that be interesting?

He looked back at her again. He could kill her anytime.

"I will come with you," he said.

She stood suddenly, reaching out her hands to take his own, drawing him up with her. They might have been lovers. "There are two more that must come with us, two like yourself who are needed," she said. "One of them is here in Culhaven. I want you to bring him to me."

Pe Ell frowned. He had already resolved to separate her from those fools camped without, misguided believers in miracles and fate who would only get in his way. Quickening belonged to him alone. He shook his head. "No."

She stepped close, her coal black eyes strangely empty. "Without them, we cannot succeed. Without them, the talisman is beyond our reach. No others need come, but they must."

She spoke with such determination that he found it impossible to argue with her. She seemed convinced that what she was saying was true. Perhaps it was, he decided; she knew more of what she was about at this point than he.

"Just two?" he asked. "No others? None of those without?"

She nodded wordlessly.

"All right," he agreed. No two men would be enough to cause him problems, to interfere with his plans. The girl would still be his to kill when he chose. "One man is here in the village, you say. Where am I to find him?"

For the first time since she had come awake, she turned away so that he could not see her.

"In the Federation prisons," she said.

VII

Morgan Leah.

That was the name of the man that Pe Ell was supposed to find and bring to the daughter of the King of the Silver River.

The streets of Culhaven were deserted save for the homeless huddled in the crooks and crannies of the shops, shapeless bundles of rags waiting out the night. Pe Ell ignored them as he made his way toward the center of town and the Federation prisons. Dawn was the better part of two hours away; he had more than sufficient time to do what was needed. He might have postponed this rescue business another night, but he saw no reason to do so. The quicker this fellow was found, the quicker they would all be on their way. He hadn't asked the girl yet where it was that they were going. It didn't matter.

He kept to the shadows as he moved ahead, mulling over in his mind the ambivalent effect she had on him. He was both exhilarated and appalled. She made him feel as if he were a man in the process of rediscovering himself and at the same time as if he were a fool. Rimmer Dall would certainly claim he was the latter, that he was playing the most dangerous of games, that he was being led about by the nose and deluding himself into thinking he was in command. But Rimmer Dall had no heart, no soul, no sense of the poetry of life and death. He cared nothing for anything or anyone—only for the power he wielded or sought to secure. He was a Shadowen, and the Shadowen were empty things. However Rimmer Dall saw it, Pe Ell was less like him than the First Seeker thought. Pe Ell understood the harsh realities of existence, the practical necessities of staying alive, and of making oneself secure; but he also could feel the beauty of things, particularly in the prospect of death. Death possessed great beauty. Rimmer Dall saw it as extinction. But when Pe Ell killed, he did so to discover anew the grace and symmetry that made it the most wondrous of life's events.

He was certain that there would be incredible beauty in the death of Quickening. It would be unlike any other killing he had ever done.

So he would not rush it, not hurry the irrevocable fact of it; he would take time to anticipate it. The feelings she invoked in him would not alter or adversely effect the course of action he had set for himself. He would not disparage himself for experiencing them; they were part of his makeup, a reaffirmation of his humanity. Rimmer Dall and his Shadowen could know nothing of such feelings; they were as unfeeling as stone. But not Pe Ell. Not ever.

He slipped past the workhouses, avoiding the lights of the compound and the Federation soldiers on watch. The surrounding forest was hushed and sleeping, a black void in which sounds were disembodied and somehow frightening. Pe Ell became a part of that void, comfortable within its cloaking as he moved soundlessly ahead. He could see and hear what no one else could; it had always been that way. He could feel what lived within the dark even though it hid from him. The Shadowen were like that; but even they could not assimilate as he could.

He paused at a lighted crossway and waited to be certain it was clear. There were patrols everywhere.

He pictured Quickening's image in the aura cast by a solitary streetlamp. A child, a woman, a magical being—she was all of these and much more. She was the embodiment of the land's most beautiful things—a sunlit woodland glen, a towering falls, a blue sky at midday, a rainbow's kaleidoscope of color, an endless sweep of stars at night viewed from an empty plain. She was a creature of flesh and blood, of human life, and yet she was a part of the earth as well, of fresh-turned soil, of mountain streams, of great old rocks that would not yield to anything but time. It baffled him, but he could sense things in her that were at once incongruous and compatible. How could that be? What was she, beyond what she claimed?

He moved swiftly through the light and melted back into the shadows. He did not know, but he was determined to find out.

The squarish dark bulk of the prisons loomed ahead. Pe Ell took a moment to consider his options. He knew the design of the Federation prisons at Culhaven; he had even been in them once or twice, though no one knew about it but Rimmer Dall. Even in prison, there were men who needed to be killed. But that was not to be the case tonight. Admittedly, he had considered killing this man he had been sent to rescue, this Morgan Leah. That would be one way to prevent the girl from insisting that he accompany them in their search for the missing talisman. Kill this one now, the other one later, and that would be the end of the matter. He could lie about how it happened. But the girl might guess the truth, might even divine it. She trusted him; why take a chance on changing that? Besides, perhaps she was right about needing these men to reclaim the talisman. He did not know enough yet of what they were about. It was better to wait and see.

He let his lean frame disappear into the stone of the wall against which he rested, thinking. He could enter the prisons directly, confront the commanding officer with his Shadowen insignia, and secure the release of the man without further fuss. But that would mean revealing himself, and he preferred not to do that. No one knew about him now besides Rimmer Dall. He was the First Seeker's private assassin. None of the other Shadowen even suspected that he existed; none had ever seen him. Those who had encountered him, Shadowen or otherwise, were all dead. He was a secret to everyone and he preferred to keep it that way. It would be better to take the man out in the usual way, in silence and stealth, alone.

Pe Ell smiled his lopsided smile. Save the man now so that he could kill him later. It was a strange world.

He eased himself out from the wall and snaked his way through the darkness toward the prisons.

Morgan Leah was not asleep. He lay wrapped in a blanket in his cell on a pallet of straw, thinking. He had been awake for most of the night, too restless to sleep, plagued by worries and regrets and a nagging sense of futility that he could not seem to banish. The cell was claustrophobic, barely a dozen feet square while more than twenty feet from floor to ceiling with an iron door several inches thick and a single barred window so high up he could not manage to reach it to look out even by jumping. The cell had not been cleaned since he had been thrown into it, so consequently it stank. His food, such as it was, was brought to him twice a day and shoved through a slot at the base of the door. He was given water to drink in the same way, but none with which to wash. He had been imprisoned now for almost a week and no one had come to see him. He was beginning to think that no one would.

It was an odd prospect. When they had caught him he had been certain they would be quick to use whatever means they had at their disposal to find out why he had gone to so much trouble to free two old Dwarf ladies. He wondered even now if Granny Elise and Auntie Jilt had escaped, if they remained free; he had no way of knowing. He had struck a Federation commander, perhaps killed him. He had stolen a Federation uniform to impersonate a Federation soldier, used a Federation major's name to secure entry to the workhouses, deceived the Federation officer on duty, and made the Federation army in general appear like a bunch of incompetents. All for the purpose of freeing two old ladies. A maligned and misused Federation command had to want to know why. They had to be anxious to repay him for the humiliation and hurt he had caused them. Yet they had left him alone.

He played mind games with the possibilities. It seemed unlikely he was going to be ignored indefinitely, that he was to be left in that cell until he was simply forgotten. Major Assomal, as he had discovered, was in the field; perhaps they were waiting for him to return to begin the questioning. But would Commander Soldt be patient enough to wait after what had been done to him? Or was he dead; had Morgan killed him after all? Or were they all waiting for someone else?

Morgan sighed. Someone else. He always came back to the

same inescapable conclusion. They were waiting for Rimmer Dall.

He knew that had to be it. Teel had betrayed Granny and Auntie to the Federation, but more particularly to the Shadowen. Rimmer Dall had to know of their connection to Par and Coll Ohmsford and all those who had gone in search of the Sword of Shannara. If someone tried to rescue them, surely he would be notified—and would come to see who it was that had been caught.

Morgan eased himself gingerly over on one side facing out from the wall into the blackness. He didn't hurt as much as he had the first few days; the aches and pains of his beating were beginning to heal. He was lucky nothing had been broken—lucky, in fact, that he was still alive.

Or not so lucky, he amended his assessment, depending on how you looked at it. His luck, it appeared, had run out. He thought momentarily of Par and Coll and regretted that he would not be able to go to them, to look after them as he had promised he would. What would become of them without him? What had happened to them in his absence? He wondered if Damson Rhee had hidden them after their escape from the Pit of Tyrsis. He wondered if Padishar Creel had found out where they were.

He wondered a thousand things, and there were no answers to be found for any of them.

Mostly he wondered how much longer he would be kept alive.

He rolled onto his back again, thinking of how different things might have been for him. In another age he would have been a Prince of Leah and one day ruled his homeland. But the Federation had put an end to the monarchy more than two hundred years ago, and today his family ruled nothing. He closed his eyes, trying to dispel any thoughts of might-have-beens and would-have-beens, finding no comfort there. He remained hopeful, his spirit intact despite all that had happened, the resiliency that had seen him through so much still in evidence. He did not intend to give up. There was always a way.

He just wished he could discover what it was.

He dozed for a bit, lost in a flow of imaginings that jumbled together in a wash of faces and voices, teasing him with their disjointed, false connectings, lies of things that never were and could never be.

He drifted into sleep.

Then a hand came down over his mouth, cutting off his exclamation of surprise. A second hand pinned him to the floor. He struggled, but the grip that held him was unbreakable.

"Quiet, now," a voice whispered in his ear. "Hush."

Morgan went still. A hawk-faced man in a Federation uniform was bent over him, peering into his eyes intently. The hands released, and the man sat back. A smile tugged at the corners of his mouth, and laugh lines wreathed his narrow face.

"Who are you?" Morgan asked softly.

"Someone who can get you free of this place if you're smart enough to do as I say, Morgan Leah."

"You know my name?"

The laugh lines deepened. "A lucky guess. Actually, I stumbled in here by chance. Can you show me the way out again?"

Morgan stared at him, a tall, gaunt fellow who had the look of a man who knew what he was about. The smile he wore seemed wired in place and there was nothing friendly about it. Morgan shoved his blanket aside and came to his feet, noticing the way the other backed off as he did so, always keeping the same amount of space between them. Cautious, thought Morgan, like a cat.

"Are you with the Movement?" he asked the man.

"I'm with myself. Put this on."

He tossed Morgan some clothing. When the Highlander examined it, he found he was holding a Federation uniform. The stranger disappeared back into the dark for a moment, then reemerged carrying something bulky over one shoulder. He deposited his burden on the pallet with a grunt. Morgan started as he realized it was a body. The stranger picked up the discarded blanket and draped it over the dead man to make it look as if he were sleeping.

"It will take them longer this way to discover you're missing," he whispered with that unnerving smile.

Morgan turned away and dressed as quickly as he could. The other man beckoned impatiently when he was finished and together they slipped out through the open cell door.

The corridor without was narrow and empty. Lamplight brightened the darkness only marginally. Morgan had seen nothing of the prisons when they brought him in, still unconscious from his beating, and he was immediately lost. He trailed after the stranger watchfully, following the passageway as it burrowed through the stone block walls past rows of cell doors identical to his own, all locked and barred. They encountered no one.

When they reached the first watch station, it was deserted as well. There appeared to be no one on duty. The stranger moved quickly to the corridor beyond, but Morgan caught a glint of metal blades through a half-open door to one side. He slowed, peering in. Racks of weapons lined the walls of a small room. He suddenly remembered the Sword of Leah. He did not want to leave without it.

"Wait a minute!" he whispered to the man ahead.

The stranger turned. Quickly Morgan pushed at the door. It gave reluctantly, dragging against something. Morgan shoved until there was enough space to get through. Inside, wedged against the back of the door, was another dead man. Morgan swallowed against what he was feeling and forced himself to search the racks for the Sword of Leah.

He found it almost immediately, still in its makeshift sheath, hung on a nail behind a brace of pikes. He strapped the weapon on hurriedly, grabbed a broadsword as well, and went out again.

The stranger was waiting. "No more delays," he said pointedly. "The shift change comes just after sunrise. It's almost that now."

Morgan nodded. They went down a second corridor, a back set of stairs supported by timbers that creaked and groaned as they descended, and out through a courtyard. The stranger knew exactly where he was going. There were no guards until they reached a post just inside the walls and even then they were not challenged. They passed through the gates and out of the prison just as the first faint tinges of light began to appear on the horizon.

The stranger took Morgan down the roadway a short distance, then into a barn through a backdoor where the shadows were so thick the Highlander had to feel his way. Inside, the stranger lit a lamp. Digging under a pile of empty feed sacks, he produced a change of clothing for each of them, woods garb, indistinguishable from what most Eastland laborers wore. They changed wordlessly, then stuffed the discarded Federation uniforms back beneath the sacks.

The stranger motioned Morgan after him and they went out again into the first light of the new day.

"A Highlander, are you?" the stranger asked abruptly as they walked eastward through the waking village.

Morgan nodded.

"Morgan Leah. Last name the same as the country. Your family ruled the Highlands once, didn't they?"

"Yes," Morgan answered. His companion seemed more relaxed now, his long strides slow and easy, though his eyes never stopped moving. "But the monarchy hasn't existed for many years."

They took a narrow bridge across a sewage-fouled tributary of the Silver River. An old woman passed them carrying a small child. Both looked hungry. Morgan glanced over at them. The stranger did not.

"My name is Pe Ell," he said. He did not offer his hand.

"Where are we going?" Morgan asked him.

The corners of the other's mouth tugged upward slightly. "You'll see." Then he added, "To meet the lady who sent me to rescue you."

Morgan thought at once of Granny Elise and Auntie Jilt. But how would they know someone like Pe Ell? The man had already said he was not a part of the Free-born Movement; it seemed unlikely that he was allied with the Dwarf Resistance either. Pe Ell, Morgan thought, was with exactly who he had said he was with—himself.

But who then was the lady on whose behalf he had come?

They passed down lanes that wound through the Dwarf cottages and shacks at the edge of Culhaven, crumbling stone and wood slat structures falling down around the heads of those who lived within. Morgan could hear the sluggish flow of the Silver River grow nearer. The houses separated as the trees thickened and soon there were few to be seen. Dwarves at work in their yards and gardens looked up at them suspiciously. If Pe Ell noticed, he gave no sign.

Sunlight was breaking through the trees ahead in widening streamers by the time they reached their destination, a small, well-kept cottage surrounded by a ragged band of men who had settled in at the edge of the yard and were in the process of completing breakfast and rolling up their sleeping gear. The men whispered among themselves and looked long and hard at Pe Ell as he approached. Pe Ell went past them without speaking, Morgan in tow. They went up the steps to the front door of the cottage and inside. A Dwarf family seated at a small table greeted them with nods and brief words of welcome. Pe Ell barely acknowledged them. He took Morgan to the back of the cottage and into a small bedroom and shut the door carefully behind them.

A girl sat on the edge of the bed.

"Thank you, Pe Ell," she said quietly and rose.

Morgan Leah stared. The girl was stunningly beautiful with

small, perfect features dominated by the blackest eyes the Highlander had ever seen. She had long, silver hair that shimmered like captured light, and a softness to her that invited protection. She wore simple clothes—a tunic, pants cinched at the waist with a wide leather belt, and boots—but the clothes could not begin to disguise the sensuality and grace of the body beneath.

"Morgan Leah," the girl whispered.

Morgan blinked, suddenly aware that he was staring. He flushed.

"I am called Quickening," the girl said. "My father is the King of the Silver River. He has sent me from his Gardens into the world of Men to find a talisman. I require your help to do so."

Morgan started to respond and stopped, not knowing what to say. He glanced at Pe Ell, but the other's eyes were on the girl. Pe Ell was as mesmerized as he.

Quickening came up to him, and the flush in his face and neck traveled down his body in a warm rush. She reached out her hands and placed her fingers gently on the sides of his face. He had never felt a touch like hers. He thought he might give anything to experience it again.

"Close your eyes, Morgan Leah," she whispered.

He did not question her; he simply did as she asked. He was immediately at peace. He could hear voices conversing somewhere without, the flow of the waters of the nearby river, the whisper of the wind, the singing of birds, and the scrape of a garden hoe. Then Quickening's fingers tightened marginally against his skin and everything disappeared in a wash of color.

Morgan Leah floated as if swept away in a dream. Hazy brightness surrounded him, but there was no focus to it. Then the brightness cleared and the images began. He saw Quickening enter Culhaven along a roadway lined with men, women, and children who cheered and called out to her as she passed, then followed anxiously after. He watched as she walked through growing crowds of Dwarves, Southlanders, and Gnomes to the barren stretch of hillside where the Meade Gardens had once flourished. It seemed that he became a part of the crowd, standing with those who had come to see what this girl would do, experiencing himself their sense of expectancy and hope. Then she ascended the hillside, buried her hands in the charred earth, and worked her wondrous magic. The earth was transformed before his eyes; the Meade Gardens were restored. The colors, smells, and tastes of her miracle filled the air, and Morgan felt an aching in his chest that was impossibly sweet. He began to cry.

The images faded. He found himself back in the cottage. He felt her fingers drop away and he brushed roughly at his eyes with the back of his hand as he opened them. She was staring at him.

"Was that real?" he asked, his voice catching in spite of his resolve to keep it firm. "Did that actually happen? It did, didn't it?"

"Yes," she answered.

"You brought back the Gardens. Why?"

Her smile was faint and sweet. "Because the Dwarves need to have something to believe in again. Because they are dying."

Morgan took a deep breath. "Can you save them, Quickening?"

"No, Morgan Leah," she answered, disappointing him, "I cannot." She turned momentarily into the room's shadows. "You can, perhaps, one day. But for now you must come with me."

The Highlander hesitated, unsure. "Where?"

She lifted her exquisite face back into the light. "North, Morgan Leah. To Darklin Reach. To find Walker Boh."

Pe Ell stood to one side in the little cottage bedroom, momentarily forgotten. He didn't like what he was seeing. He didn't like the way the girl touched the Highlander or the way the Highlander responded to it. She hadn't touched him like that. It bothered him, too, that she knew the Highlander's name. She knew the other man's name as well, this Walker Boh. She hadn't known his.

She turned to him then, drawing him back into the conversation with Morgan Leah, telling them both they must travel north to find the third man. After they found him they would leave in search of the talisman she had been sent to find. She did not tell them what that talisman was, and neither of them asked. It was a result of the peculiar effect she had on them, Pe Ell decided, that they did not question what she told them, that they simply accepted it. They believed. Pe Ell had never done that. But he knew instinctively that this girl, this child of the King of the Silver River, this creature of wondrous magic, did not lie. He did not believe she was capable of it.

"I need you to come with me," she said again to the Highlander.

He glanced at Pe Ell. "Are you coming?"

The way he asked the question pleased Pe Ell. There was a measure of wariness in the Highlander's tone of voice. Perhaps even fear. He smiled enigmatically and nodded. Of course, Highlander, but only to kill you both when it pleases me, he thought.

The Highlander turned back to the girl and began explaining something about two old Dwarf ladies he had rescued from the workhouses and how he needed to know that they were safe because of some promise he had made to a friend. He kept staring at the girl as if the sight of her gave him life. Pe Ell shook his head. This one was certainly no threat to him. He could not imagine why the girl thought he was necessary to their recovery of the mysterious talisman.

Quickening told the Highlander that among those who had come with her to the cottage was one who would be able to discover what had become of the Dwarf ladies. He would make certain that they were well. She would ask him to do so immediately.

"Then if you truly need me, I will come with you," Morgan Leah promised her.

Pe Ell turned away. The Highlander was coming because he had no choice, because the girl had captured him. He could see it in the youth's eyes; he would do anything for her. Pe Ell understood that feeling. He shared something of it as well. The only difference between them was what they intended to do about it.

Pe Ell wondered again what it would feel like when he finally killed the girl. He wondered what he would discover in her eyes.

Quickening guided Morgan toward her bed so that he could rest. Pe Ell departed the room in silence and walked out of the cottage into the light. He stood there with his eyes closed and let the sun's warmth bathe his face.

VIII

Coll Ohmsford was a prisoner at Southwatch for eight days before he discovered who had locked him away. His cell was the whole of his world, a room twenty feet square, high within the black granite tower, a stone-and-mortar box with a single metal door that never opened, a window closed off by metal shutters, a sleeping mat, a wooden bench, and a small table with two chairs. Light filtered through the shutters in thin, gray shafts when it was daytime and disappeared when it was night. He could peer through the cracks in the shutters and see the blue waters of the Rainbow Lake and the green canopy of the trees. He could catch glimpses of birds flying, cranes and terns and gulls, and he could hear their solitary cries.

Sometimes he could hear the howl of the wind blowing down out of the Runne through the canyons that channeled the Mermidon. Once or twice he could hear the howling of wolves.

Cooking smells reached him now and then, but they never seemed to emanate from the food that he was fed. His food came on a tray shoved through a hinged flap at the bottom of the iron door, a furtive delivery that lacked any discernible source. The food was consumed, and the trays remained where he stacked them by the door. There was a constant humming sound from deep beneath the castle, a sort of vibration that at first suggested huge machinery, then later something more akin to an earth tremor. It carried through the stone of the tower, and when Coll placed his hands against the walls he could feel the stone shiver. Everything was warm, the walls and floor, the door and window, the stone and mortar and metal. He didn't know how that could be with the nights sometimes chill enough to cause the air to bite, but it was. Sometimes he thought he could hear footsteps beyond his door—not when the food was delivered, but at other times when everything was still and the only other sound was the buzz of insects in the distant trees. The footsteps did not approach, but passed on without slowing. Nor did they seem to have an identifiable source; they might as easily come from below or above as without.

He could feel himself being watched, not often, but enough so that he was aware. He could feel someone's eyes fixed on him, studying him, waiting perhaps. He could not determine from where the eyes watched; it felt as if they watched from everywhere. He could hear breathing sometimes, but when he tried to listen for it he could hear only his own.

He spent most of his time thinking, for there was little else to do. He could eat and sleep; he could pace his cell and look through the cracks in the shutters. He could listen; he could smell and taste the air. But thinking was best, he found, an exercise that kept his mind sharp and free. His thoughts, at least, were not prisoners. The isolation he experienced threatened to overwhelm him, for he was closed away from everything and everyone he knew, without reason or purpose that he could discern, and by captors that kept themselves carefully hidden. He worried for Par so greatly that at times he nearly wept. He felt as if the rest of the world had forgotten him, had passed him by. Events were happening without him; perhaps everything he once knew had changed. Time stretched away in a slow, endless succession of seconds and minutes and hours and, after a while, days as well. He was lost in shadows and half-light and near-silence, his existence empty of meaning.

Thinking kept him together.

He thought constantly of how he might escape. The door and window were solidly seated in the stone of the fortress tower, and the walls and floor were thick and impenetrable. He lacked even the smallest digging tool in any event. He tried listening for those who patroled without, but the effort proved futile. He tried catching sight of those who delivered his meals, but they never revealed themselves. Escape seemed impossible.

He thought as well about what he might do to let someone know he was there. He could force a bit of cloth or a scrap of paper with a message scrawled on it through the cracks in the shutters of the window, but to what end? The wind would likely carry it away to the lake or the mountains and no one would ever find it. Or at least not in time to make any difference. He thought he might yell, but he knew he was so far up and away from any travelers that they would never hear him. He peered at the countryside unfailingly when it was light and never saw a single person. He felt himself to be completely alone.

He turned his thoughts finally to envisioning what was taking place beyond his door. He tried using his senses and when that failed, his imagination. His captors assumed multiple identities and behavioral patterns. Plots and conspiracies sprang to life, fleshed out with the details of their involvement of him. Par and Morgan, Padishar Creel and Damson Rhee, Dwarves, Elves, and Southlanders alike came to the black tower to free him. Brave rescue parties sallied forth. But all efforts failed. No one could reach him. Eventually, everyone gave up trying. Beyond the walls of Southwatch, life went on, uncaring.

After a week of this solitary existence, Coll Ohmsford began to despair.

Then, on the eighth day of his captivity, Rimmer Dall appeared.

It was late afternoon, gray and rainy, stormclouds low and heavy across the skies, lightning a wicked spider's web flashing through the creases, thunder rolling out of the darkness in long, booming peals. The summer air was thick with smells brought alive by the damp, and it felt chill within Coll's cell. He stood close against the shuttered window, peering out through the cracks in the fittings, listening to the sound of the Mermidon as it churned through the canyon rocks below.

When he heard the lock on the door to his room release he did not turn at first, certain that he must be mistaken. Then he saw the door begin to open, caught sight of the movement out of the corner of his eye, and wheeled about instantly.

A cloaked form appeared, tall and dark and forbidding, lacking face or limbs, seemingly a wraith come out of the night. Coll's first thought was of the Shadowen, and he dropped into a protective crouch, frantically searching his suddenly diminished cell for a weapon with which to defend himself.

"Don't be frightened, Valeman," the wraith soothed in an oddly familiar, whispery voice. "You are in no danger here."

The wraith closed the door behind it and stepped into the room's faint light. Coll saw by turns the black clothing marked with a white wolf's head, the left hand gloved to the elbow, and the rawboned, narrow face with its distinctive reddish beard.

Rimmer Dall.

Instantly Coll thought of the circumstances of his capture. He had gone with Par, Damson, and the Mole through the tunnels beneath Tyrsis into the abandoned palace of the old city's kings, and from there the Ohmsford brothers had gone on alone into the Pit in search of the missing Sword of Shannara. He had stood guard outside the entry to the vault that was supposed to contain the Sword, keeping watch while his brother went inside. It was the last time he had seen Par. He had been seized from behind, rendered unconscious, and spirited away. Until now he had not known who was responsible. It made sense that it should be Rimmer Dall, the man who had come for them weeks ago in Varfleet and hunted them ever since across the length and breadth of the Four Lands.

The First Seeker moved to within a few feet of Coll and stopped. His craggy face was calm and reassuring. "Are you rested?"

"That's a stupid question," Coll answered before he could think better of it. "Where's my brother?"

Rimmer Dall shrugged. "I don't know. When I last saw him he was carrying the Sword of Shannara from its vault."

Coll stared. "You were there—inside?"

"I was."

"And you let Par take the Sword of Shannara? You just let him walk away with it?"

"Why not? It belongs to him."

"You want me to believe," Coll said carefully, "that you don't care if he has possession of the Sword, that it doesn't matter to you?"

"Not in the way you think."

Coll paused. "So you let Par go, but you took me prisoner. Is that right?"

"It is."

Coll shook his head. "Why?"

"To protect you."

Coll laughed. "From what? Freedom of choice?"

"From your brother."

"From Par? You must think me the biggest fool who ever lived!"

The big man folded his arms across his chest comfortably. "To be honest with you, there is more to it than just offering you protection. You are a prisoner for another reason as well. Sooner or later, your brother will come looking for you. When he does, I want another chance to talk with him. Keeping you here assures me that I will have that chance."

"What really happened," Coll snapped angrily, "is that you

caught me, but Par escaped! He found the Sword of Shannara and slipped past you somehow and now you're using me as bait to trap him. Well, it won't work. Par's smarter than that.''

Rimmer Dall shook his head. "If I was able to capture you at the entrance to the vault, how is it that your brother managed to escape? Answer me that?'' He waited a moment, then moved over to the table with its wooden chairs and seated himself. "I'll tell you the truth of things, Coll Ohmsford, if you'll give me a chance. Will you?''

Coll studied the other's face wordlessly for a moment, then shrugged. What did he have to lose? He stayed where he was, standing, deliberately measuring the distance between them.

Rimmer Dall nodded. "Let's begin with the Shadowen. The Shadowen are not what you have been led to believe. They are not monsters, not wraiths whose only purpose is to destroy the Races, whose very presence has sickened the Four Lands. They are victims, for the most part. They are men, women and children who possess some measure of the faerie magic. They are the result of man's evolution through generations in which the magic was used. The Federation hunts them like animals. You saw the poor creatures trapped within the Pit. Do you know what they are? They are Shadowen whom the Federation has imprisoned and starved into madness, changing them so that they have become worse than animals. You saw as well the woodswoman and the giant on your journey to Culhaven. What they are is not their fault.''

The gloved hand lifted quickly as Coll started to speak. "Valeman, hear me out. You wonder how it is that I know so much about you. I will explain if you will just be patient.''

The hand came down again. "I became First Seeker in order to hunt the Shadowen—not to harm or imprison them, but to warn them, to get them to safety. That was why I came to you in Varfleet—to see that you and your brother were protected. I did not have the chance to do so. I have been searching for you ever since to explain what I know. I thought that you might return to the Vale and so placed your parents under my protection. I believed that if I could reach you first, before the Federation found you in some other way, you would be safe.''

"I don't believe any of this,'' Coll interjected coldly.

Rimmer Dall ignored him. "Valeman, you have been lied to from the beginning. That old man, the one who calls himself Cogline, told you the Shadowen were the enemy. The shade of Allanon warned you at the Hadeshorn in the Valley of Shale that the Shadowen must be destroyed. Retrieve the lost magics of the old world, you were advised. Find the Sword of Shannara. Find the missing Elfstones. Find lost Paranor and bring back the Druids. But were you told what any of this would accomplish? Of course not. Because the truth of the matter is that you are not supposed to know. If you did, you would abandon this business at once. The Druids care nothing for you and your kin and never have. They are interested only in regaining the power they lost when Allanon died. Bring them back, restore their magics, and they will again control the destiny of the Races. This is what they work for, Coll Ohmsford. The Federation, unwittingly, ignorantly, helps them. The Shadowen provide the perfect victim for both to prey upon. Your uncle recognized the truth of things. He saw that Allanon sought to manipulate him, to induce him to undertake a quest that would benefit no one. He warned you all; he refused to be part of the Druid madness. He was right. The danger is far greater than you realize.''

He leaned forward. ''I told all of this to your brother when he came into the vault after the Sword of Shannara. I was waiting there for him—had been waiting in fact for several days. I knew he would come back for the Sword. He had to; he couldn't help himself. That's what having the magic does to you. I know. I have the magic, too.''

He stood up suddenly, and Coll shrank back in alarm. The black-clad body began to shimmer in the gloom as if translucent. Then it seemed to come apart, and Coll heard himself gasp. The dark form of a Shadowen lifted slowly out of Rimmer Dall's body red eyes glinting, hung suspended in the air for a moment, and settled back again.

The First Seeker smiled coldly. ''I am a Shadowen, you see. All of the Seekers are Shadowen. Ironic, isn't it? The Federation doesn't know. They believe us ordinary men, nothing more, men who serve their twisted interests, who seek as they do to rid the land of magic. They are fools. Magic isn't the enemy of the people. They are. And the Druids. And any who would keep men and women from being who and what they must.''

One finger pointed at Coll like a dagger. ''I told this to your brother, and I told him one thing more. I told him that he, too, is a Shadowen. Ah, you still don't believe me, do you? But listen, now. Par Ohmsford is in truth a Shadowen, whether either of you cares to admit it or not. So is Walker Boh. So is anyone who possesses real magic. That's what we are, all of us— Shadowen. We are sane, rational, and for the most part ordinary

men, women, and children until we become hunted and imprisoned and driven mad by fools like the Federation. Then the
magic overwhelms us and we become animals, like the woodswoman and the giant, like the things in the Pit.''

Coll was shaking his head steadily. "No. This is all a lie."

"How is it that I know so much about you, do you think?"
Rimmer Dall persisted, his voice maddeningly calm, even now.
"I know all about your flight south down the Mermidon, your
encounters with the woodswoman and the old man, how you
met with that Highlander and persuaded him to join you, how
you journeyed to Culhaven, then to Hearthstone, and finally to
the Hadeshorn. I know of the Dwarves and Walker Boh. I know
of your cousin Wren Ohmsford. I know of the outlaws and Padishar Creel and the girl and all the rest. I knew when you were
going down into the Pit and tried to have you stopped. I knew
that you would return and waited there for you. How, Valeman?
Tell me.''

"A spy in the outlaw camp," Coll answered, suddenly unsure.

"Who?"

Coll hesitated. "I don't know."

"Then I will tell you. The spy was your brother."

Coll stared.

"Your brother, though he didn't realize it. Par is a Shadowen,
and I sometimes know what other Shadowen think. When they
use their magic, my own responds. It reveals to me their
thoughts. When your brother used the wishsong, it let me know
what he was thinking. That was how I found you. But Par's use
of his magic alerted others as well. Enemies. That was why the
Gnawl tracked you in the Wolfsktaag and the Spider Gnomes at
Hearthstone.

"Think, Valeman! All that has befallen you has been the
result of your own doing. I did not seek to harm you in Tyrsis.
It was Par's decision to go down into the Pit that brought you to
grief. I did not withhold the Sword of Shannara. Yes, I kept it
hidden—but only to force Par to come to me so that I might save
him.''

Coll stiffened. "What do you mean?"

Rimmer Dall's pale eyes were intense. "I told you that the
reason I brought you here was to protect you from your brother.
I spoke the truth. The magic of a Shadowen is as two-edged as
any sword. You have surely thought the same thing many times.
It can be either salvation or curse. It can work to help or to hurt.

But it is more complicated than that. A Shadowen can be affected by the stresses that use of the magic demands, particularly when he is threatened or hunted. The magic can grow frayed; it can escape. Remember the creatures in the Pit? Remember those you encountered on your travels? What do you think happened to them? Your brother has the wishsong as his magic. But the wishsong is only a thin shell covering the magic that lies beneath—a magic more powerful than your brother imagines. It begins to grow stronger as he runs and hides and tries to keep himself safe. If I don't reach him in time, if he continues to ignore my warnings, that magic will consume him.''

A long silence followed. Coll reflected silently. He remembered Par telling him that he believed the magic of the wishsong was capable of doing much more than creating images, that he could feel it seeking a release. He remembered the way it had responded during their first venture into the Pit, casting a light through the gloom, illuminating the scroll of the vault. He thought of the creatures trapped there, become monsters and demons.

He wondered, just for an instant, if Rimmer Dall might not be telling him the truth.

The First Seeker came forward a single step and stopped. ''Think about it, Coll Ohmsford,'' he suggested softly. He was big and dark against the gloom and frightening to look at. But his voice was reassuring. ''Reason it through. You will have time enough to do so. I intend that you remain here until your brother comes looking for you or he uses his magic. One way or the other, I have to find him and warn him. I have to protect you both and those with whom you will eventually come in contact. Help me. We must find a way to reach your brother. We must try. I know you don't believe me now, but that will change.''

Coll shook his head. ''I don't think so.''

Outside, distant and low, thunder rumbled and faded into the hissing of the rain. ''So many lies have been told to you by others,'' Rimmer Dall said. ''In time, you will see.''

He moved back toward the cell door and stopped. ''You have been kept in this room long enough. You may leave during the day. Just knock on the door when you wish to go out. Go down to the exercise yard and practice with the weapons. Someone will be there to help you. You should have some training. You need to learn better how to protect yourself. Make no mistake, though. You cannot leave. At night you will be locked in again.

I wish it could be otherwise, but it cannot. Too much is at stake.''

He paused. ''I have a short visit to make, a journey of several days. Another requires my attention. When I return, we will talk again.''

He seemed to consider Coll for a long moment, as if measuring him for something, then turned, and went out the way he had come. Coll watched him go, then walked back to the shuttered window and stood looking out again into the rain.

He slept poorly that night, plagued by dreams of dark things that bore his brother's face, haunted when he came awake by what he had been told. *Nonsense*, was his first thought. *Lies.* But his instincts told him that some part of it, at least, was true—and that, in turn, suggested the unpleasant possibility that it might all be. Par a Shadowen. The magic a weapon that could destroy him. Both of them threatened by dark forces beyond their understanding or control.

He no longer knew what to believe.

When he woke, he rapped on the door. A black-cloaked Seeker released him and walked him down to the exercise yard. Another, a gruff fellow with a shaven head and knots and scars all over him, offered to spar with him. Using padded cudgels, they trained through the morning. Coll sweated and strained. It felt good to make use of his body again.

Later, alone in his cell, the afternoon clearing as the clouds thinned and sunshine broke through to the distant south, he evaluated his new situation. He was a prisoner still, but not so much so. He was no longer confined to a single room. He had been offered the means to stay fit and strong. He did not feel as threatened.

Whether or not Rimmer Dall was playing mind games with him remained to be seen, of course. In any case, the First Seeker had made a mistake. He had given Coll Ohmsford the opportunity to explore Southwatch.

And the further opportunity to find a way to escape.

IX

Walker Boh languished at Hearthstone in a prison far more forbidding than the one that had secured Morgan Leah. He had returned from Storlock filled with a fiery determination to cure the sickness that attacked him, to drive from his body the poison that the Asphinx had injected into it, and to heal himself as even the Stors could not. Within a week he had changed completely, grown dispirited and bitter, frightened that his hopes had been in vain, that he could not save himself after all. His days were long, heat-filled stretches of time in which he wandered the valley lost in thought, desperately trying to reason out what form of magic it would take to stem the poison's flow. His nights were empty and brooding, the dark hours expended in a silent, futile effort to implement his ideas.

Nothing worked.

He tried a little of everything. He began with a series of mind sets, inward delvings of his own magic that were designed to dissolve, break apart, turn back, or at least slow the poison's advance. None of these occurred. He used channeling of the magic in the form of an assault, the equivalent of an inner summoning of the fire that he sometimes used to protect and defend. The channeling could not seem to find a ready source; it scattered and lost its potency. He attempted spells and conjurings from the lore he had accumulated over the years, both that which was innate and that he had been taught. All failed. He resorted finally to the chemicals and powders that Cogline relied upon, the sciences of the old world brought into the new. He attacked the stone ruin of his arm and tried to burn it to the flesh so that cauterization might take place. He tried healing potions that were absorbed through the skin and permeated the stone. He used magnetic and electric fields. He used antitoxins. These, too, failed. The poison was too strong. It could not be overcome. It continued to work its way through his system, slowly killing him.

Rumor stayed at his side almost constantly, trailing silently after him on his long daytime walks, stretching out next to him in the darkness of his room as he struggled in vain to employ the magic in a way that would allow him to survive. The giant moor cat seemed to sense what was happening to Walker; it watched him as if fearful he might disappear at any moment; as if by watching closely it might somehow protect against this unseen thing that threatened. The luminous yellow eyes were always there, regarding him with intelligence and concern, and Walker found himself staring into them hopefully, searching for the answers he could find nowhere else.

Cogline, too, did what he could to help Walker in his struggle. Like the moor cat, he kept watch, albeit at a somewhat greater distance, afraid that Walker would not tolerate it if he came too close or stayed too long. There was still an antagonism between the two that would not be dispelled. It was difficult for them to remain in each other's presence for more than a few minutes at a time. Cogline offered what advice he could, mixing powders and potions at Walker's request, administering salves and healing medicines, suggesting forms of magic he thought might help. Mostly he provided what little reassurance he could that an antidote would be found.

Walker, though he would not admit it to the other, was grateful for that reassurance. For the first time in many years, he did not want to be alone. He had never given much thought to his own death, always convinced it was still far away and he would be prepared for it in any case when it arrived. He discovered now that he had been wrong on both counts. He was angry and frightened and confused; his emotions careened about inside him like stones tossed in a wagon bed, the debris of some emptied load. He fought to maintain his sense of balance, a belief in himself, some small measure of hope, but without the steadying presence of Cogline he would have been lost. The old man's face and voice, his movements, his idiosyncrasies, all so familiar, were handholds on the cliff to which Walker Boh clung, and they kept him from dropping away completely. He had known Cogline a long time; in the absence of Par and Coll, and to a lesser extent Wren, Cogline was his only link with the past—a past that he had in turn scorned, reviled, and finally cast away entirely, a past he was now desperate to regain as it was his link to the use of the magic that could save him. Had he not been so quick to disparage it, so anxious to be rid of its influence, had he taken more time to understand it, to learn from it, to master it and make it serve his needs, he might not be struggling so hard now to stay alive.

But the past is always irretrievable, and so Walker Boh found it here. Yet there was some comfort to be taken from the continued presence of the old man who had given him what understanding of the magic he had. With his future become so shockingly uncertain, he discovered a strange and compelling need to reach out to those things that remained his from the past. The most immediate of those was Cogline.

Cogline had come to him during the second year of his solitary life at Hearthstone. Risse had been dead fifteen years, Kenner five. He had been on his own ever since despite the efforts of Jaralan and Mirianna Ohmsford to make him a part of their family, an outcast from everyone because his magic would not let him be otherwise. While it had disappeared with the coming of age of all the Ohmsfords since Brin, it did not do so in him. Rather, it grew stronger, more insistent, more uncontrollable. It was bad enough when he lived in Shady Vale; it became intolerable at Hearthstone. It began to manifest itself in new ways—unwanted perceptions, strange foresights, harsh sensory recognition, and frightening exhibitions of raw power that threatened to shatter him. He could not seem to master them. He didn't understand them to begin with and therefore could not find a way to decipher their workings. It was best that he was alone; no one would have been safe around him. He found his sanity slipping away.

Cogline changed everything. He came out of the trees one afternoon, materializing from the mist that spilled down off the Wolfsktaag at autumn's close, a little old man with robes that hung precariously on his stick frame, wild unkempt hair, and sharp knowing eyes. Rumor was with him, a massive, immutable black presence that seemed to foreshadow the change that was to come into the Dark Uncle's life. Cogline related to Walker the history of his life from the days of Bremen and the Druid Council to the present, a thousand years of time. It was a straightforward telling that did not beg for acceptance but demanded it. Strangely enough, Walker complied. He sensed that this wild and improbable tale was the truth. He knew the stories of Cogline from the time of Brin Ohmsford, and this old man was exactly who and what the stories had described.

"I was sleeping the Druid sleep," Cogline explained at one point, "or I would have come sooner. I had not thought it was time yet, but the magic that resides within you, brought to life with your arrival at manhood, tells me that it is. Allanon planned it so when he gave the blood trust to Brin; there would come a time when the magic would be needed again and one among the Ohmsfords would be required to wield it. I think that perhaps you are meant to be that one, Walker. If so, you will need my help in understanding how the magic works."

Walker was filled with misgivings, but recognized that the old man might be able to show him how to bring the magic under control. He needed that control desperately. He was willing to take a chance that Cogline could give it to him.

Cogline stayed with him for the better part of three years. He revealed to Walker as a teacher to a student the lore of the Druids, the keys that would unlock the doors of understanding. He taught the ways of Bremen and Allanon, of going within to harness the magic's raw power, of working mind sets so that the power could be channeled and not loosed haphazardly. Walker had some knowledge to begin with; he had lived with the magic for many years and learned something of the self-denial and restraint that was necessary to survive its demands. Cogline expanded on that knowledge, advancing it into areas that Walker had not thought to go, instructing on methods he had not believed possible. Slowly, gradually, Walker began to find that the magic no longer governed his life; unpredictability gave way to self-control. Walker began to master himself.

Cogline instructed on the sciences of the old world as well, the chemicals and potions that he had developed and utilized over the years, the powders that burned through metal and exploded like fire, and the solutions that changed the form of both liquids and solids. Another set of doors opened for Walker; he discovered an entirely different form of power. His curiosity was such that he began to explore a combining of the two—old world and new world, a blending of magic and science that no one had ever successfully tried. He proceeded slowly, cautiously, determined that he would not become another of the victims that the power had claimed over the years, from the men of the old world who had brought about the Great Wars to the rebel Druid Brona, his Skull Bearers, and the Mord Wraiths who had sparked the Wars of the Races.

Then for some reason his thinking changed. Perhaps it was the exhilaration he felt when wielding the magic. Perhaps it was the insatiable need to know more. Whatever it was, he came to believe that complete mastery over the magic was not possible, that no matter how diligently he went about protecting himself against its adverse effects, the power would eventually claim him. His attitude toward using it reversed itself overnight. He tried to back away from it, to thrust it from him. His dilemma was enormous; he sought to distance himself from the magic yet could not do so successfully because it was an integral part of him. Cogline saw what was happening and tried to reason with him. Walker refused to listen, wondering all of a sudden why it was that Cogline had come to him in the first place, no longer believing it was simply to help. An effort was being made to manipulate him, a Druidic conspiracy that could be traced all the way back to the time of Shea Ohmsford. He would not be a part of it. He quarreled with Cogline, then fought. In the end, Cogline went away.

He came back, of course, over the years. But Walker would no longer accept instruction on use of the magic, fearing that further knowledge would result in an erosion of the control he had worked so hard to gain, that enhancement would lead to usurpation. Better simply to rely on what understanding he had, limited but manageable, and keep apart from the Races as he had planned from the first. Cogline could come and go, they could maintain their uneasy alliance, but he would not give himself over to the ways of Druids or once-Druids or anyone else. He would be his own person until the end.

And now that end had come, and he was no longer so sure of the path he had chosen to take. Death had arrived to claim him, and had he not distanced himself so from the magic he might have delayed its arrival a bit longer. Admission of the possibility required swallowing a bitter dose of pride. It was harsh to second-guess himself so, but it could not be avoided. Walker Boh had never in his life shied away from the truth; he refused to begin doing so now.

On the second week of his return from Storlock, sitting before the fire in the early evening hours, the pain of his sickness a constant reminder of things left undone, he said to Cogline, who was somewhere in the shadows behind rummaging through the books he kept at the cottage for his own use, "Come sit with me, old man."

He said it kindly, wearily, and Cogline came without argument, seating himself at Walker's elbow. Together they stared into the fire's bright glow.

"I am dying," Walker said after a time. "I have tried everything to dispel the poison, and nothing has worked. Even my magic has failed. And your science. We have to accept what that means. I intend to keep working to prevent it, but it seems that I will not survive." He shifted his arm uncomfortably against his side, a stone weight that worked relentlessly to pull him down, to make an end of him. "There are things I need to say to you before I die."

Cogline turned toward him and started to speak, but Walker shook his head. "I have embittered myself against you without reasonable cause. I have been unkind to you when you have been more than kind to me. I am sorry for that."

He looked at the old man. "I was afraid of what the magic would do to me if I continued to give myself over to it; I am still afraid. I have not changed my thinking completely. I still believe that the Druids use the Ohmsfords for their own purposes, that they tell us what they wish and direct us as they choose. It is a hard thing for me to accept, that I should be made their cat's-paw. But I was wrong to judge you one of them. Your purpose has not been theirs. It has been your own."

"As much as any purpose is mine and not one of circumstance and fate," Cogline said, and his face was sad. "We use so many words to describe what happens to us, and it all amounts to the same thing. We live out our lives as we are meant to live them—with some choice, with some chance, but mostly as a result of the persons we are." He shook his head. "Who is to say that I am any freer of the Druids and their manipulations than you, Walker? Allanon came to me in the same way as he did to you, young Par and Wren, and made me his. I cannot claim otherwise."

Walker nodded. "Nevertheless, I have been harsh with you and I wish I had not been. I wanted you to be the enemy because you were a flesh-and-blood person, not a Druid dead and gone or an unseen magic, and I could strike out at you. I wanted you to be the source of the fear I felt. It made things easier for me if I thought of you that way."

Cogline shrugged. "Do not apologize. The magic is a difficult burden for any to bear, but more so for you." He paused. "I don't believe you will ever be free of it."

"Except in death," Walker said.

"If death comes as swiftly as you think it will." The old eyes blinked. "Would Allanon establish a trust that could be thwarted so easily? Would he risk a complete undoing of his work on the chance that you might die too soon?"

Walker hesitated. "Even Druids can be wrong in their judgments."

"In this judgment?"

"Perhaps the timing was wrong. Another besides myself was meant to possess the magic beyond youth. I am the mistaken recipient. Cogline, what can possibly save me now? What is there left to try?"

The old man shook his head. "I do not know, Walker. But I sense that there is something."

They were silent then. Rumor, stretched out comfortably before the fire, lifted his head to check on Walker, and then let it drop again. The wood in the fireplace snapped loudly, and a whiff of smoke tinged the air of the room.

"So you think the Druids are not finished with me yet?" Walker said finally. "You think they will not let me give up my life?"

Cogline did not reply at once. Then he said, "I think you will determine what is to become of you, Walker. I have always thought that. What you lack is the ability to recognize what you are meant to do. Or at least an acceptance of it."

Walker felt a chill run through him. The old man's words echoed Allanon's. He knew what they meant. That he was to acknowledge that Brin Ohmsford's trust was meant for him, that he was to don the magic's armor and go forth into battle—like some invincible warrior brought forth out of time. That he was to destroy the Shadowen.

A dying man?

How?

The silence returned, and this time he did not break it.

Three days later Walker's condition took a turn for the worse. The medicines of the Stors and the ministerings of Cogline suddenly gave way before the onslaught of the poison. Walker woke feverish and sick, barely able to rise. He ate breakfast, walked out onto the porch to enjoy the warmth of the sun, and collapsed.

He remembered only snatches of what happened for several days after that. Cogline put him back to bed and bathed him with cold cloths while the poison's fever raged within him, an unquenchable fire. He drank liquids but could not eat. He dreamed constantly. An endless mirage of vile, frightening creatures paraded themselves before him, threatening him as he stood helpless, stripping him of his sanity. He fought back against them as best he could, but he lacked the necessary weapons. Whatever he brought to bear the monsters withstood. In the end, he simply gave himself over to them and drifted in black sleep.

From time to time he came awake and when he did so Cogline was always there. It was the old man's reassuring presence that saved him once again, a lifeline to which he clung, pulling him back from the oblivion into which he might otherwise have been swept. The gnarled hands reached out to him, sometimes gripping as if to hold him fast, sometimes stroking as if he were a child in need of comfort. The familiar voice soothed him, speaking words without meaning but filled with warmth. He could feel the other beside him, always near, waiting for him to wake.

"You are not meant to die, Walker Boh," he thought he heard more than once, though he could not be certain.

Sometimes he saw the old man's face bending close, leathery skin wrinkled and seamed, wispy hair and beard gray and disheveled, eyes bright and filled with understanding. He could smell the other, a forest tree with ancient limbs and trunk, but leaves as fresh and new as spring. When the sickness threatened to overwhelm him, Cogline was there to lift him free. It was because of the old man that he did not give up, that he fought back against the effects of the poison and willed himself to recover.

On the fourth day he awoke at midday and took some soup. The poison had been arrested temporarily, the medicines and ministerings and Walker's own will to survive taking command once more. Walker forced himself to explore the devastation of his shattered arm. The poison had progressed. His arm was turned to stone almost to the shoulder.

He wept that night in rage and frustration. Before he fell asleep he was aware of Cogline standing over him, a fragile presence against the vast, inexorable dark, telling him quietly that all would be well.

He awoke again in the slow, aimless hours between midnight and dawn when time seems to have lost its way. It was instinct that woke him, a sense that something was impossibly wrong. He struggled up on one elbow, weak and disoriented, unable to pinpoint the source of his trepidation. An odd, unidentifiable sound rose out of the night's stillness, a buzz of activity from somewhere without that sleep and sickness rendered indistinct.

His breathing was ragged as he pushed himself into a sitting position, shivering beneath his bedclothes against the chill of the air.

Light flared sharply, suddenly visible through the breaks in his curtained window.

He heard voices. No, he thought anxiously. Not voices. Guttural, inhuman sounds.

It took what strength he had to crawl from the bedside to the window, working his way slowly and painfully through fatigue and fever. He kept still, aware of a need for caution, sensing that he should not reveal himself. Without, the sounds had risen, and an overpowering smell of decay had descended over everything.

Groping, he found the windowsill before him and pulled himself level with its edge.

What he saw through the part in the curtains turned his stomach to ice.

Cogline awoke when Rumor nudged him with his face, a rough, urgent shove that brought the old man upright instantly. He had not gone to bed until well after midnight, buried in his books of old-world science, fighting to discover some means by which Walker Boh's life could be saved. Eventually he had fallen asleep in his chair before the fire, the book he was perusing still open in his lap, and it was there that Rumor found him.

"Confound it, cat," he muttered.

His first thought was that something had happened to Walker. Then he heard the sounds, faint still, but growing louder. Growls and snarls and hisses. Animal sounds. And no effort being made to disguise their coming.

He pushed himself to his feet, taking a moment to wipe the sleep from his eyes. A single lamp burned at the dining table; the fire in the hearth had gone out. Cogline drew his robes close and shuffled toward the front door, uneasy, anxious to discover what was happening. Rumor went with him, moving ahead. The fur along the ridge of his back bristled, and his muzzle was drawn back to expose his teeth. Whatever was out there, the moor cat didn't like it.

Cogline opened the door and stepped out onto the covered porch that fronted the cottage. The sky was clear and depthless. Moonlight flooded down through the trees, bathing the valley in white luminescence. The air was cool and brought Cogline fully awake. He stopped at the edge of the porch and stared.

Dozens of pairs of tiny red lights blinked at him from out of the shadows of the forest, a vast scattering of delicate scarlet blossoms that shone in the black. They were everywhere, it seemed, ringing the cottage and its clearing.

Cogline squinted to better make them out. Then he realized that they were eyes.

He jumped as something moved amid the eyes. It was a man dressed in a black uniform with the silver insignia of a wolf's head sewn on his breast. Cogline saw him clearly as he stepped into the moonlight, big and rawboned with a face that was hollowed and pitted and eyes that were empty of life.

Rimmer Dall, he thought at once and experienced a terrible sinking feeling.

"Old man," the other said, and his voice was a grating whisper.

Cogline did not respond, staring fixedly at the other, forcing himself to keep from looking to his right, to where the window to Walker's bedroom stood open, to where Walker slept. Fear and anger raced through him, and a voice within screamed at him to run, to flee for his life. Quickly, it warned. Wake Walker. Help him escape!

But he knew it was already too late for that.

He had known for some time now that it would be.

"We are here for you, old man," whispered Rimmer Dall, "my friends and I." He motioned, and the creatures with him began to edge into the light, one after another, horrors all, Shadowen. Some were misshapen creatures like the woodswoman he had chased from the camp of Par and Coll Ohmsford weeks ago; some had the look of dogs or wolves, bent down on all fours, covered with hair, their faces twisted into animal muzzles, teeth and claws showing. The sounds they made suggested that they were anxious to feed.

"Failures," their leader said. "Men who could not rise above their weaknesses. They serve a better purpose now." He came forward a step. "You are the last, old man—the last who stands against me. All the Shannara children are gone, swept from the earth. You are all that remains, a poor once-Druid with no one to save him."

The lines that etched Cogline's face deepened. "Is that so?" he said. "Killed them all, did you?" Rimmer Dall stared at him. Not half a chance of it, Cogline decided instantly. The truth is he hasn't killed a one, just wants me to think he has.

"And you came all this way to tell me about it, did you?" he said.

"I came to put an end to you," Rimmer Dall replied.

Well, there you have it, the old man thought. Whatever the First Seeker had managed to do about the Shannara children, it wasn't enough; so now he had come after Cogline as well, easier prey, perhaps. The old man almost smiled. To think it had all come down to this. Well, it wasn't as if he hadn't known. Allanon had warned him weeks ago, warned him in fact when he'd summoned him to retrieve the Druid History from Paranor. Oh, he hadn't told Walker, of course. He had thought about it, but hadn't done it. There just didn't seem to be any point. *Know this, Cogline*, the shade had intoned, deep-voiced, prophetic. *I have read the netherworld signs; your time in this world is nearly finished. Death stalks you and she is an implacable huntress. When next you see the face of Rimmer Dall, she will have found you. Remember, then. When that time comes, take back the Druid History from Walker Boh and hold it to you as if it were your life. Do not release it. Do not give it up. Remember, Cogline.*

Remember.

Cogline collected his thoughts. The Druid History rested within a niche in the stone fireplace inside the cottage, right where Walker had hidden it.

Remember.

He sighed wearily, resignedly. He'd asked questions, of course, but the shade had given no answers. Very like Allanon. It was enough that Cogline knew what was coming, it seemed. It wasn't necessary that he know the particulars.

Rumor snarled, his fur standing on end all over. He was crouched protectively before the old man, and Cogline knew there was no way to save the big cat. Rumor would never leave him. He shook his head. Well. An odd sense of calm settled over him. His thoughts were quite clear. The Shadowen had come for him; they knew nothing at all about Walker Boh being there. That was the way he intended to keep it.

His brow furrowed. Would the Druid History, if he could reach it, aid him in this?

His eyes found Rimmer Dall's. This time he did smile. "I don't think there's enough of you to do the job," he said.

His arm swept up and silver dust flew at the First Seeker, bursting into flame as it struck him. Rimmer Dall screamed in fury and staggered away, and the creatures with him attacked.

They came at Cogline from everywhere, but Rumor met them with a lunge, stopped them short of the porch and tore the foremost to pieces. Cogline flung handfuls of the silver dust at his would-be destroyers and whole lines of them were set ablaze. The Shadowen screeched and howled, blundering into one another as they sought first to attack, then to escape. Bodies lurched wildly through the moonlight, filling the clearing with burning limbs. They began attacking each other. They died by the dozens. *Easy prey, do they think!* Cogline experienced a wild, perverse elation as he flung back his robes and sent the night exploding into white brilliance.

For an impossible moment, he thought he might actually survive.

But then Rimmer Dall reappeared, too powerful to be overcome by Cogline's small magic, and lashed out with fire of his own at the creatures he commanded, at his dogs and wolves and half-humans, at his near-mindless brutes. The Shadowen-kind, terrified of him, attacked in a renewed frenzy of hate and anger. This time they would not be driven off. Rumor savaged the first wave, quick and huge amid their smaller forms, and then they were all over him, a maelstrom of teeth and claws. Cogline could do nothing to help the gallant cat; even with the silver dust exploding all through them, the Shadowen came on. Rumor slowly began to give ground.

Despairing, Cogline used the last of his powder, dashing handfuls to the earth, igniting a wall of flame that for just an instant brought a halt to the beasts' advance. Swiftly he darted inside and snatched the Druid History from its hiding place.

Now we'll see.

He barely made the front door again before the Shadowen-kind were through the wall of fire and on him. He heard Rimmer Dall screaming at them. He felt Rumor press back against him protectively. There was nowhere to run and no point in trying, so he simply stood his ground, clutching the book to his chest, a scarecrow in tattered robes before a whirlwind. His attackers came on. When they had their hands on him, as his body was about to be ripped apart, he felt the rune markings on the book flare to life. Brilliant white fire burst forth, and everything within fifty feet was consumed.

It remains now for you, Walker, was Cogline's last thought. He disappeared in the flames.

* * *

The final explosion threw Walker clear of the curtained window an instant before it was engulfed in flame. Even so, his face and hair were singed and his clothes were left steaming. He lay in a heap as the fire licked its way across the ceiling of his room. He ignored it, no longer caring what happened. He had been helpless to aid Cogline and Rumor, too weak to summon the magic, too weak even to rise and stand with them against the Shadowen, too weak to do anything but hang there on that window ledge and watch.

Useless! He screamed the word silently in his mind, rage and grief washing through him.

He lurched to his knees in desperation and peered out through the flames. Cogline and Rumor were gone. Rimmer Dall and what remained of the Shadowen-kind were melting back into the forest. He stared after them momentarily, and then his strength left him and he collapsed again.

Useless!

The fire's heat intensified about him. Timbers crashed down, fiery brands splintering off and searing his skin. His body jerked in pain, his stone arm an anchor that dragged against the wooden floor. His fate was assured, he realized. Another minute or two and he would be consumed. No one would come for him. No one even knew he was here. The old man and the giant moor cat had concealed his presence from the Shadowen; they had given up their lives to do so. . . .

He shuddered as an image of Rimmer Dall's face appeared in his mind, the dead eyes looking at him appraisingly.

He decided he did not want to die.

Almost without realizing what he was doing, he began to crawl.

X

Quickening found him two days later. Pe Ell and Morgan Leah were with her, drawn on by the mystery of who and what she was, by her promise that they were needed to recover the talisman that she insisted she had been sent to find, by curiosity, by passion, and by a dozen other things that neither could begin to define. They had made the journey north out of Culhaven in three days' time, traveling openly and on foot along the Rabb where it bordered on the Anar, safely west of the Wolfsktaag and the dark things that lived there. Secrecy seemed the least of Quickening's concerns. She had chosen to depart in daylight rather than under cover of darkness, having told her band of would-be followers that they must remain behind and continue her work to help restore the health of the land, and she had kept to the open plains the entire way up the forestline. While Morgan Leah had been relieved that he would not have to venture into the Wolfsktaag again, he had been certain that Federation patrols along the Rabb would attempt to detain them. Curiously, that did not happen. They were seen more than once and approached, but each time the patrols got close they suddenly veered away. It was almost as if they had decided they were mistaken—as if they had decided that they hadn't seen anything after all.

It was nearing dusk when the three finally arrived at Hearthstone, the men footsore, sweaty, and vaguely disgruntled by the quick pace the girl had set and the fact that she could maintain it seemingly without effort. They had bypassed Storlock, crossed through the Pass of Jade and come down the Chard Rush into Darklin Reach. The sun was behind them, dropping quickly toward the rim of the mountains, and the skies ahead were sharply etched by the light. A column of thick black smoke rose

before them like a snake. They could see the smoke long before
they were able to determine its source. They watched it lift into
the darkening eastern skies and dissipate, and Morgan Leah
began to worry. Quickening said nothing, but it seemed to the
Highlander that her face grew more intense. By the time they
reached the rim of the valley and there was no longer any doubt,
the girl's face looked stricken.

They followed the smoke to the ruins of the cottage. Charred
rubble was all that remained; the fire that had consumed it was
so hot that it was still burning in spots, wood and ash glowing
red, sending the black smoke curling skyward. The clearing
about it was seared and lifeless, and huge knots of earth had
been exploded away. It looked as if two great armies had fought
a war in the space of a hundred yards. There was nothing left
that was recognizable. Bits and pieces were scattered about of
what once might have been something human, but it was impossible to tell. Even Pe Ell, who was usually so careful not to
reveal anything of what he was thinking, stared.

"The Shadowen were here," Quickening said, and that
brought both men about to search the shadows of the forest
behind them, until she added, "But they are gone now and will
not return."

At the girl's direction, they searched the clearing for Walker
Boh. Morgan's heart sank. He had been hoping that Walker was
not there, that the Shadowen attack had been for some other
reason. Nothing could have survived this, he thought. He
watched Pe Ell kick halfheartedly at piles of rubble, clearly of
the same mind. Morgan did not like the man. He didn't trust
him; he didn't understand him. Despite the fact that Pe Ell had
saved him from the Federation prisons, Morgan couldn't bring
himself to feel any friendship toward the other. Pe Ell had rescued him at Quickening's request; he wouldn't have lifted a
finger if the girl hadn't asked. He had already told Morgan as
much; he had made a point of telling him. Who he was remained
a mystery, but the Highlander didn't think anything good would
come of his being there. Even now, picking his way across the
blackened clearing, he had the look of a cat in search of something to play with.

Quickening found Walker Boh moments later, calling out urgently to the other two when she did. How she determined where
he was hiding was anyone's guess. He was unconscious and
buried several feet beneath the earth. Pe Ell and Morgan dug
him free, discovering when they did that he had apparently been

trapped in an underground passageway that led from the cottage
to the edge of the forest. Although the passageway had collapsed, probably during the Shadowen attack, sufficient air had
been able to reach him to allow him to survive. They pulled him
into the failing light, and Morgan saw the remains of his arm,
the lower part gone entirely, a stone stub protruding from the
shoulder. Walker's breathing was faint and shallow, his skin
drawn and white. At first, the Highlander didn't think he was
even alive.

They laid him carefully on the ground, brushed the dirt from
his face, and Quickening knelt next to him. Her two hands
reached out to take his one. She held it a moment, and his eyes
flickered open. Morgan drew back. He had never seen Walker's
eyes like this; they were terrifying to look into, filled with dark
madness.

"Don't let me die," the Dark Uncle whispered harshly.

The girl touched his face and he was instantly asleep. Morgan
took a deep breath and let it out again slowly. Walker Boh wasn't
asking for help out of fear; he was asking out of rage.

They made camp beside the ruins of the cottage that night,
backed into the shelter of the trees as the light gave way to
darkness. Quickening had a fire built close to where Walker Boh
lay sleeping and she took up a position at his side and did not
move. Sometimes she held his hand; sometimes she stroked
him. Morgan and Pe Ell were forgotten. She did not seem to
have need of them or wish that they intrude, so the Highlander
built a second fire some distance away and prepared dinner from
the supplies they carried—bread, some dried meat, cheese, and
fruit. He offered some to the girl, but she shook her head and
he moved away. He ate alone. Pe Ell took his food off into the
dark.

After a time Quickening lay down next to Walker Boh and
went to sleep, her body pressed close against his. Morgan
watched stone-faced, a surge of jealousy sweeping through him
at the thought that the Dark Uncle should be so close to her. He
studied her face in the firelight, the curve of her body, the softness of her. She was so beautiful. He could not explain the effect
she had on him; he did not think he could refuse her anything.
It wasn't that he had a reasonable hope that she felt for him as
he did for her—or even that she felt anything for him. It was the
need she roused in him. He should not have come with her once
he had escaped the prisons and made certain that Granny Elise
and Auntie Jilt were safe. He should have gone after the Vale-

men, after Par and Coll Ohmsford. He had promised himself
more than once while lying in the darkness and filth of that
Federation cell that if he ever got free, he would. Yet here he
was, chasing off into the deep Anar after this girl, searching out
a talisman she said existed but hadn't once described, caught up
with the enigmatic Pe Ell and now Walker Boh. It baffled him,
but he didn't question it. He was there because he wanted to be
there. He was there because the moment he had met Quickening
he had fallen hopelessly in love with her.

He watched her until it hurt, then forced himself to look
away. He was surprised when he saw Pe Ell standing back in
the shadows at the edge of the trees watching too.

He was surprised again moments later when the other man
came over to sit next to him by the fire. Pe Ell made it seem the
most natural thing in the world, as if there had been no distance
kept between them before, as if they were companions and not
strangers. Hatchet-faced, as lean as a wire's shadow, he was not
much more than a gathering of lines and angles that threatened
to disappear in the dark. He sat cross-legged, his thin frame
relaxed, hunched down, his mouth breaking into a faint smile
as he saw Morgan frown. "You don't trust me," he said. "You
shouldn't."

Morgan said, "Why not?"

"Because you don't know me and you never trust anyone you
don't know. You don't trust most of those you do either. That's
just the way it is. Tell me, Highlander. Why do you think I'm
here?"

"I don't know."

"I don't know either. I would be willing to bet that it is the
same with you. We're here, you and I, because the girl tells us
she needs us, but we really don't know what she means. It's just
that we can't bring ourselves to tell her no." Pe Ell seemed to
be explaining things as much to himself as to Morgan. He
glanced Quickening's way briefly, nodding. "She's beautiful,
isn't she? How can you say no to someone who looks like that?
But it's more, because she has something inside as well, something special even in this world. She has magic, the strongest
kind of magic. She brings dead things back to life—like the
Gardens, like that one over there."

He looked back at Morgan. "We all want to touch that magic,
to feel it through her. That's what I think. Maybe we can, if
we're lucky. But if the Shadowen are involved in this, if there
are things as bad as that to be dealt with, why then we're going

to have to look out for one another. So you don't have to trust me or me you—maybe we shouldn't—but we have to watch each other's backs. Do you agree?''

Morgan wasn't sure whether he did or not, but he nodded anyway. What he thought was that Pe Ell didn't seem the kind who relied on anyone to watch his back. Or who watched anyone else's back either, for that matter.

"Do you know what I am?" Pe Ell asked softly, looking down into the fire. "I am a craftsman. I get myself in and out of places without anyone knowing. I move things aside that don't want to be moved. I make people disappear." He looked up. "I have a little magic of my own. You do, too, don't you?"

Morgan shook his head, cautious. "There's the man with the magic," he offered, indicating Walker Boh.

Pe Ell smiled doubtfully. "Doesn't seem to have done him much good against the Shadowen."

"It might have kept him alive."

"Barely, it appears. And what use is he to us with that arm?" Pe Ell folded his hands carefully. "Tell me. What can he do with his magic?"

Morgan didn't like the question. "He can do a lot of what you do. Ask him yourself when he's better."

"If he gets better." Pe Ell stood up smoothly, an effortless motion that caught Morgan by surprise. Quick, the Highlander thought. Much quicker than me. The other was looking at him. "I sense the magic in you, Highlander. I want you to tell me about it sometime. Later, when we've traveled together a bit longer, when we know each other a little better. When you trust me."

He moved away into the shadows at the fire's edge, spread his blanket on the ground, and rolled into it. He was asleep almost at once.

Morgan sat staring at him for a moment, thinking it would be a long time before he trusted that one. Pe Ell smiled easily enough, but it seemed that only his mouth wanted to participate in the act. Morgan thought about what the man had said about himself, trying to make sense of it. Get in and out of places without being seen? Move things that don't want to be moved? Make people disappear? What sort of double-talk was that?

The fire burned low and everyone around him slept. Morgan thought about the past for a moment, about his friends who were dead or disappeared, about the inexorable flow of events that was dragging him along in its wake. Mostly he thought about the girl who said she was the daughter of the King of the Silver River. Quickening. He wondered about her.

What was she going to ask of him?

What was he going to be able to give?

Walker Boh came awake at sunrise, rising up from the black pit of his unconsciousness. His eyes blinked open to find the girl peering down at him. Her hands were on his face, her fingers cool and soft against his skin, and it seemed that she drew him up with no more effort than it would require to lift a feather.

"Walker Boh." She spoke his name gently.

She seemed strangely familiar to him although he was certain they had never met. He tried to speak and found he couldn't. Something forbade it, a sense of wonder at the exquisite beauty of her, at the feelings she invoked within him. He found her like the earth, filled with strange magic that was simple and complex at once, a vessel of elements, of soil, air, and water, a part of everything that gave life. He saw her differently than Morgan Leah and Pe Ell, though he couldn't know that yet. He was not drawn to her as a lover or a protector; he had no wish to possess her. Rather, there was an affinity between them that transcended passion and need. There were bonds of immediate understanding that united them as emotions never could. Walker recognized the existence of those bonds even without being able to define them. This girl was something of what he had struggled all his life to be. This girl was a reflection of his dreams.

"Look at me," she said.

His eyes locked on her. She took her fingers from his face and moved them to the shattered remnants of his arm, to the stone stump that hung inert and lifeless from his shoulder. Her fingers reached within his clothing, stroking his skin, working their way to where the skin hardened into stone. He flinched at her touch, not wanting her to feel the sickness in him, or to discover the corruption of his flesh. But her fingers persisted; her eyes did not look away.

Then he gasped as everything disappeared in a white-hot flash of pain. For an instant he saw the Hall of Kings again, the crypts of the dead, the stone slab with its rune markings, the black hole beneath, and the flash of movement as the Asphinx struck. After that he was floating, and there were only her eyes, black and depthless, folding him in a wave of sweet relief. The pain disappeared, drawing out of him in a red mist that dissipated into the air. He felt a weight lift away from him and he was at peace.

He might have slept for a time then; he was not certain. When he opened his eyes again, the girl was there beside him, looking down at him, and the dawn's light was faint and distant through the tips of the trees. He swallowed against the dryness in his mouth and throat, and she gave him water to drink from a skin. He was aware of Morgan Leah staring openmouthed at him from one side, his lean brown face a mask of disbelief. There was another man next to him, one he didn't know, hard-faced and cunning. They had both been there when the girl found him, he remembered. What were they seeing now that so astonished them?

Then he realized that something was different. His arm felt lighter, freer. There was no pain. He used what little strength he had to raise his head and look down at himself. His clothes had been pulled away from his shoulder, revealing pink, healed flesh where the stone wreckage of his sickness had been removed.

His arm was gone.

So, too, was the poison of the Asphinx.

What did he feel? His emotions jumbled together within him. He stared at the girl and tried unsuccessfully to speak.

She looked down at him, serene and perfect. "I am Quickening," she said. "I am the daughter of the King of the Silver River. Look into my eyes and discover me."

He did as he was told, and she touched him. Instantly he saw what Morgan Leah had seen before him, what Pe Ell had witnessed—the coming of Quickening into Culhaven and the resurrection of the Meade Gardens out of ash and dust. He felt the wonder of the miracle and he knew instinctively that she was who she claimed. She possessed magic that defied belief, magic that could salvage the most pitiful of life's wreckage. When the images were gone, he was struck again by the unexplainable sense of kinship he felt for her.

"You are well again, Walker Boh," she told him. "The sickness will trouble you no more. Sleep now, for I have great need of you."

She touched him once and he drifted away.

He awoke again at midday, ravenous with hunger, dry with thirst. Quickening was there to give him food and water and to help him sit up. He felt stronger now, more the man he had been before his encounter with the Asphinx, able to think clearly again for the first time in weeks. His relief at being free of the poison of the Asphinx, at simply being alive for that matter, warred with his rage at what Rimmer Dall and the Shadowen had done to Cogline and Rumor. Just an old man and a bothersome cat, he had called them. He looked out across the clearing at the devastation. The girl did not ask him what had happened; she merely touched him and knew. All the images of that night's tragic events returned in a flood of memories that left him shaking and close to tears. She touched him again, to comfort and reassure, but he did not cry. He would not let himself. He kept his grief inside, walled away behind his determination to find and destroy those responsible.

Quickening said to him, away from Morgan Leah and the one she named Pe Ell, "You cannot give way to what you feel, Walker Boh. If you pursue the Shadowen now, they will destroy you. You lack the wisdom and the strength to overcome them. You will find both only through me."

Then, before he could respond, she called the other two over, seated them before her, and said, "I will tell you now of the need I have of you." She looked at them in turn and then seemed to look beyond. "A long time ago, in an age before Mankind, before the faerie wars, before everything you know, there were many like my father. They were the first of the faerie creatures, given life by the Word, given dominion over the land. Theirs was a trust to preserve and protect, and while they could, they did. But the world changed with the fading of the faerie creatures and the rise of Man. The evolution of the world took away almost everything that had existed in the beginning including those like my father. One by one, they died away, lost in the passing of the years and the changes of the world. The Great Wars destroyed many of them. The Wars of the Races destroyed more. Finally, there was only my father, a legend by now, the faerie Lord they called the King of the Silver River."

Her face lifted. "Except that my father was not alone as he believed. There was another. Even my father did not know of him at first, believing that all his kindred had died out long ago, that he alone had survived. My father was wrong. Another like himself still lived, changed so markedly as to now be all but unrecognizable. All of the first faeries drew their magic from the elements of the land. My father's strength derived from the rivers and lakes, from the waters that fed the earth. He built his Gardens to nourish them, to give them life, and draw life back again. His brother, the one he did not know had survived along with him, took his magic from the earth's stone. Where my father found strength in fluidity and change, his brother found strength in constancy and immutability.''

She paused. ''His name is Uhl Belk. He is the Stone King. He had no name in the old days; none of my father's kindred did. There was no need for names. My father was given his name by the people of the land; he did not ask for it. Uhl Belk took his name out of fear. He took it because he felt that only in having a name could he be certain of surviving. A name implied permanency, he believed. Permanency became everything for him. All around him, the world was changing, the old dying out, giving way to the new. He could not accept that he must change, for like the stone from which he drew his strength, he was unyielding. To survive, he embedded himself deeper in the ways that had sustained him for so long, burrowing into the earth on which he relied. He hid while the Great Wars destroyed almost everything. He hid again when the wars of magic, the Wars of the Races, threatened to do the same. He took his name and wrapped himself in stone. Like my father, his world was reduced to almost nothing, to a tiny bit of existence that was all his magic could protect. He clung to it desperately while the wars of Mankind raged through the centuries and he waited for a measure of sanity to return.

''But, unlike my father, Uhl Belk put aside the trust that the Word had given him. He lost sight of his purpose in his struggle to survive; he became convinced that simply to exist at whatever cost was all that mattered. His pledge to preserve and protect the land was forgotten; his promise to care for the land's life lost meaning. He hoarded and built upon his magic with one thought in mind—that when he grew strong enough he would make certain that his existence would never be threatened by anything or anyone again.''

Quickening's eyes glanced down and lifted again, filled with wonder. ''Uhl Belk is master of Eldwist, a finger of land far north and east above the Charnal Mountains where the Eastland ends at the Tiderace. After centuries of hiding, he has come forth to claim the world of Men for his own. He does this through his magic, which grows in strength as he applies it. He applies it indiscriminately to the land—the soil, the waters, the trees, the creatures that take nourishment from them. He turns everything to stone and takes back such magic as will make him stronger still. The whole of Eldwist is stone and the land about begins to turn as well. The Tiderace holds him captive for now because it is huge, and even Uhl Belk's magic is not yet sufficient to overcome an ocean. But Eldwist connects to the East-land at its tip, and nothing prevents the magic's poison from spreading south. Except my father."

"And the Shadowen," Morgan Leah added.

"No, Morgan," she said, and it did not escape any of them that she called him by his first name alone. "The Shadowen are not Uhl Belk's enemy. My father alone seeks to preserve the Four Lands. The Shadowen, like the Stone King, would see the Lands made over in a way that would leave them unrecogniz-able—barren and stripped of life. The Shadowen and Uhl Belk leave each other alone because neither has anything to fear from the other. One day that may change, but by then it will no longer matter to any of us."

She looked at Walker. "Think of your arm, Walker Boh. The poison that claimed it is Uhl Belk's. The Asphinx belonged to him. Whatever living thing the Stone King or his creatures touch becomes as your arm did—hard and lifeless. That is the source of Uhl Belk's power, that constancy, that changelessness."

"Why did he choose to poison me?" Walker asked.

Her silver hair caught a ray of sunlight and shimmered in momentary brilliance. She shook the light away. "He stole a Druid talisman from the Hall of Kings, and he wanted to be certain that whoever discovered the theft would die before he could do anything about it. You were simply unlucky enough to be that one. The Druids, when they lived, were strong enough to challenge Uhl Belk. He waited until they were all gone to come forth again. His only enemy now is my father."

Her dark eyes shifted to Pe Ell. "Uhl Belk seeks to consume the land and to do so he must destroy my father. My father sends me forth to prevent that. I cannot do so without your help. I need you to come north with me into Eldwist. Once there, we must find and recover from the Stone King the talisman he stole from the Hall of Kings, from the Druids. That talisman is called the Black Elfstone. As long as he possesses it, Uhl Belk is invincible. We must take it away from him."

Pe Ell's long, narrow face remained expressionless. "How are we supposed to do that?" he asked.

"You will find a way," the girl said, looking at each of them in turn. "My father said you would, that you possess the means. But it will take all three of you to succeed. Each of you has the magic that is required; we have not spoken of it, but it is so. All three magics are needed. All three of you must go."

"All three." Pe Ell glanced doubtfully at Walker and Morgan. "What is it that this Black Elfstone does? What sort of magic does it possess?"

Walker leaned forward to hear her answer, and Quickening's black eyes fixed on him. "It steals away the power of other magics. It swallows them up and makes them its own."

There was stunned silence. Walker had never heard of such magic. Even in the old Druid legends, there was no mention of it. He thought about the words contained in the Druid History that Cogline had brought to him, the words that described how Paranor could be restored:

Once removed, Paranor shall remain lost to the world of men for the whole of time, sealed away and invincible within its casting. One magic alone has the power to return it—that singular Elfstone which is colored Black and was conceived by the faerie people of the old world in the manner and form of all Elfstones, combining nevertheless in one stone alone the necessary properties of heart, mind, and body. Whosoever shall have cause and right shall wield it to its proper end.

He had memorized the words before hiding the book in a crevice in the fireplace of the cottage before departing for the Hall of Kings. The words explained something of how the Black Elfstone could be used to bring back Paranor. If Druid magic had sealed it away, the Black Elfstone would negate the magic and restore the Keep. Walker frowned. That seemed awfully easy. Worse, the power of such a magic suggested that once employed, nothing could defeat it. Why would the Druids take the chance that something so powerful would fall into the hands of an enemy like Uhl Belk?

On the other hand, they had done what they could to protect it, he supposed. Almost no one could have retrieved it from the Hall of Kings. Or even known it was there. How had the Stone King discovered it? he wondered.

"If the Black Elfstone can take away other magics," Pe Ell said suddenly, putting an end to Walker's musings, "how can anything overcome it? Our own magic, any magic, will be useless against it."

"Especially mine, since I don't have any," Morgan spoke up suddenly, causing all of them to glance sharply at him. "At least, not enough to bother about."

"Is there something you can do to help us against the Stone

King?'' Walker asked. ''Can you make use of your own magic in some way?''

''No,'' the girl said, and they went silent, staring at her. ''My magic is useless until you have regained possession of the Black Elfstone from Uhl Belk. Nor must he be allowed to discover who I am. If he should, he would make a quick end of me. I will go with you and advise you when I can. I will help if possible. But I cannot use my magic—not the smallest amount, not for even the shortest time.''

''But you think that we can?'' Pe Ell demanded incredulously.

''The Stone King will find your magic of no consequence; he will not feel threatened by you.''

Pe Ell's face assumed such a black look that Walker was momentarily distracted from wondering what it was that Quickening was hiding from them. He was certain now that she was hiding something. Not lying to them, he didn't think that. But there was definitely something she wasn't telling them. The problem was, he hadn't the faintest idea what.

She said then, ''There is another reason that you should help me.'' Her eyes held them. ''All things are possible if you come with me. Walker Boh. I have driven the poison from your body and made you well. I have healed your arm, but I cannot make you whole again. Come with me in search of the Black Elfstone and you will find a way to do so. Morgan Leah. You would restore the magic of your shattered Sword. Come with me. Pe Ell. You would seek out magic greater than that of the Shadowen. Come with me. My father tells me that together you possess the keys that will unlock all of these secrets. My father knows what is possible. He would not lie.''

Her face lifted toward them. ''The Four Lands and her people are threatened by the Shadowen; but no more so than by Uhl Belk. The means of ending one threat shall be found through ending the other. The Black Elfstone is the talisman that shall enable the ending of both. I know you cannot yet understand that; I know I cannot explain it to you. I do not know how you shall fare in this quest. But I shall go with you, live or die with you, succeed or fail with you. We shall be bound forever by what happens.''

As we are somehow bound already, Walker thought to himself and wondered anew why the feeling persisted.

Silence crystallized about them. No one wanted to break its shell. There were questions yet unasked and answers yet ungiven; there were doubts and misgivings and fears to be conquered. A future that had been settled for them all not a week gone now stretched ahead, a dark and uncertain pathway that would take them where it chose. Uhl Belk, the Stone King, waited at the end of that path, and they were going to seek him out. It was already decided. Without anyone having said so, it was resolved. Such was the strength of Quickening's magic, the magic she exercised over the lives of others, a magic that not only restored life to what was believed dead and gone but also liberated hopes and dreams in the living.

It was like that now.

Morgan Leah was thinking what it would be like to have the Sword of Leah restored to him. He was remembering how it felt when its magic was his to command. Pe Ell was thinking what it would be like to have possession of a weapon that no one could stand against. He was remembering how it felt when he used the Stiehl. He was wondering if this would be the same.

But Walker Boh was thinking not so much of himself as of the Black Elfstone. It remained the key to all the locked doors. Could Paranor be restored; could the Druids be brought back again? Allanon's charge to him, part of what must be done if the Shadowen were to be destroyed. And now, for the first time since the dreams had come to him, he wanted them destroyed. More, he wanted to be the one to do it.

He looked into Quickening's black eyes, and it seemed as if she could read his thoughts. A Druid trick. A faerie gift.

And suddenly, shockingly, he remembered where he had seen her before.

He went to her later that night to tell her. It took him a long time to decide to do so. It would have been easier to say nothing because in speaking he risked jeopardizing both his newfound friendship with her and his participation in the journey to Eldwist. But keeping silent would have been the same as lying, and he could not bring himself to do that. So he waited until Morgan and Pe Ell were slumbering, until the night was cloaked in blackness and time's passage slowed to a crawl, and he rose soundlessly from beneath his blankets, still aching and stiff from his ordeal, and crossed the fire-lit clearing to where she waited.

As he passed the ruins of the cottage, he glanced over. Earlier, while it was still light, he had searched the smoldering ashes for the missing Druid History. He had found nothing.

Quickening was not asleep; he knew she wouldn't be. She

was sitting in the shadow of a massive fir where the trees that ringed the clearing were farthest from the sleepers. He was still weak and could not go far, but he did not wish to speak to her where the other two might hear. She seemed to sense this; she rose as he approached and went with him wordlessly into the forest. When they were a safe distance away, she slowed and faced him.

"What would you tell me, Walker Boh?" she asked and pulled him down with her onto the cool matting of the woodland floor.

It took him a moment to speak. He felt that odd kinship to her without yet understanding why, and it almost changed his mind, making him frightened of the words he had come to say and of the reaction they would cause.

"Quickening," he said finally, and the sound of her name coming from his lips stopped him anew. He tightened his resolve. "I was given a book of the Druid Histories by Cogline before he died. The book was destroyed in the fire. There was a passage in the book that said that the Black Elfstone is a Druid magic and possesses the power to bring back disappeared Paranor. That is the charge I was given by the shade of Allanon when I went to speak with him at the Hadeshorn some weeks ago—to restore Paranor and the Druids to the Four Lands. It was a charge that Cogline urged me to accept. He brought the Druid History to me to convince me it could be done."

"I know this," she said softly.

Her black eyes threatened to swallow him up, and he forced himself to look away. "I doubted him," he continued, the words coming harder now. "I questioned his purpose in telling me, accused him of serving the interests of the Druids. I wanted nothing to do with any of them. But my curiosity about the Black Elfstone persuaded me to pursue the matter anyway, even after he was gone. I decided to try to find out where the Elfstone was hidden. I went to see the Grimpond."

He looked up at her again and kept his gaze steady. "I was shown three visions. All three were of me. In the first I stood before the others in the company that had journeyed to the Hadeshorn to meet with the shade of Allanon and declared that I would sooner cut off my hand than help bring back the Druids. The vision mocked what I had said and showed me with my hand already gone. And now it is gone indeed. My hand and my arm both."

His voice was shaking. "The third vision is of no importance here. But in the second vision I stood at the crest of a ridgeline that looked out over the world. A girl was with me. She lost her balance and reached for me. When she did, I thrust her away, and she fell. That girl, Quickening, was you.''

He waited for her response, the silence filling the space between them until it seemed to Walker as if nothing separated them. Quickening did not speak. She kept her eyes fixed on him, her features swept clean of expression.

"Surely you know of the Grimpond!" he exclaimed to her finally in exasperation.

Then he saw her blink and realized that she had been thinking of something else entirely. "It is an exiled spirit," she said.

"One that riddles and lies, but speaks a measure of truth as well, hiding it in devious ways. It did so with the first vision. My arm is gone. I would not have the same thing happen with your life!"

She smiled faintly then, just a trace of movement at the corners of her mouth. "You will not hurt me, Walker Boh. Are you worried that you must?"

"The vision," he repeated.

"The vision is that and nothing more," she interrupted gently. "Visions are as much illusion as truth. Visions tell us of possibilities and do not speak in absolutes. We are not bound by them; they do not govern what is to be. Especially those of a creature like the Grimpond. It teases with falsehoods; it deceives. Do you fear it, Walker Boh? No, not you. Nor I. My father tells me what is to be and that is enough. You will bring no harm to me."

Walker's face felt pinched and tight. "He might be mistaken in what he says; he might not see everything that is to be."

Quickening shook her head, reached out her slim hand, and touched his own. "You will be my protector on this journey, Walker Boh—all three of you, for as long as is necessary. Do not worry. I will be safe with you."

Walker shook his head. "I could remain behind . . . ."

Her hand lifted quickly to his mouth and touched it as if to wipe away some new poison. "No." The word was sheathed in iron. "I will be safe if you are with me; I will be in danger only if you are not. You must come."

He stared at her doubtfully. "Can you tell me anything of what I am expected to do?"

She shook her head.

"Or of the means by which I am to claim the Black Elfstone from Uhl Belk?"

Again, no, firmly.

"Or even how I am to protect you when I have but one arm and . . . ?"

"No."

He let his body sag; he was suddenly very weary. The darkness was a cloak of doubt and indecision that hung about him in suffocating folds. "I am half a man," he whispered. "I have lost faith in who and what I am, in the promises I made to myself, in the tasks I set myself. I have been dragged about by Druid dreams and charges in which I do not believe. I have been stripped of my two closest friends, my home, and my sense of worth. I was the strongest of those who went to meet with Allanon, the one the others relied upon; now I am the weakest, barely able to stand on my own two feet. I cannot be as quick as you to dismiss the Grimpond's visions. I have been wrongly confident too many times. Now I must question everything."

"Walker Boh," she said.

He stared at her wonderingly as she reached out for him and brought him to his feet. "You will be strong again—but only if you believe."

She was so close he could feel the heat of her reaching out to him through the cool night air. "You are like me," she said quietly. "You have sensed as much already, though you fail to understand why it is so. It is because we are, before all other things, creatures of the magic we wield. The magic defines us, shapes us, and makes us who we are. For both of us, it is a birthright we cannot escape. You would protect me by telling me of this vision, by taking away the danger that your presence poses if the vision should be true. But, Walker Boh, we are bound in such a way that despite any vision's telling we cannot separate ourselves and survive. Do you not feel it? We must pick up the thread of this trail that leads to Eldwist and Uhl Belk and the Black Elfstone and follow it to its end. Visions of what might be cannot be allowed to deter us. Fears of our future cannot be permitted to intrude."

She paused. "Magic, Walker Boh. Magic governs my life's purpose, the magic given to me by my father. Can you say that it is any different for you?"

It wasn't a question she put to him; it was a statement of fact, of indisputable truth. He took a deep breath. "No," he acknowledged. "I cannot."

"We can neither deny it nor run from it, can we?"

"No."

"We have this in common—this, and separate charges to find the Black Elfstone and preserve the Four Lands, yours from the shade of Allanon, mine from my father. Beyond that, nothing matters. All paths lead to the Druid talisman." She lifted her face into the faint trailers of light that seeped downward through the trees from the starlit skies. "We must go in search of it together, Walker Boh."

She was so positive in her statement, so certain of what she said. Walker met her gaze, still filled with the doubts and fears she had urged him to cast aside, but comforted now in her sense of purpose and her strength of will. Once he had possessed both in equal measure. It made him ashamed and angry that he no longer did. He remembered Par Ohmsford's determination to do what was right, to find a use for his gift of magic. He thought of his own unspoken promise to the ghosts of Cogline and Rumor. He was still wary of the Grimpond's vision, but Quickening was right. He could not let it dissuade him from his quest.

He looked at her and nodded. A measure of determination returned. "We will not speak of the Grimpond's vision again," he promised.

"Not until there is need," she replied.

She took him by the arm and led him back through the darkened forest to sleep.

XI

Par Ohmsford's strength returned to him slowly. Two weeks passed while he lay bedded in the Mole's underground lair, a gaunt and motionless skeleton draped in old linen, dappled by a mingling of shadows and candlelight, and surrounded by the strange, changeless faces of the Mole's adopted children. Time had no meaning at first, for he was lost to anything remotely connected with the real world. Then the madness faded, and he began to come back to himself. The days and nights took on definition. Damson Rhee and the Mole became recognizable. The blur of darkness and light sharpened to reveal the shapes and forms of the subterranean rooms in which he rested. The stuffed castoffs grew familiar once more, button noses and eyes, thread-sewn mouths, worn cloth limbs and bodies. He was able to give them names. Words assumed meaning out of idle talk. There was nourishment and there was sleep.

Mostly, though, there were the memories. They tracked him through sleep and waking alike, wraiths that hovered at the edge of his thoughts, anxious to sting and bite. There were memories of the Pit, the Shadowen, Rimmer Dall, and the Sword of Shannara, but mostly of Coll.

He could not forgive himself. Coll was dead because of him—not simply because he had struck the fatal blow, the killing stroke of his wishsong's magic, not because he had failed to adequately protect his brother from the packs of Shadowen that roamed the Pit while he was engaged with Rimmer Dall, not for any of this, but because he had from the first, from the moment they had fled Varfleet and the Seekers, thought only of himself. His need to know the truth about the wishsong, the Sword of Shannara, the charges of Allanon, the purpose of the magic—this was what had mattered. He had sacrificed everything to discover that truth, and in the end that sacrifice had included his brother.

Damson Rhee strove mightily to persuade him otherwise, seeing his torment and instinctively recognizing its cause.

"He wanted to be there with you, Par," she would tell him, over and over, her face bent close, her red hair tumbling down about her slender shoulders, her voice soft and gentle. "It was his choice. He loved you enough that it could not have been otherwise. You did your best to keep him from coming, to keep him safe. But there was that in Coll that would not be compromised. A sense of what's right, what's necessary. He was determined to protect you from the dangers you both knew waited. He gave his life to keep you safe, don't you see? Don't be so quick to steal away what that sacrifice meant by insisting it was your fault. There were choices and he made them. He was strong-willed, and you could not have changed his mind even had you tried harder than you did. He understood, Par. He recognized the purpose and need in what you do. You believed that was true before; you must believe it now. Coll did. Don't let his death have been for nothing.''

But Coll's death might have been for exactly that, he feared, and the fear chased after him in his darkest thoughts. Exactly what had his brother's death accomplished? What did he have to show for it? The Sword of Shannara? Yes, he had gained possession of the legendary blade of his Elven-blooded ancestors, the talisman the shade of Allanon had sent him to find. And what use was it? It had failed utterly as a weapon against Rimmer Dall, even after the First Seeker had revealed himself as a Shadowen. If the Sword was a necessary magic as Allanon had claimed, why hadn't it destroyed his greatest enemy? Worse, if Dall were to be believed, the Sword of Shannara could have been his simply for the asking. There was no need for their agonizing, destructive descent into the Pit—no need, then, for the death of Coll.

And no purpose to it either if Rimmer Dall was right about one thing more—that Par Ohmsford, like himself, was a Shadowen. For if Par were the very thing they were fighting to protect the Four Lands against . . .

If Coll had died to save a Shadowen . . .

Unthinkable? He was no longer sure.

So the memories plagued him, bitter and terrible, and he was awash in a slew of anguish and disbelief and anger. He fought through that morass, struggled to keep himself afloat, to breathe, to survive. The fever disappeared, the starkness of his emotions softened, the edges dulled, and the aching of his heart and body scarred and healed.

He rose at the end of the two weeks' time, determined to lie about no longer, and began to walk short distances within the Mole's dark quarters. He washed at the basin, dressed, and took his meals at the table. He navigated the lair end to end, doorway to doorway, testing himself, feeling his way through his weakness. He pushed back the memories; he kept them carefully at bay. He did so mostly through simple motion. Doing something, anything, helped to keep him from dwelling so much on what was over and done. He made note of the smells and tastes that hung upon the trapped air. He studied the texture of the ruined furniture, of the various discards of the upper world, and of the walls and floors themselves. His resolution stiffened. He was alive and there was a reason for it. He shifted in and out of the candlelight and shadows, a ghost impelled by an inner vision. Even when he was too tired to move about further he was reluctant to rest. He spent hours seated on the edge of his bed examining the Sword of Shannara, pondering its mystery.

Why had it failed to respond to him when he had touched its blade to Rimmer Dall?

"Is it possible," Damson asked him at one point, her voice cautious, "that you have been deceived in some way and that this is not the Sword of Shannara?"

He thought carefully before he answered. "When I saw it in the vault, Damson, and then when I touched it, I knew it was the Sword. I was certain of it. I have sung the story of it so many times, pictured it so often. There was no doubt in my mind." He shook his head slowly. "I still feel it to be so."

She nodded. She was seated next to him on the bed, legs folded beneath her, green eyes intense. "But your anticipation of finding it might have colored your judgment, Par. You might have wanted it so badly that you allowed yourself to be fooled."

"It might have happened like that, yes," he agreed. "Then. But now, as well? Look at the blade. See here. The handle is worn, aged—yet the blade shines like new. Like Morgan's sword—magic protects it. And see the carving of the torch with its flame . . ."

His enthusiasm trailed off with a sigh. He saw the doubt mirrored in her eyes. "Yet it doesn't work, it's true. It doesn't do a thing. I hold it, and it seems right, what it should be—and it doesn't do anything, give back anything, or let me feel even the slightest hint of its magic. So how can it be the Sword?"

"Counter-magic," the Mole said solemnly. He was crouched in a corner of the room close to them, almost invisible in the shadows. "A mask that hides." He stretched his face with his hands to change its shape.

Par looked at him and nodded. "A concealment of some kind. Yes, Mole. It might be. I have considered the possibility. But what magic exists that is strong enough to suppress that of the Sword of Shannara? How could the Shadowen produce such a magic? And if they could, why not simply use it to destroy the blade? And shouldn't I be able to break past any counter-magic if I am the rightful bearer of the Sword?"

The Mole regarded him solemnly, voiceless. Damson gave no reply.

"I don't understand," he whispered softly. "I don't understand what's wrong."

He wondered, too, at how willingly Rimmer Dall had let him depart with the Sword. If it were truly the weapon it was supposed to be, the weapon that could destroy the Shadowen, Dall would surely not have let Par Ohmsford have it. Yet he had given it to the Valeman without argument, almost with encouragement in fact, telling him instead that what he had been told of the Shadowen and the Sword was a lie.

And then virtually proved it by demonstrating that the touch of the Sword would not harm him.

Par wandered the Mole's quarters with the blade in hand, hefting it, balancing it, working to invoke the magic that lay within. Yet the secret of the Sword of Shannara continued to elude him.

Periodically Damson left their underground concealment and went up into the streets of Tyrsis. It was odd to think of an entire city existing just overhead, just beyond sight and sound, with people and buildings, sunlight and fresh air. Par longed to go with her, but she wisely counseled against it. He lacked strength yet for such an undertaking, and the Federation was still searching.

A week after Par had left his sickbed and begun moving about on his own, Damson returned with disquieting news.

"Some weeks ago," she advised, "the Federation discovered the location of the Jut. A spy in the outlaw camp apparently betrayed it. An army was dispatched from Tyrsis to penetrate the Parma Key and lay siege. The siege was successful. The Jut fell. It was taken close to the time, Par, when you escaped the Pit." She paused. "Everyone found there was killed."

Par caught his breath. "Everyone?"

"So the Federation claims. The Movement, it says, is finished."

There was momentary silence. They sat at the Mole's long table surrounded by his voiceless, unseeing children, saucers and cups set before them. It had become a midafternoon ritual.

"More tea, lovely Damson?" the Mole asked softly, his furry face poking up from the table's edge. She nodded without taking her eyes from Par.

Par frowned. "You don't seem distressed by this," he responded finally.

"I think it odd that it took weeks for word of this victory to reach the city."

"So it isn't true, then?"

She bit into one of the crackers that the Mole had provided for them and chewed. "It may be true that the Jut was taken. But I know Padishar Creel. It doesn't seem likely that he would let himself be trapped in his own lair. He's much too clever for that. More to the point, friends of the Movement here in the city with whom I spoke tell me that line soldiers with the army claim they killed almost no one, several dozen at most, and those were already dead when the Jut's summit was breached. What happened, then, to the others? There were three hundred men in that camp. Besides, if the Federation really had Padishar Creel, they'd spike his head atop the city gates to prove it.''

"But there's no message from Padishar?''

She shook her head.

"And no word of Morgan or Steff or any of the others?''

She shook her head again. "They've vanished.''

"So.'' He let the word hang.

She smiled ruefully. They finished their tea without speaking.

The following day, his body stronger, his mind determined, Par again announced that he wanted to go up into Tyrsis. He had been shut away long enough; he needed to see something of his own world again. He needed to feel sunlight on his skin and breathe fresh air. Besides, as long as he remained hidden away, nothing was being accomplished. It was time for him to *do* something.

Damson objected strongly, pointing out that he was not yet fully recovered and that it was extremely dangerous for him to go anywhere. The Federation knew who he was now; his description was everywhere. After his escape from the Pit, Seekers had begun searching the lower levels of the old palace and discovered the tunnels leading in. Now they were searching the tunnels as well. There were miles of tunnel and sewer to search, but the risk of discovery remained. For now, it was best to lie low.

In the end, they compromised. Par would be allowed to go into the tunnels close at hand as long as he was in the company of Damson or the Mole. He would not go aboveground, even for a moment. He would go where he was told and do what he was advised. But at least he would be out of his sickrooms. Par agreed.

He began his exploration eagerly, studying the lay of the tunnels as he trailed after Damson and the Mole, mapping it all out carefully in his mind. He tired quickly the first day and had to return early. He was stronger the second and continued to improve. He began to grow comfortable with his understanding of how the tunnels and sewers wove together—enough so that he believed he could find his way to the surface on his own should the need arise. The Mole advised him cautiously, watched him with intense, glittery eyes, and nodded in satisfaction. Damson stayed close, her hands constantly touching him, as if to shield against danger. He smiled inwardly at their protectiveness.

A week passed away. He was much better now, almost completely recovered. More than a month had elapsed since he had been carried beneath the city of Tyrsis and placed in hiding. He thought constantly of leaving, of picking up again the threads of his life.

At the same time he found himself wondering where he would begin.

In the end the decision was made for him.

It was late afternoon ten days after he had begun his exploration of the tunnels surrounding the Mole's lair. He was seated on the edge of his bed, once again examining the Sword of Shannara. Damson had gone up to the city to see what news she could learn of Padishar and the Federation. The Mole was a furtive shadow as he passed from room to room, straightening, arranging, and fussing with his possessions. Teatime had come and gone without the girl, and the Mole was unsettled. Par might have been if he had allowed himself to dwell on the matter, but as it was he was consumed with something else. His memory of the events surrounding the discovery of the Sword of Shannara and the death of Coll was still incomplete, the fragments piecing themselves back in place only intermittently as he recovered to form a complete picture. Now and then a new piece would recall itself. One did so now.

It had to do with the wishsong, actually. He remembered all too clearly how his magic had gathered within him, summoned on its own almost, when Coll—the thing that had been Coll—threatened him. Then, after Coll was gone and the others of the Shadowen in the Pit came for him, the wishsong had given him a flaming sword, a weapon unlike anything the magic had ever produced. It had destroyed the Shadowen effortlessly. For a few moments he had been possessed, infused with fury and madness, driven beyond any semblance of reason. He remembered how that had felt. But there was something more, something he had forgotten completely until now. When the Shadowen were destroyed and he had reached down to retrieve the Sword of Shannara from where it had fallen, the Sword had burned him—had seared his hand like fire. And instantly his own magic had died, and he had been unable to summon it again.

Why had the Sword of Shannara done that? What had happened to produce such a reaction?

He was pondering this, trying to make it fit with what little he knew of the mystery of the Sword, when Damson burst through the entry to the Mole's subterranean refuge, long hair disheveled, her breathing quick and frightened.

"Federation soldiers!" she announced, rushing up to Par, pulling him to his feet. "Dozens of them, hunting through the sewers, making a thorough sweep! Not at the palace, but here. I barely slipped in ahead of them. I don't know if someone betrayed us or if I was simply seen. But they have found the entry down and they're coming!" She paused, steadying herself. "If we stay, they will find us. We have to get out right away."

Par slung the Sword of Shannara over his shoulder and began shoving his few possessions into a sling pack. His thoughts scattered. He had been anxious to leave, but not like this.

"Mole!" Damson called out, and the furry fellow skittered quickly up to her. "You have to come with us. They will find you as well."

But the Mole shook his head solemnly, and his voice was calm. "No, beautiful Damson. This is my home. I will stay."

Damson knelt hurriedly. "You can't do that, Mole. You will be in great danger. These men will hurt you."

Par hurried over. "Come with us, Mole. Please. It is our fault that you are threatened."

The Mole regarded him quizzically. "I chose to bring you here. I chose to care for you. I did it for Damson—but for myself as well. I like you. I like how you make . . . lovely Damson feel."

Par saw Damson flush out of the corner of his eye and kept his gaze focused on the Mole. "None of that matters now. What matters is that we are your friends, and friends look out for one another. You have to come with us."

"I will not go back into the world above," the Mole insisted quietly. "This is my home. I must look out for it. What of my children? What of Chalt and little Lida and Westra and Everlind? Would you have me leave them?"

"Bring them, if you must!" Par was growing desperate.

"We will help you find a new home," Damson added quickly.

But the Mole shook his head stubbornly. "The world up there wants nothing to do with any of us. We do not belong there, lovely Damson. We belong down here. Do not worry for us. We know these tunnels. There are places to hide where we will never be found. We will go to them if we must.'' He paused. ''You could come with us, both of you. You would be safe.''

Damson rose, her brow furrowed. ''It will be enough if you are safe, Mole. We have brought too much danger already into your life. Just promise me that you will go to one of these hiding places now. Take your children and stay there until this hunt is finished and the tunnels are safe again. Promise me.''

The Mole nodded. ''I promise, sweet Damson.''

Damson flew to gather her own possessions, then joined Par at the entryway. The Mole stood looking at them from out of the shadows, little more than a pair of glittering eyes lost in the jumble of discarded goods and faint candlelight.

Damson shouldered her pack. ''Goodbye, Mole,'' she called softly, then lowered her pack, walked to where he waited, and reached down to embrace him. When she returned to Par, she was crying.

''I owe you my life, Mole,'' Par told him. ''Thank you for everything you have done for me.''

One small hand lifted in a faint wave.

''Remember your promise!'' Damson warned almost angrily. ''Hide yourself!''

Then they were through the entry and into the tunnel beyond, slipping soundlessly ahead. Damson carried no torch, but instead produced one of the strange stones that glowed when warmed by her hand. She used its small, sure light to guide them, opening her fingers to provide direction, closing them again to protect against discovery. They moved swiftly away from the Mole's lair, down one tunnel and into another, then up a metal ladder and into a pit.

From somewhere distant, they heard the sound of boots scraping.

Damson led Par away from the sound, along a tunnel that was dank and slick with moisture. Already the temperature was rising and the air filling with sewer smells. Rats skittered about in the dark recesses, and water trickled along the crevices of the rock. They wound their way steadily through the maze. Voices reached them once, unfocused, indistinct. Damson ignored them.

They arrived at a joining of several sewer ways, a ringed pit with water collecting in a deep, shadowed well. A central convergence, Par thought. He was breathing heavily, his strength failing already in the face of this sudden activity. The muscles of his legs and back ached, and he stretched himself gingerly to relieve them.

Damson glanced back at him, concern mirrored in her eyes. She hesitated, then guided him forward.

The voices rose again, closer now, coming from more than one direction. Torchlight flared behind them. Damson took Par up another ladder and into a tunnel that was so narrow they were forced to crawl to get through. Dampness and filth soaked into Par's clothing and clung to his skin. He forced himself to breathe through his mouth and then only when he could hold his breath no longer.

They emerged at the beginning of a wider tunnel, this one trenched down its middle so that there were stone walkways to either side of where the sewer water flowed. A pair of smaller tunnels intersected. There was a flicker of torchlight in each. Damson hurried on. They rounded a bend and found torchlight waiting ahead as well. Damson stopped, shoving Par back against the rock wall.

When she faced him, there was a hint of desperation in her eyes. "The only way out," she whispered, her mouth close to his ear, "lies ahead. If we go back, we'll be trapped."

She stepped back so that she could see his response. He glanced past her to the lights, approaching rapidly now, and heard the thudding of boots and the first hint of voices. Fear welled within and threatened to drown him. It felt as if the Federation had been hunting him forever; it seemed that the hunting would never stop. So many times he had escaped capture. It could not go on. Sooner or later his luck was going to run out. He had barely survived the Pit and the Shadowen. He was worn and sick at heart and he just wanted to be left alone. But the Federation would never leave him alone; the cycle was endless.

For an instant despair claimed him completely. Then abruptly he thought of Coll. He remembered his vow that someone would pay for what had become of his brother. Anger replaced the despair instantly. No, he would not be taken prisoner, he swore silently. He would not be given over to Rimmer Dall.

He thought momentarily to summon the magic that had aided him in the Pit, to call forth that fiery sword that would cut his enemies to pieces. He brushed the impulse aside. It was too much power to face again so soon and still with so little understanding. Cunning, not brute force, was needed here. He remembered suddenly how he had escaped from the Federation

that night in the People's Park. Pulling Damson after him, he
hastened to a shadowed niche in the tunnel wall formed by the
bracing. Crouched in the darkness with the girl, he put a finger
to his lips and signaled for her to remain still.

The Federation soldiers approached, five strong, torches lifted
to provide sufficient light for their search, the metal of their
weapons glinting. Par took a deep breath and slipped down
within himself. He would have only one chance. Just one.

He waited until they were almost upon them, then used the
wishsong. He kept it tightly in check, taking no chances with
what it might do, carefully controlling its release. He cast a net
about the soldiers of whispered warnings, a hint of something
that disturbed the waters of the sewer farther ahead, a shadowy
movement. He infused them with a need to hurry if they were
to catch it.

Almost as one, the soldiers broke into a run and hastened
past without looking. The Valeman and the girl pressed back
against the tunnel rock, breathless. In moments the soldiers were
gone.

Slowly Damson and Par came back to their feet. Then Damson reached out impulsively and hugged the Valeman. "You are
well again, Par Ohmsford," she whispered, and kissed him.
"This way, now. We're almost free."

They hurried down the passageway, crossed a confluent, and
entered a dry well. The torches and boots and voices had receded into silence. There was a ladder leading up. Damson went
first, pausing at the top to push up against a trapdoor. Twilight
seeped through the crack. She listened, peered about, then
climbed through. Par followed.

They stood within a shed, slat-walled and closed away. A
single door led out. Damson moved to it, opened it cautiously
and with Par in tow stepped out.

The city of Tyrsis rose around them, fortress walls, spiraled
towers, jumbled buildings of stone and wood. The air was thick
with smells and sounds. It was early evening, the day gone west,
the city's people turned homeward. Life was slow and weary in
the stillness of the summer heat. Overhead the sky was turning
to black velvet, and stars were beginning to spread like scattered
bits of crystal. A wondrously bright full moon beamed cold
white light across the world.

Par Ohmsford smiled, the aches forgotten, his fears momentarily behind him. He adjusted the weight of the Sword of Shannara across his shoulders. It felt good to be alive.

Damson reached over and took his hand, squeezing it gently.

Together they turned down the street and disappeared into the night.

XII

Quickening kept her little company at Hearthstone for several days to allow Walker Boh to regain his strength. It returned quickly, the healing process augmented as much by the girl's small touches and sudden smiles, by the very fact of her presence, as by nature's hand. There was magic all about her, an invisible aura that surrounded her, that reached out to everything with which she came in contact, and that restored and renewed with a thoroughness and rapidity that was astounding. Walker grew strong again almost overnight, the effects of his poisoning gone into memory, to some small extent at least joined by the pain of losing Cogline and Rumor. The haunted look disappeared from his eyes, and he was able to put away his anger and his fear, to lock them in a small dark corner of his mind where they would not disturb him and yet not be forgotten when the time came to remember. His determination returned, his confidence, his sense of purpose and resolve, and he became more like the Dark Uncle of old. His magic aided him in his recovery, but it was Quickening who provided the impetus, moment by moment, a warmth that outshone the sun.

She did more. The clearing where the cottage had stood became cleansed of its scars and burns, and the signs of the battle with the Shadowen slowly disappeared. Grasses and flowers blossomed and filled the emptiness, swatches of color and patches of fragrance that soothed and comforted. Even the ruins of the cottage settled into dust and at last faded from view completely. It seemed that whenever she chose she could make the world over again.

Morgan Leah began to talk to Walker when Pe Ell was not around, the Highlander still uneasy, admitting to Walker that he was not certain yet who the other really was or why Quickening had brought him along. Morgan had grown since Walker had seen him last. Brash and full of himself when he had first come to Hearthstone, he seemed subdued now, more controlled, a cautious man without lacking courage, a well-reasoned man. Walker liked him better for it and thought that the events that had conspired to separate him from the Ohmsfords and bring him to Culhaven had done much to mature him. The Highlander told Walker what had befallen Par and Coll, of their joining Padishar Creel and the Movement, their journey to Tyrsis and attempts to recover the Sword of Shannara from the Pit, their battles with the Shadowen, and their separation and separate escapes. He told Walker of the Federation assault on the Jut, Teel's betrayal, her death and Steff's, and the outlaw's flight north.

"She gave us all away, Walker," Morgan declared when he had finished his narrative. "She gave up Granny and Auntie in Culhaven, the Dwarves working with the Resistance that she knew about, everyone. She must have given Cogline up as well."

But Walker did not believe so. The Shadowen had known of Cogline and Hearthstone since Par had been kidnapped from the valley by Spider Gnomes some months earlier. The Shadowen could have come for Cogline at any time, and they had not chosen to do so until now. Rimmer Dall had told Cogline before he killed him that the old man was the last who stood against the Shadowen, and that meant that he believed Cogline had become a threat. More worrisome to him than how Rimmer Dall had found them was the First Seeker's claim that the children of Shannara were all dead. Obviously he was mistaken about Walker, but what of Par and Wren, the others of the Shannara line dispatched by the shade of Allanon in search of those things lost and disappeared that would supposedly save the Four Lands? Was Rimmer Dall mistaken about them as well or had they, too, gone the way of Cogline? He hadn't the means to discover the truth and he kept what he was thinking to himself. There was no point in saying anything to Morgan Leah, who was already struggling with the imagined consequences of his decision to follow after Quickening.

"I know I should not be here," he told Walker in confidence

one afternoon. They were sitting within the shade of an aged white oak, listening to and watching the songbirds that darted overhead. "I kept my word to Steff and saw to the safety of Granny Elise and Auntie Jilt. But this! What of my promise to Par and Coll that I would protect them? I shouldn't be here; I should be back in Tyrsis looking for them!"

But Walker said, "No, Highlander, you should not. What good could you do even if you found them? How much help would you be against the Shadowen? You have a chance here to do something far more important—indeed, a need, if Quickening is right in what she says. Perhaps, too, you may find a way to restore the magic to your Sword, just as I may find a way to restore my arm. Slim hopes for those of us with pragmatic minds, yet hopes nevertheless. We feel her need, Highlander, and we respond to it; we are her children, aren't we? I think we cannot dismiss such stirrings so easily. For now at least, we belong with her."

He had come to believe that, swayed by his midnight talk with Quickening when he had told her of the Grimpond's vision and his fear that it would come to pass, won over by her insistence and determination that it would not. Morgan Leah was no less thoroughly bound, mesmerized by her beauty, chained by his longings, drawn to her in ways he could not begin to understand but could not deny. For each of the three, the attraction to Quickening was different. Morgan's was physical, a fascination with the look and movement of her, with the exquisite line and curve of her face and body, and with a loveliness that transcended anything he had ever known or even imagined. Walker's was more ethereal, a sense of kinship with her born of their common birthright of magic, an understanding of the ways in which she was compelled to think and act because of it, a binding together through a common chain of links where each link was a shared experience of reasoning grown out of the magic's lure.

Pe Ell's purpose in coming was the most difficult to discern. He called himself an artist, at various times of sleight-of-hand and escape, but he was clearly something more. That he was extremely dangerous was no mystery to anyone, yet he kept any truths about himself carefully concealed. He seldom spoke to any of them, even to Quickening, though he was as attracted to her as either Walker or Morgan and looked after her as carefully as they. But Pe Ell's attraction was more that of a man for his possessions than a man for his lover or a kindred spirit. He seemed drawn to Quickening in the way of a craftsman to something he has created and offers up as evidence of his skill. It was an attitude that Walker found difficult to understand, for Pe Ell had been brought along in the same way as the rest of them and had done nothing to make Quickening who or what she was. Yet the feeling persisted in him that Pe Ell viewed the girl as his own and when the time was right he would attempt to possess her.

The days of the week played themselves out until finally Quickening decided Walker was well enough to travel, and the company of four departed Hearthstone. Traveling afoot, for the country would permit nothing better, they journeyed north through Darklin Reach and the forests of the Anar along the western edge of Toffer Ridge to the Rabb, crossed where the waters narrowed, and proceeded on toward the Charnals. Progress was slow because the country was heavily wooded, choked with scrub and slashed by ravines and ridges, and they were forced constantly to alter their direction of travel away from their intended course to find passable terrain. The weather was good, however, warm days of sunshine and soft breezes, the summer's close, a slow, lazy winding down of hours that made every day seem welcome and endless. There was sickness even this far north, wilting and poisoning of the earth and its life, yet not as advanced as in the middle sections of the Four Lands, and the smells and tastes, the sights and sounds, were mostly fresh and new and unfouled. Streams were clear and forests green, and the life within both seemed unaffected by the gathering darkness with which the Shadowen threatened to blanket everything.

Nights were spent camped in wooded clearings by ponds or streams that provided fresh water and often fish for a meal, and there was talk now and then between the men, even by Pe Ell. It was Quickening who remained reticent, who kept herself apart when the day's travel was completed, who secluded herself back in the shadows, away from the firelight and the presence of the other three. It wasn't that she disdained them or hid from them; it was more that she needed the solitude. The wall went up early in their travels, an invisible distancing that she established the first night out and did not relinquish after. The three she had brought with her did not question, but instead watched her and each other surreptitiously and waited to see what would transpire. When nothing did, thrown together by her forced separation from them, they began to loosen up in each other's presence and to speak. Morgan would have talked in any case, an open and relaxed youth who enjoyed stories and the company of others. It was different with Walker and Pe Ell, both of whom were by nature and practice guarded and cautious. Conversations frequently became small battlegrounds between the two with each attempting to discover what secrets the other hid and neither willing to reveal anything about himself. They used their talk as a screen, careful to keep the conversation away from anything that really mattered.

They all speculated now and again on where they were going and what they were going to do when they got there. Those conversations ended quickly every time. No one would discuss what sort of magic he possessed, though Walker and Morgan already had some idea of each other's strengths, and no one would advance any plan of action for retrieving the talisman. They fenced with each other like swordsmen, probing for strengths and weaknesses, feinting with their questions and their suggestions, and trying to discover what sort of iron fortified the others. Walker and Pe Ell made little progress with each other, and while it became clear enough that Morgan was there because of the magic contained in the Sword of Leah it was impossible to learn anything substantive with the weapon shattered. Pe Ell, particularly, asked questions over and over again about what it was the Sword of Leah could do, what sort of materials it could penetrate, and how much power it contained. Morgan used all of his considerable talents to be both charming and confusing with his answers and to give the impression that the magic could do either anything or nothing. Eventually, Pe Ell left him alone.

The close of the first week of travel brought them north above the Anar to the foothills leading into the Charnals where for days thereafter they journeyed, always in the shadow of the mountains as they wound their way northeast toward the Tiderace. By now, they were beyond the lands any of them knew. Neither Morgan nor Pe Ell had ever been north of the Upper Anar, and Walker had not gone farther than the lower regions of the Charnals. In any case, it was Quickening who led them, seemingly unperturbed by the fact that she knew less of the country than any of them, responding to some inner voice that none of them could hear, to instincts that none of them could feel. She admitted that she did not know exactly where she was going, that she could sense enough to lead them for now, but that eventually they would have to cross the Charnals, and then she would be lost as the mountains would prove unfathomable to her. Eldwist lay beyond the Charnals, and they would have to have help in finding it.

"Have you the magic for that, Walker?" Pe Ell teased when she finished, but Walker only smiled and wondered the same thing.

Rain caught up with them as the second week ended and followed them relentlessly into the third, dampening their trail, their packs and clothing, and their spirits. Clouds massed overhead along the line of the peaks and refused to budge, dark and persistent. Thunder boomed and lightning flashed against the wall of the mountains as if giants were playing shadow games with their hands. There were not many travelers this far north; most of those they encountered were Trolls. Few spoke and fewer still had anything useful to tell. There were several passes that led through the mountains a day or two ahead, all of them beginning at a town high in the foothills called Rampling Steep. Yes, some of the passes led all the way east to the Tiderace. No, they had never heard of Eldwist.

"Makes you wonder if it really exists," Pe Ell muttered, persisting in his role as agitator, a smile creasing his narrow face, cold and empty and devoid of humor. "Makes you think."

That night, two days short of the completion of their third week of travel, he broached the subject in a manner that left no one in doubt as to his feelings. The rains were still falling, a gray haze that chilled and numbed the senses, and tempers had grown short.

"This town, Rampling Steep," he began, an edge to his voice that brought them all around in the stillness of the twilight, "that's where we lose any idea of where we're going, isn't it?" He asked the question of Quickening, who made no response. "We're lost after that, and I don't like being lost. Maybe it's time we talked a bit more about this whole business."

"What would you know, Pe Ell?" the girl asked quietly, unperturbed.

"You haven't told us enough about what lies ahead," he said. "I think you should. Now."

She shook her head. "You ask for answers I do not have to give. I have to discover them as well."

"I don't believe that," he said, shaking his head for emphasis, his voice low and hard. Morgan Leah was looking at him with undisguised irritation and Walker Boh was on his feet. "I know something about people, even ones who have the magic like yourself and I know when they're telling me everything they know and when they're not. You're not. You better do so.''

''Or you might turn around and go back?'' Morgan challenged sharply.

Pe Ell looked at him expressionlessly.

''Why don't you do that, Pe Ell? Why don't you?''

Pe Ell rose, his eyes flat and seemingly disinterested. Morgan stood up with him. But Quickening stepped forward, coming swiftly between them, moving to separate them without seeming to mean to do so, but as if she sought only to face Pe Ell. She stood before him, small and vulnerable, silver hair swept back as she tilted her face to his. He frowned and for a moment looked as if he felt threatened and might lash out. Whip-thin and sinewy, he curled back like a snake. But she did not move, either toward him or away, and the tension slowly went out of him.

''You must trust me,'' she told him softly, speaking to him as if he were the only other person alive in all the world, holding him spellbound by the force of her voice, the intensity of her black eyes, and the closeness of her body. ''What there is to know of Uhl Belk and Eldwist, I have told you. What there is to know of the Black Elfstone, I have told you. As much, at least, as I am given to know. Yes, there are things I keep from you just as you keep things from me. That is the way of all living creatures, Pe Ell. You cannot begrudge me my secrets when you have your own. I keep nothing back that will harm you. That is the best I can do.''

The lean man stared down at her without speaking, everything closed away behind his eyes where his thoughts were at work.

''When we reach Rampling Steep, we will seek help in finding our way,'' she continued, her voice still barely above a whisper, yet bell-clear and certain. ''Eldwist will be known and someone will point the way.''

And to the surprise of both Walker and Morgan Leah, Pe Ell simply nodded and stepped away. He did not speak again that night to any of them. He seemed to have forgotten they existed.

The following day they reached a broad roadway leading west into the foothills and turned onto it. The roadway wound ahead snakelike into the light and then into shadow when the sun dropped behind the peaks of the Charnals. Night descended and they camped beneath the stars, the first clear sky in many days. They talked quietly as the evening meal was consumed, a sense of balance restored with the passing of the rains. No mention was made of the previous night's events. Pe Ell seemed satisfied with what Quickening had told him, although she had told him almost nothing. It was the way in which she had spoken to him, Walker thought on reflection. It was the way she employed her magic to turn aside his suspicion and anger.

They set out again early the following morning, traveling northeast once more, the sunrise bright and warming. By late afternoon they had climbed high into the foothills, close against the base of the mountains. By sunset they had arrived at the town of Rampling Steep.

The light was nearly gone by then, a dim glow from behind the mountains west that colored the skyline in shades of gold and silver. Rampling Steep was hunkered down in a deep pool of shadows, cupped in a shallow basin at the foot of the peaks where the forest trees began to thin and scatter into isolated clumps between the ridges of mountain rock. The buildings of the town were a sorry bunch, ramshackle structures built of stone foundations and wooden walls and roofs with windows and doors all shuttered and barred and closed away like the eyes of frightened children. There was a single street that wound between them as if looking for a way out. The buildings of the town crouched down on either side save for a handful of shacks and cottages that were settled back on the high ground like careless sentries. Everything was desperately in need of repair. Boards from walls were broken and hung loose, roofing shingles had slipped away, and porch fronts sagged and buckled. Slivers of light crept through cracks and crevices. There were teams of horses hitched to wagons pulled up close against the buildings, each looking a little more ruined than the one before, and shadowed figures on two legs moved between them like wraiths.

As the company drew nearer Walker saw that the figures were mostly Trolls, great, hulking figures in the twilight, their bark-like faces impossible to read. A few glanced at the four as they passed down the roadway, but none bothered to speak or to give a second look. The sound of voices reached out to them now, disembodied grunts and mutterings and laughter that the dilapidated walls could not keep in. But despite the talk and the laughter and the movement of men, Rampling Steep had an empty feel to it, as if it had long ago been abandoned by the living.

Quickening took them up the roadway without pausing, glancing neither left nor right, as sure of herself now as she had

been from the start. Morgan followed no more than a step behind, staying close, keeping watch, being protective although
there was probably no need for him to do so. Pe Ell had drifted
out to the right, distancing himself. Walker trailed.

There was a series of ale houses at the center of Rampling
Steep, and it appeared that everyone had gathered there. Music
came from some, and men lurched and swaggered through the
doors, passing in and out of the light in faceless anonymity. A
few women passed as well, worn and hard looking. Rampling
Steep appeared to be a place of ending rather than beginning.

Quickening took them into the first of the ale houses and
asked the keeper if he knew of someone who could guide them
through the mountains to Eldwist. She asked the question as if
there were nothing unusual about it. She was oblivious to the
stir her presence caused, to the stares that were directed at her
from every quarter, and to the dark hunger that lay behind a
good many of the eyes that fixed upon her, or at least she seemed
to be. Perhaps, Walker thought, as he watched her, it was all
simply of no consequence to her. He saw that no one tried to
approach and no one threatened. Morgan stood protectively at
her back, facing that unfriendly, rapacious gathering—as if one
man could make a difference if they should decide to do something—but it was not the Highlander that deterred them or Walker
or even the forbidding Pe Ell. It was the girl, a creature so
stunning that like a thing out of some wild imagining it could
not be disturbed for fear it would prove false. The men gathered
in the ale house watched, that crowd of wild-eyed men, not quite
believing but not willing to prove themselves wrong.

There was nothing to be learned at the first ale house, so they
moved on to the next. No one followed. The scenario of the first
ale house was repeated at the second, this one smaller and closer
inside, the smoke of pipes and the smell of bodies thicker and
more pungent. There were Trolls, Gnomes, Dwarves, and Men
in Rampling Steep, all drinking and talking together as if it were
the natural order of things, as if what was happening in the rest
of the Four Lands was of no importance here. Walker studied
their faces dispassionately, their eyes when their faces told him
nothing, and found them secretive and scared, the faces and
eyes of men who lived with hardship and disappointment yet
ignored both because to do otherwise would mean they could
not survive. Some seemed dangerous, a few even desperate. But
there was an order to life in Rampling Steep as there was in most
places, and not much happened to disturb that order. Strangers

came and went, even ones as striking as Quickening, and life went on nevertheless. Quickening was something like a falling star—it happened a few times and you were lucky if you saw it but you didn't do anything to change your life because of it.

They moved on to a third ale house and then a fourth. At each ale house, the answers to Quickening's questions were the same. No one knew anything of Eldwist and Uhl Belk and no one wanted to. There were maybe eight drinking houses in all along the roadway, most offering beds upstairs and supplies from storerooms out back, a few doubling as trading stations or exchanges. Because Rampling Steep was the only town for days in either direction that fronted the lower side of the Charnals and because it was situated where the trails leading down out of the mountains converged, a lot of traffic passed through, trappers and traders mostly, but others as well. Every ale house was filled and most gathered were temporary or sometime residents on their way to or from somewhere else. There was talk of all sorts, of business and politics, of roads traveled and wonders seen, of the people and places that made up the Four Lands. Walker listened without appearing to and thought that Pe Ell was doing the same.

At the fifth ale house they visited—Walker never even noticed the name—they finally got the response they were looking for. The keeper was a big, ruddy-complexioned fellow with a scarred face and a ready smile. He sized up Quickening in a way that made even Walker uncomfortable. Then he suggested that the girl should take a room with him for a few days, just to see if maybe she might like the town enough to stay. That brought Morgan Leah about with fire in his eyes, but Quickening screened him away with a slight shifting of her body, met the keeper's bold stare, and replied that she wasn't interested. The keeper did not press the suggestion. Instead, to everyone's amazement in the face of the rejection he had just been handed, he told her that the man she was seeking was down the street at the Skinned Cat. His name, he said, was Horner Dees.

They went back out into the night, leaving the keeper looking as if he wasn't at all sure what he had just done. The look was telling. Quickening had that gift; it was the essence of her magic. She could turn you around before you realized it. She could make you reveal yourself in ways you had never intended. She could make you want to please her. It was the kind of thing a beautiful woman could make a man do, but with Quickening it was something far more than her beauty that disarmed you. It was the creature within, the elemental that seemed human but was far more, an embodiment of magic that Walker thought reflected the father who had made her. He knew the stories of the King of the Silver River. When you met him, you told him what he wished to know and you did not dissemble. His presence alone was enough to make you *want* to tell him. Walker had seen how Morgan and Pe Ell and the men in the ale houses responded to her. And he as well. She was most certainly her father's child.

They found the Skinned Cat at the far end of the town, tucked back within the shadow of several massive, ancient shagbarks. It was a large, rambling structure that creaked and groaned simply from the movement of the men and women inside and seemed to hang together mostly out of stubbornness. It was as crowded as the others, but there was more space to fill and it had been divided along its walls into nooks and partitions to make it feel less barnlike. Lights were scattered about like distant friends reaching out through the gloom, and the patrons were gathered in knots at the serving bar and about long tables and benches. Heads turned at their entrance as they had turned at the other ale houses, and eyes watched. Quickening moved to find the keeper, who listened and pointed to the back of the room. There was a man sitting at a table there, alone in a shadowed nook, hunched over and faceless, pushed away from the light and the crowd.

The four walked over to stand before him.

"Horner Dees," Quickening said in that silken voice.

Massive hands brought an ale mug slowly away from a bearded mouth and back to the tabletop, and a large, shaggy head lifted. The man was huge, a great old bear of a fellow with the better part of his years behind him. There was hair all over him, on his forearms and the backs of his hands, at his throat and on his chest, and on his head and face, grown over him so completely that except for his eyes and nose his features were obscured almost entirely. It was impossible to guess how old he was, but the hair was silver gray, the skin beneath it wrinkled and browned and mottled, and the fingers gnarled like old roots.

"I might be," he rumbled truculently from out of some giant's cave. His eyes were riveted on the girl.

"My name is Quickening," she said. "These are my companions. We search for a place called Eldwist and a man named Uhl Belk. We are told you know of both."

"You were told wrong."

"Can you take us there?" she asked, ignoring his response.
"I just said . . ."

"Can you take us there?" she repeated.

The big man stared at her without speaking, without moving, with no hint of what he was thinking. He was like a huge, settled rock that had survived ages of weathering and erosion and found them to be little more than a passing breeze. "Who are you?" he asked finally. "Who, other than your name?"

Quickening did not hesitate. "I am the daughter of the King of the Silver River. Do you know of him, Horner Dees?"

The other nodded slowly. "Yes, I know him. And maybe you are who you say. And maybe I am who you think. Maybe I even know about Eldwist and Uhl Belk. Maybe I'm the only one who knows—the only one who's still alive to tell about it. Maybe I can even do what you ask and take you there. But I don't see the point. Sit."

He gestured at a scattering of empty chairs, and the four seated themselves across the table from him. He looked at the men in turn, then his eyes returned to the girl. "You don't look as if you're someone who doesn't know what they're doing. Why would you want to find Uhl Belk?"

Quickening's black eyes were fathomless, intense. "Uhl Belk stole something that doesn't belong to him. It must be returned."

Horner Dees snorted derisively. "You plan to steal it back, do you? Or just ask him to return it? Do you know anything about Belk? I do."

"He stole a talisman from the Druids."

Dees hesitated. His bearded face twitched as he chewed on something imaginary. "Girl, nobody who goes into Eldwist ever comes out again. Nobody except me, and I was just plain lucky. There's things there that nothing can stand against. Belk, he's an old thing, come out of some other age, full of dark magic and evil. You won't ever take anything away from him, and he won't ever give anything back."

"Those who are with me are stronger than Uhl Belk," Quickening said. "They have magic as well, and theirs will overcome his. My father says it will be so. These three," and she named them each in turn, "will prevail."

As she spoke their names, Horner Dees let his eyes shift to identify each, passing over their faces quickly, pausing only once—so briefly that Walker wasn't sure at first that there had been a pause at all—on Pe Ell.

Then he said, "These are men. Uhl Belk is something more. You can't kill him like an ordinary man. You probably can't even find him. He'll find you and by then it will be too late." He snapped his fingers and sat back.

Quickening eyed him momentarily across the table, then reached out impulsively and touched the table's wooden surface. Instantly a splinter curled up, a slender stem forming, leafing out and finally flowering with tiny bluebells. Quickening's smile was as magical as her touch. "Show us the way into Eldwist, Horner Dees," she said.

The old man wet his lips. "It will take more than flowers to do in Belk," he said.

"Perhaps not," she whispered, and Walker had the feeling that for a moment she had gone somewhere else entirely. "Wouldn't you like to come with us and see?"

Dees shook his head. "I didn't get old being stupid," he said. He thought a moment, then sat forward again. "It was ten years ago when I went into Eldwist. I'd found it some time before that, but I knew it was dangerous and I wasn't about to go in there alone. I kept thinking about it though, wondering what was in there, because finding out about things is what I do. I've been a Tracker, a soldier, a hunter, everything there is to be, and it all comes down to finding out what's what. So I kept wondering about Eldwist, about what was in there, all those old buildings, all that stone, everywhere you looked. I went back finally because I couldn't stand not knowing anymore. I took a dozen men with me, lucky thirteen of us. We thought we'd find something of value in there, a place as secret and old as that. We knew what it was called; there's been legends about it for years in the high country, over on the other side of the mountains where some of us had been. The Trolls know it. It's a peninsula—just a narrow strip of land, all rock, jutting out into the middle of the Tiderace. We went out there one morning, the thirteen of us. Full of life. By dawn of the next day, the other twelve were dead, and I was running like a scared deer!"

He hunched his shoulders. "You don't want to go there," he said. "You don't want anything to do with Eldwist and Uhl Belk."

He picked up his mug, drained it, and slammed it down purposefully. The sound brought the keeper immediately, a fresh drink in hand, and away again just as quickly. Dees never looked at him, his eyes still fixed on Quickening. The evening was wearing on toward midnight by now, but few among the ale-house customers had drifted away. They clustered as they had since sunset, since long before in some cases, their talk more liquid and disjointed than earlier and their posture more relaxed. Time had lost its hold on them momentarily, victims of all forms of strife and misadventure, refugees huddled within the shelter of their intoxication and their loose companionship. Dees was not one of them; Walker Boh doubted that he ever would be.

Quickening stirred. "Horner Dees," she said, saying his name as if she were examining it, a young girl trying on an old man's identity. "If you do nothing, Uhl Belk will come for you."

For the first time, Dees looked startled.

"In time, he will come," Quickening continued, her voice both gentle and sad. "He advances his kingdom beyond what it was and it grows more swiftly with the passing of time. If he is not stopped, if his power is not lessened, sooner or later he will reach you."

"I'll be long dead," the old man said, but he didn't sound sure.

Quickening smiled, magical once again, something perfect and wondrous. "There are mysteries that you will never solve because you will not have the chance," she said. "That is not the case with Uhl Belk. You are a man who has spent his life finding out about things. Would you stop doing so now? How will you know which of us is right about Uhl Belk if you do not come with us? Do so, Horner Dees. Show us the way into Eldwist. Make this journey."

Dees was silent for a long time, thinking it through. Then he said, "I would like to believe that monster could be undone by something . . ." He shook his head. "I don't know."

"Do you need to?" the girl asked softly.

Dees frowned, then smiled, a great, gap-toothed grin that wreathed his broad face in weathered lines. "Never have," he said and laughed. The grin disappeared. "This is a hard walk we're talking about, not some stroll across the street. The passes are tough going any time of the year and once we're over and beyond, we'll be on our own. No help over there. Nothing but Trolls, and they don't care spit about outsiders. Nothing to help us but us. Truth is, none of you look strong enough to make it."

"We might be stronger than you think," Morgan Leah said quietly.

Dees eyed him critically. "You'll have to be," he said. "A

lot stronger.'' Then he sighed. ''Well, well. Come to this, has it? Me, an old man, about to go out into the far reaches one more time.'' He chuckled softly and looked back at Quickening. ''You have a way about you, I'll say that. Talk a nut right out of its shell. Even a hard old nut like me. Well, well.''

He shoved his chair back from the table and came to his feet. He was even bigger standing than he had been sitting, like some pitted wall that refused to fall down even after years of enduring adverse weather. He stood before them, hunched over and hoary looking, his big arms hanging loose, and his eyes squinting as if he had just come into the light.

''All right, I'll take you,'' he announced, leaning forward to emphasize his decision, keeping his voice low and even. ''I'll take you because it's true that I haven't seen everything or found all the answers and what's life for if not to keep trying—even when I don't believe that trying will be enough. You meet me back here at sunrise, and I'll give you a list of what you need and where to find it. You do the gathering, I'll do the organizing. We'll give it a try. Who knows? Maybe some of us will even make it back.''

He paused and looked at them as if seeing them for the first time. There was a hint of laughter around the edges of his voice as he said, ''Won't it be a good joke on Belk if you really do have the stronger magic?''

Then he eased his way out from behind the table, shambled across the room and out the door, and disappeared into the night.

XIII

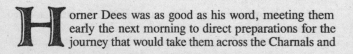

Horner Dees was as good as his word, meeting them early the next morning to direct preparations for the journey that would take them across the Charnals and into Eldwist. He met them at the door of the rooming house on which they had finally settled for their night's lodgings, a creaky two-storied rambler that in former times had been first a residence then later a store, and without bothering to explain how he had found them provided a list of supplies they would need and directions on where to obtain them. He was even more rumpled and bearish seeming than he had been the previous night, wider than the door he stood before and hunched over like some sodden jungle shrub. He muttered and grumbled, and his instructions were delivered as if he were suffering from too much drink. Pe Ell thought him a worthless sot, and Morgan Leah found him just plain unpleasant. Because they could see that Quickening expected it, they accepted their instructions wordlessly. A little of Horner Dees went a long way. But Walker Boh saw something different. To begin with, he had worried enough the previous night about Dees to take Quickening aside after the old man's departure and suggest to her that maybe this wasn't the man they were looking for. After all, what did they know about Dees beyond what he had told them? Even if he actually had gone into Eldwist, that was ten years ago. What if he had since forgotten the way? What if he remembered just enough to get them hopelessly lost? But Quickening had assured him in that way she had of dispelling all doubt that Horner Dees was the man they needed. Now, as he listened to the old Tracker, he was inclined to agree. Walker had made a good many journeys in his time and he understood the kinds of preparations that were required. It was clear that Dees understood as well. For all of his gruff talk and his grizzled look, Horner Dees knew what he was doing.

The preparation time passed quickly. Walker, Morgan, and Pe Ell gathered together the foodstuffs, bedding, canvases, ropes, climbing tools, cooking implements, clothing, and survival gear that Dees had sent them to find. Dees himself arranged for pack animals, shaggy mules that could carry the heavy loads they would need and weather the mountain storms. They brought everything to an old stable situated at the north end of Rampling Steep, a building that seemed to serve Dees as both workshop and home. He lived in the tack room and when he wasn't issuing orders or checking on their efforts to carry them out he kept himself there.

Quickening was even more reclusive. When she wasn't with them, which was most of the time, they had no idea where she was. She seemed to drift in the manner of an errant cloud, more shadow than substance. She might have walked the woodlands away from the town, for she would have been more comfortable there. She might have simply hidden away. Wherever she went, she disappeared with the completeness of the sun at day's end, and they missed her as much. Only when she returned did they feel warmed again. She spoke to them each day, always singly, never together. She gave them a measure of herself, some small reassurance that they could not quite define but not mistake either. Had she been someone else, they would have suspected her of game playing. But she was Quickening, the daughter of the King of the Silver River, and there was no time or wish or even need for games in her life. She transcended such behavior, and while they did not fully understand her and sensed that perhaps they never would, they were convinced that deception and betrayal were beyond her. Her presence alone kept them together, bound them to her so that they would not turn away. She was incandescent, a creature of overpowering brilliance, so magical that they were as captivated by her as they would have been by a rainbow's arc. She caused them to look for her everywhere. They watched for her to appear and when she did found themselves beguiled anew. They waited for her to speak to them, to touch them, for even the briefest look. She spun them in the vortex of her being, and even as they found themselves spellbound they yearned for it to go on. They watched each other like hawks, uncertain of their roles in her plans, of their uses, and of their needs. They fought to learn something of her that would belong only to them and they measured the time they spent with her as if it were gold dust.

Yet they were not entirely without doubts or misgivings. In the secrecy of their most private thoughts they still worried—about her wisdom in selecting them, about her foresight in the quest they had agreed to undertake, and about whether wanting to be near her was sufficient reason for them to go on.

Pe Ell's ruminations were the most intense. He had come on this journey in the first place because the girl intrigued him, because she was different from the others he had been sent to kill, because he wanted to learn as much about her as he could before he used the Stiehl, and because he wanted to discover, too, if this talisman of which she spoke, this Black Elfstone, was as powerful as she believed and if so whether he could make it his own. It had annoyed him when she had insisted on bringing along the brash Highlander and the tall, pale one-armed man. He would have preferred that they go alone, because in truth he believed that he was all she would need. Yet he had held his tongue and remained patient, convinced that the other two would cause him no problem.

But now there was Horner Dees to contend with as well, and there was something about this old man that bothered Pe Ell. It was odd that Dees should trouble him like this; he seemed a worthless old coot. The source of his discomfort, he supposed, was the fact that he was beginning to feel crowded. How many more did the girl intend to add to their little company? Soon, he would be stumbling over cripples and misfits at every turn, none of them worth even the small effort it would eventually require to eliminate them. Pe Ell was a loner; he did not like groups. Yet the girl persisted in swelling their number and all for a rather vague purpose. Her magic seemed almost limitless; she could do things no one else could, not even him. He was convinced that despite her protestations to the contrary her magic was sufficient to guide them into Eldwist. Once there, she had no need of anyone but him. What was the purpose then of including the others?

Two nights earlier, just before the rains had ended, Pe Ell had confronted her out of frustration and discontent, intending to force from her the truth of the matter. Quickening had turned him aside somehow, calmed him, stripping him of his determination to unmask her. The experience had left him perplexed at the ease with which she had manipulated him, and for a time afterward he had thought simply to kill her and be done with it. He had discovered her purpose, hadn't he? Why not do as Rimmer Dall had advised and be finished with this business, forget the Black Elfstone, and leave these fools to chase after it without him? He had decided to wait. Now he was glad he had. For as he considered the irritating presence of Dees and the others, he began to think that he understood their purpose. Quickening had brought them to serve as a diversion, nothing more. After all, what other service could they provide? One's strength was contained in a broken sword, the other's in a broken body. What were such paltry magics compared to that of the Stiehl? Wasn't he the assassin, the master killer, the one whose magic could bring down anything? That was most certainly why she had brought him. She had never said as much, but he knew it was so. Rimmer Dall had been wrong to think she would not recognize what he was. Quickening, with her formidable insight and intuition, would not have missed such an obvious truth. Which was why she had brought him, of course—why she had come to him before any of the others. She needed him to kill Belk; he was the only one who could. She needed the magic of the Stiehl. The others, Dees included, were so much kindling to be thrown into the fire. In the end, she would have to depend on him.

Morgan Leah, if Pe Ell had bothered to ask him, might have agreed. He was the youngest and despite his brash attitude the most insecure. He was still closer to being a boy than a grown man, a fact he was forced to admit to himself if to no one else. He had traveled fewer places and done fewer things. He knew less about practically everything. Almost the whole of his life had been spent in the Highlands of Leah, and although he had found ways to make occupation of his homeland unpleasant for the Federation officials who sought to govern, he had done little else of note. He was hopelessly in love with Quickening and he had nothing to offer her. The Sword of Leah was the weapon she needed in her quest for the Black Elfstone, the talisman whose magic could defeat Uhl Belk. Yet the Sword had lost the better part of its magic when it had shattered against the rune-marked doors leading from the Pit, and what remained was insufficient and, worse, unpredictable. Without it, he did not see how he would be of much use in this business. Perhaps Quickening was right when she said he might regain the Sword's magic if he went with her. But what would happen if she were threatened before then? Who among them would protect her? He had only a shattered Sword. Walker Boh, without his arm, seemed less formidable than he had before, a man in search of himself. Horner Dees was old and gray. Only Pe Ell, with his still secret magic and enigmatic ways, seemed capable of defending the daughter of the King of the Silver River.

Nevertheless Morgan was determined to continue the quest. He was not entirely certain why. Perhaps it was pride, perhaps a stubborn refusal to give up on himself. Whatever it was, it kept alive a dim hope that somehow he would prove useful to this strange and wondrous girl he had fallen in love with, that he would somehow be able to protect her against whatever threatened, and that with time and patience he would discover a way to restore the magic to the Sword of Leah. He worked diligently at the tasks Horner Dees gave him to aid in outfitting the little company for its journey north, trying a little harder most times than the others. He thought of Quickening constantly, playing with images of her in his mind. She was a gift, he knew. She was the possibility of everything he had always hoped might one day be. It was more than the fact that she was beautiful, or the look or feel or way of her, or that she had rescued him from the Federation prisons or restored the Meade Gardens to the Dwarves of Culhaven. It was what he sensed lay between them, an intangible bond different than that linking her to the others. It was there when she spoke to him, when she called him by his first name as she did not do with the others. It was there in the way she looked at him. It was something incredibly precious.

He made up his mind that he would not let it go, whatever it was, whatever it might turn out to be. It became, to his surprise and even his joy, the most important thing in his life.

Walker Boh had hold of something as well, but it was not as easily identifiable. As with Morgan's determination to love and Pe Ell's to kill, there was a bond that linked him to Quickening. There was that strange kinship between them, that sharing of magics that gave them insights into each other no one else possessed. Like the Highlander and the assassin, he believed his relationship with her different than that of the others, more personal and important, more lasting. He did not feel love for her as Morgan did and he had no wish to possess her like Pe Ell. What he needed was to understand her magic because in doing so he was convinced he would come to understand his own.

The dilemma lay in determining whether or not this was a good idea. It was not enough that his need was compelling; the deaths of Cogline and Rumor had made it that. He knew that he needed to understand the magic if he were to destroy the Shadowen. But he was frightened still of the consequences of such knowledge. With the magic, there was always a price. He had been intrigued with it since he had discovered he possessed it—and frightened of it as well. Fear and curiosity had pulled him in two directions all his life. It had been so when his father had told him of his legacy, when he had struggled unsuccessfully to make his home with the people of Shady Vale, when Cogline had come to him and offered to teach him how the magic worked, and when he had learned of the existence of the Black Elfstone from the pages of the Druid History and known that the charge given him by the shade of Allanon might be fulfilled. It was always the same. It was so now.

He had worried for a time that he had lost the magic entirely, that it had been destroyed by the poison of the Asphinx. But with the healing of his arm, his sense of himself had returned and with it an awareness that the magic had survived. He had tested it on this journey in little ways. He knew it was there, for example, when something within him reacted to Quickening's presence, to the way she used her own magic to bind Morgan and Pe Ell and himself to her, and to the effect she had on others. It was there, too, in the way he sensed things. He had caught the hesitation in the look Horner Dees gave Pe Ell—just a hint of recognition. He could feel the interaction between the members of the company and Quickening, a sense of the feelings that lay just beneath the surface of the looks and words they exchanged. He had insight, intuition, and foreknowledge in some cases. There was no doubt. The magic was still there.

Yet it was weakened and no longer the formidable weapon it had once been. That gave Walker pause. Here was an opportunity to move away from its influence, from the shadow it cast upon his life, from the legacy of Brin Ohmsford and the Druids, and from everything that had made him the Dark Uncle. If he did not probe, there would be no hurt. The magic would lie dormant, he believed, if it were not stirred. If left alone, it might let him break free.

But without it the Shadowen would be left free as well. And what purpose would it serve to make this journey into Eldwist and confront Uhl Belk if he did not intend to employ the magic? What use would he ever make of the Black Elfstone?

So they prowled within cages of their own making, Walker Boh and Morgan Leah and Pe Ell, suspicious cats with sharp eyes and hungry looks, their minds made up as to what they would do in the days that lay ahead and at the same time still quizzing themselves to make certain. They kept each other's company without ever getting close. Supplies were gathered and packs assembled, and the time passed quickly. Horner Dees seemed satisfied, but he was the only one. The other three chafed against the constraints of their uncertainty, impatience, and doubt despite their resolve to do otherwise, and nothing they could do or think would relieve them. There was a darkness that lay ahead, building upon itself like a stormcloud, and they could not see what waited beyond. They could see it rising up before them like a wall, a coming together of event and circumstance, an explosion of magic and raw strength, a revelation of need and purpose. Black and impenetrable, it would seek to devour them.

When it did, they sensed, not everyone would survive.

Three days later they departed Rampling Steep. They went out at sunrise, the skies thick with clouds that scraped against the mountains and shut away the light. The smell of rain was in the air, and the wind was sharp and chill as it swept down off the peaks. The town slept as they climbed away from it, hunkered down against the dark like a frightened animal, closed and still. A few forgotten oil lamps burned on porches and through the cracks of windows, but the people did not stir. As Walker Boh passed into the rocks he looked back momentarily at the cluster of colorless buildings and was reminded of locust shells, hollow and abandoned and fascinatingly ugly.

The rain began at midday and continued for a week without stopping. At times it slowed to a drizzle but never quit completely. The clouds remained locked in place overhead, thunder rumbled all about, and lightning flashed in the distance. They were cold and wet, and there was nothing they could do to relieve their discomfort. The foothills were forested lower down, but bare at the higher elevations. The wind swept over them unhindered and without the sun's warmth remained frost-edged and chill. Horner Dees set a steady pace, but the company could not travel rapidly while afoot and with mules in tow, and progress was slow. At night they slept beneath canvas shelters that kept the rain off and were able to strip away their wet clothing and wrap themselves in blankets. But there was no wood for a fire and the dampness persisted. They woke cramped and cold each morning, ate because it was necessary, and pressed ahead.

The foothills gave way to mountains after several days, and the path became less certain. The trail they had been following, broad and clear before, disappeared completely. Dees took them into a maze of ridges and defiles, along the rims of broad slides, and around massive boulders that would have dwarfed the buildings of Rampling Steep. The slope steepened dangerously, and they were forced to watch their footing at every turn. The clouds swept downward, filling the air with clinging moisture that sought to envelop them, that twisted about the rocks like some huge, substanceless worm, its skin a damp ooze. Thunder crashed, and it seemed as if they were at its center. Rain descended in torrents. They lost sight of everything that lay behind, and they could not discern what waited ahead.

Without Dees to guide them, they would have been lost. The Charnals swallowed them as an ocean would a stone. Everything looked the same. Cliffs were impassable walls through the mist and rain, canyons dropped into vast chasms of black emptiness, and the mountains spread away in a seemingly endless huddle of snowcapped peaks. It was so cold their skin grew numb. At times the rain turned to sleet and even to snow. They wrapped themselves in great cloaks and heavy boots and trudged on. Through it all Horner Dees remained steady and certain, a great shaggy presence they quickly learned to rely upon. He was at home in the mountains, comfortable despite the forbidding climate and terrain, at peace with himself. He hummed as he went, lost in private reveries of other times and places. He paused now and then to point something out that they would not have otherwise seen, determined that nothing should be missed. That he understood the Charnals was clear from the beginning; that he loved them soon became apparent. He spoke freely of that love, of the mix of wildness and serenity he found there, and of their vastness and permanency. His deep voice rumbled and shook as if filled with the tremors of the storms and the wind. He told stories of what life was like in the Charnals and he gave them a part of himself in the telling.

He gained no converts, however—except, perhaps, for Quickening, who as usual gave no indication of what she was thinking. The other three simply grumbled now and again, kept a studied silence the rest of the time, and fought a hopeless battle to ignore their discomfort. The mountains would never be their home; the mountains were simply a barrier they needed to get past. They labored stoically and waited for the journey to come to an end.

It did not do so. Instead it went on rather as if it were a lost dog searching for its master, the scent firmly in mind, yet distracted by other smells. The rains diminished and finally passed, but the air stayed frosty, the wind continued to buffet them, and the mountains stretched on. The men, the girl, and the animals trudged forward, shoved and pushed by the weather and the land. Midway through the second week Dees said they were starting down, but there was no way of knowing if that were true; nothing in the rocks and scrub about them indicated it was so. Wherever they looked, the Charnals were still there.

Twelve days out they were caught in a snowstorm high in a mountain pass and nearly died. The storm came on them so quickly that even Dees was caught by surprise. He quickly roped them together and because there was no shelter to be found in the pass he was forced to take them through. The air became a sheet of impenetrable white and everything about them disappeared. Their feet and hands began to freeze. The mules broke away in terror when part of the slope slid away, braying and stumbling past the frantic men until they tumbled over the mountainside and were lost. Only one was saved, and it carried no food.

They found shelter, survived the storm, and pushed on. Even Dees, who had shown himself to be the most durable among them, was beginning to tire. The remaining mule had to be destroyed the next day when it stepped in a snow-covered crevice and broke its leg. The heavy weather gear had been lost, and they were reduced to backpacks which contained a meager portion of food and water, some rope, and not much else.

That night the temperature plummeted. They would have frozen if Dees had not managed to find wood for a fire. They sat huddled together all night, pushed close to the flames, rubbing their hands and feet, talking to stay awake, afraid if they didn't they would die in their sleep. It was an odd tableau, the five of them settled back within the rocks, crouched close together about the tiny blaze, still wary of one another, protective of themselves, and forced to share space and time and circumstance. Yet the words they spoke revealed them, not so much for what was said as for how and when and why. It drew them together in a strange sort of way, bonding them as not much else could, and while the closeness that developed was more physical than emotional and decidedly limited in any case, it at least left them with a sense of fellowship that had been missing before.

The weather improved after that, the clouds breaking up and drifting on, the sun returning to warm the air, and the snow and rain disappearing at last. The Charnals began to thin ahead of them, and there was no mistaking the fact that they had begun their descent. Trees returned, a scattering at first, then whole groves, and finally forests for as far as the eye could see, spilling down into distant valleys. They were able to fish and hunt game for food, to sleep in warm arbors, and to wake dry and rested. Spirits improved.

Then, fifteen days out of Rampling Steep, they arrived at the Spikes.

They stood for a long time on a ridgeline and looked down onto the valley. It was nearing midday, the sun bright, the air warm and sweet smelling. The valley was broad and deep and shadowed by mountains that rose about it on either side. It was shaped like a funnel, wide mouth at the south end and narrow at the north where it disappeared into a line of distant hills. Trees grew thick upon its floor, but down its middle a jagged ridgeline rose, and the trees there had suffered a blight that had left them stripped of their foliage, bare trunks and branches jutting upward like the hackles on the back of a cornered animal.

Like spikes, Morgan Leah thought.

He glanced at Horner Dees. "What's down there?" he asked. His attitude toward the old Tracker had changed during the past two weeks. He no longer thought of him as an unpleasant old man. It had taken him longer than Walker Boh, but he had come to recognize that Dees was a thorough professional, better at what he did than anyone the Highlander had ever encountered. Morgan would have liked to be just half as good. He had begun paying attention to what the old man said and did.

Dees shrugged. "I don't know. It's been ten years since I passed this way." Dees, for his part, liked Morgan's enthusiasm and willingness to work. He liked the fact that Morgan wasn't afraid to learn. He narrowed his brows thoughtfully as he returned the other's glance. "I'm just being careful, Highlander."

They studied the valley some more.

"Something is down there," Pe Ell said quietly.

No one disputed him. Pe Ell had remained the most secretive among them, yet they knew enough of him by now to trust his instincts.

"We have to pass this way," Dees said finally, "or skirt the mountains on one side or the other. If we do that, we'll lose a week's time."

They continued their vigil for long moments without speaking, thinking the matter through separately, until finally Horner Dees said, "Let's get on with it."

They worked their way downward, discovering a pathway that led directly toward the center of the valley and the barren ridge. They moved quietly, Dees leading, Quickening behind him, Morgan, Walker, and Pe Ell bringing up the rear. They passed out of sunlight into shadow, and the air turned cool. The valley rose up to meet them and for a time swallowed them up. Then the trail lifted onto the ridgeline, and they found themselves in the midst of the blighted trees. Morgan studied the lifeless skeletons for a time, the blackening of the bark, the wilting of leaves and buds where there were any to be seen at all, and turned instinctively to look at Walker. The Dark Uncle's pale, drawn face lifted, and the hard eyes stared back at him. They were both thinking the same thing. The Spikes had been sickened in the same way as the rest of the land. The Shadowen were at work here, too.

They crossed a band of sunlight that had slipped through a break in the peaks and then dipped downward into a hollow. It was abnormally still there, a pool of silence that magnified the sound of their footsteps as they worked their way ahead. Morgan had grown increasingly edgy, reminded of his encounter with the Shadowen on the journey to Culhaven with the Ohmsfords. His nose tested the air for the rank smell that would warn of the other's presence, and his ears strained to catch even the smallest sound. Dees moved ahead purposefully, Quickening's long hair a slender bit of silver trailing after. Neither exhibited any sign of hesitation. Yet there was tension in all of them; Morgan could feel it.

They passed out of the hollow and back onto the open ridge. For a time they were high enough above the trees that Morgan could see the valley from end to end. They were more than halfway through now, approaching the narrow end of the funnel where the mountains split apart and the trees thinned with the beginning of the hills beyond. Morgan's edginess began to dissipate and he found himself thinking of home, of the Highlands of Leah, and of the countryside he had grown up in. He missed the Highlands, he realized—much more than he would have expected. It was one thing to say that his home no longer belonged to him because the Federation occupied it; it was another to make himself believe it. Like Par Ohmsford, he lived with the hope that things might one day change.

The trail dipped downward again and another hollow appeared, this one shaggy with brush and scrub that had filled the gaps left with the passing of the trees. They moved into it, shoving their way past brambles and stickers, angling for the open spaces where the trail wound ahead. Shadows lay thick across the hollow as the light began to creep westward. The forests about them formed a wall of dark silence.

They had just entered a clearing at the center of the hollow when Quickening suddenly slowed. "Stand still," she said.

They did so instantly, looking first at her, then at the brush all about them. Something was moving. Figures began to detach themselves, breaking their concealment, moving into the light. There were hundreds of them—small, squat creatures with hairy, gnarled limbs and bony features. They looked as if they had grown out of the scrub, so like it were they, and it was only the short pants and weapons that seemed to separate the two. The weapons were formidable—short spears and strangely shaped throwing implements with razor edges. The creatures held them threateningly as they advanced.

"Urdas," Horner Dees said quietly. "Don't move."

No one did, not even Pe Ell who was crouched in much the same way as the creatures who menaced him.

"Who are they?" Morgan asked of Dees, at the same time backing protectively toward Quickening.

"Gnomes," the other said. "With a little Troll thrown in. No one has ever been sure of the exact mix. You don't find them anywhere south of the Charnals. They're Northlanders as much as the Trolls. Tribal like the Gnomes. Very dangerous."

The Urdas were all about them now, closing off any chance of escape. They had thickly muscled bodies with short, powerful legs and long arms, and their faces were blunt and expressionless. Morgan tried to read something of what they might be thinking in their yellow eyes, but failed.

Then he noticed that they were all looking at Quickening.

"What do we do?" he asked Dees in an anxious whisper, worried now.

Dees shook his head.

The Urdas moved to within a dozen feet of the company and stopped. They did not threaten; they did not speak. They simply stood there, watching Quickening for the most part, but waiting as well.

Waiting for what? Morgan asked himself silently.

And at almost the same moment the brush parted, and a golden-haired man stepped into view. Instantly the Urdas dropped to one knee, heads bowed in recognition. The golden-haired man looked at the five beleaguered members of the surrounded company and smiled.

"The King has come," he said brightly. "Long live the King."

XIV

Would you lay down your weapons, please?" the man called out to them cheerfully. "Just put them on the ground in front of you. Don't worry. You can pick them up again in a moment."

He sang:

> *"Nothing given freely is ever given up.*
> *It will be given back to you*
> *Through others' love and trust."*

The five from Rampling Steep stared at him.

"Please?" he said. "It will make things so much easier if you do."

Dees glanced at the others, shrugged, and did as he was asked. Neither Walker nor Quickening carried any weapons. Morgan hesitated. Pe Ell didn't move at all.

"This is only for the purpose of demonstrating your friendship," the man went on encouragingly. "If you don't lay down your weapons, my subjects won't allow me to approach. I'll have to keep shouting at you from over here."

He sang:

> *"High, low, wherever we may go,*
> *I'll have to keep on shouting out to you."*

Morgan, after a sharp glance from Dees, complied. It was hard to tell what Pe Ell might have done if Quickening hadn't turned to him and whispered, "Do as he says." Pe Ell hesitated even then before unstrapping his broadsword. The look on his hard face was unmistakable. The broadsword notwithstanding,

Morgan was willing to bet that Pe Ell still had a weapon concealed on him somewhere.

"Much better," the stranger announced. "Now step back a pace. There!" He beckoned, and the Urdas came quickly to their feet. He was a man of average height and build, his movements quick and energetic, and his clean-shaven face handsome beneath his long blond hair. His blue eyes twinkled. He gestured at the Urdas and then at the weapons on the ground. The odd-looking creatures muttered agreeably and heads began to nod. He sang again, a short piece that the Urdas seemed to recognize, his voice full and rich, his handsome face beaming. When he finished, the circle parted to let him pass. He came directly up to Quickening, bowed low before her, took her hand in his own and kissed it. "My lady," he said.

He sang:

> *"Five travelers crossed field and stream*
> *And Eastland forests wide.*
> *They crossed the Charnal Mountain range*
> *To gain the Northland side.*
> *Tra-la-la-diddie-oh-day.*
>
> *Five travelers came from afar*
> *And entered Urda Land.*
> *They braved the dangers of the Spikes*
> *To meet King Carisman.*
> *Tra-la-la-diddie-oh-day."*

He bowed to Quickening again. "That is my name, Lady. Carisman. And yours?"

Quickening gave it to him and those of her companions as well. She seemed unconcerned that he knew. "Are you indeed a king?" she asked.

Carisman beamed. "Oh, yes, Lady. I am king of the Urdas, lord of all those you now survey and many, many more. To be honest, I did not seek out the job. It was thrust upon me, as they say. But come now. Time enough to tell that tale later. Pick up your weapons—carefully, of course. We mustn't alarm my subjects; they are very protective of me. I shall take you to my palace and we shall talk and drink wine and eat exotic fruits and fishes. Come now, come. It shall be a royal feast!"

Dees tried to say something, but Carisman was gone as swiftly as a feather caught by the wind, dancing away, singing some new song, and beckoning them to follow. The Tracker, Morgan, and Pe Ell retrieved their weapons and with Walker and Quickening in tow, started after. Urdas surrounded them on all sides, not pressing in on them, but staying uncomfortably close nevertheless. The odd creatures did not speak, but merely gestured to one another, their eyes shifting from Carisman to the travelers, inquisitive and cautious. Morgan returned the gaze of those closest and tried a smile. They did not smile back.

The gathering went down off the Spikes into the forested valley below, west of the ridgeline where the shadows were deepest. There was a narrow trail that wound through the trees, and the procession followed it dutifully, Carisman in the lead, singing as he went. Morgan had encountered some odd characters in his time, but Carisman struck him as odder than most. He could not help wondering why anyone, even the Urdas, would make this fellow their king.

Dees had dropped back a pace to walk with him, and he asked the old Tracker. "As I said, a tribal folk. Superstitious, like most Gnomes. Believe in spirits and wraiths and other nonsense."

"But Carisman?" Morgan questioned.

Dees shook his head. "I admit I can't figure it. Urdas usually don't want anything to do with outlanders. This one seems goofy as a week-old loon, but he's obviously found some way of gaining their respect. I never heard of him before this. Don't think anyone has."

Morgan peered over the heads of the Urdas at the prancing Carisman. "He seems harmless enough."

Dees snorted. "He probably is. Anyway, it isn't him you have to worry about."

They worked their way west toward the wall of the mountains, daylight fading rapidly now, dusk spreading until the whole of the forestland was enveloped. Morgan and Dees continued to exchange comments, but the other three kept their thoughts to themselves. Walker and Pe Ell were gaunt shadows, Quickening a burst of sunlight. The Urdas filtered out about them, appearing and disappearing in the heavy brush, strung out ahead, behind, and to either side. Carisman's words had suggested that they were guests, but Morgan couldn't shake the feeling that they were really prisoners.

After a little more than a mile, the trail ended at a clearing in which the village of the Urdas was settled. A stockade had been built to protect the village from raiders, and its gates opened now to let the hunters and those they shepherded pass through. A sea of women, children, and old people waited within, bony-faced and staring, their voices a low, inaudible buzz. The village consisted of a cluster of small huts and open-sided shelters surrounding a lodge constructed of notched logs and a shingled roof. Trees grew inside the stockade, shading the village and providing supports for treeways and lifts. There were wells scattered about and smokehouses for curing meat. The Urdas, it appeared, had at least rudimentary skills.

The five from Rampling Steep were taken to the main lodge and led to a platform on which a rough-hewn chair draped with a garland of fresh flowers was situated. Carisman seated himself ceremoniously and beckoned his guests to take their places next to him on mats. Morgan and the others did as they were asked, keeping a wary eye on the Urdas, a large number of whom entered as well and took seats on the floor below the platform. When everyone was settled, Carisman came to his feet and sang some more, this time in a tongue that Morgan found impossible to identify. When he was finished, a handful of Urda women began to bring out platters of food.

Carisman sat down. "I have to sing to get them to do anything," he confided. "It is so tedious sometimes."

"What are you doing here anyway?" Horner Dees asked bluntly. "Where did you come from?"

"Ah," Carisman said with a sigh.

He sang:

> *"There was a young tunesmith from Rampling,*
> *Who felt it was time to take wing.*
> *He decided to hike,*
> *North into the Spikes,*
> *To the Urdas, who made him their king!"*

He grimaced. "Not very original, I'm afraid. Let me try again."

He sang:

> *"Come hither, my fellows, and lady, come nigh,*
> *There are worlds to discover more'n what meets the eye.*
> *Far reaches to travel and people to see,*
> *Wonders to gaze on and lives for to lead,*
> *A million adventures to try.*

Come hither, my fellows, and lady, come nigh,
A tunesmith's a man who must sing for to fly.
He searches the byways for songs telling truth,
Seeks out hidden meanings and offers of proof,
Of the reasons for being alive.

Come hither, my fellows, and lady, come nigh,
For life's to be found in the rivers and skies.
In the forests and mountains that lie far away,
In the creatures that frolic and gambol and play,
And beg me my songs to apply."

"Considerably better, don't you think?" he asked them, blue eyes darting from one face to the next, anxiously seeking their approval.

"A tunesmith, are you?" Dees grunted. "From Rampling Steep?"

"Well, by way of Rampling Steep. I was there a day or so once several years back." Carisman looked sheepish. "The rhyme works, so I use it." He brightened. "But a tunesmith, yes. All my life. I have the gift of song and the wit to make use of it. I have talent."

"But why are you here, Carisman?" Quickening pressed.

Carisman seemed to melt. "Lady, chance has brought me to this place and time and even to you. I have traveled the better part of the Four Lands, searching out the songs that would give wings to my music. There is a restlessness in me that will not let me stay in any one place for very long. I have had my chances to do so, and even ladies who wished to keep me—though none was as beautiful as you. But I keep moving. I wandered first west, then east, and finally north. I passed through Rampling Steep and found myself wondering what lay beyond. Finally I set out across the mountains to see."

"And survived?" Horner Dees asked incredulously.

"Just barely. I have a sense of things; it comes from my music, I think. I was well provisioned, for I had traveled in rough country before. I found my way by listening to my heart. I had the good fortune of encountering favorable weather. When I was finally across—exhausted and close to starving, I admit—I was found by the Urdas. Not knowing what else to do, I sang for them. They were enchanted by my music and they made me their king."

"Enchanted by limericks and snippets of rhyme?" Dees refused to let go of his skepticism. "A bold claim, Carisman."

Carisman grinned boyishly. "Oh, I don't claim to be a better man than any other."

He sang:

> *"No matter how high or lofty the throne,*
> *What sits on it is the same as your own."*

He brushed the matter aside. "Eat now, you must be very hungry after your journey. There is as much food and drink as you want. And tell me what brings you here. No one from the Southland ever comes this far north—not even the trappers. I never see anyone except Trolls and Gnomes. What brings you?"

Quickening told him that they were on a quest, that they had come in search of a talisman. It was more than Morgan would have revealed, but it seemed to matter little to Carisman, who did not even bother asking what the talisman was or why they needed it but only wanted to know if Quickening could teach him any new songs. Carisman was quick and bright, yet his focus was quixotic and narrow. He was like a child, inquisitive and distracted and full of the wonder of things. He seemed to genuinely need approval. Quickening was the most responsive, so he concentrated his attention on her and included the others in his conversation mostly by implication. Morgan listened disinterestedly as he ate, then noticed that Walker wasn't listening at all, that he was studying the Urdas below the platform. Morgan began studying them as well. After a time he saw that they were seated in carefully defined groups, and that the foremost group consisted of a mixed gathering of old and young men to whom all the others deferred. Chiefs, thought Morgan at once. They were talking intently among themselves, glancing now and then at the six seated on the platform, but otherwise ignoring them. Something was being decided, without Carisman.

Morgan grew nervous.

The meal ended and the empty plates were carried away. There was a sustained clapping from the Urdas, and Carisman rose to his feet with a sigh. He sang once more, but this time the song was different. This time it was studied and intricate, a finely wrought piece of music filled with nuances and subtleties that transcended the tune. Carisman's voice filled the lodge, it soared and swept aside everything that separated it from the senses, reaching down through the body to embrace and cradle the heart. Morgan was astounded. He had never been so affected—not even by the music of the wishsong. Par Ohmsford could capture your feeling for and sense of history in his song, but Carisman could capture your soul.

When the tunesmith was finished, there was utter silence. Slowly he sat down again, momentarily lost in himself, still caught up in what he had sung. Then the Urdas began thumping their hands on their knees approvingly.

Quickening said, "That was beautiful, Carisman."

"Thank you, Lady," he replied, sheepish again. "I have a talent for more than limericks, you see."

The silver-haired girl looked suddenly at Walker. "Did you find it beautiful, Walker Boh?"

The pale face inclined in thought. "It makes me wonder why someone who possesses such abilities chooses to share them with so few." The dark eyes fixed Carisman.

The tunesmith squirmed uncomfortably. "Well." The words suddenly would not seem to come.

"Especially since you said yourself that there is a restlessness in you that will not allow you to stay in one place. Yet you stay here among the Urdas."

Carisman looked down at his hands.

"They will not let you leave, will they?" Walker said quietly.

Carisman looked as if he would sink into the earth. "No," he admitted reluctantly. "For all that I am, a king notwithstanding, I remain a captive. I am allowed to be king only so long as I sing my songs. The Urdas keep me because they believe my song is magic."

"And so it is," Quickening murmured so softly that only Morgan, seated next to her, heard.

"What about us?" Dees demanded sharply. He shifted his bulk menacingly. "Are we captives as well? Have you brought us here as guests or prisoners, King Carisman? Or do you even have a say in the matter?"

"Oh, no!" the tunesmith exclaimed, clearly distraught. "I mean, yes, I have a say in the matter. And, no, you are not prisoners. I need only speak with the council, those men gathered there below us." He pointed to the group that Walker and Morgan had been observing earlier. Then he hesitated as he caught the black look on Pe Ell's face and came hurriedly to his feet. "I shall speak to them at once. If need be, I shall sing. A special song. You shall not remain here any longer than you wish, I promise. Lady, believe me, please. Friends."

He rushed from the platform and knelt next to the members of the Urda council, addressing them earnestly. The five who waited to discover whether they were guests or prisoners looked at one another.

"I don't think he can do anything to help us," Horner Dees muttered.

Pe Ell edged forward. "If I put a knife to his throat they will release us quick enough."

"Or kill us on the spot," Dees replied with a hiss. The two glared at each other.

"Let him have his chance," Walker Boh said, looking calmly at the assemblage. His face was unreadable.

"Yes," Quickening agreed softly. "Patience."

They sat silently after that until Carisman returned, detaching himself from the council, stepping back onto the platform to face them. His face told them everything. "I . . . I have to ask you to stay the night," he said, struggling to get the words out, discomforted beyond measure. "The council wishes to . . . debate the matter a bit. Just a formality, you understand. I simply require a little time . . ."

He trailed off uncertainly. He had positioned himself as far as possible from Pe Ell. Morgan held his breath. He didn't think the distance separating the two offered the tunesmith much protection. He found himself wondering, almost in fascination, what Pe Ell would do, what he *could* in fact do against so many.

He would not find out on this occasion. Quickening smiled reassuringly at Carisman and said, "We will wait."

They were taken to one of the larger huts and given mats and blankets for sleeping. The door was closed behind them, but not locked. Morgan didn't think it mattered either way. The hut sat in the center of the village, and the village was enclosed by the stockade and filled with Urdas. He had taken the trouble of asking Dees about the strange creatures during dinner. Dees had told him that they were a tribe of hunters. The weapons they carried were designed to bring down even the swiftest game. Two-legged intruders, he said, would not prove much of a challenge.

Pe Ell stood looking out through chinks in the hut's mud walls. "They are not going to let us leave," he said. No one spoke. "It doesn't matter what that play-king says, they'll try to keep us. We had better get away tonight."

Dees sat back heavily against one wall. "You make it sound as if leaving were an option."

Pe Ell turned. "I can leave whenever I choose. No prison can hold me."

He said it so matter-of-factly that the others, save Quickening, just stared at him. Quickening was looking off into space. "There is magic in his song," she said.

Morgan remembered her saying something like that before. "Real magic?" he asked.

"Close enough to be called so. I do not understand its source; I am not even certain what it can do. But a form of magic nevertheless. He is more than an ordinary tunesmith."

"Yes," Pe Ell agreed. "He is a fool."

"We might think you one as well if you persist in suggesting we can get out of here without him," Horner Dees snapped.

Pe Ell wheeled on him. There was such rage in his face that Dees came to his feet much more quickly than Morgan would have thought possible. Walker Boh, a dark figure at the hut's far end, turned slowly. Pe Ell seemed to consider his options, then stalked to where Quickening stood looking at him from beside Morgan. It was all the Highlander could do to stand his ground. Pe Ell's black look dismissed him with barely a flicker of a glance and fell instead on the girl.

"What do we need any of them for?" he whispered, his voice a hiss of fury. "I came because you asked me to; I could easily have chosen otherwise."

"I know that," she said.

"You know what I am." He bent close, his gaunt face hawk-like above her, his lean body taut. "You know I have the magic you need. I have all the magic you need. Be done with them. Let us go on alone."

Around him, the room seemed to have turned to stone, the others frozen into statues that could only observe and never act. Morgan Leah's hand moved a fraction of an inch toward his sword, then stopped. He would never be quick enough, he knew. Pe Ell would kill him before he could pull the blade clear.

Quickening seemed completely unafraid. "It is not yet time for you and I, Pe Ell," she whispered back, her voice soothing, cool. Her eyes searched his. "You must wait until it is."

Morgan did not understand what she was saying and he was reasonably certain that Pe Ell didn't either. The narrow face pinched and the hard eyes flickered. He seemed to be deciding something.

"My father alone has the gift of foresight," Quickening said softly. "He has foreseen that I shall have need of all of you when we find Uhl Belk. So it shall be—even though you might wish it otherwise, Pe Ell. Even though.''

Pe Ell shook his head slowly. "No, girl. You are wrong. It shall be as I choose. Just as it always is.'' He studied her momentarily, then shrugged. "Nevertheless, what difference does it make? Another day, another week, it shall all come out the same in the end. Keep these others with you if you wish. At least for now.''

He turned and moved away by himself, settling into a darkened corner.

The others stared after him in silence.

Night descended and the village of the Urdas grew quiet as its inhabitants drifted off to sleep. The five from Rampling Steep huddled within the darkened confines of their shelter, separated from each other by the privacy of their thoughts. Horner Dees slept. Walker Boh was a shapeless bundle in the shadows, unmoving. Morgan Leah sat next to Quickening, neither speaking, eyes closed against the faint light of moon and stars that penetrated from without.

Pe Ell watched them all and raged silently against circumstance and his own stupidity.

What was *wrong* with him? he wondered bleakly. Losing his temper like that, exposing himself, nearly ruining his chance of accomplishing what he had set out to do. He was always in control. *Always!* But not this time, not when he was giving way to frustration and impatience, threatening the girl and all of her precious charges as if he were some schoolboy bully.

He was calm now, able to analyze what he had done, to sift through his emotions and sort out his mistakes. There were many of both. And it was the girl who was responsible, who undid him each time, he knew. She was the bane of his existence, an irritation and an attraction pulling him in opposite directions, a creature of beauty and life and magic that he would never understand until the moment he killed her. His yearning to do so grew stronger all the time, and it was becoming increasingly difficult to restrain. Yet he knew he must if he expected to gain possession of the Black Elfstone. The difficulty was in knowing how to withstand his obsession for her in the meantime. She incensed him, enflamed him, and left him twisted inside like fine wire. Everything that seemed obvious and uncomplicated to him appeared to be just the opposite to her. She insisted on having these fools accompany them—the one-armed man, the Highlander, and the old Tracker. *Shades! Useless foils!* How much longer would he have to tolerate them?

He felt the anger begin again and moved quickly to quell it. *Patience.* Her word, not his—but he had better try it on for size.

He listened to the sounds of the Urdas without, the guards, more than a dozen of them, crouched down in the darkness about the hut. He couldn't see them, but he could feel their presence. His instincts told him they were there. There was no sign of the tunesmith yet—not that it made any difference. The Urdas weren't about to set them free.

So many intrusions on what really matters!

His sharp eyes fixed momentarily on Dees. That old man. He was the worst of the lot, the hardest to figure out. There was something about him . . .

He caught himself again. Be patient. Wait. Events would undoubtedly continue to conspire to force him to do otherwise, but he must overcome them. He must remain in control.

Except that it was so difficult here. This was not his country, these were not his people, and the familiarity of surroundings and behavior, of people and customs that he had always been able to rely upon before was missing here. He was scaling a cliff he had never seen before and the footing was treacherous.

Perhaps staying in control this time would prove impossible.

He shook his head uneasily. The thought stayed with him and would not be dispelled.

It was after midnight when Carisman reappeared. Quickening brought Morgan awake with a touch of her hand to his cheek. He came to his feet and found the others already standing. The door unlatched and opened, and the tunesmith slipped inside.

"Ah, you are awake. Good." He moved at once to stand next to Quickening, hesitant to speak, uncertain in their presence, like a boy forced to confess something he would prefer to keep secret.

"What has the council decided, Carisman?" Quickening prodded him gently, taking his arm and bringing him about to face her.

The tunesmith shook his head. "Lady, the best and the worst, I am afraid." He glanced at the others. "All of you are free to go when you choose." He turned back to Quickening. "Except you."

Morgan remembered at once the way the Urdas had looked

at Quickening, recalling their fascination with her. "Why?" he demanded heatedly. "Why isn't she released as well?"

Carisman swallowed. "My subjects find her beautiful. They think she may be magic, like myself. They . . . wish her to marry me."

"Well now, this is an inventive tale!" Horner Dees snapped, his bristled face screwing up in disbelief.

Morgan seized Carisman by the tunic front. "I have seen the way you look at her, tunesmith! This is your idea!"

"No, no, I swear it is not!" the other cried in dismay, his handsome face contorted in horror. "I would never do such a thing! The Urdas . . ."

"The Urdas couldn't care less about . . ."

"Let him go, Morgan," Quickening said, interrupting, her voice low and steady. Morgan released his grip and stepped back instantly. "He speaks the truth," she said. "This is not his doing."

Pe Ell had shoved forward like a knife blade. "It doesn't matter whose doing it is." His eyes fixed Carisman. "She goes with us."

Carisman's face went pale, and his eyes shifted anxiously from one determined face to the next. "They won't let her," he whispered, his gaze dropping. "And if they don't, she will end up like me."

He sang:

"Long ago, in times gone by, there was a fair, fair maiden.
She wandered fields and forest glens,
With all the world her haven.
A mighty Lord a fancy took, demanded that she wed him.
When she refused, he took her home,
And locked her in his dungeon.
She pined away for what she'd lost, a life beyond her prison.
She promised everything she owned,
If she could have her freedom.
A fairy imp her plea did hear and quickly broke the door in.
Yet freed her not as she had asked,
But claimed her his possession.

The moral is: If you offer to give up everything,
Be prepared to keep nothing."

Horner Dees threw up his hands in exasperation. "What is it you are trying to say, Carisman?" he snapped.

"That your choices often undo you. That seeking everything sometimes costs you everything." It was Walker Boh who answered. "Carisman thought that in becoming a king he would find freedom and has instead found only shackles."

"Yes," the tunesmith breathed, sadness flooding his finely chiseled features. "I don't belong here any more than Quickening. If you would take her when you go, then you must take me as well!"

"No!" Pe Ell cried instantly.

"Lady," the tunesmith begged. "Please. I have been here for almost five years now—not just several as I claimed. I am caged as surely as that maiden in my song. If you do not take me with you, I shall be kept captive until I die!"

Quickening shook her head. "It is dangerous where we go, Carisman. Far more dangerous than it is here. You would not be safe."

Carisman's voice shook. "It doesn't matter! I want to be free!"

"No!" Pe Ell repeated, circling away like a cat. "Think, girl! Yet another fool to burden us? Why not an army of them, then? Shades!"

Morgan Leah was tired of being called a fool and was about to say so when Walker Boh caught him firmly by the arm and shook his head. Morgan frowned angrily, but gave way.

"What do you know of the country north, Carisman?" Horner Dees asked suddenly, his bulk backing the tunesmith away. "Ever been there?"

Carisman shook his head. "No. It doesn't matter what's there. It is away from here." His eyes darted furtively. "Besides, you have to take me. You can't get away if I don't show you how."

That stopped them. Everyone turned. "What do you mean?" Dees asked cautiously.

"I mean that you will be dead a dozen times over without my help," the tunesmith said.

He sang:

> "Sticks and stones will break your bones,
> But only if the spears don't.
> There's traps and snares placed everywhere,
> And none to warn if I don't.
> Fiddle-de-diddle-de-de."

Pe Ell had him by the throat so quickly that no one else had time to intervene. "You'll tell everything you know before I'm done with you or wish you had!" he threatened furiously.

But Carisman held steady, even forced back as he was, the hard eyes inches from his own. "Never," he gasped. "Unless . . . you agree . . . to take me with you."

His face lost all its color as Pe Ell's hand tightened. Morgan and Horner Dees glanced uncertainly at each other and then at Quickening, hesitating in spite of themselves. It was Walker Boh who stepped in. He moved behind Pe Ell and touched him in a manner they could not see. The gaunt man jerked back, his face rigid with surprise. Walker was quickly by him, his arm coming about Carisman and lifting him away.

Pe Ell whirled, cold rage in his eyes. Morgan was certain he was going to attack Walker, and nothing good could come of that. But Pe Ell surprised him. Instead of striking out, he simply stared at Walker a moment and then turned away, his face suddenly an expressionless mask.

Quickening spoke, diverting them. "Carisman," she said. "Do you know a way out of here?"

Carisman nodded, swallowing to speak. "Yes, Lady."

"Will you show it to us?"

"If you agree to take me with you, yes." He was bargaining now, but he seemed confident.

"Perhaps it would be enough if we helped you escape the village?"

"No, Lady. I would lose my way and they would bring me back again. I must go to wherever it is that you are going—far away from here. Perhaps," he said brightly, "I may turn out to be of some use to you."

When pigs fly, Morgan thought uncharitably.

Quickening seemed undecided, strange for her. She looked questioningly at Horner Dees.

"He's right about the Urdas bringing him back," the old Tracker agreed. "Us, too, if we aren't quick enough. Or smart enough."

Morgan saw Pe Ell and Walker Boh glaring at each other from opposite corners of the hut—harsh, dark wraiths come from exacting worlds, their silent looks full of warning. Who would survive a confrontation between those two? And how could the company survive while they were at such odds?

Then suddenly an idea occurred to him. "Your magic, Quickening!" he burst out impulsively. "We can use your magic to escape! You can control all that grows within the earth. That is enough to make the Urdas give way. With or without Carisman, we have your magic!''

But Quickening shook her head and for an instant she seemed almost to dissolve. ''No, Morgan. We have crossed the Charnals into the country of Uhl Belk, and I cannot use my magic again until after we find the talisman. The Stone King must not discover who I am. If I use the magic, he will know.''

The hut went silent again. ''Who is the Stone King?'' Carisman asked, and they all looked at him.

''I say we take him,'' Horner Dees said finally, bluff and to the point as always. His bulky figure shifted. ''If he really can get us out of here, that is.''

''Take him,'' Morgan agreed. He grinned. ''I like the idea of having a king on our side as well—even if all he can do is make up songs.''

Quickening glanced at the silent antagonists behind her. Pe Ell shrugged his indifference. Walker Boh said nothing.

''We will take you, Carisman,'' Quickening said, ''though I am afraid to guess what this choice might cost you.''

Carisman shook his head emphatically. ''No price is too great, Lady, I promise you.'' The tunesmith was elated.

Quickening moved toward the door. ''The night flies. Let us hurry.''

Carisman held up his hand. ''Not that way, Lady.''

She turned. ''There is another?''

''Indeed.'' He was beaming mischievously. ''As it happens, I am standing on it.''

XV

The Spikes and the lands surrounding were filled with tribes of Urdas and other species of Gnomes and Trolls. Since they were all constantly at war with one another, they kept their villages fortified. A lot of hard lessons had been learned over the years, and one of them was that a stockade needed more than one way out. Carisman's bunch had dug tunnels beneath the village that opened through hidden trap-doors into the forests beyond. If the village were threatened by a prolonged siege or by an army of overwhelming numbers, the inhabitants still had a means of escape.

One of the entrances to the tunnels that lay inside the village was under the floor of the hut in which the five from Rampling Steep had been placed. Carisman showed them where it lay, buried a good foot beneath the earthen floor, sealed so tightly by weather and time that it took Horner Dees and Morgan working together to pull it free. It had clearly never seen use and perhaps been all but forgotten. In any case, it was a way out and the company was quick to seize upon it.

"I would feel better about this if we had a light," Dees muttered as he stood looking down into the blackness.

"Here," Walker Boh whispered impatiently, moving forward to take his place. He slipped down into the blackness where the walls of the tunnel shielded his actions and made a snapping motion with his fingers. Light blazed up about his hand, an aura of brightness that had no visible source. The Dark Uncle has at least a little of his magic left, Morgan thought.

"Carisman, is there more than one passage down here?" Walker's voice sounded hollow. The tunesmith nodded. "Then stay close to me and tell me how we are to go."

They dropped into the hole one by one, Carisman following

Walker, Quickening and Morgan after them, Dees and Pe Ell
last. It was black in the tunnel, even with Walker's light, and
the air was close and full of earth smells. The tunnel ran in a
straight line, then branched in three directions. Carisman took
them right. It branched again, and this time he took them left.
They had gone far enough, Morgan thought, that they must be
beyond the stockade walls. Still the tunnel continued. Tree roots
penetrated its walls, tangling their arms and feet, slowing their
progress. At times the roots grew so thick that they had to be
severed to permit passage. Even when the passageway was completely clear, it was hard for Horner Dees to fit through. He
grunted and huffed and pushed ahead determinedly. Other tunnels intersected and passed on. Dirt and silt from their movements began to choke the air, and it grew hard to breathe.
Morgan buried his face in his tunic sleeve and would not allow
himself to think about what would happen if the tunnel walls
collapsed.

After what seemed an impossibly long time they slowed and
then stopped altogether. "Yes, this is it," Morgan heard Carisman say to Walker. He listened as the two struggled to free
the trapdoor that sealed them in. They labored in wordless silence, grunting, digging, and shifting about in the cramped
space. Morgan and the others crouched down in the blackness
and waited.

It took them almost as long to loosen the trapdoor as it had
to navigate the tunnel. When it finally fell back, fresh air rushed
in and the six scrambled up into the night. They found themselves in a heavily wooded glen, the limbs of the trees grown so
thick overhead that the sky was masked almost completely.

They stood wordlessly for a moment, breathing in the clean
air, and then Dees pushed forward. "Which way to the Spikes?"
he whispered anxiously to Carisman.

Carisman pointed and Dees started away, but Pe Ell reached
out hurriedly and yanked him back. "Wait!" he warned. "There
will be a watch!"

He gave the old Tracker a withering look, motioned them all
down and melted into the trees. Morgan sank back against the
trunk of a massive fir, and the others became vague shadows
through the screen of its shaggy limbs. He closed his eyes wearily. It seemed days since he had rested properly. He thought
about how good it would feel to sleep.

But a touch on his shoulder brought him awake again almost
immediately. "Easy, Highlander," Walker Boh whispered. The

tall man slid down next to Morgan, dark eyes searching his own. "You tread on dangerous ground these days, Morgan Leah. You had better watch where you step."

Morgan blinked. "What do you mean?"

Walker's face inclined slightly, and Morgan could see the lines of tension and strain that creased it. "Pe Ell. Stay away from him. Don't taunt him, don't challenge him. Have as little to do with him as you can. If he chooses, he can strike you down faster than a snake in hiding."

The words were spoken in a whisper that was harsh and chilling in its certainty, a brittle promise of death. Morgan swallowed what he was feeling and nodded. "Who is he, Walker? Do you know?"

The Dark Uncle glanced away and back again. "Sometimes I am able to sense things by touching. Sometimes I can learn another's secrets by doing nothing more than brushing up against him. It happened that way when I took Carisman away from Pe Ell. He has killed. Many times. He has done so intentionally rather than in self-defense. He enjoys it. I expect he is an assassin."

A pale hand reached up to hold a startled Morgan in place. "Listen, now. He conceals a weapon of immense power beneath his clothing. The weapon he carries is magic. It is what he uses to kill."

"Magic?" Morgan's voice quivered in surprise despite his effort to keep it steady. His mind raced. "Does Quickening know?"

"She chose him, Highlander. She chose us all. She told us we possessed magic. She told us our magic was needed. Of course, she knows."

Morgan was aghast. "She deliberately brought an assassin? Is this how she plans to regain the Black Elfstone?"

Walker stared fixedly at him. "I think not," he said finally. "But I can't be sure."

Morgan slumped back in disbelief. "Walker, what are we doing here? Why has she brought us?" Walker did not respond. "I don't know for the life of me why I agreed to come. Or maybe I do. I am drawn to her, I admit; I am enchanted by her. But what sort of reason is that? I shouldn't be here. I should be back in Tyrsis searching for Par and Coll."

"We have had this discussion," Walker reminded him gently.

"I know. But I keep questioning myself. Especially now. Pe Ell is an assassin; what do we have to do with such a man? Does

Quickening think us all the same? Does she think we are all killers of other men? Is that the use to which we are to be put? I cannot believe it!''

"Morgan." Walker spoke his name to calm him, then eased back against the tree until their heads were almost touching. Something in the way the Dark Uncle's body was bent reminded Morgan for a moment of how broken he had been when they had found him amid the ruins of his cottage at Hearthstone. "There is more to this than what you know," Walker whispered. "Or I, for that matter. I can sense things but not see them clearly. Quickening has a purpose beyond what she reveals. She is the daughter of the King of the Silver River—do not forget that. She has forbidden insight. She has magic that transcends any that we have ever seen. But she is vulnerable as well. She must walk a careful path in her quest. I think that we are here in part, at least, to see that she is able to keep to that path."

Morgan thought it over a moment and nodded, listening to the stillness of the night about them, staring out through the boughs of the old fir at the shadowy figures beyond, picking out Quickening's slim, ethereal form, a slender bit of movement that the night might swallow with no more than a slight shifting of the light.

Walker's voice tightened. "I have been shown a vision of her—a vision as frightening as any I have ever experienced. The vision told me that she will die. I warned her of this before we left Hearthstone; I told her that perhaps I should not come. But she insisted. So I came." He glanced over. "It is the same with all of us. We came because we knew we must. Don't try to understand why that is, Morgan. Just accept it."

Morgan sighed, lost in the tangle of his feelings and his needs, wishing for things that could never be, for a past that was lost and a future he could not determine. He thought of how far things had gone since the Ohmsfords had come to him in Leah, of how different they all now were.

Walker Boh rose, a rustle of movement in the silence. "Remember what I said, Highlander. Stay away from Pe Ell."

He pushed through the curtain of branches without looking back. Morgan Leah stared after him.

Pe Ell was gone a long time. When he returned, he spoke only to Horner Dees. "It is safe now, old man," he advised softly. "Lead on."

They departed the glen wordlessly, following Carisman as he

led them back toward the ridgeline, a silent procession of wraiths in the forest night. No one challenged them, and Morgan was certain that no one would. Pe Ell had seen to that.

It was still dark when they again caught sight of the Spikes. They climbed to the crest of the ridgeline and turned north. Dees moved them forward at a rapid pace, the pathway clear, the spine of the land bare and open to the light of moon and stars, empty save where the skeletal trees threw the spindly shadow of their trunks and branches crosswise against the earth like spiders' webs. They followed the Spikes through the narrow end of the valley's funnel and turned upward into the hills beyond. Daybreak was beginning to approach, a faint lightening of the skies east. Dees moved them faster still. No one had to bother asking why.

By the time the sun crested the mountains they were far enough into the hills that they could no longer see the valley at all. They found a stream of clear water and stopped to drink. Sweat ran down their faces and their breathing was labored.

"Look ahead," Horner Dees said, pointing. A line of peaks jutted into the sky. "That's the north edge of the Charnals, the last we have to cross. There's a dozen passes that lead over and the Urdas can't know which one we will take. It's all rock up there, hard to track anything."

"Hard for you, you mean," Pe Ell suggested unkindly. "Not necessarily hard for them."

"They won't go out of their mountains." Dees ignored him. "Once we're across, we'll be safe."

They hauled themselves back to their feet and went on. The sun climbed into the cloudless sky, a brilliant ball of white fire that turned the earth beneath into a furnace. It was the hottest Morgan could remember it being since he had left Culhaven. The hills rose toward the mountains, and the trees began to give way to scrub and brush. Once Dees thought he saw something moving in the forestlands far behind them, and once they heard a wailing sound that Carisman claimed was Urda horns. But midday came and went, and there was no sign of pursuit.

Then clouds began to move in from the west, a large threatening bank of black thunderheads. Morgan slapped at the gnats that flew against his sweat-streaked face. There would be a storm soon.

They stopped again as midafternoon approached, exhausted from their flight and hungry now as well. There was little to eat, just some roots and wild vegetables and fresh water. Horner

Dees went off to scout ahead, and Pe Ell decided to backtrack to a bluff that would let him study the land behind. Walker sat by himself. Carisman began speaking with Quickening again about his music, insistent upon her undivided attention. Morgan studied the tunesmith's handsome features, his shock of blond hair, and his uninhibited gestures and was annoyed. Rather than show what he was feeling, the Highlander moved into the shade of a spindly pine and faced away.

Thunder rumbled in the distance, and the clouds pushed up against the mountains. The sky was a peculiar mix of sunshine and darkness. The heat was still oppressive, a suffocating blanket as it pressed down against the earth. Morgan buried his face in his hands and closed his eyes.

Both Horner Dees and Pe Ell were back quickly. The former advised that the passage that would take them across the last of the Charnals lay less than an hour ahead. The latter reported that the Urdas were after them in force.

"More than a hundred," he announced, fixing them with those hard, unreadable eyes. "Right on our heels."

They resumed their march at once, pressing ahead more quickly, a sense of urgency driving them now that had not been present before. No one had expected the Urdas to catch up with them this fast, certainly not before they were across the mountains. If they were forced to stand and fight here, they knew, they were finished.

They worked their way upward into the rocks, scrambling through huge fields of boulders and down narrow defiles, struggling to keep their footing on slides that threatened to send them careening away into jagged, bottomless fissures. The clouds scraped over the mountain peaks and filled the skies from horizon to horizon. Heavy drops of rain began to fall, spattering against the earth and their heated skin. Darkness settled over everything, an ominous black that echoed with the sound of thunder as it rolled across the empty, barren rock. Dusk was approaching, and Morgan was certain they would be caught in the mountains at nightfall, a decidedly unpleasant prospect. His entire body ached, but he forced himself to keep going. He glanced ahead to Carisman and saw that the tunesmith was in worse shape, stumbling and falling regularly, gasping for breath. Fighting back against his own exhaustion, he caught up with the other man, put an arm about him, and helped him to go on.

They had just gained the head of the pass that Dees had been shepherding them toward when they caught sight of the Urdas.

The rugged, shaggy creatures appeared out of the rocks behind them, still more than a mile off, but charging ahead as if maddened, screaming and crying out, shaking their weapons with an unmistakable promise of what they would do with those they were pursuing when they finally caught up with them. The company, after no more than a moment's hesitation, fled into the pass.

The pass was a knife cut that sliced upward through the cliffs, a narrow passageway filled with twists and turns. The company spread out, snaking its way forward. The rain began to fall in earnest now, turning from a slow spattering into a heavy downpour. The footing became slippery, and tiny streams began to flow down out of the rocks, cutting away at the earth beneath their feet. They passed from the shadow of the cliffs and found themselves on a barren slope that angled left into a high-walled defile that was as black as night. Wind blew across the slope in frenzied gusts that sent silt flying into their faces. Morgan let go of Carisman and brought his cloak across his head to protect himself.

It required a tremendous effort to gain the defile, the wind beating against them so hard that they could progress only a little at a time. As they reached the darkened opening, the Urdas reappeared, very close now, come that last mile all too quickly. Darts, lances, and the razor-sharp throwing implements whizzed through the air, falling uncomfortably close. Hurriedly the company charged into the passageway and the protection of its walls.

Here, the rain descended in torrents and the light was almost extinguished. Jagged rock edges jutted out from the floor and walls of the narrow corridor and cut and scraped them as they passed. Time slowed to a standstill in the howl of wind and the roll of the thunder, and it seemed as if they would never get free. Morgan moved ahead to be with Quickening, determined to see that she was protected.

When they finally worked their way clear of the defile, they found themselves standing on a ledge that ran along a seam midway down a towering cliff face that dropped away into a gorge through which the waters of the Rabb raged in a churning, white-foamed maelstrom. Dees took them onto the ledge without hesitation, shouting something back that was meant to be encouraging but was lost in the sound of the storm. The line spread out along the broken seam, Dees in the lead, Carisman, Quickening, Morgan, and Walker Boh following, and Pe Ell last. The rain fell in sheets, the wind tore at them, and the sound of the river's rush was an impenetrable wall of sound.

When the foremost of the Urdas appeared at the mouth of the defile, no one saw. It wasn't until their weapons began to shatter against the rocks about the fleeing company that anyone realized they were there. A dart nicked Pe Ell's shoulder and spun him about, but he kept his footing and struggled on. The others began to advance more quickly, trying desperately to distance themselves from their pursuers, hastening along the ledge, booted feet slipping and sliding dangerously. Morgan glanced back and saw Walker Boh turn and throw something into the storm. Instantly the air flared with silver light. Darts and lances that were hurled into the brightness fell harmlessly away. The Urdas, frightened by the Dark Uncle's magic, fell back into the defile.

Ahead, the ledge broadened slightly and sloped downward. The far side of the mountains came into view, a sweeping stretch of forested hills that ran into the distance until it disappeared into a wall of clouds and rain. The Rabb churned below, cutting back on itself, rushing eastward through the rocks. The trail followed its bend, some fifty feet above its banks, the barren rock giving way to the beginnings of earth and scrub.

Morgan looked around one final time and saw that the Urdas were not following. Either Walker had frightened them off, or Horner Dees had been right about them not leaving their mountains.

He turned back.

In the next instant the entire cliff face was rocked with tremors as parts of it gave way under the relentless pounding of the wind and rain. The trail in front of him, an entire section of earth and rock, disappeared completely and took Quickening with it. She fell back against the slope, grasping. But there was nothing to hold on to, and she began to slide in a cloud of silt and gravel toward the river. Carisman, directly in front of her, almost went, too, but managed to throw himself forward far enough to clutch a tangle of roots from some mountain scrub and was saved.

Morgan was directly behind. He saw that Quickening could not save herself and that there was no one who could reach her. He didn't hesitate. He jumped from the crumbling trail into the gap, hurtling down the mountainside after her, the trailing shouts of his companions disappearing almost instantly. He struck the waters of the Rabb with jarring force, went under, and came up again gasping in shock at the cold. He caught a flash of Quick-

ening's silver hair bobbing in a shower of white foam a few feet
away, swam to her, seized her clothing, and drew her to him.

Then the current had them both, and they were swept away.

XVI

It was all that Morgan Leah could do to keep himself and
Quickening afloat in the churning river, and while he might
have considered trying to swim for shore if he had been
unencumbered he gave no thought of doing so here. Quickening
was awake and able to lend some assistance to his effort, but it
was mostly Morgan's strength that kept them away from the
rocks and out of the deep eddies that might have pulled them
down. As it was, the river took them pretty much where it chose.
It was swollen by the rains and overflowing its banks, and its
surface waters were white with foam and spray against the darkness of the skies and land. The storm continued to rage, thunder
rumbling down the canyon depths, lightning flashing against the
distant peaks, and the rains falling in heavy sheets. The cliff
face they had tumbled down disappeared from view almost immediately and with it their companions. The Rabb twisted and
turned through the mountain rocks, and soon they lost any sense
of where they were.

After a time a tree that had been knocked into the river washed
by and they caught hold of it and let it carry them along. They
were able to rest a bit then, clutching the slippery trunk side by
side, doing what they could to protect their bodies from the
rocks and debris, searching the river and the shoreline for a
means to extract themselves. They did not bother trying to speak;
they were too exhausted to expend the effort and the river would
likely have drowned out their words in any case. They simply
exchanged glances and concentrated on staying together.

Eventually the river broadened, tumbling down out of the

peaks into the hill country north, emptying into a forested basin where it pooled before being swept into a second channel that carried it south again. There was an island in the center of the basin, and the tree they were riding ran aground against it, spinning and bumping along its banks. Morgan and Quickening shoved away from their make-do raft and stumbled wearily ashore. Exhausted, their clothing hanging in tatters, they crawled through weeds and grasses for the shelter of the trees that grew there, a cluster of hardwoods dominated by a pair of monstrous old elms. Streams of water eddied and pooled on the ground about them as they fought their way along the island's rain-soaked banks, and the wind howled around their ears. Lightning struck the mainland shore nearby with a thunderous crack, and they flattened themselves while the thunder rolled past.

At last they gained the trees, grateful to discover that it was comparatively dry beneath the canopy of limbs and sheltered against the wind. They stumbled to the base of the largest of the elms and collapsed, sprawling next to each other on the ground, gasping for breath. They lay without moving for a time, letting their strength return. Then, after exchanging a long look that conveyed their unspoken agreement to do so, they pulled themselves upright against the elm's rough trunk and sat shoulder to shoulder, staring out into the rain.

"Are you all right?" Morgan asked her.

It was the first thing either of them had said. She nodded wordlessly. Morgan checked himself carefully for injuries, and finding none, sighed and leaned back—relieved, weary, cold, and unexplainably hungry and thirsty, too, despite being drenched. But there was nothing to eat or drink, so there was no point in thinking about it.

He glanced over again. "I don't suppose you could do anything about a fire, could you?" She shook her head. "Can't use magic of any kind, huh? Ah, well. Where's Walker Boh when you need him?" He tried to sound flippant and failed. He sighed.

She reached over and let her hand rest on his, and it warmed him despite his discomfort. He lifted his arm and placed it about her shoulders, easing her close. It brought them both some small measure of warmth. Her silver hair was against his cheek, and her smell was in his nostrils, a mix of earth and forest and something else that was sweet and compelling.

"They won't find us until this storm ends," she said.

Morgan nodded. "If then. There won't be any trail to follow.

Just the river." He frowned. "Where are we, anyway? North or south of where we went into the river?"

"North and east," she advised.

"You know that?"

She nodded. He could feel her breathing, the slight movement of her body against him. He was shivering, but having her close like this seemed to make up for it. He closed his eyes.

"You didn't have to come after me," she said suddenly. She sounded uncomfortable. "I would have been all right."

He tried unsuccessfully to stifle a yawn. "I was due for a bath."

"You could have been hurt, Morgan."

"Not me. I've already survived attacks by Shadowen, Federation soldiers, Creepers, and other things I'd just as soon forget about. A fall into a river isn't going to hurt me."

The wind gusted sharply, howling through the branches of the trees, and they glanced skyward to listen. When the sound died away, they could hear the rush of the river again as it pounded against the shoreline.

Morgan hunched down within his sodden clothing. "When this storm blows itself out, we can swim to the mainland, get off this island. The river is too rough to try it now. And we're too tired to make the attempt in any case. But that's all right. We're safe enough right here. Just a little damp."

He realized that he was talking just to be doing something and went still again. Quickening did not respond. He could almost feel her thinking, but he hadn't a clue as to what she was thinking about. He closed his eyes again and let his breathing slow. He wondered what had become of the others. Had they managed to make it safely down that trail or had the collapse of the ledge trapped Walker and Pe Ell on the upper slope? He tried to envision the Dark Uncle and the assassin trapped with each other and failed.

It was growing dark now, dusk chasing away what little light remained, and shadows began to spread across the island in widening black stains. The rains were slowing, the sounds of thunder and wind receding in the distance, and the storm was beginning to pass. The air was not cooling as Morgan had expected, but instead was growing warm again, thick with the smells of heat and humidity. Just as well, he thought. They were too cold as it was. He thought about what it would feel like to be warm and dry again, to be secluded in his hunting lodge in the Highlands with hot broth and a fire, seated on the floor with the Ohmsfords, swapping lies of what had never been.

Or seated perhaps with Quickening, saying nothing because speaking wasn't necessary and just being together was enough, just touching . . .

The ache of what he was feeling filled him with both longing and fear. He wanted it to continue, wanted it to be there always, and at the same time he did not understand it and was certain that it would betray him.

"Are you awake?" he asked her, anxious suddenly for the sound of her voice.

"Yes," she replied.

He took a deep breath and breathed out slowly. "I have been thinking about why I'm here," he said. "Wondering about it since Culhaven. I haven't any magic anymore—not really. All I ever had was contained in the Sword of Leah, and now it's broken and what magic remains is small and probably won't be of much help to you. So there's just me, and I . . ." He stopped. "I just don't know what it is that you expect of me, I guess."

"Nothing," she answered softly.

"Nothing?" He could not keep the incredulity from his voice.

"Only what you are able and wish to give," she answered vaguely.

"But I thought that the King of the Silver River said . . ." He stopped. "I thought that your father said I was needed. Isn't that what you said? That he told you we were needed, all of us?"

"He did not say what it was that you were to do, Morgan. He told me to bring you with me in my search for the talisman and that you would know what to do, that we all would." She lifted away slightly and turned to look at him. "If I could tell you more, I would."

He scowled at her, frustrated with the evasiveness of her answers, with the uncertainty he was feeling. "Would you?"

She almost smiled. Even rain-streaked and soiled by the river's waters, she was the most beautiful woman he had ever seen. He tried to speak and failed. He simply sat there, mute and staring.

"Morgan," she said softly. "My father sees things that are hidden from all others. He tells me what I must know of these things, and I trust him enough to believe that what he tells me is enough. You are here because I need you. It has something to do with the magic of your Sword. I was told by my father and told you in turn that you will have a chance to make the Sword whole again. Perhaps then it will serve us both in a way we cannot foresee.''

"And Pe Ell?'' he pressed, determined now to know everything.

"Pe Ell?''

"Walker says he is an assassin—that he, too, carries a weapon of magic, a weapon that kills.''

She studied him for a long moment before she said, "That is true.''

"And he is needed, too?''

"Morgan.'' His name was spoken as a caution.

"Tell me. Please.''

Her perfect features lowered into shadow and lifted again, filled with sadness. "Pe Ell is needed. His purpose, as yours, must reveal itself.''

Morgan hesitated, trying to decide what to ask next, desperate to learn the truth but unwilling to risk losing her by crossing into territory in which he was not welcome.

His face tightened. "I would not like to think that I had been brought along for the same reason as Pe Ell,'' he said finally. "I am not like him.''

"I know that,'' she said. She hesitated, wrestling with some inner demon. "I believe that each of you—Walker Boh included—is here for a different reason, to serve a different purpose. That is my sense of things.''

He nodded, anxious to believe her, finding it impossible not to do so. He said, "I just wish I understood more.''

She reached up and touched his cheek with her fingers, letting them slide down his jaw to his neck and lift away again. "It will be all right,'' she said.

She lay back again, folding into him, and he felt his frustration and doubt begin to fade. He let them go without a fight, content just to hold the girl. It was dark now, daylight gone into the west, night settled comfortably over the land. The storm had moved east, and the rains had been reduced to mist. The clouds were still thick overhead but empty now of thunder, and a blanket of stillness lay across the land as if to cover a child preparing for sleep. In the invisible distance the Rabb continued to churn, a sullen, now sluggish flow that lulled and soothed with its wash. Morgan peered into the night without seeing, finding its opaque curtain lowered to enclose him, to wrap about him as if an invisible shroud. He breathed the clean air and let his thoughts drift free.

"I could eat something," he mused after a time. "If there were anything to eat."

Quickening rose without speaking, took his hands in hers, and pulled him up after her. Together, they walked into the darkness, picking their way through the damp grasses. She was able to see as he could not and led the way with a sureness that defied him. After a time she found roots and berries that they could eat and a plant that when properly cut yielded fresh water. They ate and drank what they found, crouched silently next to each other, saying nothing. When they were finished, she took him out to the riverbank where they sat in silence watching the Rabb flow past in the dim, mysterious half-light, a murky sheen of movement against the darker mainland.

A light breeze blew into Morgan's face, filled with the rich scent of flowers and grasses. His clothes were still damp, but he was no longer chilled. The air was warm, and he felt strangely light-headed.

"It is like this sometimes in the Highlands," he told her. "Warm and filled with earth smells after a summer storm, the nights so long you think they might never end and wish they wouldn't." He laughed. "I used to sit up with Par and Coll Ohmsford on nights like this. I'd tell them that if a man wished hard enough for it, he could just . . . melt into the darkness like a snowflake into skin, just disappear into it, and then stay as long as he liked."

He glanced over to judge her reaction. She was still beside him, lost in thought. He brought his knees up to his chest and wrapped his arms around them. A part of him wanted to melt into this night so that it would go on forever, wanted to take her with him, away from the world about them. It was a foolish wish.

"Morgan," she said finally, turning. "I envy you your past. I have none."

He smiled. "Of course you . . . ."

"No," she interrupted him. "I am an elemental. Do you know what that means? I am not human. I was created by magic. I was made from the earth of the Gardens. My father's hand shaped me. I was born full-grown, a woman without ever having been a child. My purpose in being has been determined by my father, and I have no say in what that purpose is to be. I am not saddened by this because it is all I know. But my instincts, my human feelings, tell me there is more, and I wish that it were mine as it has been yours. I sense the pleasure you take in remembering. I sense the joy.''

Morgan was speechless. He had known she was magic, that she possessed magic, but it had never occurred to him that she might not be . . . He caught himself. Might not be what? As real as he was? As human? But she was, wasn't she? Despite what she thought, she was. She felt and looked and talked and acted human. What else was there? Her father had fashioned her in the image of humans. Wasn't that enough? His eyes swept over her. It was enough for him, he decided. It was more than enough.

He reached out to stroke her hand. ''I admit I don't know anything about how you were made, Quickening. Or even anything about elementals. But you are human. I believe that. I would know if you weren't. As for not having any past, a past is nothing more than the memories you acquire, and that's something you're doing right now, acquiring memories—even if they're not the most pleasant in the world.''

She smiled at the idea. ''The ones of you will always be pleasant, Morgan Leah,'' she said.

He held her gaze. Then he leaned forward and kissed her, just a brief touching of their lips, and lifted away. She looked at him through those black, penetrating eyes. There was fear mirrored there, and he saw it.

''What frightens you?'' he asked.

She shook her head. ''That you make me feel so much.''

He felt himself treading on dangerous ground, but went forward nevertheless. ''You asked me before why I came after you when you fell. The truth is, I had to. I am in love with you.''

Her face lost all expression. ''You cannot be in love with me,'' she whispered.

He smiled bleakly. ''I'm afraid I have no choice in the matter. This isn't something I can help.''

She looked at him for a long time and then shuddered. ''Nor can I help what I feel for you. But while you are certain of your feelings, mine simply confuse me. I do not know what to do with them. I have my father's purpose to fulfill, and my feelings for you and yours for me cannot be allowed to interfere with that.''

''They don't have to,'' he said, taking her hands firmly now. ''They can just be there.''

Her silver hair shimmered as she shook her head. "I think not. Not feelings such as these."

He kissed her again and this time she kissed him back. He breathed her in as if she were a flower. He had never felt so certain about anything in his life as how he felt about her.

She broke the kiss and drew away. "Morgan," she said, speaking his name as if it were a plea.

They rose and went back through the damp grasses to the sheltering trees, to the elm where they had waited out the storm earlier, and sank down again by its roughened trunk. They held each other as children might when frightened and alone, protecting against nameless terrors that waited just beyond the bounds of their consciousness, that stalked their dreams and threatened their sleep.

"My father told me as I left the Gardens of my birth that there were things he could not protect me against," she whispered. Her face was close against Morgan's, soft and smooth, her breath warm. "He was not speaking of the dangers that would threaten me—of Uhl Belk and the things that live in Eldwist or even of the Shadowen. He was speaking of this."

Morgan stroked her hair gently. "There isn't much of anything that you can do to protect against your feelings."

"I can close them away," she answered.

He nodded. "If you must. But I will tell you first that I am not capable of closing my feelings away. Even if my life depended on it, I could not do so. It doesn't make any difference who you are or even what you are. Elemental or something else. I don't care how you were made or why. I love you, Quickening. I think I did from the first moment I saw you, from the first words you spoke. I can't change that, no matter what else you ask of me. I don't even want to try."

She turned in his arms, and her face lifted to find his. Then she kissed him and kept on kissing him until everything around them disappeared.

When they woke the next morning the sun was cresting the horizon of a cloudless blue sky. Birds sang and the air was warm and sweet. They rose and walked to the riverbank and found the Rabb slow-moving and placid once more.

Morgan Leah looked at Quickening, at the curve of her body, the wild flow of her silver hair, the softness of her face, and the smile that came to his face was fierce and unbidden. "I love you," he whispered.

She smiled back at him. "And I love you, Morgan Leah. I will never love anyone again in my life the way I love you."

They plunged into the river. Rested now, they swam easily the distance that separated the island from the mainland. On gaining the far shore, they stood together for a moment looking back, and Morgan fought to contain the sadness that welled up within him. The island and their solitude and last night were lost to him except as memories. They were going back into the world of Uhl Belk and the Black Elfstone.

They walked south along the river's edge for several hours before encountering the others. It was Carisman who spied them first as he wandered the edge of a bluff, and he cried out in delight, summoning the rest. Down the steep slope he raced, blond hair flying, handsome features flushed. He skidded the last several yards on his backside, bounded up, and raced to intercept them. Throwing himself at Quickening's feet, he burst into song.

He sang:

> *"Found are the sheep who have strayed from the fold,*
> *Saved are the lambs from the wolves and the cold,*
> *Wandering far, they have yet found their way,*
> *Now, pray we all, they are here for to stay.*
> *Tra-la-la, tra-la-la, tra-la-la!"*

It was a ridiculous song, but it made Morgan smile nevertheless. In moments, the others had joined them as well, gaunt Pe Ell, his dark anger at having lost Quickening giving way to relief that she had been found again; bearish Horner Dees, gruffly trying to put the entire incident behind them; and the enigmatic Walker Boh, his face an inscrutable mask as he complimented Morgan on his rescue. All the while, an exuberant Carisman danced and sang, filling the air with his music.

When the reunion finally concluded the company resumed its journey, moving away from the Charnals and into the forestlands north. Somewhere far ahead, Eldwist waited. The sun climbed into the sky and hung there, brightening and warming the lands beneath as if determined to erase all traces of yesterday's storm.

Morgan walked next to Quickening, picking his way through the slowly evaporating puddles and streams. They didn't speak. They didn't even look at each other. After a time, he felt her hand take his.

At her touch, the memories flooded through him.

XVII

They walked north for five days through the country beyond the Charnals, a land that was green and gently rolling, carpeted by long grasses and fields of wildflowers, dotted by forests of fir, aspen, and spruce. Rivers and streams meandered in silver ribbons from the mountains and bluffs, pooling in lakes, shimmering in the sunlight like mirrors, and sending a flurry of cooling breezes from their shores. It was easier journeying here than it had been through the mountains; the terrain was far less steep, the footing sure, and the weather mild. The days were sun-filled, the nights warm and sweet smelling. The skies stretched away from horizon to horizon, broad and empty and blue. It rained only once, a slow and gentle dampening of trees and grasses that passed almost unnoticed. The spirits of the company were high; anticipation of what lay ahead was tempered by renewed confidence and a sense of well-being. Doubts lay half-forgotten in the dark grottos to which they had been consigned. There was strength and quickness in their steps. The passage of the hours chipped away at uncertain temperaments with slow, steady precision and like a stonecutter's chisel etched and shaped until the rough edges vanished and only the smooth surface of agreeable companionship remained.

Even Walker Boh and Pe Ell called an unspoken truce. It could never be argued reasonably that they showed even the remotest inclination toward establishing a friendship, but they kept apart amiably enough, each maintaining a studied indifference to the other's presence. As for the remainder of the company, constancy was the behavioral norm. Horner Dees continued reticent and gruff, Carisman kept them all entertained with stories and songs, and Morgan and Quickening feinted and boxed with glances and gestures in a lovers' dance that was a mystery to everyone but them. There was in all of them, save perhaps Carisman, an undercurrent of wariness and stealth. Carisman, it seemed, was incapable of showing more than one face. But the others were circumspect in their dark times, anxious to keep their doubts and fears at bay, hopeful that some mix of luck and determination would prove sufficient to carry them through to the journey's end.

The beginning of that end came the following day with a gradual change in the character of the land. The green that had brightened the forests and hills south began to fade to gray. Flowers disappeared. Grasses withered and dried. Trees that should have been fully leafed and vibrant were stunted and bare. The birds that had flown in dazzling bursts of color and song just a mile south were missing here along with small game and the larger hoofed and horned animals. It was as if a blight had fallen over everything, stripping the land of its life.

They stood at the crest of a rise at midmorning and looked out over the desolation that stretched away before them.

"Shadowen," Morgan Leah declared darkly.

But Quickening shook her silvery head and replied, "Uhl Belk."

It grew worse by midday and worse still by nightfall. It was bad enough when the land was sickened; now it turned completely dead. All trace of grasses and leaves disappeared. Even the smallest bit of scrub disdained to grow. Trunks lifted their skeletal limbs skyward as if searching for protection, as if beseeching for it. The country appeared to have been so thoroughly ravaged that nothing dared grow back, a vast wilderness gone empty and stark and friendless. Dust rose in dry puffs from their boots as they stalked the dead ground, the earth's poisoned breath. Nothing moved about them, above them, beneath them—not animals, not birds, not even insects. There was no water. The air had a flat, metallic taste and smell to it. Clouds began to gather again, small wisps at first, then a solid bank that hung above the earth like a shroud.

They camped that night in a forest of deadwood where the air was so still they could hear each other breathe. The wood would not burn, so they had no fire. Light from a mix of elements in the earth reflected off the ceiling of clouds and cast the shadows of the trees across their huddled forms in clinging webs.

"We'll be there by nightfall tomorrow," Horner Dees said as they sat facing each other in the stillness. "Eldwist."

Dark stares were his only reply.

Uhl Belk's presence became palpable after that. He huddled next to them there in the fading dusk, slept with them that night, and walked with them when they set out the following day. His breath was what they breathed, his silence their own. They could feel him beckoning, reaching out to gather them in. No one said so, but Uhl Belk was there.

By midday, the land had turned to stone. It was as if the whole of it, sickened and withered and gone lifeless, had been washed of every color but gray and in the process petrified. It was all preserved perfectly, like a giant piece of sculpture. Trunks and limbs, scrub and grasses, rocks and earth— everything as far as the eye could see had been turned to stone. It was a starkly chilling landscape that despite its coldness radiated an oddly compelling beauty. The company from Rampling Steep found itself entranced. Perhaps it was the solidity that drew them, the sense that here was something lasting and enduring and somehow perfectly wrought. The ravages of time, the changing of the seasons, the most determined efforts of man—it seemed as if none of these could affect what had been done here.

Horner Dees nodded and the members of the company went forward.

A haze hung about them as they walked across this tapestry of frozen time, and it was only with difficulty that they were able, after several hours, to distinguish something else shimmering in the distance. It was a vast body of water, as gray as the land they passed through, blending into its bleakness, a backdrop merging starkly into earth and sky as if the transition were meaningless.

They had reached the Tiderace.

Twin peaks came into view as well, jagged rock spirals that lifted starkly against the horizon. It was apparent that the peaks were their destination.

Now and again the earth beneath them rumbled ominously, tremors reverberating as if the land were a carpet that some giant had taken in his hands and shaken. There was nothing about the tremors to indicate their source. But Horner Dees knew something. Morgan saw it in the way his bearded face tightened down against his chest and fear slipped into his eyes.

After a time the land about them began to narrow on either side and the Tiderace to close about, and they were left with a shrinking corridor of rock upon which to walk. The corridor was taking them directly toward the peaks, a ramp that might at its end drop them into the sea. The temperature cooled, and there was moisture in the air that clung to their skin in faint droplets. Their booted feet were strangely noiseless as they trod the hard surface of the rock, climbing steadily into a haze. Soon they became a line of shadows in the approaching dusk. Dees led, ancient, massive, and steady. Morgan followed with Quickening, the tall Highlander's face lined with wariness, the girl's smooth and calm. Handsome Carisman hummed beneath his breath while his gaze shifted about him as rapidly as a bird's. Walker Boh floated behind, pale and introspective within his long cloak. Pe Ell brought up the rear, his stalker's eyes seeing everything.

The ramp began to break apart before them, an escarpment out of which strange rock formations rose against the light. They might have been carvings of some sort save for the fact that they lacked any recognizable form. Like pillars that had been hewn apart by weather's angry hand over thousands of years, they jutted and angled in bizarre shapes and images, the mindless visions of a madman. The company passed between them, anxious in their shadow, and hurried on.

They arrived finally at the peaks. There was a rift between them, a break so deep and narrow that it appeared to have been formed by some cataclysm that had split apart what had once been a single peak to form the two. They loomed to either side, spirals of rock that thrust into the clouds as if to pin them fast. Beyond, the skies were murky and misted, and the waters of the Tiderace crashed and rumbled against the rocky shores.

Horner Dees moved ahead and the others followed until all had been enveloped in shadows. The air was chill and unmoving in the gap, and the distant shrieks of seabirds echoed shrilly. What sort of creatures besides those of the sea could possibly live here? Morgan Leah wondered uneasily. He drew his sword. His whole body was rigid with tension, and he strained to catch some sign of the danger he sensed threatening them. Dees was hunched forward like an animal at hunt, and the three behind the Highlander were ghosts without substance. Only Quickening seemed unaffected, her head held high, her eyes alert as she scanned the rock, the skies, the gray that shrouded everything.

Morgan swallowed against the dryness in his throat. *What is it that waits for us?*

The walls of the break seemed to join overhead, and they were left momentarily in utter blackness with only the thin line of the passageway ahead to give them reassurance that they had not been entombed. Then the walls receded again, and the light returned. The rift opened into a valley that lay cradled between the peaks. Shallow, rutted, choked with the husks of trees and brush and with boulders many times the size of any man, it was an ugly catchall for nature's refuse and time's discards. Skeletons lay everywhere, vast piles of them, all sizes and shapes, scattered without suggestion of what creatures they might once have been.

Horner Dees brought them to a halt. "This is Bone Hollow," he said quietly. "This is the gateway to Eldwist. Over there, across the Hollow, through the gap in the peaks, Eldwist begins."

The others crowded forward for a better look. Walker Boh stiffened. "There's something down there."

Dees nodded. "Found that out the hard way ten years ago," he said. "It's called a Koden. It's the Stone King's watchdog. You see it?"

They looked and saw nothing, even Pe Ell. Dees seated himself ponderously on a rock. "You won't either. Not until it has you. And it won't matter much by then, will it? You could ask any of those poor creatures down there if they still had tongues and the stuff of life to use them."

Morgan scuffed his boot on a piece of deadwood as he listened. The deadwood was heavy and unyielding. Stone. Morgan looked at it as if understanding for the first time. Stone. Everything underfoot, everything surrounding them, everything for as far as the eye could see—it was all stone.

"Kodens are a kind of bear," Dees was saying. "Big fellows, live up in the cold regions north of the mountains, keep pretty much to themselves. Very unpredictable under any conditions. But this one?" He made his nod an enigmatic gesture. "He's a monster."

"Huge?" Morgan asked.

"A *monster*," Dees emphasized. "Not just in size, Highlander. This thing isn't a Koden anymore. You can recognize it for what it's supposed to be, but just barely. Belk did something to it. Blinded it, for one thing. It can't see. But its ears are so sharp it can hear a pin drop."

"So it knows we are here," Walker mused, edging past Dees for a closer look at the Hollow. His eyes were dark and introspective.

"Has for quite a while, I'd guess. It's down there waiting for us to try to get past."

"If it's still there at all," Pe Ell said. "It's been a long time since you were here, old man. By now it might be dead and gone."

Dees looked at him mildly. "Why don't you go on down there and take a look?"

Pe Ell gave him that lopsided, chilling smile.

The old Tracker turned away, his gaze shifting to the Hollow. "Ten years since I saw it and I still can't forget it," he whispered. He shook his grizzled head. "Something like that you don't ever forget."

"Maybe Pe Ell is right; maybe it is dead by now," Morgan suggested hopefully. He glanced at Quickening and found her staring fixedly at Walker.

"Not this thing," Dees insisted.

"Well, why can't we see it if it's all that big and ugly?" Carisman asked, peering cautiously over Morgan's shoulder.

Dees chuckled. His eyes narrowed. "You can't see it because it looks like everything else down there—like stone, all gray and hard, just another chunk of rock. Look for yourself. One of those mounds, one of those boulders, something that's down there that doesn't look like anything—that's it. Just lying there, perfectly still. Waiting."

"Waiting," Carisman echoed.

He sang:

> *"Down in the valley, the valley of stone.*
> *The Koden lies waiting amid shattered bone.*
> *Amid all its victims,*
> *Within its gray home,*
> *The Koden lies waiting to make you its own."*

"Be still, tunesmith," Pe Ell said, a warning edge to his voice. He scowled at Dees. "You got past this thing before, if we're to believe what you tell us. How?"

Dees laughed aloud. "I was lucky, of course! I had twelve other men with me and we just walked right in, fools to the last. It couldn't get us all, not once we started running. No, it had to settle for three. That was going in. Coming out, it only got one. Of course, there were just two of us left by then. I was the one it missed."

Pe Ell stared at him expressionlessly. "Like you said, old man—lucky for you."

Dees rose, as bearish as any Koden Morgan might have imagined, sullen and forbidding when he set his face as he did now. He faced Pe Ell as if he meant to have at him. Then he said, "There's all sorts of luck. Some you've got and some you make. Some you carry with you and some you pick up along the way. You're going to need all kinds of it getting in and out of Eldwist. The Koden, he's a thing you wouldn't want to dream about on your worst night. But let me tell you something. After you see what else is down there, what lies beyond Bone Hollow, you won't have to worry about the Koden anymore. Because the dreams you'll have on your worst nights after that will be concerned with other things!"

Pe Ell's shrug was scornful and indifferent. "Dreams are for frightened old men, Horner Dees."

Dees glared at him. "Brave words now."

"I can see it," Walker Boh said suddenly.

His voice was soft, almost a whisper, but it silenced the others instantly and brought them about to face him. The Dark Uncle was staring out across the broken desolation of the Hollow, seemingly unaware that he had spoken.

"The Koden?" Dees asked sharply. He came forward a step.

"Where?" Pe Ell asked.

Walker's gesture was obscure. Morgan looked anyway and saw nothing. He glanced at the others. None of them appeared to be able to find it either. But Walker Boh was paying no attention to any of them. He seemed instead to be listening for something.

"If you really can see it, point it out to me," Pe Ell said finally, his voice carefully neutral.

Walker did not respond. He continued to stare. "It feels . . ." he began and stopped.

"Walker?" Quickening whispered and touched his arm.

The pale countenance shifted away from the Hollow at last and the dark eyes found her own. "I must find it," he said. He glanced at each of them in turn. "Wait here until I call for you."

Morgan started to object, but there was something in the other man's eyes that stopped him from doing so.

Instead, he watched silently with the others as the Dark Uncle walked alone into Bone Hollow.

The day was still, the air windless, and nothing moved in the ragged expanse of the Hollow save Walker Boh. He crossed the broken stone in silence, a ghost who made no sound and left no mark. There were times in the past few weeks when he had thought himself little more. He had almost died from the poison of the Asphinx and again from the attack of the Shadowen at Hearthstone. A part of him had surely died with the loss of his arm, another part with the failure of his magic to cure his sickness. A part of him had died with Cogline. He had been empty and lost on this journey, compelled to come by his rage at the Shadowen, his fear at being left alone, and his wish to discover the secrets of Uhl Belk and the Black Elfstone. Even Quickening, despite ministering to his needs, both physical and emotional, had not been strong enough to give him back to himself. He had been a hollow thing, bereft of any sense of who and what he was supposed to be, reduced to undertaking this quest in the faint hope that he would discover his purpose in the world.

And now, here within this vast, desolate stretch of land, where fears and doubts and weaknesses were felt most keenly, Walker Boh thought he had a chance to come alive again.

It was the presence of the Koden that triggered this hope. Until now the magic had been curiously silent within him, a worn and tired thing that had failed repeatedly and at last seemed to have given up. To be sure, it was there still to protect him when he was threatened, to frighten off the Urdas when they came too close, to deflect their hurled weapons. Yet this was a poor and sorry use when he remembered what it had once been able to do. What of the empathy it had given him with other living things? What of his sense of emotions and thoughts? What of the knowledge that had always just seemed to come to him? What of the glimpses of what was to be? All of these had deserted him, gone away as surely as his old world, his life with Cogline and Rumor at Hearthstone. Once he had wished it would be so, that the magic would disappear and he would be left in peace, a man like any other. But it had become increasingly clear to him on this journey, his sense of who and what he was heightened by the passing of Cogline and his own physical and emotional devastation, that his wish had been foolish. He would never be like other men, and he would never be at peace without the magic. He could not change who and what he was; Cogline had known that and told him so. On this journey he had discovered it was true.

He needed the magic.

He required it.

Now he would test whether or not he could still call it his own. He had sensed the presence of the Koden before Pe Ell had. He had sensed what it was before Horner Dees had de-

scribed it. Amid the strewn rock, hunched down and silent, it
had reached out to him as creatures once had when he approached. He could feel the Koden call to him. Walker Boh was
not certain of its purpose in doing so, yet knew he must respond.
It was more than the creature's need that he was answering; it
was also his own.

He moved directly through the jumble of boulders and petrified wood to where the Koden waited. It had not moved, not
even an inch, since the company had arrived. But Walker knew
where it lay concealed nevertheless, for its presence had brought
the magic awake again. It was an unexpected, exhilarating, and
strangely comforting experience to have the power within him
stir to life, to discover that it was not lost as he had believed,
but merely misplaced.

Or suppressed, he chided harshly. Certainly he had worked
hard at denying it even existed.

Mist curled through the rocks, tendrils of white that formed
strange shapes and patterns against the gray of the land. Far
distant, beyond and below the peaks and the valley they cradled,
Walker could hear the crash of the ocean waters against the
shoreline, a dull booming that resonated through the silence.
He slowed, conscious now that the Koden was just ahead, unable to dispel entirely his apprehension that he was being lured
to his doom, that the magic would not protect him, and he would
be killed. Would it matter if he was? he wondered suddenly. He
brushed the thought away. Within, he could feel the magic burning like a fire stoked to life.

He came down from between two boulders into a depression,
and the Koden rose up before him, cat-quick. It seemed to materialize out of the earth, as if the dust that lay upon the rock
had suddenly come together to give it form. It was huge and old
and grizzled, three times his own size, with great shaggy limbs
and ragged yellow claws that curled down to grip the rock. It
lifted onto its hind legs to show itself to him, and its twisted
snout huffed and opened to reveal a glistening row of teeth.
Sightless white eyes peered down at him. Walker stood his
ground, his life a slender thread that a single swipe of one huge
paw could sever. He saw that the Koden's head and body had
been distorted by some dark magic to make the creature appear
more grotesque and that the symmetry of shape that had once
given grace to its power had been stripped away.

Speak to me, thought Walker Boh.

The Koden blinked its eyes and dropped down so close that

the huge muzzle was no more than inches from the Dark Uncle's face. Walker forced himself to meet the creature's empty gaze. He could feel the hot, fetid breath.

Tell me, he thought.

There was an instant's time when he was certain that he was going to die, that the magic had failed him entirely, that the Koden would reach out and strike him down. He waited for the claws to rend him, for the end to come. Then he heard the creature answer him, the guttural sounds of its own language captured and transformed by the magic.

Help me, the Koden said.

A flush of warmth filled Walker. Life returned to him in a way he found difficult to describe, as if he had been reborn and could believe in himself again. A flicker of a smile crossed his face. The magic was still his.

He reached out slowly with his good arm and touched the Koden on its muzzle, feeling beneath his fingertips more than the roughness of its hide and fur, finding as well the spirit of the creature that was trapped beneath. The Dark Uncle read its history in that touch and felt its pain. He stepped close to study its massive, scarred body, no longer frightened by its size or its ugliness or its ability to destroy. It was a prisoner, he saw— frightened, angered, bewildered, and despairing in the manner of all prisoners, wanting only to be free.

"I will make you so," Walker Boh whispered.

He looked to discover how the Koden was bound and found nothing. Where were the chains that shackled it? He circled the beast, testing the weight and texture of the air and earth. The great head swung about, seeking to follow him, the eyes fixed and staring. Walker completed his circuit and stopped, frowning. He had found the invisible lines of magic that the Stone King had fashioned and he knew what it would take to set the creature free. The Koden was a prisoner of its mutation. It would have to be changed back into a bear again, into the creature it had been, and the stigma of Uhl Belk's touch cleansed. But Walker hadn't the magic for that. Only Quickening possessed such power, magic strong enough to bring back the Meade Gardens out of the ashes of the past, to restore what once was, and she had already said she could not use her magic again until the Black Elfstone was recovered. Walker stood looking at the Koden helplessly, trying to decide if there were anything he could do. The beast shifted to face him, its great, ragged bulk a shimmer of rock dust against the landscape.

Walker reached out once more, and his fingers rested on the Koden's muzzle. His thoughts became words. *Let us pass, and we will find a way to set you free.*

The Koden stared out at him from the prison of its ruined body, sightless eyes hard and empty. *Go,* it said.

Walker lifted his hand away long enough to beckon his companions forward, then placed it back again. The others of the company came hesitantly, Quickening in the lead, then Morgan Leah, Horner Dees, Carisman, and Pe Ell. He watched them pass without comment, his arm outstretched, his hand steady. He caught a glimpse of what was in their eyes, a strange mix of emotions, understanding in Quickening's alone, fear and awe and disbelief in the rest. Then they were past. They walked from the rubble of Bone Hollow to the break in the cliffs beyond which they turned to wait for him.

Walker took his hand away and saw the Koden tremble. Its mouth gaped wide, and it appeared to cry out soundlessly. Then it wheeled away from him and lumbered down into the rocks.

"I won't forget," the Dark Uncle called after it.

The emptiness he felt made him shiver. Pulling his cloak close, he walked from the Hollow.

Morgan and the others, all but Quickening, asked Walker Boh when he reached them what had happened. How had he managed to charm the Koden so that they could pass? But the Dark Uncle refused to answer their questions. He would say only that the creature was a prisoner of the Stone King's magic and must be freed, that he had given his promise.

"Since you made the promise, you can worry about keeping it," Pe Ell declared irritably, anxious to dismiss the matter of the Koden now that the danger was behind them.

"We'll have trouble enough keeping ourselves free of the Stone King's magic," Horner Dees agreed.

Carisman was already skipping ahead, and Morgan suddenly found himself facing Walker Boh with no reply to give. It was Quickening who spoke instead, saying, "If you gave your promise, Walker Boh, then it must be kept." She did not, however, say how.

They turned away from Bone Hollow and passed into the break that opened out through the peaks to the Tiderace. The passage was shadowed and dark in the fading afternoon light, and a chill, rough-edged wind blew down off the slopes of the cliffs above, thrusting into them like a giant hand, shoving them relentlessly ahead. The sun had dropped into the horizon west, caught in a web of clouds that turned its light scarlet and gold. The smell of salt water, fish, and kelp filled the air, sharp and pungent.

Morgan glanced back once or twice at Walker Boh, still amazed at how he had been able to keep the Koden from attacking them, to walk right up to it as he had and touch it without coming to harm. He recalled the stories of the Dark Uncle, of the man before he had suffered the bite of the Asphinx and the loss of Cogline and Rumor, the man who had taught Par Ohmsford not to be frightened of the power of the Elven magic. Until now, he had thought Walker Boh crippled by the Shadowen attack on Hearthstone. He pursed his lips thoughtfully. Perhaps he had been wrong. And if wrong about Walker, why not wrong about himself as well? Perhaps the Sword of Leah could be made whole again and his own magic restored. Perhaps there was a chance for all of them, just as Quickening had suggested.

The defile opened suddenly before them, the shadows which had caged them brightened into gray, misty light, and they peeked through a narrow window in the cliffs. The Tiderace spread away below in an endless expanse, its waters roiling and white-capped as they churned toward the shoreline. The company moved ahead, back into the shadows. The trail they followed began to descend, to twist and turn through the rocks, damp and treacherous from the mist and the ocean spray. The walls split apart once more, this time forming ragged columns of stone that permitted brief glimpses of sky and sea. Underfoot, the rock was loose, and it felt as if everything was on the verge of breaking up.

Then they turned onto a slide so steep that they were forced to descend sitting and found themselves in a narrow passageway that curled ahead into a tunnel. They stooped to pass through, for the tunnel was filled with jagged rock edges. At its far end, the walls fell away, and the tunnel opened onto a shelf that lifted toward the sky. The company moved onto the shelf, discovered a pathway, and climbed to where it ended at a rampart formed of stone blocks.

They stood at the edge of the rampart and looked down. Morgan felt his stomach lurch. From where they stood, the land dropped away to a narrow isthmus that jutted into the sea. Connected to the isthmus was a peninsula, broad and ragged about the edges, formed all of cliffs against which the waters of the Tiderace pounded relentlessly. Atop the cliffs sat a city of tow-

ering stone buildings. The buildings were not of this time, but
of the old world, of the age before the Great Wars destroyed the
order of things and the new Races were born. They rose hundreds
of feet into the air, smooth and symmetrical and lined with
banks of windows that yawned blackly against the gray light.
Everything was set close together, so that the city had the look
of a gathering of monstrous stone obelisks grown out of the
rock. Seabirds wheeled and circled about the buildings, crying
out mournfully in the failing light.

"Eldwist," Horner Dees announced.

Far west, the sun was sinking into the waters of the sea, losing
its brightness and its color with the coming of night, the scarlet
and gold fading to silver. The wind howled down off the cliffs
behind them in a steady crescendo, and it felt as if even the
pinnacle of rock on which they stood was being shaken. They
huddled together against its thrust and the fall of night and
watched raptly as Eldwist turned black with shadow. The wind
howled through the city as well, down the canyons of its streets,
across the drops of its cliffs. Morgan was chilled by the sound
of it. Eldwist was empty and dead. There was only its stone,
hard and unyielding, unchanging and fixed.

Horner Dees called out to them over the sound of the wind
as he turned away. He led them back to where a set of steps had
been carved into the cliff face to lead downward to the city. The
steps ran back against the wall, angling through the crevices and
nooks, twisting once more into shadow. Night closed about as
they descended, the sun disappearing, the stars winking into
view in a sky that was clear and bright. Moonlight reflected off
the Tiderace, and Morgan could see the stark, jutting peaks of
the city lifting off the rocks. Mist rose in gauzy trailers, and
Eldwist took on a surrealistic look—as if come out of time and
legend. The seabirds flew away, the sound of their cries fading
into silence. Soon there was only the roll of the waves as they
slapped against the rocky shores.

At the base of the stairs they found an alcove sheltered by the
rocks. Horner Dees brought them to a halt. "No sense in trying
to go farther," he advised, sounding weary. The wind did not
reach them here, and he talked in a normal tone of voice. "Too
dangerous to try to go in at night. There's a Creeper down
there . . ."

"A Creeper?" Morgan, who had been examining bits of grass
and shrub that were perfectly preserved in stone, looked up
sharply.

"Yes, Highlander," the other continued. "A thing that sweeps the streets of the city after dark, gathering up any stray bits and pieces of living refuse . . ."

A rumbling within the earth cut short the rest of what he was about to say. The source of the rumbling was Eldwist, and the members of the company turned quickly to look. The city stood framed against the night sky, all black save for where the light reflected off the stone. It was larger and more forbidding when viewed from below, Morgan thought as he peered into its shadows. More impenetrable . . .

Something huge surged out of the dark recesses he searched, a thing of such monstrous size as to give the momentary illusion that it dwarfed even the buildings. It rose from between the monoliths as if kindred, all bulk and weight, but long and sinewy like a snake as well, stone blocks turned momentarily liquid to reshape and re-form. Then jaws gaped wide—Morgan could see the jagged edge of the teeth clearly against the backdrop of the moon—and they heard a horrifying cry, like a strangled cough. The earth reverberated with that cry, and the members of the company from Rampling Steep dropped into a protective crouch—all but Quickening, who remained erect, as if she alone were strong enough to withstand this nightmare.

A second later it was gone, dropping away as quickly and smoothly as it had come, the rumble of its passing hanging faintly in the air.

"That was no Creeper," Morgan whispered.

"And it wasn't here ten years ago either," a white-faced Horner Dees whispered back. "I'd bet on it."

"No," Quickening said softly, turning to face them now. Her companions came slowly to their feet. "It is newly born," she said, "barely five years old. It is still a baby."

"A baby!" Morgan exclaimed incredulously.

Quickening nodded. "Yes, Morgan Leah. It is called the Maw Grint." She smiled sadly. "It is Uhl Belk's child."

XVIII

𝒯he six that formed the company from Rampling Steep spent the remainder of the night huddled in the shelter of the cliffs, crouched silently in the darkness, hidden away from the Maw Grint and whatever other horrors lay in wait within Eldwist. They built no fire—indeed, there was no wood to be gathered for one—and they ate sparingly of their meager food. Food and water would be a problem in the days to come since there was little of either to be found in this country of stone. Fish would become the staple of their diet; a small stream of rainwater that tumbled down off the rocks behind would quench their thirst. If the fish proved elusive or the stream dried up, they would be in serious trouble.

No one slept much in the aftermath of the Maw Grint's appearance. For a long while no one even tried. Their uneasiness was palpable as they waited out the night. Quickening used that time to relate to the others what she knew of the Stone King's child.

"My father told me of the Maw Grint when he sent me forth from his Gardens," she began, her black eyes distant as she spoke, her silver hair gleaming brightly in the moonlight. They sat in a half-circle, their backs settled protectively against the rocks, their eyes shifting warily from time to time toward the forbidding shadow of the city. All was silent now, the Maw Grint disappeared as mysteriously as it had come, the seabirds gone to roost, and the wind faded away.

Quickening's voice was carefully hushed. "As I am the child of the King of the Silver River, so the Maw Grint is the child of Uhl Belk. Both of us were made by the magic, each to serve a father's needs. We are elementals, beings of earth's life, born out of the soil and not of woman's flesh. We are much the same, the Maw Grint and I.''

It was such a bizarre statement that it was all Morgan Leah could do to keep from attacking it. He refrained from doing so only because there was nothing to be gained by voicing an objection and diverting the narration from its intended course.

"The Maw Grint was created to serve a single purpose," Quickening went on. "Eldwist is a city of the old world, one which escaped the devastation of the Great Wars. The city and the land on which it is settled mark the kingdom of Uhl Belk, his haven, his fortress against all encroachment of the world beyond. For a while, they were enough. He was content to burrow in his stone, to remain secluded. But his appetite for power and his fear of losing it were constant obsessions. In the end, they consumed him. He became convinced that if he did not change the world without, it would eventually change him. He determined to extend his kingdom south. But to do so he would have to leave the safety of Eldwist, and that was unacceptable. Like my father, his magic grows weaker the farther he travels from its source. Uhl Belk refused to take such a risk. Instead, he created the Maw Grint and sent his child in his place.

"The Maw Grint," she whispered, "once looked like me. It was human in form and walked the land as I do. It possessed a part of its father's magic as I do. But whereas I was given power to heal the land, the Maw Grint was given power to turn it to stone. A simple touching was all it took. By touching it fed upon the earth and all that lived and grew upon it, and everything was changed to stone.

"But Uhl Belk grew impatient with his child, for the transformation of the lands surrounding was not proceeding quickly enough to suit him. Surrounded by the waters of the Tiderace, which his magic could not affect, he was trapped upon this finger of land with only the way south open to him and only the Maw Grint to widen the corridor. The Stone King infused his child with increasingly greater amounts of his own magic, anxious for quicker and more extensive results. The Maw Grint began to change form as a result of the infusions of power, to transform itself into something more adaptable to what its father demanded. It became molelike. It began to tunnel into the earth, finding that change came quicker from beneath than above. It grew in size as it fed and changed again. It became a massive slug, a burrowing worm of immense proportions.''

She paused. "It also went mad. Too much power, too quickly

fed, and it lost its sanity. It evolved from a thinking, reasoning creature to one so mindless that it knew only to feed. It swept into the land south, burrowing deeper and deeper. The land changed quickly then, but the Maw Grint changed more quickly yet. And then one day Uhl Belk lost control of his child completely.''

She glanced at the dark silhouette of the city and back again. ''The Maw Grint began to hunt its father when it was not feeding off the land, aware of the power that the Stone King possessed and eager to usurp it. Uhl Belk discovered that he had fashioned a two-edged sword. On the one hand, the Maw Grint was tunneling into the Four Lands and changing them to stone. On the other, it was tunneling beneath Eldwist as well, searching for a way to destroy him. So powerful had the Maw Grint grown that father and son were evenly matched. The Stone King was in danger of being dispatched by his own weapon.''

''Couldn't he simply change his son back again?'' Carisman asked, wide-eyed. ''Couldn't he use the magic to restore him to what he was?''

Quickening shook her head. ''Not by the time he thought to do anything. By then it was too late. The Maw Grint would not let itself be changed—even though, my father tells me, a part of it realized the horror of what it had become and longed for release. That part, it seems, was too weak to act.''

''So now it burrows the earth and sorrows over its fate,'' the tunesmith murmured.

He sang:

> *''Made in the shape of humankind,*
> *To serve the Stone King's dark design,*
> *The Maw Grint tunnels 'neath the land,*
> *A horror wrought by father's hand,*
> *Become a monster out of need,*
> *With no true hope of being freed,*
> *It hunts.''*

''Hunts, indeed,'' Morgan Leah echoed. ''Hunts us, probably.''

Quickening shook her head. ''It isn't even aware that we exist, Morgan. We are too small, too insignificant to catch its attention. Until we choose to use magic, of course. Then it will know.''

There was a studied silence. "What was it doing when we saw it tonight?" Horner Dees asked finally.

"Crying out what it feels—its rage, frustration, hatred, and madness." She paused. "Its pain."

"Like the Koden, it is a prisoner of the Stone King's magic," Walker Boh said. His sharp eyes fixed the girl. "And somehow Uhl Belk has managed to keep that magic his own, hasn't he?"

"He has gained possession of the Black Elfstone," she replied. "He went out from Eldwist long enough to steal it from the Hall of Kings and replace it with the Asphinx. He took it back into his keep and used it against his child. Possession of the Elven magic shifted the balance of power back to Uhl Belk. Even the Maw Grint was not powerful enough to defeat the Stone."

"A magic that can negate the power of other magics," Pe Ell recited thoughtfully. "A magic that can turn them to its own use."

"The Maw Grint still threatens its father, but it cannot overcome the Elfstone. It lives because Uhl Belk wishes it to continue feeding on the land, to continue transforming living matter to stone. The Maw Grint is a useful, if dangerous, slave. By night, it tunnels the earth. By day, it sleeps. Like the Koden, it is blind—made so by the magic and the nature of what it does, burrowing within darkness, seldom seeing light." She looked again toward the city. "It will probably never know we are here if we are careful."

"So all we have to do is to steal the Elfstone." Pe Ell smiled. "Steal the Elfstone and let father and son feed on each other. Nothing complicated about it, is there?" He glanced sharply at Quickening. "Is there?"

She met his gaze without flinching, but did not answer. Pe Ell's smile turned cold as he leaned back into the shadows.

There was a moment of strained silence, and then Morgan said to Horner Dees, "What about this Creeper you mentioned?"

Dees was looking sullen as well. He leaned forward ponderously, his eyes narrowed suspiciously. "Maybe the girl can tell you more about it than me," he answered quietly. "I've a feeling there's a great deal she knows and isn't telling."

Quickening's face was devoid of expression, coldly perfect as she faced the old Tracker. "I know what my father told me, Horner Dees—nothing more."

"King of the Silver River, Lord of the Gardens of Life," Pe Ell growled from the shadows. "Keeper of dark secrets."

"As you say, there is a Creeper in the city of Eldwist," Quickening went on, ignoring Pe Ell, her eyes on Dees. "Uhl Belk calls it the Rake. The Rake has been there for many years, a scavenger of living things serving the needs of its master. It comes out after dark and sweeps the streets and walkways of the city clean. We will have to be careful to avoid it when we go in."

"I've seen it at work," Dees grunted. "It took half a dozen of us on the first pass ten years ago, another two shortly after. It's big and quick." He was remembering now, and his anger at Quickening seemed to dissipate. He shook his head doubtfully. "I don't know. It hunts you out, finds you, finishes you. Goes into the buildings if it needs to. Did then, anyway."

"So it would be wise for us to find the Black Elfstone quickly, wouldn't it?" Pe Ell whispered.

They fell silent then, and after a few moments drifted away from each other into the shadows. They spent the remainder of the night attempting to sleep. Morgan dozed, but never for long. Walker was seated at the edge of the rocks watching the city when the Highlander nodded off and was still there when he woke. They were all tired and disheveled—all but Quickening. She stood fresh and new in the weak light of the morning sunrise, as beautiful as in the moment of their first meeting. Morgan found himself disturbed by the fact. In that way, certainly, she was something more than ordinary. He watched her, then looked quickly away when she turned toward him, afraid she would see. It bothered him to think that there might be differences between them after all and, worse, that those differences might be substantial.

They ate breakfast with the same lack of interest with which they had eaten dinner the night before. The land was a stark and ominous presence that watched them through hidden eyes. Fog hung across the peninsula, rising from the cliffs on which the city rested to the peaks of the tallest towers, giving the impression that Eldwist sat within the clouds. The seabirds had returned, gulls, puffins, and terns, wheeling and calling out above the dark waters of the Tiderace. A dampness had settled into the air with dawn's coming, and the water beaded on the faces of the six.

Having been warned by Dees of what lay ahead, they gathered rainwater from pools high in the rocks, wrapped what little food they still possessed against the wet, and set out to cross the isthmus.

It took them longer than they expected. The distance was short, but the path was treacherous. The rock was crisscrossed with crevices, its surface broken apart by ancient upheavals, damp and slick beneath their feet from the ocean's constant pounding. The wind gusted sharply, blowing spray in their faces, chilling their skin. Progress was slow. The sun remained a hazy white ball behind the low-hanging clouds, and the land ahead was filled with shadows. Eldwist rose before them, a cluster of vague shapes, dark and forbidding and silent. They watched it grow larger as they neared, rising steadily into the bleak skies, the sound of the wind echoing mournfully through its canyons.

Sometimes, as they walked, they could feel a rumbling beneath their feet, far distant, but ominously familiar. Apparently the Maw Grint didn't always sleep during the daylight hours.

Midday neared. The isthmus, which had been so narrow at points that the rock dropped away to either side of where they walked into dark cauldrons and whirlpools, broadened finally onto the peninsula and the outskirts of the city. The cliffs on which Eldwist had been built lifted before them, and the company was forced to climb a broad escarpment. Winding through a jumble of monstrous boulders along a pathway littered with loose stone, with their feet constantly sliding out from under them, they struggled resolutely ahead.

It took them the better part of two hours to gain the heights. By then the sun was already arcing west.

They paused to catch their breath at the city's edge, standing together at the end of a stone street that ran between rows of towering, vacant-windowed buildings and narrowed steadily until it disappeared into mist and shadow. Morgan Leah had never seen a city such as this one, the buildings flat and smooth, all constructed of stone, all symmetrically arranged like squares on a checkerboard. Broken rock littered the street, but beneath the rubble he could see the hard, even surface. It seemed as if it ran on forever, as if it had no end, a long, narrow corridor that disappeared only when the mist grew too thick for the eye to penetrate.

They began to walk it, a slow and cautious passage, spreading out along its corridor, listening and watching like cats at hunt. Other streets bisected it from out of the maze of tall buildings, these in turn disappearing right and left into shadow. There were no protective walls about Eldwist, no watchtowers or battlements or gates, only the buildings and the streets that fronted them. There appeared to be nothing living there. The streets and buildings came and went as the company pressed deeper, and the only sounds were those of the ocean and the wind and the seabirds. The birds flew overhead, the only sign of movement, winging their way past the caps of the buildings, down into the streets, across intersections and catwalks. Some roosted on the window ledges high overhead. After a time, Morgan saw that some of those he had believed roosting had been turned to stone.

Much of the debris that lay strewn about had once been something other than stone although most of it was not unrecognizable. Odd-looking poles stood at every street corner, and it was possible to surmise that these might have once been some form of lamps. The carcass of a monstrous carriage lay on its side against one building, a machine whose bones had been stripped of their flesh. Scattered pieces of engines had survived time and weather, gear wheels and cylinders, flywheels and tanks. All had turned to stone. There were no growing things, no trees or shrubs, or even the smallest blade of grass.

They looked inside a few of the buildings and found the rooms cavernous and empty. Stairways ran upward into the stone shells, and they climbed one set all the way to the top so that they could look out across Eldwist and orient themselves. It was impossible to tell much, even as little as where the city began and ended. Clouds and mist obscured everything, revealing only glimpses of facings and roofs in a sea of swirling gray.

They did sight an odd dome at Eldwist's center, a structure unlike the tall obelisks that formed the balance of the city, and they chose to explore it next.

But coming down again into the streets they lost their sense of direction and turned the wrong way. They walked for the better part of an hour before deciding they had made a mistake; then they were forced to climb the stairs of another building in order to regain their bearings.

While they were doing so, the sun set. None of them had been paying any attention to how quickly the daylight had been fading.

When they emerged from their climb they were stunned to find the city in darkness.

"We'd better find a place to hide right now," Horner Dees admonished, glancing around uneasily. "The Rake will be out soon if it isn't already. It if finds us unprotected . . ."

He didn't have to finish the thought. For a moment they stared wordlessly at one another. None of them had bothered looking for a nighttime shelter.

Then Walker Boh said, "There was a small building several streets back with no windows on the lower levels, a small entry, a maze of corridors and rooms inside—like a warren."

"Safe enough for the moment," Pe Ell muttered, already heading down the street.

They began to backtrack through the city. It was so dark by now that they could barely find their way. The buildings loomed to either side in a wall made more solid by the thickening of the mist. The seabirds had again gone to roost, and the sound of ocean and wind had faded into a distant lull. The city was uncomfortably still.

Beneath them, the stone shell of the earth rumbled and shook.

"Something's awake and hungry," Pe Ell murmured and smiled coldly at Carisman.

The tunesmith laughed nervously, his handsome face white and drawn.

He sang:

> *"Slip away, slip away, slip away home,*
> *Run for your bedcovers, no more to roam,*
> *Steal away quick from the things of the night,*
> *Keep yourself hidden and well out of sight."*

They crossed an intersection that was flooded with pale moonlight that had found a break in the clouds and was streaming down in a splash of white fire. Pe Ell stopped abruptly, bringing the rest of them up short as well, listened for a moment, shook his head, and moved on. The rumbling beneath them came and went, sometimes close, sometimes far, never in one spot at any given time, seemingly all around. Morgan Leah peered ahead through mist and shadows. Was this the same street they had been on before? It didn't look quite the same . . .

There was a loud click. Pe Ell, still in the lead, catapulted backward, careening into Horner Dees and Quickening, who were closest, the force of his thrust knocking them both from their feet. They tumbled down in a heap, inches from the edge of a gaping hole that had opened in the street.

"Get back against the buildings!" he snapped, leaping to his feet and sweeping Quickening up with him as he raced from the chasm's edge.

The others were only a step behind. Another section of the street gave way, this one behind them, falling with a crash into blackness. The rumbling beneath crescendoed into a roar that deafened them, and they could hear the passing of something massive below. Morgan crouched deep within a shadowed alcove, pressed up against the stone wall, fighting to keep from screaming against his fear. The Maw Grint! He saw Horner Dees next to him, his bearded face all but invisible as it turned away into the shadows. The thunder of the monster moving below peaked and then began to fade. Seconds later, it was gone.

The members of the little company came out of hiding then, one after another, white-faced and staring. They moved cautiously into the street, then started violently as the holes in the streets closed up again, the fallen sections lifting smoothly back into place.

"Trapdoors!" Pe Ell spat. There was fear and loathing in his face. Morgan caught sight of something white in his hand, a knife of some sort, its metal bright and shining. Then it was gone.

Pe Ell released Quickening from his grasp and turned away from them, moving back along the street, this time staying well up on the walkways that fronted the buildings. Wordlessly, eyes darting from one pool of shadows to the next, the others followed. They hastened down the walkway in single file, crossed the next intersection the same way, and hurried on. The rumbling sounded again, but far away now. The streets about them were quiet and empty once more.

Morgan Leah was still shaking. Those trapdoors had been placed there either to snare intruders or to let the Maw Grint into the city. Probably both. He swallowed against the dryness in his throat. They had been careless back there. They had better not be so again.

A heavy wall of mist blocked the way forward. Pe Ell hesitated as they approached it, then stopped. He looked back at Walker Boh, his eyes hard and penetrating. Some unspoken communication passed between them, a shared look that Morgan found almost feral. Walker glanced right. Pe Ell, after a moment's hesitation, turned that way.

They walked ahead, slowly now, listening to the silence again. The mist was all about them, fallen out of the clouds, seeped up from the stone, and come out of nowhere to envelop them. They moved with their hands stretched out to brush against the walls of the buildings for reassurance. Pe Ell was studying the path ahead carefully, aware now that the city was probably one vast collection of traps, that any part of the stone could drop away beneath their feet without warning.

Ahead, the mist began to clear.

Morgan thought he heard something, then decided he hadn't heard it, that he had sensed it instead. What?

They emerged from the shadow of the building next to them and the answer was waiting. The Rake stood in the center of the street, a huge, splay-legged metal monster with dozens of tentacles and feelers, pincers that gaped from its maw, and a whip-like tail. It was a Creeper like the one the outlaws of the Movement had faced at the Jut, comprised of metal and flesh, a hybrid nightmare of machine and insect. Except that this one was much bigger.

And much quicker. It came for them so fast that it was almost upon them before they had begun to scatter. Its wide, bent legs skittered like a centipede's. Tentacles swept out in a flurry of movement, the sound of metal scraping against stone a horrid rasp. The tentacles caught Dees and Carisman almost instantly, wrapping about them as they tried to flee. Pe Ell shoved Quickening across the walkway toward an open doorway, feinted as if to rush the monster, then darted away. Morgan drew his sword and would have attacked, having lost all sense of what he was doing at the thought of Quickening in danger, when Walker Boh caught hold of him and threw him back against the wall.

"Get inside!" the Dark Uncle cried, motioning toward a set of massive stone doors that gaped open.

Then Walker Boh threw back his cloak and his single arm came up. The Rake was almost on top of him when the arm lowered and a sheet of white light ignited. Morgan shrank back against the wall, blinded. He heard a harsh shriek and realized it was the Creeper. His vision cleared enough to see the creature's metal arms windmilling violently and caught a glimpse of Carisman and Horner Dees running from it. Then he was seized in an iron grip and thrust back through the black opening of the doorway.

It was Pe Ell who had yanked him inside. Quickening was already there. The white light of Walker's magic still burned through the darkness without, and they could hear the Rake thrashing against the building, the force of its attack so violent that stone chips were scattered everywhere. Walker burst into view, Carisman and Horner Dees running before him, stunned but freed. They stumbled across the floor and fell, then regained their feet instantly as the Rake tore the giant entry doors from their hinges, ripped the stone facing apart and shoved inside.

There was a broad staircase leading upward behind them, and they bolted for it. The Rake came after them, staggering slightly. If Walker's magic had done nothing else, it had momentarily disoriented the beast. Its tentacles lashed out wildly in an effort to snare its prey. The six dashed up the stairs. A single whiplash movement from below brought one arm across the steps before them, but Pe Ell's strange knife flashed into view, slicing across the arm and all but severing it. The arm withdrew. They raced upward, springing from one landing to the next, fleeing without looking back.

Finally, at a landing ten floors up, Walker brought them to a ragged halt. Behind them there was only silence. They stood in a knot, their breathing ragged as they listened.

"Perhaps it's given up," Carisman whispered, sounding hopeful.

"Not that thing," Horner Dees replied, his voice a muffled rasp as he fought to catch his breath. "That thing won't ever quit. I've seen what it can do."

Pe Ell thrust forward. "Since you claim to know so much about it, tell us what it might do here!" he snarled.

Dees shook his bearish head obstinately. "I don't know. We never made it as far as the buildings last time." Then he shuddered. "Shades! I can still feel those arms coming tight about me!" He glanced sideways at Quickening. "I should never have let you talk me into coming back here!"

"Hsssst!" Walker Boh was standing at the top of the stairs, head cocked. "There's something . . ." he started to say and stopped.

Pe Ell was next to him in a moment, crouched next to the stair railing. Suddenly he jerked upright. "It's outside!" he snarled and whirled about.

The once-glassed floor-to-ceiling latticework shattered into pieces across the landing as the Rake clawed its way in. Morgan was aghast. While the company had looked for it to come up the stairs, the Rake had climbed the wall!

For a second time, it almost had them. Tentacles whipped across the small space and knocked most of them from their feet. Pe Ell was too quick for it, however, and the strange knife materialized in his hand, shredding the nearest arm. The Creeper flinched away, then came for him. But the diversion had given Walker Boh time to act. A fistful of Cogline's black powder appeared in his hand. He threw it at the beast and fire exploded forth.

The company raced up the stairs once more—one floor, two, three. Behind them, the Creeper thrashed against the fire. Then everything went still. They could no longer hear it; but they all knew where it was. There were openings through the walls on each floor where the windows had fallen away over the years. The Creeper could attack through any of them. It would keep coming after them, and sooner or later it would have them.

"We'll have to stand and fight!" Morgan cried out to the others, snatching free his broadsword.

"Do that and we'll all die, Highlander!" Horner Dees shouted back.

Then Pe Ell brought them up short, lunging ahead and wheeling to face them. "Back down those stairs, the bunch of you! Now! Stay close and I'll see you out of this!"

No one stopped to argue, not even Walker. They retraced their steps in a rush, descending in leaps and bounds, eyes on the window openings at each floor. Two flights down they caught a glimpse of the Rake as it pulled itself level with the frame. Tentacles snaked out, falling short. As they darted away, they could hear the monstrous thing reverse itself against the stone and start after them.

Another three flights, still far from the ground, Pe Ell brought them to a halt once more. "Here! This is the spot!" He pushed them down a long, high-ceilinged corridor. Behind them, the Rake gained the landing and lumbered swiftly in pursuit. The creature seemed to elongate as it came, changing the shape of its body to allow it access. Morgan was terrified. This Creeper could adapt to any situation. Narrow passageways and long climbs were not nearly enough to stop it.

At the end of the corridor was an enclosed catwalk that crossed over to another building. "Get across as fast as you can!" Pe Ell snapped.

Morgan and the others did as they were told. But the Highlander despaired of escape this way. Narrow as the catwalk might be, it would not stop the Rake.

He reached the other side and turned with the others. Pe Ell was kneeling at the far end of the walk where it joined to the other building and sawing at the stone bracing with his strange knife. Morgan stared. Had Pe Ell lost his mind? Did he actually think his knife—any knife—could cut through stone? The Rake was almost on top of him before he was back on his feet. Cat-quick, he darted across the walk. He reached them just as the Rake eased into view, snakelike now as it entered the narrow tunnel opening.

And then the impossible happened. The bracing that Pe Ell had been sawing snapped and gave way. The catwalk lurched downward, held momentarily, then collapsed completely be-neath the weight of the Rake. Down it plunged to the street, shattering into fragments, dust and debris rising to mix with the mist and the night.

The six from Rampling Steep stared downward, waiting. Then they heard something—a scraping movement, the sound of metal on stone.

"It's not dead!" Dees whispered in horror.

They stepped back hurriedly from the opening and slipped down to the ground floor, exiting from a door on the far side of the building onto the street. With Pe Ell and Walker in the lead, they made their way silently through the dark. Behind them, they could hear the Creeper beginning to search again.

Less than five blocks away they came upon the building Walker Boh had been seeking, a squat, virtually windowless bunker. They entered with anxious backward glances and peered about. It was indeed a warren, a maze of rooms and corridors with several sets of stairs and half a dozen entries. They climbed four stories, settled themselves in a central room away from any windows, and crouched down to wait.

The minutes passed and the Rake did not appear. An hour came and went. They ate a cold meal and settled back. No one slept.

In the silence, their breathing was the only sound.

Toward dawn, Morgan Leah grew restless. He found himself thinking of Pe Ell's knife, a blade that could cut through stone. The knife intrigued him. Like Pe Ell's presence on this journey, it was an unsolved mystery. The Highlander took a deep breath. Despite Walker's warning to stay clear of the man, he decided to see what he could learn. Climbing to his feet he moved to the darkened corner where the other sat with his back to the wall. He could see Pe Ell's eyes track him as he approached.

"What do you want?" Pe Ell asked coldly.

Morgan crouched down in front of him, hesitating in spite of his resolve. "I was curious about your knife," he admitted after a moment.

Their voices were barely audible whispers in the stillness. In the darkened room, no one else could hear.

Pe Ell's smile was cold. "You are, are you?"

"We all saw what it did."

Pe Ell had the knife out instantly, the blade held inches from Morgan's nose. Morgan held his breath and did not move. "The only thing you need to know about this," Pe Ell swore, "is that it can kill you before you can blink. You. Your one-armed friend. Anyone."

Morgan swallowed hard. "Even the Stone King?" He forced the question out, angry with himself for being frightened.

The blade disappeared back into the shadows. "Let me tell you something. The girl says you have magic about you. I don't believe it. You have nothing. One-arm is the only one among you who has magic, and his magic doesn't do anything! It doesn't kill. *He* doesn't kill. I can see it in his eyes. None of you matters in this business, whether you know it or not. You're nothing but a pack of fools."

He jabbed at Morgan with his finger. "Don't get in my way, Highlander. Any of you. And don't expect me to save you the next time that Creeper comes hunting. I'm all done with the lot of you." He withdrew his hand scornfully. "Now get away from me."

Morgan retreated wordlessly. He glanced briefly at Walker as he went, ashamed he had ignored the other's warning about Pe Ell. It was impossible to tell if the Dark Uncle had been watching. Dees and Carisman were asleep. Quickening was a faceless, barely distinguishable shadow.

Morgan sat cross-legged in a corner by himself, seething. He had learned nothing. All he had done was humiliate himself. His mouth tightened. One day he would have the use of his sword again. One day he would find a way to make it whole and recapture its magic—just as Quickening had said he would.

Then he would deal with Pe Ell.

He made himself a promise of it.

XIX

The company emerged from its concealment at daybreak. Clouds masked the skies over Eldwist from horizon to horizon, morning's arrival bleak and gray. A faint brightening of the damp, misty air was the best that dawn could manage, and night's shadows merely retreated into the city's alcoves and nooks to await their mistress' return.

There was no sign of the Rake. The six from Rampling Steep scanned the gloom cautiously. The buildings rose about them, massive and silent. The streets stretched away, canyons of stone. The only sounds were the howl of the wind, the crashing of the ocean, and the cries of the high-flying seabirds. The only movements were their own.

"As if it were never here," Horner Dees muttered as he shouldered his way past Morgan. "As if it were all a dream."

They began the search again for Uhl Belk. Rain fell through a curtain of smoky mist that tasted and smelled of the sea, and they were soaked through in minutes. A damp sheen settled across the stone walkways and streets, the walls of the buildings, the rubble and debris, a coating that mirrored the gloom and the shadows and played tricks with the light. The wind blew in sharp gusts, darting out of hiding at corners and alleyways, racing down the city's corridors with shrieks of delight, chasing itself endlessly. The morning wore on, a slow grinding of gears in some vast machine that could only be heard in the mind and felt in the wearing of the spirit. Time stole from them, they sensed. Time was a thief.

They found no trace of the Stone King. The city was vast and filled with hiding places, and even if they were sixty instead of six a thorough search could take weeks. None of them had any idea where to look for Uhl Belk or, worse, any idea what he looked like. Even Quickening could offer no help. Her father had not told her how the Stone King might appear. Did he look as they did? Was he human in form? Was he large or small? Morgan asked these questions as they trudged through the gloom, keeping well back on the walkways, close to the building walls. No one knew. They were searching for a ghost.

Midday passed. The buildings and streets of the city came and went in an endless procession of obelisks and gleaming black ribbons. The rain lessened, then increased. Thunder rumbled overhead, slow and ominous. The six ate a cold meal and drank a little in the dank, shadowed entry of one of the buildings while the rain turned into a downpour that flooded the streets with several inches of churning water. They peered outside and watched as the water gathered and flowed in small rivers to stone drains that swallowed it up.

They resumed walking when the rainfall lessened again and shortly afterward came upon the strange dome they had seen from the top of the building they had climbed the previous day. It sat amid the stone spires, a monstrous shell, its surface pitted and worn and cracked. They walked its circumference, searched for an entry, and found none. There were no doors, no stairs, no windows, nor openings of any kind. There were alcoves and niches and insets of varying sizes and shapes that gave its armor a sculpted look, but no way in or out. There were no footholds or ladders that would allow them to climb to its top. It was impossible to determine what it might have been used for. It sat there in the gloom and damp and defied them.

Mindful of time's rapid passing after yesterday's debacle, they returned early to their shelter. No one had much to say. They sat in the growing darkness, mostly apart from each other, mostly silent, and kept their thoughts to themselves.

There had been no sign of either the Maw Grint or the Rake that day. Nightfall brought them both out. They heard the Rake first, a skittering of metal legs on the stone street below, passing by without stopping as they held their collective breath. The Maw Grint came later, the sound of its approach a low rumbling that quickly became a roar. The monster burst forth, howling as it rose into the night. It was uncomfortably close; the stone of the building in which they hid shook with its cry. Then, just as quickly as it had come, it was gone again. No one made any attempt to try to catch a glimpse of it. Everyone stayed carefully put.

They slept better that night, perhaps because they were grow-

ing used to the city's night sounds, perhaps because they were
so exhausted. They posted a watch and took turns standing it.
The watch proved uneventful.

For three days afterward they continued their search. Fog and
mist and rain hunted with them, persistent and unwelcome, and
the city haunted their dreams. Eldwist was a stone forest filled
with shadows and secrets, its towering buildings the trees that
hemmed them in and closed them about. But unlike the green,
living forests of the lands south the city was empty and lifeless.
The girl and the men could form no affinity with Eldwist; they
were trespassers here, unwanted and alone. Everything about
the world in which they hunted was hard and unyielding. There
were no recognizable signs, no familiar markings, and no
changes in color or shape or smell or taste that would reveal to
them even the smallest clue. There was only the enigma of the
stone.

It began to affect the little company despite its resolve. Conversation diminished, tempers grew short, and there was a
growing uncertainty as to what they were about. Horner Dees
became more sullen and taciturn, his skills as a Tracker rendered
useless, his experience from ten years previous used up. Pe Ell
continued to distance himself, his eyes suspicious, his movements furtive and tense, a prowling cat at the edges of a jungle
determined not to be brought to bay. Carisman quit singing
almost completely. Morgan Leah found himself jumping at the
smallest sound and was preoccupied with thoughts of the magic
he had lost when the Sword of Leah had shattered. Walker Boh
was a voiceless ghost, pale and aloof, floating through the gloom
as if at any moment he might simply fade away.

Even Quickening changed. It was barely perceptible, a faint
blurring of her exquisite beauty, an odd shading of her voice
and movements, and a vague weariness in her eyes. Morgan,
ever aware of what the girl was about, thought that he alone
could tell.

But once, as they paused in their search in the shadow of a
carriage husk, Walker Boh eased down beside the Highlander
and whispered, "This city consumes us, Morgan Leah. Can you
feel it? It has a life beyond what we understand, an extension of
the Stone King's will, and it feeds on us. The magic is all about.
If we do not find Uhl Belk soon, we will be in danger of being
swallowed up entirely. Do you see? Even Quickening is affected."

And she was, of course. Walker drifted away again, and Mor-

gan was left to wonder to what end they had been brought here.
So much effort expended to reach this place and it all seemed
for nothing. They were being drained of life, sapped of energy
and purpose and will. He thought to speak of it to Quickening,
but changed his mind. She knew what was happening. She always did. When it was time to do something, she would do it.

But it was Walker Boh who acted first. The fourth day of their
hunt for the Stone King had concluded in the same manner as
the previous three, without any of them having found even the
smallest trace of their quarry. They were huddled in the shadows
of their latest shelter; Pe Ell had insisted they change buildings
in an effort to avoid discovery by the Rake, who still hunted
them each night. They had not eaten a hot meal or enjoyed a
fire's warmth since their arrival in Eldwist, and their water sup-
ply was in need of replenishing. Footsore and discouraged, they
sat mired in silence.

"We need to search the tunnels beneath the city," the Dark
Uncle said suddenly, his soft voice distant and cold.

The others looked up. "What tunnels?" Carisman wearily
asked. The tunesmith, less fit than the others, was losing
strength.

"The ones that honeycomb the rock beneath the buildings,"
Walker answered. "There are many of them. I have seen the
stairways leading down from the streets."

Bearish Horner Dees shook his shaggy head. "You forget.
The Maw Grint is down there."

"Yes. Somewhere. But it is a huge, blind worm. It won't even
know of us if we're careful. And if the Maw Grint hides within
the earth, maybe the Stone King hides there as well."

Morgan nodded. "Why not? They might both be worms.
Maybe both are blind. Maybe neither likes the light. Goodness
knows, there will be little enough of it down there. I think it is
a good idea."

"Yes," Quickening agreed without looking at any of them.

Pe Ell stirred in the shadows and said nothing. The others
muttered their assent. The darkness of their refuge went quickly
still again.

That night Quickening slept next to Morgan Leah, something
she had not done since their arrival in Eldwist. She came to him
unexpectedly and burrowed close, as if she feared something
would attempt to steal her away. Morgan reached around and
held her for a time, listening to the sound of her breathing,
feeling the pulse of her body against his own. She did not speak.

After a time, he fell asleep holding her. When he awoke, she was gone again.

At dawn they departed their shelter and entered the catacombs beneath the city. A stairwell leading down from the building next to the one in which they were housed placed them on the first level. Other stairs ran deeper into the rock, spiraling down black holes of stone into emptiness. The tunnels on the first level were shaped from stone blocks and rails sat on beds of stone and cross ties as they disappeared into the dark. All had been turned to stone. There was no light beneath the city, so Walker Boh used one of Cogline's powders to coat the head of a narrow wedge of stone and create a firebrand. They moved ahead into the tunnels, following the line of the rails as they wound through the darkness. The rails passed platforms and other stairs leading up and down, and the tunnels branched and diverged. The air smelled musty, and loose stone crunched beneath their feet. After a time they came upon a giant carriage that lay upon its side, its wheels grooved to fit the rails, but broken and splintered now and fused to the axle and body by the magic's transformation. Once this carriage had ridden the rails, propelled in some mysterious way, carrying people of the old world from building to building, and from street to street. The members of the company paused momentarily to gaze upon the wreck, then hurried on.

There were other carriages along the way, once an entire chamber full of them, some still seated upon the rails, some fallen and smashed along the way. There were piles of debris fallen by the rails that could not be identified and bits and pieces of what had been iron benches on the platforms they passed. Once or twice they ascended the stairs back to the streets of the city to regain their bearings before going down again. Below, far from where they walked, they could hear the rumble of the Maw Grint. Farther down still there was the sound of the ocean.

After several hours of exploring the network of tunnels without encountering any sign of the Stone King, Pe Ell brought them up short. "This is a waste of time," he said. "There's nothing to be found at this level. We need to go farther down."

Walker Boh glanced at Quickening, then nodded. Morgan caught sight of the looks on the faces of Carisman and Horner Dees and decided the same look was probably on his own.

They descended to the next level, winding down the stairwell into a maze of sewers. The sewers were empty and dry, but there was no mistaking what they had once been. The pipes that formed them were more than twenty feet high. Like everything else, they had been turned to stone. The company began following them, the light of Walker's makeshift torch a silver flare against the black, and the sound of their boots thudding harshly in the stillness. Not more than a hundred yards from where they had entered the sewers, a giant hole had been torn in the side of the stone pipe, shattering it apart as if it were paper. Something massive had burrowed through the rock and out again, something so huge that the sewer pipe had been no more than a blade of grass in its path.

From down the black emptiness of the burrowed tunnel came the rumble of the Maw Grint. The company crossed quickly through the rubble-strewn opening and continued on.

For two hours they wandered the sewers beneath the city, searching in vain for the lair of the Stone King. They twisted and wound about, and soon any sense of direction was irretrievably lost. There were fewer stairs leading up from this level, and many of them were nothing more than ladders hammered into the walls of drains. They came across the burrowings of the Maw Grint several times in the course of their hunt, the massive, jagged openings ripping upward through the earth and then disappearing down into it again, chasms of blackness large enough to swallow whole buildings. Morgan Leah stared into those chasms, realized they must honeycomb the peninsula rock, and wondered why the entire city didn't simply collapse into them.

Shortly after midday they stopped to rest and eat. They found a set of steps leading up to the first level and climbed to where an abandoned platform offered a set of battered stone benches. Seated there, Walker's odd torch planted in the rubble so that its light spilled over them like a halo, they stared wordlessly into the shadows.

Morgan finished before the others and moved over to where a thin shaft of daylight knifed down a stairwell leading to the streets of the city. He seated himself and stared upward, thinking of better times and places, wondering despondently if he would ever find them again.

Carisman came over to sit beside him. "It would be nice to see the sun again," the tunesmith mused and smiled faintly as Morgan glanced over. "Even for just a moment."

He sang:

"Darkness is for bats and cats and frightened little mice,
It's not for those of us who find the sunshine rather nice,

So stay away from Eldwist's murk and take this good advice,
Go someplace where your skin is warm instead of cold as
    ice.''

He grinned rather sadly. "Isn't that a terrible piece of dog-
gerel? It must be the worst song I've ever composed."

"Where did you come from, Carisman?" Morgan asked him.
"I mean, before the Urdas and Rampling Steep. Where is your
home?"

Carisman shook his head. "Anywhere. Everywhere. I call
wherever I am my home, and I have been most places. I have
been traveling since I was old enough to walk."

"Do you have a family?"

"No. Not that I know about." Carisman drew his knees up
to his chest and hugged them. "If I am to die here, there is no
one who will wonder what has become of me."

Morgan snorted. "You're not going to die. None of us are.
Not if we're careful." The intensity of Carisman's gaze made
him uncomfortable. "I have a family. A father and mother back
in the Highlands. Two younger brothers as well. I haven't seen
them now in weeks."

Carisman's handsome face brightened. "I traveled the Highlands some years back. It was beautiful country, the hills all
purple and silver in the early light, almost red when the sun set.
It was quiet up there, so still you could hear the sound of the
birds when they called out from far away." He rocked slightly.
"I could have been happy there if I had stayed."

Morgan studied him a moment, watched him stare off into
space, caught up in some inner vision. "I plan to go back when
we're done with this business," he said. "Why don't you come
home with me?"

Carisman stared at him. "Would that be all right? I would
like that."

Morgan nodded. "Consider it done. But let's not have any
more talk about dying."

They were silent for a moment before Carisman said, "Do
you know that the closest thing I ever had to a family was the
Urdas? Despite the fact that they kept me prisoner, they took
care of me. Cared about me, too. And I cared about them. Like
a family. Strange."

Morgan thought about his own family for a moment, his father and mother and brothers. He remembered their faces, the
sound of their voices, the way they moved and acted. That led

him to think of the Valemen, Par and Coll. Where were they? Then he thought of Steff, dead several weeks now, already becoming a memory, fading into the history of his past. He thought of the promise he had made to his friend—that if he found a magic that could aid the Dwarves in their struggle to be free again, he would use it—against the Federation—against the Shadowen. A rush of determination surged through him and dissipated again. Maybe the Black Elfstone would prove to be the weapon he needed. If it could negate other magics, if it were indeed powerful enough to bring back disappeared Paranor by counteracting the spell of magic that bound it . . .

"They liked the music, you know, but it was more than just that," Carisman was saying. "I think they liked me as well. They were a lot like children in need of a father. They wanted to hear all about the world beyond their valley, about the Four Lands and the peoples that lived there. Most of them had never been anywhere beyond the Spikes. I had been everywhere."

"Except here," Morgan said with a smile.

But Carisman only looked away. "I wish I had never come here," he said.

The company resumed its search of the sewers of Eldwist and continued to find them empty of life. They discovered nothing—not the smallest burrowing rodent, not a bat, not even the insects that normally thrived underground. There was no sign of Uhl Belk. There was only the stone that marked his passing. They wandered for several hours and then began to retrace their steps. Daylight would be gone shortly, and they had no intention of being caught outside when the Rake began its nocturnal scavenging.

"It may be, however, that it doesn't come down into the tunnels," Walker Boh mused.

But no one wanted to find out, so they kept moving. They followed the twisting catacombs, recrossed the burrowings of the Maw Grint, and pushed steadily ahead through the darkness. Grunting and huffing were the only sounds to be heard. Tension lined their faces. Their eyes reflected their discouragement and discontent. No one spoke. What they were thinking needed no words.

Then Walker brought them to a sudden halt and pointed off into the gloom. There was an opening in the tunnel, one that they had somehow missed earlier, smaller than the sewers and virtually invisible in the dimness. Walker crouched down to peer inside, then disappeared into the dark.

A moment later he returned. "There is a cavern and a stairwell leading down," he reported. "It appears there is yet another set of tunnels below."

They followed him through the opening to the chamber beyond, a cave whose walls and floors were studded with jagged projections and rent with deep clefts. They found the stairwell and looked down into its gloom. It was impossible to see anything. They exchanged uneasy glances. Wordlessly, Walker moved to the head of the stairs. Holding the makeshift torch out in front of him, he started down. After a moment's hesitation, the others followed.

The stairs descended a long way, ragged and slick with moisture. The smell of the Tiderace was present here, and they could hear the trickle of seawater in the blackness. When they reached the end of the stairs, they found themselves standing in the middle of a broad, high tunnel in which the rock was crystallized and massive stone icicles hung from the ceiling in clusters, dripping water into black pools. Walker turned right, and the company moved ahead. The dampness chilled the air to ice, and the six pulled their cloaks tightly about them for warmth. Echoes of their footsteps reverberated through the stone corridor, chasing the silence.

Then suddenly there was something else, a sort of squealing that reminded Morgan Leah of a rusted iron lever being shifted after a long period of disuse. The members of the company stopped as one at its sound and stood in the faint silver glow of the torchlight, listening. The squealing continued; it was coming from somewhere behind them.

"Come," Walker Boh said sharply and began hurrying ahead. The others hastened after, spurred on by the unexpected urgency in his voice. Walker had recognized something in the sound that they had not. Morgan glanced over his shoulder as he went. What was back there?

They crossed a shallow stream of water that tumbled from a fissure in the rock wall, and Walker turned, motioning the rest of them past. The squealing sound was deafening now and coming closer. The Dark Uncle passed the torch to Morgan wordlessly, then lifted his arm and threw something into the black. A white fire flared to life, and the tunnel behind them was suddenly filled with light.

Morgan gasped. There were rats everywhere, a churning, scrambling mass of furred bodies. But these rats were giants, grown to three and four times their normal size, all claws and teeth. Their eyes were white and sightless, like everything else the company had encountered in Eldwist, and their bodies were sleek with the dampness of the sea. They looked ravenous. And maddened. They poured out of the rocks and came for the men and the girl.

"Run!" Walker cried, snatching the torch back from Morgan.

And run they did, charging frantically through the darkness with the sound of the squealing chasing after them in gathering waves, struggling to keep at the edges of the torchlight as they fought to escape the horror that pursued. The tunnel rose and fell in ragged slopes, and the rocks cut and scraped at them. They fell repeatedly, scrambled up again, and ran on.

A ladder! That was all that Morgan Leah could think. *We've got to find a ladder!*

But there was none. There were only the rock walls, the streams and pools of seawater, and the rats. And themselves, trapped.

Then from somewhere ahead came a new sound, the booming of waves against a shoreline, the pounding of the ocean against land.

They broke from the blackness of the tunnel into a faint, silvery brightness and staggered to a ragged halt. Before them a cliff dropped sharply into the Tiderace. The ocean churned and swirled below, crashing into the rocks, foaming white as it spilled over them. They were in an underground cavern so massive that its farthest reaches were lost in mist and shadow. Daylight spilled through clefts in the rock where the ocean had breached the wall. Other tunnels opened into the cavern as well, black holes far to the right and left. All were unreachable. The cliffs to either side were impassable. The drop below led to the rocks and the roiling sea. The only way left was back the way they had come.

Through the rats.

The rats were almost on top of the company now, their squeals rising up to overwhelm the thunder of the ocean's waters, their masses filling the lower half of the tunnel as they bit and clawed ahead. Morgan yanked out his broadsword, knowing even as he did so how futile the weapon would be. Pe Ell had moved to one side, clear of the others, and his strange silver knife was in his hand. Dees and Carisman were backed to the edge of the drop, crouched as if to jump.

Quickening stepped forward beside Morgan, her beautiful face strangely calm, her hands steady on his arm.

Then Walker Boh cast aside his torch and hurled a fistful of black powder into the horde of rats. Fire exploded everywhere, and the first rank was incinerated. But there were hundreds more behind that one, thousands of churning dark bodies. Claws scraped madly on the rocks, seeking to find a grip. Teeth and sightless eyes gleamed. The rats came on.

"Walker!" Morgan cried out desperately and shoved Quickening behind him.

But it wasn't the Dark Uncle who responded to Morgan's plea, or Pe Ell, or Horner Dees, or even Quickening. It was Carisman, the tunesmith.

He rushed forward, pushing past Morgan and Quickening, coming up beside Walker just as the rats burst through the tunnel opening onto the narrow ledge. Lifting his wondrous voice, he began to sing. It was a song that was different than any they had ever heard; it scraped like the rub of metal on stone, shrieked like the tearing of wood, and broke through the thunder of the ocean and the squeal of the rats to fill the cavern with its sound.

"Come to me!" Quickening cried out to the rest of them.

They bunched close at once, even Pe Ell, flattening themselves against one another as the tunesmith continued to sing. The rats poured out of the tunnel and swept toward them in a wave of struggling bodies. But then the wave split apart, flowing to either side of the tunesmith, passing by without touching any of them. Something in Carisman's song was turning them away. They twisted to either side, a churning mass. Onward they scrambled, heedless of everything, whether fleeing or being called it was impossible to tell, and tumbled into the sea.

Moments later, the last of them had been swallowed up or swept away. Carisman went still, then collapsed into Morgan's arms. The Highlander propped him up, and Quickening wiped cold seawater onto his face with the sleeve of her tunic. The others glanced about breathlessly, cautiously, scanning the dark tunnel opening, the empty rock, the waters of the sea.

"It worked," Carisman whispered in surprise as his eyes fluttered open again. "Did you see? It worked!" He struggled up and seized Quickening jubilantly by the arms. "I'd read something about it once, or heard about it maybe, but I had never thought I would . . . I mean, I had never tried such a thing before! Never! It was a cat song, Lady! A cat song! I didn't know what else to do, so I made those horrid rodents think we were giant cats!''

Everyone stared in disbelief. Only then did Morgan Leah appreciate how truly miraculous their escape had been.

XX

With the destruction of the rats, they were able to retrace their steps through the tunnel that had brought them to the underground cavern, climb back into the sewers of Eldwist, climb from there to the level of tunnels above, and finally reach the streets of the city. It was already growing dark, and they hurried quickly through the descending gloom to gain the safety of their nighttime refuge. They only just succeeded. The Rake appeared almost at once, an invisible presence beyond the walls of the building, its armored legs scraping across the stone below, searching for them still. They sat huddled silently in the dark listening to it hunt until it had gone. Walker said he thought the creature could track by smell, only the rain and the number of trails they had left was confusing it. Sooner or later it would figure out where they were hiding.

Exhausted and aching and shaken by what had befallen them, they ate their dinner in silence and went quickly off to sleep.

The next morning Pe Ell, who following their escape from the tunnels had descended into a mood so black that no one dared approach him, announced that he was going out on his own.

''There are too many of us stumbling about to ever find anything,'' he declared, his voice calm and expressionless, his narrow face unreadable. He spoke to Quickening, as if only she mattered. ''If there truly is a Stone King, he knows by now that we are here. This is his city; he can hide in it forever if he chooses. The only way to find him is to catch him off guard, sneak up on him, and surprise him. There will be none of that if we continue to hunt like a pack of dogs.''

Morgan started to intervene, but Walker's fingers closed about his arm like iron bands.

Pe Ell glanced around. ''The rest of you can keep bumbling about as long as you wish. But you'll do it without me. I've spent enough time shepherding you around. I should have gone off on my own from the first. If I had, this business would be finished by now.'' He turned back to Quickening. ''When I have found Uhl Belk and the Black Elfstone, I will come back for you.'' He paused, meeting her gaze squarely. ''If you are still alive.''

He strode past them contemptuously and disappeared down the hall. His boots thudded softly on the stairs and faded into silence.

Horner Dees spit. ''We're well rid of that one,'' he muttered.

''He is correct, though,'' Walker Boh said, and they all turned to look at him. ''In one respect at least. We must divide ourselves up into groups if we are ever to complete this search. The city is too large, and we are too easy to avoid while we stay together.''

''Two groups then,'' Dees agreed, nodding his shaggy head. ''No one goes out alone.''

''Pe Ell doesn't seem worried about hunting alone,'' Morgan noted.

''He's a predator, sure enough,'' Dees replied. He looked at Quickening speculatively. ''How about it, girl? Does he have any chance of finding Belk and the Elfstone on his own?''

But Quickening only said, ''He will return.''

They seated themselves to work out a strategy, a method by which the city could be searched from end to end. The buildings ran mostly north of where they were concealed, so it was decided to divide Eldwist in two with one group taking the east half and the other the west. The search would concentrate on the buildings and streets, not the tunnels. If nothing were found aboveground, they would change their approach.

''Pe Ell may be wrong when he says that the Stone King must know we are here,'' Quickening said in closing. She brought her slender fingers up in a quick, birdlike movement. ''We are insignificant in his eyes, and he may not yet have even noticed us. We are the reason he keeps the Rake in service. Besides, the Maw Grint occupies his time.''

"How do we divide ourselves up?" Carisman asked.

"You will go with me," Quickening answered at once. "And Walker Boh."

Morgan was surprised. He had expected her to choose him. The disappointment he felt cut deeply. He started to dispute her choice, but her black eyes fixed him with such intensity that he went instantly still. Whatever her reasons for making this decision, she did not want it questioned.

"That leaves you and me, Highlander," Horner Dees grunted and clapped one heavy hand on Morgan's shoulder. "Think we can manage to disappoint Pe Ell and keep our skins whole?"

His sudden laugh was so infectious that Morgan found himself smiling in response. "I'd bet on it," he replied.

They gathered up their gear and went down into the street. Sheets of gloom draped the buildings, hung from skies thick with clouds and mist. The air was damp and chill, and their breath exhaled in a haze of white. They wished each other well and began moving off in separate directions, Morgan and Horner Dees going west, Quickening, Walker, and Carisman east.

"Take care of yourself, Morgan," Quickening whispered, her exquisite face a mix of shadow and light beneath the sweep of her silver hair. She touched him softly on the shoulder and hurried after Walker Boh.

"Tra-la-la-la, a-hunting we will go!" Carisman sang merrily as they disappeared.

Rain began to fall in a steady drizzle. Morgan and Horner Dees slogged ahead with their cloaks pulled tightly about their shoulders and their heads bent. They had agreed that they would follow the street to its end, until they were at the edge of the city, then turn north to track the peninsula's shoreline. There had been little enough found within the core of the city; perhaps there was something outside—particularly if the Stone King's magic was ineffective against water. They kept to the walkways and glanced cautiously down the darkened corridors of the side-streets they passed. Rainwater collected on the city's stone skin in puddles and streams, shimmering darkly in the gloom. Seabirds huddled in nooks and crevices, waiting out the storm. In the shadows, nothing moved.

It was nearing midmorning when they reached the Tiderace, the land ending in cliffs which dropped hundreds of feet into the sea. Craggy outcroppings of rock rose out of the churning waters, worn and pitted. Waves crashed against the cliffs, the sound of their pounding mixing with the wind as it swept off the water in a rising howl. Morgan and Dees melted back into the shelter of the outer buildings, seeking to protect themselves. Rain and ocean spray soaked them quickly through, and they were soon shivering beneath their clothes. For two hours they skirted the city's western boundaries without finding anything. By midday, when they stopped to eat, they were disgruntled and worn.

"There's nothing to be found out here, Highlander," Dees observed, chewing on a bit of dried beef—his last. "Just the sea and the wind and those confounded birds, shrieking and calling like madwomen."

Morgan nodded without answering. He was trying to decide whether he could eat a seabird if he had to. Their food supplies were almost exhausted. Soon they would be forced to hunt. What else was there besides those birds? Fish, he decided firmly. The birds looked too rangy and tough.

"You miss the Highlands?" Dees asked him suddenly.

"Sometimes." He thought about his home and smiled faintly. "All the time."

"Me, too, and I haven't seen them in years. Thought they were the most beautiful piece of work nature ever made. I liked how they made me feel when I was in them."

"Carisman said he liked it there, too. He said he liked the quiet."

"The quiet. Yes, I remember how quiet it was in those hills." They had found shelter in a building's shadowed entry. The big man shifted himself away from a widening stain where the rain had trickled down the wall and collected on the steps where they were seated, backs to the wall, facing out into the weather.

He leaned forward. "Let me tell you something," he said softly. "I know this fellow, Pe Ell."

Morgan looked over, intrigued. "From where?"

"From before. Long before. Almost twenty years. He was just a kid then; I was already old." Dees chuckled darkly. "Some kid. A killer even then. An assassin right from the beginning— as if that was what he was born to be and he couldn't ever be anything else but." He shook his grizzled head. "I knew him. I knew it was bad luck if you crossed him."

"Did you?"

"Cross him? Me? No, not me. I know well enough who to stand up to and who to back away from. Always have. That's how I've stayed alive. Pe Ell is the kind who once he takes a dislike to you will keep coming till you're dead. Doesn't matter how long it takes him or how he gets the job done. He'll just keep at it.'' He pointed at Morgan. ''You better understand something. I don't know what he's doing here. I don't know why the girl brought him. But he's no friend to any of you. You know what he is? He's a Federation assassin. Their best, in fact. He's Rimmer Dall's favorite boy.''

Morgan froze, the blood draining from his face. ''That can't be.''

''Can and is,'' Dees said emphatically. ''Unless things have changed from how they used to be, and I doubt they have.''

Morgan shook his head in disbelief. ''How do you know all this, Horner?''

Horner Dees smiled, a wide, hungry grin. ''Funny thing about that. I remember him even though he doesn't remember me. I can see it in his eyes. He's trying to figure out what it is I know that he doesn't. Have you seen the way he looks at me? Trying to figure it out. Been too long, I guess. He's killed too many men, has too many faces in his past to remember many of them. Me, I been gone a long time. I don't have so many ghosts to worry about.'' He paused. ''Truth is, Highlander, I was one of them myself.''

''One of them?'' Morgan asked quietly.

The other gave a sharp laugh, like a bark. ''I was with the Federation! I tracked for them!''

As quick as that Morgan Leah's perception of Horner Dees changed. The big, bearish fellow was no longer just a gruff, old Tracker whose best days were behind him; he was no longer even a friend. Morgan started to back away and then realized there was nowhere to back to. He reached for his broadsword.

''Highlander!'' Dees snapped, freezing him. The big man clenched one massive fist, then relaxed it. ''Like I said, that was long ago. I been gone from those people twenty years. Settle back. You haven't any reason to fear me.''

He placed his hands in his lap, palms up. ''Anyway, that's how I came to see the Highlands, believe it or not—in the service of the Federation. I was tracking Dwarf rebels for them, hunting the Rainbow Lake and Silver River country. Never found much. Dwarves are like foxes; they go to ground quick as a wink when they know they're being hunted.'' He smiled unexpectedly. ''I didn't try very hard in any case. It was a worthless sort of job.''

Morgan released his grip on the broadsword and sat back again.

''I was with them long enough to find out about Pe Ell,'' the other went on, and now his eyes were distant and troubled. ''I knew most of what was happening back then. Rimmer Dall had me slated to be a Seeker. Can you imagine? Me? I thought that wolf's head stuff was nonsense. But I learned about Pe Ell while Dall was working on me. Saw him come and go once, when he didn't know it. Dall arranged for me to see because he liked putting one over on Pe Ell. It was a sort of game with the two of them, each trying to show up the other. Anyway, I saw him and heard what he did. A few others heard things, too. Everyone knew to stay away from him.''

He sighed. ''Just a little while after that, I quit the bunch of them. Left when no one was looking, came north through the Eastland, traveled about until I reached Rampling Steep, and decided that was where I'd live. Away from the madness south, the Federation, the Seekers, all of it.''

''All of it?'' Morgan repeated doubtfully, still trying to decide what to make of Horner Dees. ''Even the Shadowen?''

Dees blinked. ''What do you know of the Shadowen, Morgan Leah?''

Morgan leaned forward. Windblown mist had left Horner's face damp and shining, and droplets of water clung to his hair and beard. ''I want to know something from you first. Why are you telling me all this?''

The other's smile was strangely gentle. ''Because I want you to know about Pe Ell, and you can't know about him without knowing about me. I like you, Highlander. You remind me a little of myself when I was your age—kind of reckless and headstrong, not afraid of anything. I don't want there to be secrets about me that might come out in a bad way. Like if Pe Ell should remember who I am. I want you for a friend and ally. I don't trust anyone else.''

Morgan studied him wordlessly for a moment. ''You might do better with someone else.''

''I'll chance it. Now, how about it? I've answered your question. You tell me how you know about the Shadowen.''

Morgan drew up his knees and hugged them to his chest, making up his mind. Finally, he said, ''My best friend was a Dwarf named Steff. He was with the Resistance. The woman he loved was a Shadowen, and she killed him. I killed her.''

Horner Dees arched his eyebrows quizzically. ''I was given to understand that nothing but magic could kill those things.''

Morgan reached down and drew out the shattered end of the Sword of Leah. ''There was magic in this Sword once,'' he said. ''Allanon put it there himself—three hundred years ago. I broke it during a battle with the Shadowen in Tyrsis before the start of all this. Even so, there was still enough magic left to avenge Steff and save myself.'' He studied the blade speculatively, hefted it, waited in vain to feel its warmth, then looked back at Dees. ''Maybe there's still some. Anyway, that's why Quickening brought me along. This Sword. She said there was a chance it could be restored.''

Horner Dees frowned. ''Are you to use it against Belk then?''

''I don't know,'' Morgan admitted. ''I haven't been told anything except that it could be made whole again.'' He slipped the broken blade back into its scabbard. ''Promises,'' he said and sighed.

''She seems like the kind who keeps hers,'' the other observed after a moment's thought. ''Magic to find magic. Magic to prevail over magic. Us against the Stone King.'' He shook his head. ''It's too complicated for me. You just be sure you remember what I said about Pe Ell. You can't turn your back on him. And you mustn't go up against him either. You leave that to me.''

''You?'' Morgan declared in surprise.

''That's right. Me. Or Walker Boh. One-armed or not, he's a match for Pe Ell or I've misjudged him completely. You concentrate on keeping the girl safe.'' He paused. ''Shouldn't be too hard, considering how you feel about each other.''

Morgan flushed in spite of himself. ''It's mostly me that's feeling anything,'' he muttered awkwardly.

''She's the prettiest thing I've ever seen,'' the old man said, smiling at the other's discomfort. ''I don't know what she is, human or elemental or what, but she can charm the boots right off you. She looks at you, that face softens, she speaks the way she does, and you'll do anything for her. I should know. I wasn't ever going to come back to this place and here I am. She's done it to all of us.''

Morgan nodded. ''Even to Pe Ell. He's as much hers as the rest of us.''

But Dees shook his head. ''I don't know, Highlander. You look careful next chance you get. He's hers, but he isn't. She walks a fine line with that one. He could turn quick as a cat. That's why I tell you to look after her. You remember what he is. He's not here to do us any favors. He's here for himself. Sooner or later, he'll revert to form.''

''I think so, too,'' Morgan agreed.

Dees gave a satisfied smirk. "But it won't be so easy for him now, will it? Because we'll be watching."

They packed up, tightened their cloaks against the weather, and stepped back out into the downpour. They continued to follow the shoreline as the afternoon lengthened, reaching the northernmost point of the peninsula without finding anything, and turned back again into the city. The rain finally ended, changing to a fine mist that hung like smoke against the gray sky and buildings. The air warmed. Shadows yawned and stretched in alleyways and nooks like waking spirits, and steam rose off the streets.

From somewhere underground the rumble of the Maw Grint sounded, a distant thunder that shook the earth.

"I'm beginning to think we're not ever going to find anything," Horner Dees muttered at one point.

They followed the dark corridors of the streets and searched the brume that lay all about, the doorways and windows that gaped open like mouths in search of food, and the flat, glistening walkways and passages. Everywhere the city lay abandoned and dead, stripped of life and filled with hollow, empty sounds. It walled them away with its stone and its silence; it wrapped about them with such persistence that despite memory and reason it seemed that the world beyond must have fallen away and that Eldwist was all that remained.

They grew weary with the approach of evening; the sameness of their surroundings dulled their senses and wore against their resistance. They began to stray a bit, to wander closer to the walkway's edge, to look upward more often at the stone heights that loomed all about, and to give themselves over to a dangerous and persistent wish that something—*anything*—would happen. Their boredom was acute, their sense of being unable to change or affect the things about them maddening. They had been in Eldwist almost a week. How much longer would they be forced to remain?

Ahead, the street deadended. They rounded the corner of the building they were following and discovered that the street widened into a square. At the square's center was an odd depression with steps leading down on all sides to a basin from which a statue rose, a winged figure with streamers and ribbons trailing from its body. Almost without thinking, they turned into the square, beguiled by its look, so different from anything else they had seen. *A park*, they thought to themselves without speaking. What was it doing here?

They were halfway across the street when they heard the catch that secured the trapdoor beneath them release.

They had no chance of saving themselves. They were standing in the center of the door when it dropped, and they plunged into the void beneath. They fell a long way, struck the side of a chute, and began to slide head-downward. The chute was rough, its surface littered with loose rock that cut and bit into their faces and hands. They clawed frantically in an attempt to slow their descent, heedless of the pain. Boots and knees dug in; hands and fingers grasped. The slide broadened and its slope decreased. They quit rolling, flattened themselves in a spread-eagle position, and came to a grinding halt.

Morgan lifted his head gingerly and peered about. He lay facedown on a slab of rock that stretched so far away into the shadows on either side that he could not see its end. Loose rock lay upon the slide like a carpet, bits and pieces of it still tumbling away. There was a faint glimmer of light from somewhere above, a narrow shaft that sought in vain to penetrate the gloom, so thin that it barely reached to where Morgan lay. He forced himself to look down. Horner Dees lay some twenty feet below him on his right, sprawled on his back with his arms and legs thrown wide, unmoving. Farther down, like a giant, hungry mouth, was a chasm of impenetrable blackness.

Morgan swallowed against the dust in his throat. "Horner?" he whispered hoarsely.

"Here," the other said, his voice a faint rasp.

"Are you all right?"

There was a grunt. "Nothing broken, I think."

Morgan took a moment to look about. All he could see was the slide, the shaft of light above, and the chasm below. "Can you move?" he called down softly.

There was silence for a moment, then the sound of rocks clattering away into the dark. "No," the reply came. "I'm too fat and old, Highlander. If I try to get up to you, I'll start sliding and won't be able to stop."

Morgan heard the strain in his voice. And the fear. Dees was helpless, laying on that loose rock like a leaf on glass; even the slightest movement would send him spinning away into the void.

Me, too, if I make any attempt to help, the Highlander thought darkly.

Yet he knew that he had to try.

He took a deep breath and brought his hand up slowly to his mouth. A shower of loose rock rattled away, but his body stayed in place on the slide. He brushed at the silt on his lips and closed his eyes, thinking. There was a rope in his backpack, a thin, strong coil, some fifty feet of it. His eyes opened again. Could he find a way to fasten it to something and haul himself up?

A familiar rumbling shook the earth, rising from below, shaking the carpet of rock about him so that small showers of it slid into the abyss. There was a thunderous huffing and a great, long sigh as if an enormous amount of air was being released.

Morgan Leah glanced down, cold to the bone. In the depths below, right beneath where they hung, the Maw Grint lay sleeping.

Morgan looked up again quickly. His breath came in short, frantic gasps, and he had to struggle to overcome an almost overpowering urge to claw his way out of there as fast as he could. The Maw Grint. That close. It was huge beyond belief; even his vague glimpse of it had been enough to tell him that. He couldn't begin to guess how much of it there was, where it began and ended, how far it stretched away.

He gripped at the rock until his hands hurt, fighting back against his fear and nausea. He had to get out of there! He had to find a way!

Almost without thinking about what he was doing, he reached beneath his stomach and began working free the broken remains of the Sword of Leah. It was a slow, agonizing process, for he was unable to lift up without fear of beginning his slide down again. And now, more than he had ever wanted anything, he did not want that.

"Don't try to move, Horner!" he called down softly, his voice dry and rough. "Stay where you are!"

There was no response. Morgan inched the Sword of Leah clear of its scabbard and out from under him, bringing it level with his face. The polished metal surface of the broken blade glittered brightly in the faint light. He pushed it above his head with one hand, then reached up with the other until he could grip it firmly with both. Turning the jagged end of the blade downward, he began to slide it into the rock. He felt it bite into the stone slab beneath.

Please! he begged.

Jamming the Sword of Leah into the stone, he hauled himself up. The blade held, and he pulled his face level with its handle. Bits of rock fell away beneath him, tumbling and sliding into the void. The Maw Grint did not stir.

Morgan freed the Sword, reached upward to jam it into the

rock again, gripped it with every ounce of strength he possessed, and pulled himself level once more. He closed his eyes and lay next to it panting, then felt a rush of heat surge through his body. *The magic?* He opened his eyes quickly to see, searching the Sword's gleaming length. Nothing.

Holding himself in place with one hand, he used the other to dive into his pack and secure the length of rope and a grappling hook. A handful of cooking implements and a blanket worked free in the process and fell onto the chute. Ignoring them, the Highlander slipped the rope about his waist and shoulders and tied it in a harness.

"Horner!" he whispered.

The old Tracker looked up, and Morgan threw the rope to him. It fell across his body, and he seized it with both hands. He started to slip almost immediately, swinging over until he was beneath Morgan. Then the rope went taut, catching him. The shock to Morgan's body was staggering, an immense, wrenching weight that threatened to pull him down. But he had both hands fastened once more on the Sword of Leah, and the blade held firm.

"Climb to me!" he whispered down harshly.

Horner Dees began to do so, slowly, torturously, hand over hand up the rope and the slide. As he passed the cooking implements and blanket that had fallen from Morgan's pack, he kicked them free, and they tumbled farther down in a shower of rock.

This time the Maw Grint coughed and came awake.

It grunted, a huffing sound that reverberated against the stone walls. It lifted itself, its massive body thudding against the walls of the tunnel in which it slept, shaking the earth violently. It rolled and pitched and began to move. Morgan hung on to the pommel of his sword, and Dees clung to the slender rope, both gritting their teeth against the strain on muscle and bone. The Maw Grint shook itself, and Tracker and Highlander could hear a spraying sound and then a hiss of steam.

The Maw Grint slid away into the black and the sound of its passing faded. Morgan and Dees looked down cautiously.

An odd, greenish stain was working its way up the stone of the chute, just visible at the far edge of the shaft of light several dozen feet below Dees. It glistened darkly and steamed like a fire advancing through brush. They watched as it reached the blanket that had fallen from Morgan's pack. When it touched it, the rough wool turned instantly to stone.

Horner Dees began climbing again at once, a furious assault
on the loose stone of the slide. When he was almost to Morgan,
the Highlander stopped him, beckoned for slack on the rope,
and began his own ascent, jamming the Sword blade down into
the rock, pulling himself up, jamming and pulling, over and
over again.

They went on that way for what seemed an endless span of
time. Daylight beckoned them, drawing them like a beacon toward the surface of the city and safety. Sweat ran down Morgan's
face and body until he was drenched in it. His breathing grew
labored, and his entire body was wracked with pain. It grew so
bad at one point that he thought he must quit. But he could not.
Below, the stain continued to advance, the poison given off by
the Maw Grint's body solidifying everything in its path. The
blanket went first, then the handful of cooking implements that
hadn't fallen into the abyss. Soon there was nothing left save
Morgan and Horner Dees.

And it was gaining steadily on them.

They struggled on, hauling themselves upward foot by foot.
Morgan's mind closed down on his thoughts like an iron lid on
a trunk of useless relics, and all of his efforts became concentrated on the climb. As he labored, he felt the heat spread through
him once more, stronger this time, more insistent. He could feel
it turning inside him like an auger, boring and twisting at the
core of his being. It reached from head to heels and back again,
from fingers to toes, through the muscles and bone and blood,
until it was all he knew. At some point—he never knew exactly
when—he looked at the Sword of Leah and saw it glowing as
bright as day, the white fire of its magic burning through the
shadows. *Still there*, he thought in furious determination. *Still
mine!*

Then suddenly there was a ladder, rungs lining the walls of
the chute above him, rising up from the darkness of their prison
toward the fading daylight and the city. The light, he saw, came
from a narrow airshaft. He scrambled toward it, jamming, hauling, releasing, starting all over again. He heard Horner Dees
calling to him from below, his hoarse voice almost a sob, and
looked down long enough to see the poison of the Maw Grint
inches from the old Tracker's boots. He reached down impulsively with one hand and calling on a strength he didn't know
he possessed, hauled upward on the rope, pulling Dees clear.
The other kicked and scrambled toward him, bearded face a
mask of dust and sweat. Morgan's hand released the rope and

closed over the bottommost rung of the ladder. Dees continued to climb, digging his boots into the loose stone. The light was failing quickly now, gone gray already, slipping rapidly into darkness. Below, the Maw Grint's muffled roar shook the earth.

Then they were both on the ladder, scrambling upward, feet and hands gripping, bodies pressing against the stone. Morgan jammed the Sword of Leah back into his belt, safely in place. *Still magic!*

They burst from the airshaft into the street and fell on the walkway in exhaustion. Together, they crawled to the doorway of the nearest building and collapsed in the cool of its shadows.

"I knew . . . I was right . . . in wanting you for a friend," Horner Dees gasped.

He reached over, this great bearish man, and pulled the Highlander close. Morgan Leah could feel him shake.

XXI

Pe Ell spent the day sleeping.

After he walked out on Quickening and the others of the little company from Rampling Steep he went directly to a building less than a block away that he had chosen for himself two days earlier. Rounding the corner of the building so that he was out of sight of anyone who might be watching, he entered through a side door, climbed the stairs one floor, followed the hallways to the front of the building, and turned into a large, well-lighted chamber with windows that ran almost floor to ceiling and opened on the street below and the buildings across, one of which was where his once-companions were presently hiding.

He permitted himself a brief smile. They were such a pack of fools.

Pe Ell had a plan. He believed, as Quickening did, that the

Stone King was hidden somewhere in the city. He did not believe the others of the company would find him even if they searched from now until next summer. He alone could do so. Pe Ell was a hunter by instinct and experience; the others were something less—each to a varying degree, but all hopeless. He had not lied when he told them he would be better off on his own. He would. Horner Dees was a Tracker, but a Tracker's skills were useless in a city of stone. Carisman and Morgan Leah had no skills worth talking about. Quickening disdained the use of her magic—maybe with good reason, although he wasn't convinced of that yet. The only one who might have been useful to him was Walker Boh. But the man with one arm was his most dangerous enemy, and he did not want to have to worry about watching his back.

His plan was simple. The key to finding Uhl Belk was the Rake. The Creeper was the Stone King's house pet, a giant watchdog that kept his city free of intruders. He turned it loose at night, and it swept the streets and buildings clean. What it missed one night, it went after the next. But only at night, not during the day. Why was that? Pe Ell asked himself. And the answer was obvious. Because like everything else that served the Stone King, willingly or not, it could not see. It hunted by using its other senses. The night was its natural ally. Daylight might even hinder it.

Where did it go during the day? Pe Ell then asked. Again, the answer seemed obvious. Like any house pet, it went back to its master. That meant that if Pe Ell could manage to follow the Rake to its daytime lair he had a good chance of finding the Stone King.

Pe Ell thought he could do so. The night was his ally as well; he had done most of his own hunting in the dark. His own senses were as sharp as those of the Creeper. He could hunt the Rake as easily as the Rake could hunt him. The Rake was a monster; there was no point in thinking he stood a chance against such a beast in a face-to-face confrontation, even with the aid of the Stiehl. But Pe Ell could be a shadow when he chose, and nothing could bring him to bay. He would take his chances; he would play cat and mouse with the Rake. Pe Ell was feeling many things, but fear wasn't one of them. He had a healthy respect for the Creeper, but he was not frightened of it. After all, he was the smarter of the two.

Come nightfall, he would prove it.

So he slept the daylight hours away, stretched out of sight just beneath the windows where he could feel the faint, hazy sunlight on his face and hear the sounds of anyone or anything passing in the street below.

When it grew dark, the shadows cooling the air to a damp chill, the light fading away, he rose and slipped down the stairs and out the door. He stood listening in the gloom for a long time. He had not heard the others of the company return from their daytime hunt; that was odd. Perhaps they had come into their shelter through another door, but he thought he would have heard them nevertheless. For a moment he considered stealing in for a quick look, but abandoned the idea almost immediately. What happened to them had nothing to do with him. Even Quickening no longer mattered as much. Now that he was away from her, he discovered, she had lost something of her hold over him. She was just a girl he had been sent to kill, and kill her he would if she was still alive when he returned from his night's hunt.

He would kill them all.

The cries of the seabirds were distant and mournful in the evening stillness, faint whimpers carried on the ocean wind. He could hear the dull pounding of the waters of the Tiderace against Eldwist's shores and the low rumble of the Maw Grint somewhere deep beneath the city.

He could not hear the Creeper.

He waited until it was as black as it would get, the skies obscured by clouds and mist, the gloom settled down about the buildings, spinning shadow webs. He had listened to and identified all of the dark's sounds by then; they were as familiar as the beating of his pulse. He began to move, just another shadow in the night. He slipped down the streets in quick, cautious dartings that carried him from one pool of darkness to the next. He did not carry any weapon but the Stiehl, and the Stiehl was safely sheathed within the covering of his pants. The only weapons he needed right now were instinct and stealth.

He found a juncture of streets where he could crouch in wait within a deeply shadowed entry that opened out of a tunnel stairwell and gave him a clear view of everything for almost two blocks. He settled himself back against the stone centerpost and waited.

Almost immediately, he began thinking of the girl.

Quickening, the daughter of the King of the Silver River— she was a maddening puzzle who stirred such conflicting feelings within him that he could barely begin to sort them out. It would have been better simply to brush them all aside and do as Rimmer Dall had said he must—kill her. Yet he could not quite bring himself to do so. It was more than defiance of Dall and his continued attempts to subvert him to the Shadowen cause, more than his determination that he would handle matters in his own way; it was the doubt and hesitation she roused in him, the feeling that somehow he wasn't as much in control of matters as he believed, that *she* knew things about him he did not. Secrets—she was a harborer of so many. If he killed her, those secrets would be lost forever.

He pictured her in his mind as he had done for so many nights during their journey north. He could visualize the perfection of her features, the way the light's movement across her face and body made every aspect seem more stunning than the one before. He could hear the music in her voice. He could feel her touch. She was real and impossible at once: an elemental by her own admission, a thing made of magic, yet human as well. Pe Ell was a man whose respect for life had long since been deadened by his killings. He was a professional assassin who had never failed. He did not understand losing. He was a wall that could not be breached; he was unapproachable by others save for those brief moments he chose to tolerate their presence.

But Quickening—this strange, ephemeral girl—threatened all of that. She had it in her, he believed, to ruin everything he was and in the end to destroy him. He didn't know how, but he believed it was so. She had the power to undo him. He should have been anxious to kill her then, to do as Rimmer Dall had asked. Instead, he was intrigued. He had never encountered anyone until now who he felt might threaten him. He wanted to rid himself of that threat; yet he wanted to get close to it first.

He stared out into the streets of Eldwist, down the corridors between the silent, towering buildings, and into the tunnels of endless gloom, unbothered by the seeming contradiction in his wants. The shadows reached out to him and drew him close. He was as much at home here as he had been at Southwatch, a part of the night, the emptiness, the solitude, the presence of death and absence of life. How little difference there was, he marveled, between the kingdoms of Uhl Belk and the Shadowen.

He relaxed. He belonged in the anonymity of darkness.

It was *she* and those who stayed with her that required the light.

He thought of them momentarily. It was a way to pass the

time. He pictured each as he had pictured Quickening and considered the potential of each as a threat to him.

Carisman. He dismissed the tunesmith almost immediately.

Horner Dees. What was it about that old man that bothered him so? He hated the way the bearish Tracker looked at him, as if seeing right through skin and bone. He reflected on it momentarily, then shrugged it away. Dees was used up. He wielded no magic.

Morgan Leah. He disliked the Highlander because he was so obviously Quickening's favorite. She might even love him in her own way, although he doubted she was capable of real feeling— not her—not the elemental daughter of the King of the Silver River. She was simply using him as she was using them all, her reasons her own, carefully concealed. The Highlander was young and rash and probably would find a way to kill himself before he became a real problem.

That left Walker Boh.

As always, Pe Ell took an extra measure of time to ponder him. Walker Boh was an enigma. He had magic, but he didn't seem comfortable using it. Quickening had practically raised him from the dead, yet he seemed almost uninterested in living. He was preoccupied with matters of his own, things that he kept hidden deep down inside, secrets as puzzling as those of the girl. Walker Boh had a sense of things that surprised Pe Ell; he might even be prescient. Once, some years ago, Pe Ell had heard of a man who lived in the Eastland and could commune with animals and read the changes in the Lands before they came to pass. This man, perhaps? He was said to be a formidable opponent; the Gnomes were terrified of him.

Pe Ell rocked forward slowly and clasped his hands together. He would have to be especially careful of One-arm, he knew. Pe Ell wasn't frightened of Walker Boh, but neither was Walker Boh frightened of him.

Yet.

The minutes drifted away, the night deepened, and the streets remained empty and still. Pe Ell waited patiently, knowing the Rake would eventually come as it had come each night, searching for their hiding place, seeking them out, and determined to exterminate them as it had been trained to do. Tonight would be no exception.

He let himself consider for a time the implications of having possession of a magic like the Black Elfstone—a magic that could negate all other magics. Once he had it in his grasp—as he eventually would—what would he do with it? His narrow, sharp features crinkled with amusement. He would use it against Rimmer Dall for starters. He would use it to negate Dall's own magic. He would slip into Southwatch, find the First Seeker, and put an end to him. Rimmer Dall had grown more annoying than useful; Pe Ell no longer cared to tolerate him. It was time to sever their partnership once and for all. After that, he might use the talisman against the rest of the Shadowen, perhaps make himself their leader. Except that he really didn't want anything to do with them. Better, perhaps, simply to eliminate them all— or as many as he could reach. He smiled expectantly. That would be an interesting challenge.

He leaned back contentedly in the shadows of his shelter. He would have to learn how to use the magic of the Elfstone first, of course. Would that prove difficult? Would he have to rely on Quickening to instruct him? Would he have to find a way to keep her alive awhile longer? He shivered with anticipation. The solution would present itself when it was time. For now, he must concentrate on gaining possession of the Elfstone.

Almost an hour passed before he finally heard the approach of the Rake. The Creeper came from the east, its metal legs scraping softly on the stone as it slipped through the gloom. It came right toward Pe Ell, and the assassin melted back into the darkness of the stairwell until his eyes were level with the street. The creature looked enormous from this angle, its immense body balanced on iron-encased legs, its whiplike tail curled and ready, and its tentacles outstretched and sweeping the damp air like feelers. Steam rose from its iron shell, the heat of its body reacting to the cool air, condensation forming and dripping onto the street. It sent its tentacles snaking into doorways and windows, along the gutters below the walkways, down the sewers, and into the wrecks of the ancient skeletons of the toppled stone carriages. For an instant Pe Ell thought the beast would spy him out, but then something caught the Creeper's attention and it scuttled past and disappeared into the night.

Pe Ell waited until he could just barely hear it, then slipped from his hiding place in pursuit.

He tracked the Rake for the remainder of the night, down streets and alleyways, through the foyers and halls of massive old buildings, and along the edges of the cliffs that bounded the city west and north. The Creeper went everywhere, a beast at hunt, constantly on the move. Pe Ell stalked it relentlessly. Most of the time he could only hear it, not see it. He had to be very sure he did not get too close. If he did, the creature would sense his presence and come after him. Pe Ell made himself a part of the shadows, just another piece of an endless stone landscape, a thing of vapor and nonbeing that not even the Rake could detect. He kept on the walkways and close to the building walls, avoided the streets and their maze of trapdoors, and stayed clear of any open spaces. He did not hurry; he kept his pace steady. Playing cat and mouse required a careful exercise of patience.

And then suddenly, near dawn, the Rake disappeared. He had glimpsed it only minutes earlier as it skittered away down a street in the central section of the city, rather close to where the others of the company were hiding. He could hear its legs and tentacles scrape, its body turn, and then there was nothing. Silence. Pe Ell slowed, stopped, and listened. Still there was nothing. He moved ahead cautiously, following a narrow alleyway until it emerged into a street. Still concealed within the shadows of the alleyway, he peered out. Left, the street tunneled into the gloom past rows of buildings that stretched skyward, flat faced and unrevealing. Right, the street was bisected by a cross street and bracketed by twin towers with huge, shadowed foyers that disappeared into complete blackness.

Pe Ell searched the street both ways, listened again, and began to fume. How could he have lost it so suddenly? How could it have just disappeared?

He was aware again of a brightening of the air, a hint of the sun's pending emergence into the world beyond the clouds and mist and gloom of Eldwist. It was daybreak. The Rake would go into hiding now. Perhaps it already had. Pe Ell frowned, then scanned the impenetrable shadows of the buildings across the way. Was that its hiding place? he wondered.

He started from his own concealment for a look when that sixth sense he relied upon so heavily warned him what was happening. The Rake was in hiding all right, but not for the reason he had first imagined. It was in hiding because it was setting a trap. It knew the intruders were still loose in the city, somewhere close. It knew they would have to kill it or it would kill them. So on the chance that they had followed, it had set a trap. It was waiting now to see if anything fell into it.

Pe Ell felt a rush of cold determination surge through him as he shrank back into the gloom of the alleyway. Cat and mouse, that's all it was. He smiled and waited.

Long minutes passed and there was only silence. Pe Ell continued to wait.

Then abruptly the Rake emerged from the shadows of the building across the street to the left, dancing almost gracefully into view, body poised. Pe Ell held his breath as the monster tested the air, turning slowly about. Satisfied, it moved on. Pe Ell exhaled slowly and followed.

It was growing brighter now, and the night air evolved into a sort of gray haze that reflected the dampness so that it became even more difficult to see what lay ahead. Yet Pe Ell did not slow, relying on his hearing to warn him of any danger, always conscious of the sound of the Rake moving ahead. It was no longer worrying about pursuit. Its night's work was finished; it was headed home.

To the lair of the Stone King, Pe Ell thought, impatient for the first time since his hunt had begun.

He caught up with the Rake as it slowed before a flat-sided building with a shadowed alcove thirty feet high and twice that across. The Rake's feelers probed the stone at the top of the alcove, and a section of the wall within swung silently away, lifting into the gloom. Without a backward glance, the Rake slipped through the opening. When it was inside, the wall swung back into place.

Got you! Pe Ell thought fiercely.

Nevertheless, he stood where he was for almost an hour afterward, waiting to see if anything else would happen, making certain that this was not another trap. When he was sure that it was safe, he emerged and darted along the edge of the buildings, following the walkways until he stood before the hidden entry.

He took a long time to study it. The stone facing was flat and smooth. He could trace the seams of the opening from within the frame of the alcove, but he would never have noticed the door without first knowing it was there. Far above him, just visible against the gray of the stone, he could detect a kind of lever. A release, he thought triumphantly. A way in.

He stood there for a while longer, thinking. Then he moved away, searching the buildings across the street for a hiding place. Once safely concealed, he would sit down and figure out a way to trip that lever. Then he would sleep again until it was dark. When night came, he would wake and wait for the Rake to go out.

When it did, he would go in.

XXII

Night lay across the Westland in a humid, airless pall, the heat of the day lingering with sullen determination long after the sun's fiery ball had disappeared into the horizon. Darkness disdained to offer even the smallest measure of relief, empty of cool breezes, devoid of any suggestion of a drop in the temperature. The day's swelter was rooted in the earth, a stubborn presence that would not be dispelled, breathing fire out of its concealment like an underground dragon. Insects buzzed and hummed and flew in erratic, random bursts. Trees were heat-ravaged giants, drooping and exhausted. A full moon crawled across the southern horizon, gibbous and shimmering against the haze. The only sounds that broke the stillness were those dredged from the throats of hunted creatures an instant before their hunters silenced them forever.

Even on the hottest of nights, the game of life and death played on.

Wren Ohmsford and the big Rover Garth turned their horses down the rutted trail that led into the town of Grimpen Ward. It had taken them a week to journey there from the Tirfing, navigating hidden passes of the Irrybis that only the Rovers knew, following the trails of the Wilderun north and west, shying well clear of the treacherous Shroudslip, winding at last over Whistle Ridge and down into the dank mire of the Westland's most infamous lair.

When there was nowhere else to run or hide, it was said, there was always Grimpen Ward. Thieves, cutthroats, and misfits of all sorts came to the outlaw town to find refuge. Walled away by the Irrybis and the Rock Spur, swallowed up by the teeming jungle of the Wilderun, Grimpen Ward was a haven for renegades of every ilk.

It was also a deathtrap from which few escaped, a pit of vipers preying on one another because there was no one else, devouring their own kind with callous indifference and misguided amusement, feeding in a frenzy of need and boredom. Of those who came to Grimpen Ward seeking to stay alive, most ended up disappointed.

The town grew visible through the trees, and Wren and Garth slowed. Lights burned through the window glass of buildings black with grime, their shutters sagging and broken, their walls and roofs and porches so battered and ravaged by time and neglect that they seemed in immediate danger of collapse. Doors stood ajar in a futile effort to dispel the heat trapped within. Laughter broke sharply against the forest silence, rough, forced, desperate. Glasses clinked and sometimes shattered. Now and again, a scream sounded, solitary and disembodied.

Wren glanced at Garth and then signed, *We'll leave the horses hidden here.* Garth nodded. They turned their mounts into the trees, rode them some distance from the road until a suitable clearing was found, and tethered them in a stand of birch.

"Softly," Wren whispered, fingers moving.

They worked their way back to the roadway and continued down. Dust rose from beneath their boots and settled in a dark sheen on their faces. They had been riding all day, a slow journey through impossible heat, unable to force the pace without risking the health of their horses. The Wilderun was a morass of midsummer dampness and decay, the wood of the forests rotting into mulch, the ground soft and yielding and treacherous, the streams and drinking pools dried or poisoned, and the air a furnace that parched and withered. No matter how terrible the heat might be in other parts of the Four Lands, it was always twice as bad here. A stagnant, inhospitable cesspool, the Wilderun had long been regarded as a place to which the discards of the population of the Four Lands were welcome.

Bands of Rovers frequently came to Grimpen Ward to barter and trade. Accustomed to the vagaries and treacheries of Men, outsiders themselves from society, branded outlaws and troublemakers everywhere, the Rovers were right at home. Even so, they traveled in tight-knit families and relied on strength of numbers to keep themselves safe. Seldom did they venture into Grimpen Ward alone as Wren and Garth were doing.

A chance encounter with a small family of coin traders had persuaded the girl and her giant protector to accept the risk. Just a day after Garth's unsuccessful attempt to backtrack and trap their shadow, they had come upon an old man and his sons and their wives traveling north out of the passes, returning from a journey through the Pit. Eating with them, sharing tales, Wren had asked simply out of habit if any among them knew of the fate of the Westland Elves, and the old man had smiled, broken-toothed and wintry, and nodded.

"Not me, girl, you understand," he had rasped softly, chewing at the end of the pipe he smoked, his gray eyes squinting against the light. "But at the Iron Feather in Grimpen Ward they be an old woman that does. The Addershag, she's called. Haven't spoke to her myself, for I don't frequent the ale houses of the Ward, but word has it the old woman knows the tale. A seer, they say. Queer as sin, maybe mad." He'd leaned into the fire's glow. "They's making use of her someway, I hear. A pack of them snakes. Making her give them secrets to take others' money." He shook his head. "We stayed clear."

Later, they had talked it over, Wren and Garth, when the family was asleep and they were left alone. The reasons to stay out of the Wilderun were clear enough; but there were reasons to go in as well. For one, there was the matter of their shadow. It was back there still, just out of view and reach, carefully hidden away like the threat of winter's coming. They could not catch it and despite all their efforts and skill they could not shake it. It clung to them, a trailing spider's web floating invisibly in their wake. The Wilderun, they reflected, might be less to its taste and might, with a bit of luck, bring it to grief.

For another, of course, there was the indisputable fact that this was the first instance since Wren had started asking about the Elves that she had received a positive response. It seemed unreasonable not to test its merit.

So they had come, just the two of them, defying the odds, determined to see what sort of resolution a visit to Grimpen Ward would bring. Now, a week's journey later, they were about to find out.

They passed down through the center of the town, eyes quick but thorough in their hunt. Ale houses came and went, and there was no Iron Feather. Men lurched past them, and a handful of women, tough and hard all, reeking of ale and the stale smell of sweat. The shouts and laughter grew louder, and even Garth seemed to sense how frantic they were, his rough face grim-set and fierce. Several of the men approached Wren, drunken, un-seeing, anxious for money or pleasure, blind to the danger that mirrored in Garth's eyes. The big Rover shoved them away.

At a juncture of cross-streets, Wren caught sight of a cluster of Rovers working their way back toward their wagons at the end of an unlit road. She hailed them down and asked if they knew of the Iron Feather. One made a face and pointed. The band hurried off without comment. Wren and Garth continued on.

They found the ale house in the center of Grimpen Ward, a sprawling ramshackle structure framed of splitting boards and rusting nails, the veranda fronting painted a garish red and blue. Wide double doors were tied open with short lengths of rope; within, a crush of men sang and drank against a long bar and about trestle benches. Wren and Garth stepped inside, peering through the haze of heat and smoke. A few heads turned; eyes stared momentarily and looked away again. No one wanted to meet Garth's gaze. Wren moved up to the bar, caught the attention of the server, and signaled for ale. The server, a narrow-faced man with sure, steady hands brought the mugs over and waited for his money.

"Do you know a woman called the Addershag?" Wren asked him.

Expressionless, the man shook his head, accepted his money, and walked away. Wren watched him stop and whisper something to another man. The man slipped away. Wren sipped at her mug, found the ale unpleasantly warm, and moved down the serving bar, repeating her question as she went. No one knew of the Addershag. One grinned, leered, and made an unimaginative suggestion. Then he saw Garth and hurried off. Wren continued on. A second man reached out at her, and she flicked his arm away. When he reached again, she brought the heel of her hand into his face so hard he was knocked unconscious. She stepped around him, anxious to be done with this business. It was dangerous to continue on, even with Garth to protect her.

She reached the end of the serving bar and slowed. At the very back of the room a group of men occupied a table in the shadows. One of them beckoned, waited until he was certain she had seen, then beckoned again. She hesitated, then moved forward, pushing through the crowd, Garth at her back. She came up to the table and stopped when she was just out of reach of the men seated there. They were a rough bunch—dirty, unshaven, their skin the color of paste, their eyes ferretlike and dangerous. Ale mugs sat before them, sweating.

The man who had beckoned said, "Who is it you're looking for, girl?"

"A seer called the Addershag," she answered and then waited, certain that he already knew who she was looking for and probably where she would look.

"What do you want with her?"

"I want to ask her about the Elves."

The man snorted. "There aren't any Elves."

Wren waited.

The man eased forward in his chair. He was thick-featured, and his eyes were empty of feeling. "Suppose I decided to help you. Just suppose. Would you do something for me in turn?" The man studied her face a moment and grinned insolently. "Not that. I just want you to talk to her for me, ask her something. I can tell what you are by your clothes. You're a Rover. See, the Addershag is a Rover, too." He paused. "Didn't know that, did you? Well, she doesn't feel like talking to us, but she might feel different about you, one of her own." His gaze on her was hard and sullen. All pretense was gone now, the game under way. "So if I take you to her, then you have to ask a question or two for me. That a deal?"

Wren knew already that the man was planning to kill her. It was simply a question of how and when he and his friends would try. But she also knew he might really be able to take her to the Addershag. She weighed the risks and rewards momentarily, then said, "Agreed. But my friend goes with me."

"Whatever you say." The man smirked. "Course, my friends go, too. So I'll feel safe. Everyone goes."

Wren looked at the man appraisingly. Heavyset, muscular, an experienced cutthroat. The others the same. If they got her in a tight place . . .

"Garth," she said, looking back at him. She signed quickly, screening her movements from the men at the table. Garth nodded. She turned back to the table. "I'm ready."

The speaker rose, the others with him, an anxious, hungry-looking bunch. There was no mistaking what they were about. The speaker began ambling along the rear wall toward a door leading out. Wren followed, cautious, alert. Garth was a step behind; the remainder of the table trailed. They passed through the door into an empty hall and continued toward a back entrance. The sounds of the ale house disappeared abruptly as the door closed.

The man spoke over his shoulder. "I want to know how she reads the gaming cards like she does. How she reads the dice roll. I want to know how she can see what the players are thinking.'' He grinned. ''Something for you, girl; something for me. I have to make a living, too.''

He stopped unexpectedly before a side door, and Wren tensed. But the man ignored her, reaching into his pocket to extract a key. He inserted it in the lock and twisted. The lock released with a click and the door swung open. There were stairs beyond leading down. The man groped inside and brought forth an oil lamp, lit it, and handed it to Wren.

''She's in the cellar,'' he said, motioning through the door. ''That's where we're keeping her for the moment. You talk to her. Take your friend if you want. We'll wait here.'' His smile was hard and unpleasant. ''Just don't come back up without something to trade for my helping you out. Understand?''

The men with him had crowded up behind them, and the reek of them filled the narrow hall. Wren could hear the ragged sound of their breathing.

She moved close to the speaker and put her face inches from his own. ''What I understand is that Garth will remain here with you.'' She held his gaze. ''Just in case.''

He shrugged uncomfortably. Wren nodded to Garth, indicating the door and the gathering of men. Then holding the lamp before her, she started down the steps.

It was a shadowy descent. The stairway wound along a dirt wall shored up with timbers, the earth smell thick and pungent. It was cooler here, if only marginally. Insects skittered from underfoot. Strands of webbing brushed her face. The steps angled left along a second wall and ended. The cellar opened up before her in the lamplight.

An old woman sat slumped against the far wall, almost lost in the gloom. Her body was a dried husk, and her face had withered into a maze of lines and furrows. Ragged white hair tumbled down about her frail shoulders, and her gnarled hands were clasped before her. She wore a cloth shift and old boots. Wren approached and knelt before her. The ancient head lifted, revealing eyes that were milky and fixed. The old woman was blind.

Wren placed the oil lamp on the floor beside her. ''Are you the seer they call the Addershag, old mother?'' she asked softly.

The staring eyes blinked and a thin voice rasped, ''Who wishes to know? Tell me your name.''

''My name is Wren Ohmsford.''

The white head tilted, shifting toward the stairway and the door above. ''Are you with them?''

Wren shook her head. "I'm with myself. And a companion. Both of us are Rovers."

Aged hands reached out to touch her face, exploring its lines and hollows, scraping along the girl's skin like dried leaves. Wren did not move. The hands withdrew.

"You are an Elf."

"I have Elven blood."

"An Elf!" The old woman's voice was rough and insistent, a hiss against the silence of the ale house cellar. The wrinkled face cocked to one side as if reflecting. "I am the Addershag. I am the seer of the future and what it holds, the teller of truths. What do you wish of me?"

Wren rocked back slightly on the heels of her boots. "I am searching for the Westland Elves. I was told a week ago that you might know where to find them—if they still exist."

The Addershag cackled softly. "Oh, they exist, all right. They do indeed. But it's not to everyone they show themselves—to none at all in many years. Is it so important to you, Elf-girl, that you see them? Do you search them out because you have need of your own kind?" The milky eyes stared unseeing at Wren's face. "No, not you. Despite your blood, you're a Rover before everything, and a Rover has need of no one. Yours is the life of the wanderer, free to travel any path you choose, and you glory in it." She grinned, nearly toothless. "Why, then?"

"Because it is a charge I have been given—a charge I have chosen to accept," Wren answered carefully.

"A charge, is it?" The lines and furrows of the old woman's face deepened. "Bend close to me, Elf-girl."

Wren hesitated, then leaned forward tentatively. The Addershag's hands came up again, the fingers exploring. They passed once more across Wren's face, then down her neck to her body. When they touched the front of the girl's blouse, they jerked back as if burned and the old woman gasped. "Magic!" she howled.

Wren started, then seized the other's wrists impulsively. "What magic? What are you saying?"

But the Addershag shook her head violently, her lips clamped shut, and her head sunk into her shrunken breast. Wren held her a moment longer, then let her go.

"Elf-girl," the old woman whispered then, "who sends you in search of the Westland Elves?"

Wren took a deep breath against her fears and answered, "The shade of Allanon."

The aged head lifted with a snap. "Allanon!" She breathed the name like a curse. "So! A Druid's charge, is it? Very well. Listen to me, then. Go south through the Wilderun, cross the Irrybis and follow the coast of the Blue Divide. When you have reached the caves of the Rocs, build a fire and keep it burning three days and nights. One will come who can help you. Do you understand?"

"Yes," Wren replied, wondering at the same time if she really did. Rocs, did the old woman say? Weren't they supposed to have been a form of giant coastal bird?

"Beware, Elf-girl," the other warned, a stick-thin hand lifting. "I see danger ahead for you, hard times, and treachery and evil beyond imagining. My visions are in my head, truths that haunt me with their madness. Heed me, then. Keep your own counsel, girl. Trust no one!"

She gestured violently, then slumped back again, her blind gaze fixed and hard. Wren glanced down the length of her body and started. The Addershag's worn dress had slipped back from her boots to reveal an iron chain and clamp fastened to her leg.

Wren reached out and took the aged hands in her own. "Old mother," she said gently. "Let me get you free of this place. My friend and I can help you, if you'll let us. There is no reason for you to remain a prisoner."

"A prisoner? Ha!" The Addershag lurched forward, teeth bared like an animal at bay. "What I look and what I am are two very different things!"

"But the chain . . ."

"Holds me not an instant longer than I wish!" A wicked smile creased the wrinkled face until its features almost disappeared. "Those men, those fools—they take me by force and chain me in this cellar and wait for me to do their bidding!" Her voice lowered. "They are small, greedy men, and all that interests them is the wealth of others. I could give them what they want; I could do their bidding and be gone. But this is a game that interests me. I like the teasing of them. I like the sound of their whining. I let them keep me for a time because it amuses me. And when I am done being entertained, Elf-girl, when I tire of them and decide again to be free, why . . . this!"

Her stick hands freed themselves, then twisted sharply before Wren's eyes and were transformed into writhing snakes, tongues darting, fangs bared, hissing into the silence. Wren jerked away, shielding her face. When she looked again, the snakes had disappeared.

She swallowed against her fear. "Were . . . they real?" she asked thickly, her face flushed and hot.

The Addershag smiled with dark promise. "Go, now," she whispered, shrinking back into the shadows. "Take what I told you and use it as you will. And guard yourself closely, Elf-girl. Beware."

Wren hesitated, pondering whether she should ask answers to the rush of questions that flooded through her. She decided against it. She picked up the oil lamp and rose. "Goodbye, old mother," she said.

She went back through the darkness, squinting into the light of the oil lamp to find the stairs, feeling the sightless gaze of the Addershag follow after her. She climbed the steps swiftly and slipped back through the cellar doorway into the ale house hall.

Garth was waiting for her, facing the knot of men who had come with them from the front room. The sounds of the ale house filtered through the closed door beyond, muffled and raucous. The eyes of the men glittered. She could sense their hunger.

"What did the old woman tell you?" the leader snapped.

Wren lifted the oil lamp to shed a wider circle of light and shook her head. "Nothing. She doesn't know of the Elves or if she does, she keeps it to herself. As for gaming, she won't say a word about that either." She paused. "She doesn't seem any kind of a seer to me. I think she's mad."

Anger reflected in the other man's eyes. "What a poor liar you are, girl."

Wren's expression did not change. "I'll give you some good advice, cutthroat. Let her go. It might save your life."

A knife appeared in the other's hand, a glint of metal come out of nowhere. "But not yours . . ."

He didn't finish because Wren had already slammed the oil lamp onto the hallway floor before him, shattering the glass, spilling the oil across the wood, exploding the flames everywhere. Fire raced across the wooden planks and up the walls. The speaker caught fire, shrieked, and stumbled back into the unwilling arms of his fellows. Garth and Wren fled the other way, reaching the backdoor in seconds. Shoulder lowered, Garth hammered into the wooden barrier and it flew from its hinges as if made of paper. The girl and the big Rover burst through the opening into the night, howls of rage and fear chasing after them. Down between the buildings of the town they raced, swift

and silent, and moments later emerged back onto the main street
of Grimpen Ward.

They slowed to a walk, glanced back, and listened. Nothing.
The shouts and laughter of the ale houses nearest them drowned
out what lay behind. There was no sign of fire. There was no
indication of pursuit.

Side by side, Wren and Garth walked back up the roadway in
the direction they had come, moving through the revelers, the
heat and the gloom, calm and unhurried.

"We're going south to the Blue Divide," Wren announced as
they reached the edge of the town, signing the words.

Garth nodded and made no response.

Swiftly they disappeared into the night.

XXIII

When Walker Boh, Quickening, and Carisman left
Morgan and Horner Dees, they traveled only a
short distance east through the darkened streets of
Eldwist before slowing to a halt. Walker and the girl faced each
other. Neither had said anything about stopping; it was as if they
had read each other's mind. Carisman looked from one face to
the other in confusion.

"You know where the Stone King is hiding," Quickening
said. She made it a statement of fact.

"I think I do," Walker answered. He stared into the depthless
black eyes and marveled at the assurance he found there. "Did
you sense that when you chose to come with me?"

She nodded. "When he is found, I must be there."

She didn't explain her reasoning, and Walker didn't ask. He
glanced into the distance, trying futilely to penetrate the gloom,
to see beyond the mist and darkness, and to find something of
what he was meant to do. But there was nothing to be found out

there, of course. The answers to his questions lay somewhere within.

"I believe the Stone King hides within the dome," he said quietly. "I suspected as much when we were there several days ago. There appear to be no entrances, yet as I touched the stone and walked about the walls I sensed life. There was a presence that I could not explain. Then, yesterday, when we were beneath the earth, trapped in that underground cavern, I again sensed that presence—only it was above us this time. I took a quick calculation when we emerged from the tunnels. The dome is seated directly above the cavern."

He stopped momentarily and glanced about. "Eldwist is the creation of its master. Uhl Belk has made this city of the old world his own, changing to stone what wasn't already, expanding his domain outward symmetrically where the land allows it. The dome sits centermost, a hub in a wheel of streets and buildings, walls and wreckage."

His pale face turned to meet hers. "Uhl Belk is there."

He could almost see the life brighten in her eyes. "Then we must go to meet him," she said.

They started off again, following the walkway to the end of the block and then turning abruptly north. Walker led, keeping them carefully back from the streets, against the walls of the buildings, clear of the open spaces, and away from the danger of trapdoors. Neither he nor Quickening spoke; Carisman hummed softly. They watched the gloom like hawks, listened for strange sounds, and smelled and tasted the damp, stale air warily. A brief rain caught up with them and left them shedding water from their cloaks and hoods, their feet chilled within their boots.

Walker Boh thought of home. He had done so increasingly of late, driven by the constant, unrelenting pressure of being hemmed about by the city's stone and darkness to seek out something of what had once been pleasant and healing. For a time he had sought to banish all thoughts of Hearthstone; its memories cut at him like broken glass. The cottage that he had adopted as his home had been burned to the ground in the battle with the Shadowen. Cogline and Rumor had died there. He had barely escaped dying himself, and keeping his life had cost him his arm. He had once believed himself invulnerable to the intrusions of the outside world. He had been vain and foolish enough to boast that what lay beyond Hearthstone presented no danger to him. He had denied the dreams that Allanon had sent him from the spirit world, the pleas that Par Ohmsford had extended for his help, and in the end the charge he had been given to go in search of Paranor and the Druids. He had encased himself in imaginary walls and believed himself secure. When those walls began collapsing, he had found that they could not be replaced and those things he had thought secure were lost.

Yet there were older memories of Hearthstone that transcended the recent tragedies. There were all those years when he had lived in peace in the valley, the seasons when the world outside did not intrude and there was time enough for everything. There were the smells of flowers, trees, and freshwater springs; the sounds of birds in early spring and insects on warm summer nights; the taste of dawn on a clear autumn morning; the feeling of serenity that came with the setting sun and the fall of night. He could reach back beyond the past few weeks and find peace in those memories. He did so now because they were all he had left to draw on.

Yet even his strongest memories provided only a momentary haven. The harsh inevitabilities of the present pressed in about him and would not be banished. He might escape for brief moments into the past, into the world that had sheltered him for a time before he was swept away by the tide of events he had sought foolishly to ignore. Escape might soothe and strengthen the spirit, but it was transitory and unresolving. His mind darted away into his memories only to find the past forever beyond his reach and the present forever at hand. He was struggling with his life, he discovered. He was adrift, a castaway fighting to keep afloat amid the wreckage of his confusion and doubt. He could almost feel himself sinking.

They reached the dome at midmorning and began their search. Working together, not willing to separate if there was any chance at all that the Stone King waited within, they began to explore the dome's surface, walking its circumference, feeling along its walls, and searching even the ground it sat upon. It was perfectly formed, although its ageing shell was pitted and cracked, rising several hundred feet into the air at its peak, spreading from wall to wall several hundred feet more. Depressions that had the look of giant thumbprints decorated the dome's peak along its upper surface, laid open like the petals of a flower, separated by bands of stone that curved downward to the foundation. Niches and alcoves indented its walls at ground level, offering no way inside, leading nowhere. Sculpted designs marked its stone, most of them almost completely worn away by time's passage, no longer decipherable, the runes of a world that had long since passed away.

"I can feel a presence still," Walker Boh said, slowing, folding his cloak about him. He glanced skyward. It was raining again, a slow, persistent drizzle. "There's something here. Something."

Quickening stood close beside him. "Magic," she whispered.

He stared at her, surprised that she had been so quick to recognize a truth that had eluded him. "It is so," he murmured. His hand stretched forth, searching. "All about, in the stone itself."

"He is here," Quickening whispered.

Carisman stepped forward and stroked the wall tentatively. His handsome brow furrowed. "Why does he not respond? Shouldn't he come out long enough to see what we want?"

"He may not even know we are here. He may not care." Quickening's soft face lifted. "He may even be sleeping."

Carisman frowned. "Then perhaps a song is needed to wake him up!"

He sang:

> "Awake, awake, oh aged King of Stone,
> Come forth from your enfolding lair,
> We wait without, a worn and tired band,
> So lacking in all hope and care.
>
> Awake, awake, oh aged King of Stone,
> Be not afraid of what we bring,
> 'Tis nothing more than finite spirit,
> A measure of the song I sing.
>
> Awake, awake, oh aged King of Stone,
> You who have seen all passing time,
> Share with us weak and mortal creatures,
> The truths and secrets of Mankind."

His song ended, and he stood looking expectantly at the broad expanse of the dome. There was no response. He glanced at Quickening and Walker and shrugged. "Not his choice of music, perhaps. I shall think of another."

They moved away from the dome and into the shelter of an entry in a building that sat adjacent. Seating themselves with their backs to the wall so that they could look out at the dome, they pooled from their backpacks a collection of old bread and dried fruit for their lunch. They ate silently, staring out from the shadows into the gray rain.

"We are almost out of food," Walker said after a time. "And water. We will have to forage soon."

Carisman brightened. "I shall fish for us. I was a very good fisherman once—although I only fished for pleasure. It was a pleasing way to pass the time and compose. Walker Boh, what did you do before you came north?"

Walker hesitated, surprised by the question, unprepared to give an answer. What did he do? he asked himself. "I was a caretaker," he decided finally.

"Of what?" Carisman pressed, interested.

"Of a cottage and the land about it," he said softly, remembering.

"Of an entire valley and all the creatures that lived within it," Quickening declared, her eyes drawing Carisman's. "Walker Boh preserved life in the manner of the Elves of old. He gave of himself to replenish the land."

Walker stared at her, surprised once again. "It was a poor effort," he suggested awkwardly.

"I will not permit you to be the judge of that," the girl replied. "It is for others to determine how successful you have been in your work. You are too harsh in your criticism and lack the necessary distancing to be fair and impartial." She paused, studying him, her black eyes calm and reasoning. "I believe it will be judged that you did all that you could."

They both knew what she was talking about. Walker was strangely warmed by her words, and once again he experienced that sense of kinship. He nodded without responding and continued to eat.

When they had finished their meal they stood facing the dome once more, debating what approach to take next.

"Perhaps there is something to be seen from above," Quickening suggested. "An opening through the top of the dome or an aberration in the stone that would suggest a way in."

Walker glanced about. There was an ornate building less than a block distant that opened at its top into a belltower and gave a clear view of the dome below. They crossed to it cautiously, forever wary of trapdoors, and gained its entrance. Sculptures of winged angels and robed figures decorated its walls and ceilings. They moved inside cautiously. The central chamber was vast, the glass of its windows long disintegrated, the furnishings turned to dust. They found the stairway leading to the belltower and began to climb. The stairs had fallen away in spots, and only the bracing remained. They maneuvered along its spans, working their way upward. Floors came and went, most ragged with holes and cluttered with debris, all turned to stone, their collapse preserved in perfect relief.

They gained the belltower without difficulty and walked to the windows facing out. The city of Eldwist spread away on all sides, misted and gray, filled with the shadows of daylight's passing and night's approach. The rain had diminished, and the buildings rose like stone sentries across the span of the peninsula. The clouds had lifted slightly, and the choppy slate surface of the Tiderace and the ragged cliffs of the mainland beyond the isthmus could be seen in snatches through gaps in the lines of stone walls.

The dome sat directly below them, as closed and unrevealing at its top as it had been at its bottom. There was nothing to see, no hint of an opening, no suggestion of a way in. Nonetheless, they studied it for some time, hoping to discover something they had missed.

In the midst of their study a horn sounded, startling them.

"Urdas!" Carisman cried.

Walker and Quickening looked at each other in surprise, but Carisman had already dashed to the south window of the tower and was peering in the direction of the isthmus and the cliffs leading down.

"It must be them; that is their call!" he shouted, excitement and concern reflecting in his voice. He shaded his eyes against the glare of the dampened stone. "There! Do you see them?"

Walker and Quickening hastened to join him. The tunesmith was pointing to where the stairway descending the cliffs from the overlook was barely visible through the mist. There were glimpses of movement to be seen on the stairs, small, hunched figures crouched low as if to hide even from the shadows. Urdas, Walker recognized, and they were coming down.

"What is it that they think they are doing!" Carisman exclaimed, obviously upset. "They cannot come here!"

The Urdas faded into a patch of fog and were lost from view. Carisman wheeled on his companions, stricken. "If they are not stopped, they will all be killed!"

"The Urdas are no longer your responsibility, Carisman," Walker Boh declared softly. "You are no longer their king."

Carisman looked unconvinced. "They are children, Walker! They have no understanding of what lives down here. The Rake or the Maw Grint, either one will destroy them. I can't imagine how they slipped past the Koden . . ."

"In the same way as Horner Dees did ten years ago," Walker cut him short. "With a sacrifice of lives. And still they come ahead. They are not as worried about themselves, it appears, as you are."

Carisman wheeled on Quickening. "Lady, you've seen the way they react to things. What do they know of the Stone King and his magic? If they are not stopped . . ."

Quickening seized his arms and held them. "No, Carisman. Walker Boh is right. The Urdas are dangerous to you now as well."

But Carisman shook his head vehemently. "No, Lady. Never to me. They were my family before I abandoned them."

"They were your captors!"

"They cared for me and protected me in the only way they knew how. Lady, what am I to do? They have come here to find me! Why else would they be taking such a risk? I think they have never come so far away from home. They are here because they think you stole me away. Can I abandon them a second time, this time to die for a mistake that I can prevent them from making?" Carisman pulled free, slowly, gently. "I have to go to them. I have to warn them."

"Carisman . . ."

The tunesmith was already backing toward the belltower stairs. "I have been an orphan of the storm all of my life, blown from one island to the next, never with family or home, always in search of somewhere to belong and someone to belong to. The Urdas gave me what I have of both, little as it may seem to you. I cannot let them die needlessly."

He turned and started quickly down the stairs. Quickening and Walker exchanged wordless glances and hurried after.

They caught up with him on the street below. "We'll come with you then," Walker said.

Carisman whirled about at once. "No, no, Walker! You cannot show yourselves to them! If you do, they might think I am threatened by you—perhaps even that I am a prisoner! They might attack, and you could be hurt! No. Let me deal with them. I know them; I can talk with them, explain what has happened, and turn them back before it is too late." His handsome features crinkled with worry. "Please, Walker? Lady?"

There was nothing more to be said. Carisman had made up his mind and would not allow them to change it. As a final concession they demanded that they be allowed to accompany him at least as far as was reasonable to assure that they would be close at hand in case of trouble. Carisman was reluctant to agree even to that much, concerned that he was taking them away from work that was more important, that he was delaying their search for the Stone King. Both Quickening and Walker refused to argue the point. They walked in silence, single file along the walkways, down the tunneled streets, traveling south through the city. He would meet the Urdas at the city's south edge, Carisman told them, sweeping back his blond hair, squaring himself for his encounter. Walker found him odd and heroic at once, a strange parody of a man aspiring to reality yet unable quite to grasp it. Give thought to what you are doing, he begged the tunesmith at one point. But Carisman's answering smile was cheerfully beguiling and filled with certainty. He had done all the thinking he cared to do.

When they neared the boundaries of the city, the rocky flats of the isthmus peeking through the gaps in the buildings, Carisman brought them to a halt.

"Wait for me here," he told them firmly. Then he made them promise not to follow after him. "Do not show yourselves; it will only frighten the Urdas. Give me a little time. I am certain I can make them understand. As I said, my friends—they are like children."

He clasped their hands in farewell and walked on. He turned at one point to make certain they were doing as he had asked, then waved back to them. His handsome face was smiling and assured. They watched the mist curl about him, gather him up, and finally cause him to disappear.

Walker glanced at the buildings surrounding them, chose a suitable one, and steered Quickening toward it. They entered, climbed the stairs to the top floor, and found a room where a bank of windows gaped open to the south. From there they could watch the Urdas approach. The gnarled figures were strung out along the isthmus, making their way cautiously past the crevices and ruts. There were perhaps twenty of them, several obviously injured.

They watched until the Urdas reached the edge of the city and disappeared into the shadow of the buildings.

Walker shook his head. "I find myself wishing we had not agreed to this. Carisman is almost a child himself. I cannot help thinking he would have been better off not coming with us at all.''

"He chose to come," Quickening reminded him. Her face tilted into the light, out of a striping of shadows. "He wanted to be free, Walker Boh. Coming with us, even here, was better than staying behind."

Walker glanced through the windows a final time. The stone of the isthmus flats and the streets below glistened with the damp, empty and still. He could hear the distant thunder of the ocean, the cries of the seabirds, and the rushing of the wind down the cliffs. He felt alone.

"I wonder sometimes how many like Carisman there are," he said finally. "Orphans, as he called himself. How many left to roam the land, made outcasts by Federation rule, their magic not the gift it was intended to be, but a curse they must disguise if they would keep their lives."

Quickening seated herself against the wall and studied him. "A great many, Walker Boh. Like Carisman. Like yourself."

He eased down beside her, folding his cloak about him, lifting his pale face toward the light. "I was not thinking of myself."

"Then you must do so," she said simply. "You must become aware."

He stared at her. "Aware of what?"

"Of the possibilities of your life. Of the reasons for being who you are. If you were an elemental, you would understand. I was given life for a specific purpose. It would be terrifying to exist without that purpose. Is it not so for you?"

Walker felt his face tighten. "I have purpose in my life."

Her smile was unexpected and dazzling. "No, Walker Boh, you do not. You have thrust from you any sense of purpose and made yourself an outcast twice over—first, for having been born with the legacy of Brin Ohmsford's magic, and second, for having fallen heir to her trust. You deny who and what you are. When I healed your arm, I read your life. Tell me this is not so."

He took a deep breath. "Why is it that I feel we are so much alike, Quickening? It is neither love nor friendship. It is something in between. Am I joined to you somehow?"

"It is our magic, Walker Boh."

"No," he said quickly. "It is something more."

Her beautiful face masked all traces of the emotion that flickered in her eyes. "It is what we have come here to do."

"To find the Stone King and take back from him the stolen

Black Elfstone. Somehow.'' Walker nodded solemnly. "And for me, to regain the use of my arm. And for Morgan Leah, to regain the magic of the Sword of Leah. All somehow. I have listened to your explanations. Is it true that you have not been told how any of this is to be accomplished? Or are there secrets that you hide from us as Pe Ell charges?''

"Walker Boh," she said softly. "You turn my questions into your own and ask of me what I would ask of you. We both keep something of the truth at bay. It cannot be so for much longer. I will make a bargain with you. When you are ready to confront your truth, I shall confront mine.''

Walker struggled to understand. "I no longer fear the magic I was born with," he said, studying the lines of her face, tracing its curves and angles as if she were in danger of disappearing before he could secure a memory of her. "I listened once to my nephew Par Ohmsford admonish me that the magic was a gift and not a curse. I scorned him. I was frightened of the implications of having the magic. I feared . . .''

He caught himself, an iron grip that tightened on his voice and thoughts instantly. A shadow of something terrifying had shown itself to him, a shadow that had grown familiar to him over the years. It had no face, but it spoke with the voices of Allanon and Cogline and his father and even himself. It whispered of history and need and the laws of Mankind. He thrust it away violently.

Quickening leaned forward and with gentle fingers touched his face. "I fear only that you will continue to deny yourself," she whispered. "Until it is too late.''

"Quickening . . .''

Her fingers moved across his mouth, silencing him. "There is a scheme to life, to all of its various happenings and events, to everything we do within the time allotted to us. We can understand that scheme if we let ourselves, if we do not become frightened of knowing. Knowledge is not enough if there is not also acceptance of that knowledge. Anyone can give you knowledge, Walker Boh, but only you can learn how to accept it. That must come from within. So it is that my father has sent me to summon you and Pe Ell and Morgan Leah to Eldwist; so it is that the combination of your magics shall free the Black Elfstone and begin the healing process of the Lands. I know that this is to be. In time, I shall know how. But I must be ready to accept its truths when that happens. It is so as well for you.''

"I will . . .''

"No, you will not be ready, Walker," she anticipated him, "if you continue to deny truths already known to you. That is what you must realize. Now speak no more of it to me. Only think on what I have said."

She turned away. It was not a rebuff; she did not intend it that way. It was a simple breaking off, an ending of talk, done not to chastise but to allow him space in which to explore himself. He sat staring at her for a time, then turned introspective. He gave himself over to the images her words conjured. He found himself thinking of other voices in other times, of the world he had come from with its false measure of worth, its fears of the unknown, its subjugation to a government and rules it did not wish to comprehend. *Bring back the Druids and Paranor,* Allanon had charged him. And would that begin a changing back of the world, of the Four Lands, into what they had been? And would that make things better? He doubted, but he found his doubts founded more in a lack of understanding than in his fears. What was he to do? He was to recover the Black Elfstone, carry it to disappeared Paranor, and somehow, in some way, bring back the Keep. Yet what would that accomplish? Cogline was gone. All of the Druids were gone. There was no one . . .

But himself.

No! He almost screamed the word aloud. It bore the face of the thing he feared, the thing he struggled so hard to keep from himself. It was the terrifying possibility that had scratched and clawed around the edges of his self-imposed shield for as long as he could remember.

He would not take up the Druid cause!

Yet he was Brin Ohmsford's last descendent. He was bearer of the trust that had been left to her by Allanon. *Not in your lifetime. Keep it safe for generations to come. One day it will be needed again.* Words from the distant past, spoken by the Druid's shade after death, haunting, unfulfilled.

I haven't the magic! he wailed in desperation, in denial. *Why should it be me? Why?*

But he already knew. Need. Because there was need. It was the answer that Allanon had given to all of the Ohmsfords, to each of them, year after year, generation after generation. Always.

He wrestled with the specter of his destiny in the silence of his thoughts. The moments lengthened. Finally he heard Quickening say, "It grows dark, Walker Boh."

He glanced up, saw the failing of the light as dusk approached. He climbed to his feet and peered south into the flats. The isthmus was empty. There was no sign of the Urdas.

"It's been too long," he muttered and started for the stairs.

They descended quickly, emerged from the building, and began following the walkway south toward the city's edge. Shadows were already spreading into dark pools, the light chased west to the fringes of the horizon. The seabirds had gone to roost, and the pounding of the ocean had faded to a distant moan. The stone beneath their feet echoed faintly with their footsteps as if whispering secrets to break the silence.

They reached the fringe of the city and slowed, proceeding more cautiously now, searching the gloom for any signs of danger. There was no movement to be found. The mist curled its damp tendrils through vacant windows and down sewer grates, and there was a sense of a hidden presence at work. Ahead, the isthmus flats stretched out into the darkness, broken and ragged and lifeless.

They stepped clear of the building walls and stopped.

Carisman's body was slumped against a pillar of rock at the end of the street, pinned fast by a dozen spears. He had been dead for some time, the blood from his wounds washed away by the rain.

It appeared that the Urdas had gone back the way they had come.

They had taken Carisman's head with them.

Even children can be dangerous, Walker Boh thought bleakly. He reached over for Quickening's hand and locked it in his own. He tried to imagine what Carisman's thoughts had been when he realized his family had disowned him. He tried to tell himself that there was nothing he could have done to prevent it.

Quickening moved close to him. They stood staring at the dead tunesmith wordlessly for a moment more, then turned and walked back into the city.

XXIV

They did not return to their normal place of concealment that night; it was already dusk when they departed the flats and the distance back through the city
was too great to cover safely. Instead, they found a building
close at hand, a low, squat structure with winding, narrow halls
and rooms with doors opening through at both ends to provide
a choice of escape routes if the Rake should appear. Settled deep
within the stone interior of the building, shut away with barely
enough light to see each other at arm's length, they ate their
dinner of dried fruits and vegetables, stale bread, and a little
water and tried to banish the ghost of Carisman from their presence. The dead tunesmith surfaced in memories, in unspoken
words, and in the faint, soft roll of the ocean's distant waters.
His face blossomed in the shadows they cast, and his voice
whispered in the sound of their breathing. Walker Boh regarded
Quickening without seeing her; his thoughts were of Carisman
and of how he had let the tunesmith go when he could have
stopped him from doing so. When Quickening touched him on
the arm, he was barely aware of the pressure of her fingers.
When she read his thoughts in the touch, he was oblivious. He
felt drained and empty and impossibly alone.

Later, while she slept, he grew aware of her again. His self-
reproach had exhausted itself, his sorrow had dried up; Carisman's shade was banished, consigned at last to the place and
time in which it belonged. He sat in a box of darkness, the stone
of the walls and ceiling and floor pressing in around him, the
silence a blanket that would suffocate him, time the instrument
by which he measured the approach of his own death. Could it
be far away now for any of them? He watched the girl sleeping
next to him, watched the rise and fall of her breast as she

breathed, turned on her side, her face cradled in the crook of her arm, her silver hair fanned back in a sweep of brightness. He watched the slow, steady beat of her pulse along the slim column of her throat, searched the hollows of her face where the shadows draped and pooled, and traced the line of her body within the covering of clothes that failed to hide its perfection. She was a fragile bit of life whatever her magic, and he could not escape the feeling that despite the confidence she evidenced in her father and the command with which she had brought them north she was in peril. The feeling was elusive and difficult to credit, but it took life in his instincts and his prescience, born of the magic that he had inherited from Brin Ohmsford, magic that still ebbed and flowed within him as the tide of his belief in himself rose and fell. He could not disregard it. Quickening was at risk, and he did not know how to save her.

The night deepened and still he did not sleep. They were all at risk, of course. What he sensed of danger to the daughter of the King of the Silver River was possibly no more than what he sensed of danger to them all. It had caught up with Carisman. It would eventually catch up with Quickening as well. Perhaps what he feared was not that Quickening would die, but that she would die before she revealed the secrets she knew. There were many, he suspected. That she hid them so completely infuriated him. He was surprised at the anger his realization provoked. Quickening had brought him face to face with the darkest of his fears and then left him to stand alone against it. His entire life had been shadowed by his apprehension that Allanon's mysterious trust to the Ohmsfords, given over three hundred years ago to Brin and passed unused from generation to generation, might somehow require fulfillment by him. He had lived with the specter of it since childhood, aware of its existence as all of his family had been, finding it a ghost that would not be banished, that instead grew more substantial with the passing of the years. The magic of the Ohmsfords was alive in him as it had not been in his ancestors. The dreams of Allanon had come only to him. Cogline had made him his student and taught him the history of his art and of the Druid cause. Allanon had told him to go in search of the Druids and lost Paranor.

He shivered. Each step took him closer to the inevitable. The trust had been held for him. The phantom that had haunted him all these years had revealed a terrifying face.

He was to take the Black Elfstone and bring back Paranor.

He was to become the next Druid.

He could have laughed at the ridiculousness of the idea if he had not been so frightened of it. He despised what the Druids had done to the Ohmsfords; he saw them as sinister and self-serving manipulators. He had spent his life trying to rid himself of their curse. But it was more than that. Allanon was gone—the last of the real Druids. Cogline was gone—the last of those who had studied the art. He was alone; who was to teach him what a Druid must know? Was he to divine the study of magic somehow? Was he to teach himself? And how many years would that take? How many centuries? If the magic of the Druids was required to combat the Shadowen, such magic could not be drawn leisurely from the Histories and the tomes that had taught all the Druids who had gone before. Time did not permit it.

He clenched his teeth. It was foolish to think that he could become a Druid, even if he were willing, even if he wished it, even if the specter he had feared so for all these years turned out to be himself.

Foolish!

Walker's eyes glittered as he searched the shadows of the room for an escape from his distress. Where were the answers that he needed? Did Quickening hide those answers? Were they a part of the truths she concealed? Did she know what was to become of him? He started to reach for her, intending to shake her awake. Then he caught himself and drew back. No, he reasoned. Her knowledge was as small and imperfect as his own. With Quickening, it was more a sensing of possibilities, a divining of what might be, a prescience like his own. It was a part of the reason he felt her to be kindred; there was that sharing of abilities and uses of the magics they wielded. He forced his thoughts to slow and his mind to open and he gazed upon her as if his eyes might swallow her up. He felt something warm and generous touch him, her sleep presence, unbidden and revealed. It reminded him of his mother's when he was small and still in need of her reassurance and comfort. She was in some way a rendering of his future self. She opened him up to the possibilities of what he might be. He saw the colors of his life, the textures and the patterns that might be woven, and the styles that might be tried. He was cloth to be cut and shaped, but he lacked the tools and understanding. Quickening was doing what she could to give him both.

He dozed then for a time, still upright against the chamber wall, his legs and arms folded tightly together against his body, his face tilted forward into his cloak. When he came awake again, Quickening was looking at him. They studied each other wordlessly for a moment, each searching the other's eyes, seeking out some reading of the other's needs.

"You are afraid, Walker Boh," the girl said finally.

Walker almost smiled. "Yes, Quickening. I have been afraid forever. Afraid of this—of what is happening now—all of my life. I have run from it, hidden from it, wished it away, begged that it would disappear. I have fought to contain it. Exercising a strict and unyielding control over my life was the technique that seemed to work best. If I could dictate my own fate, then it could have no power over me. The past would be left for others; the present would belong to me."

He let his legs unfold and straightened them gingerly before him. "The Druids have affected the lives of so many of the Ohmsfords, of the children of Shannara, for generations. We have been used by them; we have been made over to serve their causes. They have changed what we are. They have made us slaves of the magic rather than simply wielders. They have altered the composition of our minds and bodies and spirits; they have subverted us. And still they are not satisfied. Look at what they expect of us now! Look at what is expected of me! I am to transcend the role of slave and become master. I am to take up the Black Elfstone—a magic I do not begin to understand. I am to use it to bring back lost Paranor. And even that is not enough. I am to bring back the Druids as well. But there are no Druids. There is only me. And if there is only me, then . . ."

He choked on the words. His resolve faltered. His patience failed him. His anger returned, a raw and bitter echo in the silence.

"Tell me!" he begged, trying to contain his urgency.

"But I do not know," she whispered.

"You must!"

"Walker . . ."

There were tears in his eyes. "I cannot be what Allanon wants me to be—what he demands that I be! I cannot!" He took a quick, harsh breath to steady himself. "Do you see, Quickening? If I am to bring back the Druids by becoming one, if I must because there is no other way that the Races can survive the Shadowen, must I then be as they once were? Must I take control of the lives of those I profess to help, those others who are Ohmsfords, Par and Coll and Wren? For how many generations yet to come? If I am to be a Druid, must I do this? Can I do anything else?"

"Walker Boh." When she spoke his name her voice was soft and compelling. "You will be what you must, but you will still be yourself. You are not trapped in some spider's web of Druid magic that has predetermined your life, that has fated you to be but one way and one way only. There is always a choice. Always."

He had the sudden sense that she was talking of something else completely. Her perfect face strained against some inner torment, and she paused to reshape it, chasing quickly the furrows and lines. "You are frightened of your fate without knowing what it is to be. You are paralyzed by doubts and misgivings that are of your own making. Much has happened to you, Dark Uncle, and it is enough to make any man doubt. You have lost loved ones, your home, a part of your body and spirit. You have seen the specter of a childhood fear take form and threaten to become real. You are far from everything you know. But you must not despair."

His eyes were haunted. "But I do. I am adrift, Quickening. I feel myself slipping away completely."

She reached out her hand and took his own. "Then cling to me, Walker Boh. And let me cling to you. If we keep hold of each other, the drifting will stop."

She moved against him, her silver hair spilling across his dark cloak as her head lowered into his chest. She did not speak, but simply rested there, still holding his hand, her warmth mixing with his own. He lowered his chin to her hair and closed his eyes.

He slept then, and there were no dreams or sudden wakings, only a gentle cradling by soft, invisible threads that held him firm. His drifting ceased, just as she had promised it would. He was no longer plagued by troubling and uncertain visions; he was left at peace. Calm enfolded him, soothing and comforting. It had a woman's hands, and the hands belonged to Quickening.

He woke again at daybreak, easing from the chilly stone floor to his feet as his eyes adjusted to the thin gray light. From beyond the maze of rooms and corridors that buffered him from the outside world, he could hear the soft patter of rain. Quickening was gone. Vaguely worried, he searched until he found her standing at a bank of windows on the north wall, staring out into the haze. The stone buildings and streets shimmered wetly, reflecting their own images in grotesque parody, mirroring their deadness. Eldwist greeted the new day as a corpse, sightless and stiff. It stretched away into the distance, rows of buildings, ribbons of streets, a symmetry of design and construction that was flat and hard and empty of life. Walker stood next to Quickening and felt the oppressiveness of the city close about him.

Her black eyes shifted to find his own, her mane of silver hair the sole brightness in the gloom. "I held you as tightly as I could, Walker Boh," she told him. "Was it enough?"

He took a moment to answer. The stump of his missing arm ached and the joints of his body were stiff and slow to respond. He felt himself to be a large shell in which his spirit had shriveled to the size of a pebble. Yet he was strangely resolved.

"I am reminded of Carisman," he said finally, "determined to be free at any cost. I would be free as well. Of my fears and doubts. Of myself. Of what I might become. That cannot be until I have learned the secret of the Black Elfstone and the truth behind the dreams of the shade of Allanon."

Quickening's faint smile surprised him. "I would be free, too," she said softly. She seemed anxious to explain, then looked quickly away. "We must find Uhl Belk," she said instead.

They departed their shelter and went out into the rain. They walked the silent streets of Eldwist north through the shadows and gloom, hunched within the protection of their forest cloaks, lost in their private thoughts.

Quickening said, "Eldwist is a land in midwinter waiting for spring. She is layered in stone as other parts of the earth at times are layered in snow. Can you feel her patience? There are seeds planted, and when the snow melts those seeds can be brought to bloom."

Walker wasn't sure what she was talking about. "There is only stone in Eldwist, Quickening. It runs deep and long, from shore to shore, the length and breadth of the peninsula. There are no seeds here, nothing of the woodlands or the fields, no trees, no flowers, no grasses. Only Uhl Belk and the monsters that serve him. And us."

"Eldwist is a lie," she said.

"Whose lie?" he asked. But she wouldn't answer.

They followed the street for close to an hour, keeping carefully to the walkways, listening for the sound of anything moving. Except for the steady patter of the rain, there was only silence. Even the Maw Grint slept, it seemed. Water pooled and was channeled into streams, and it swept down the gutters in sluggish torrents that eddied and splashed and washed away the silt and dust the wind had blown in. The buildings watched in mute and indifferent testimony, unfeeling sentinels. Clouds and mist mixed and descended to wrap them about, easing steadily downward until they scraped the earth. Things began to disappear, towers first, then entire walls, then bits and pieces of the streets themselves. Walker and Quickening felt a changing in the world, as if a presence had been loosed. Phantasms came out to play, dark shadows risen from the earth to dance at the edges of their vision, never entirely real, never quite completely formed. Eyes watched, peering downward from the heights, staring upward through the stone. Fingers brushed at their skin, droplets of rain, trailers of mist, and something more. Walker let himself become one with what he was feeling, an old trick, a blending of self with external sensations, all to gain a small measure of insight into the origin of what was unseen. He could sense a presence after a time, dark, brooding, ancient, a thing of vast power. He could hear it breathing. He could almost see its eyes.

"Walker," Quickening whispered.

A figure appeared out of the haze before them, cloaked and hooded as they were and uncomfortably close. Walker stepped in front of Quickening and stopped. The figure stopped as well. Wordlessly, they faced each other. Then the clouds shifted, changing the slant of the light, the shadows re-formed, and a voice called out uncertainly. "Quickening?"

Walker Boh started forward again. It was Morgan Leah.

They clasped hands on meeting, and Quickening hugged the sodden and disheveled Highlander close, kissing his face passionately. Walker watched without speaking, already aware of the attraction shared by the two, surprised that Quickening would allow it to be. He watched the way her eyes closed when Morgan held her and thought he understood. She was letting herself feel because it was all still new. She was no older than the time of her creation, and even if her father had given her human feelings she would not have experienced them firsthand until now. He felt an odd twinge of sadness for her. She was trying so hard to live.

"Walker." Morgan moved over to him, one arm still wrapped about the girl. "I've been searching everywhere. I thought something had happened to you as well."

He told them what had befallen Horner Dees and himself, how they had been snared by the trapdoor and tumbled onto the slide, and how they had found themselves confronted by the horror of the Maw Grint slumbering directly below. His eyes were fierce and bright as he struggled to describe how he had somehow managed to release the magic of the Sword of Leah once again, magic he had feared lost. With its aid they had escaped. They had taken refuge for the night close by, then made their way at dawn to where they had left the others of the little company. But the building had been empty and there had been no sign of anyone's return. Worried for Quickening—for all of them, he hastened to add—he had left Dees to keep watch for them in case they returned and gone hunting alone.

"Horner Dees was prepared to come as well, but I refused to allow it. The truth is, he would never move again if he could arrange it—at least not until it was time to leave this place." The Highlander smiled broadly. "He's had enough of Eldwist and its traps; he wants the ale house at Rampling Steep again!" He paused then, looking past them speculatively. "Where's Carisman?"

It was their turn to speak, and Quickening did so, her voice steady and strangely comforting as she related the events that had led to the death of the tunesmith. Even so, Morgan Leah's face was lined with despair and anger by the time she had finished.

"He never understood anything, did he?" the Highlander said, the emotions he was holding inside threatening to choke him. "He just never understood! He thought his music was a cure for everything. Shades!"

He looked away a moment, shielding his expression, hands clasped on his hips defiantly, as if stubbornness might somehow change what had happened. "Where do we go now?" he asked finally.

Walker glanced at Quickening. "We believe that Uhl Belk hides within the dome." The girl spoke for him. "We were looking for a way in when the Urdas appeared. We are returning to continue the search."

Morgan turned, his face set. "Then I am coming with you. Horner will be better off resting right where he is. We can rejoin him at nightfall." The look he gave them was almost defiant. "That's the way it should be anyway. Just the three of us."

"Come if you wish, Morgan," Quickening soothed, and Walker nodded without comment.

They resumed walking, three rain-soaked figures nearly lost in the mist and shadows. Walker led, a lean and white-faced ghost against the gloom, leader now because Quickening had moved a step back to be with Morgan, content to follow. He hunched his narrow shoulders against the weather, felt the bite of the wind as it gusted momentarily, and felt the emptiness inside threaten to engulf him. He reached into that emptiness and tried to secure some part of his magic, a strength he could rely upon. It eluded him, like a snake in flight. He peered ahead through the thin curtain of the rain and watched the shadows chase after the light. The specter of his fate leered at him, a faint shimmer in a pool of water, a wisp of fog in a doorway, a darkening of stone where the dampness reflected like a mirror. In each instance, it wore the face of Allanon.

The street ended, and the dark bulk of the dome lifted before them like the shell of some sleeping crustacean. The three stepped down off the walkway and crossed to stand before it, dwarfed by its size. Walker stared at the dome without speaking, aware that Morgan and Quickening were waiting on him, conscious that something else was waiting on him as well. *It.* The presence he had sensed before was back again, stronger here, readier, more assured. And watching. Silently watching. Walker did not move. He felt eyes all around him, as if there were nowhere he might run that he could not be seen. The stone of the city was a hand that cradled him yet might close without warning to crush out his life. The presence wanted him to know that. It wanted him to know how insignificant he was, how futile his quest, and how purposeless his life. It bore down on him, pressed about like the mist and rain. Go home, he heard it whisper. Leave while you can.

He did not leave. He did not even step away. He had faced enough threats in his time, enough dark things that roamed the land, to know when he was being tested. The effort was not a crushing one; it was teasing and fey, as if designed to insinuate an opposite effect than the one indicated. Don't really leave, it seemed to say. Just remember that you were asked.

Walker Boh stepped forward to where the wall was broadest between the bands of stone. Death brushed up against him, a soft sprinkle of rain caught in the wind. It was odd, but he sensed Cogline close beside him, the old man's ghost risen from the ashes of Hearthstone, come to watch his student practice the craft he had taught him, come perhaps to judge how well he performed. You will never be free of the magic, he could hear the other say. He stared momentarily at the pitted, worn surface of the wall, watching the rainwater snake downward along its irregular paths, silver streamers that glistened like strands of Quickening's hair. He reached down again within himself for the magic and this time fastened on it. He drew its strength about him like armor, banded himself with it as if to match the stone of the shell before him, then reached out with his one remaining hand and pressed his fingers to the wall.

He felt the magic rise within him, flowing hot like fire, extending from his chest to his arm to the tips of his fingers to . . .

There was a shudder, and the stone before him drew back, flinching away as if human flesh that had been burned. There was a long, deep groan that was the sound of stone grating on stone and a thin shriek as if a life had been pressed between. Quickening crouched like a startled bird, her silver hair flung back, her eyes bright and strangely alive. Morgan Leah drew out the broadsword strapped across his back in a single swift motion.

The wall before them opened—not as a door would swing wide or a panel lift, but as a cloth torn asunder. It opened, stretched wide from foundation to apex, a mouth that sought to feed. When it was twenty feet across, it stopped, immobile once more, the stone edges smooth and fixed, imbued with the look of a doorway that had always been there and clearly belonged.

A way in, thought Walker Boh. Exactly what they had come searching for.

Quickening and Morgan Leah stood beside him expectantly. He did not look at either of them. He kept his eyes focused on the opening before him, on the darkness within, on its sea of impenetrable shadows. He searched and listened, but nothing revealed itself.

Still, he knew what waited.

Carisman's voice sang softly in his mind. *Come right in, said the spider to the fly.*

With the girl and the Highlander flanking him, Walker Boh complied.

XXV

Shadows enveloped them almost immediately, layers of darkness that began less than a dozen feet inside the opening to the dome and entirely concealed everything that lay beyond. They slowed on Walker's lead, waiting for their eyes to adjust, listening to the hollow echoes of their booted feet fade into the silence. Then there was only the sound of their breathing. Behind them, the faint gray daylight was a slender thread connecting them to the world without, and an instant later it was severed. Stone grated on stone once more, and the opening that had admitted them disappeared. No one moved to prevent it from happening; indeed, they had all expected as much. They stood together in the silence that followed, each conscious of the reassuring presence of the others, each straining to hear the sound of any foreign movement, each waiting for some small measure of sight to return. The sense of emptiness was complete. The interior of the dome had the feel of a monstrous tomb in which nothing living had walked in centuries. The air had a stale and musty smell, devoid of any recognizable scents, and it was cold, a bone-biting chill that entered through the mouth and nostrils and worked its way instantly to the pit of the stomach and lodged there. They began to shiver almost immediately. Even in the impenetrable darkness it seemed to Walker Boh that he could see the clouding of his breath.

The seconds dragged by, heartbeats in the unbroken stillness. The three waited patiently. Something would happen. Someone would appear. Unless they had been brought into the dome to be killed, Walker speculated in the silence of his thoughts. But he didn't think that was the case. In fact, he no longer believed as he had in the beginning that there was any active effort being made to eliminate them. The character of their relationship with Eldwist suggested on close study that the city functioned in an impersonal way to rid itself of intruders, but that it did not exert any special effort if it immediately failed. Eldwist did not rely on speed; it relied on the law of averages. Sooner or later intruders would make a mistake. They would grow incautious and either the trapdoors or the Rake would claim them. Walker was willing to wager that Quickening had guessed right, that until very recently the Stone King hadn't even been aware of their presence—or if he had, hadn't bothered himself about it. It wasn't until Walker had used magic against the shell of his enclosure that he had roused himself. Not even using magic against the Rake had made any difference to him. But now, Walker believed, he was curious—and that was why they had been brought inside . . .

Walker caught himself. He had missed something. Nothing was going to happen if they just stood there in the darkness, not if they waited all that day and all the next. The Stone King had brought them inside for a reason. He had brought them inside to see what they would do.

Or, perhaps, *could* do.

He reached out with his good arm to grip first Morgan and then Quickening and bent their heads gently to press close against his own. "Whatever happens, Quickening," he whispered, speaking only to the girl, his voice so soft it was barely audible, "remember your vow to do nothing to reveal that you have any use of the magic."

Then he released them, stepped away, brought up his hand, snapped his fingers, and sparked a single silver flame to life.

They looked about. They were standing in a tunnel that ran forward a short distance to an opening. Holding the flame before him, Walker led them forward. When they reached the tunnel's end, he extinguished the flame, summoned his magic a second time, and sent a scattering of silver fire into the darkness.

Walker inhaled sharply. The shower of light flew into the unknown, soaring through the shadows, chasing them as it went, and rising until everything about them lay revealed. They stood at the entrance to a vast rotunda, an arena ringed by row upon row of seats that lifted away into the gloom. The roof of the dome stretched high overhead, its rafters of stone arcing downward from peak to foundation. Lines of stairs ran upward to the rows of seats, and railings encircled the arena. The arena and stands, like the rafters, were stone, ancient and worn by time, hard and flat against the darkness that cloaked them. A string of shadowed tunnels similar to the one that had admitted them opened through the stands, black holes that burrowed and disappeared.

At the very center of the arena stood a massive stone statue, rough-hewn and barely recognizable, of a man hunched over in thought.

Walker let the fire settle in place, its light extending. The dome was vast and empty, silent save for the sound of their footfalls, seemingly bereft of any life but their own. Out of the corner of his eye he saw Morgan start forward and reached out quickly to hold him back. Quickening moved over to take the Highlander's arm protectively in her own. Walker's gaze swept the arena, the black tunnels that opened onto it, the stands that surrounded it, the rafters and ceiling, and then the arena again. He stopped when he reached the statue. Nothing moved. But there was something there. He could feel it, more strongly now than before, the same presence he had sensed when he had stood without.

He started forward, slowly, cautiously. Morgan and Quickening trailed. He was momentarily in command of matters now, Quickening's deference in some way become an acknowledgment of her need. She was not to use magic. She was to rely on him. He discovered an unexpected strength of resolution in the fact that he had made her dependent on him. There was no time now for drifting, for self-doubts and fears, or for the uncertainties of who and what he was meant to be. A fiery determination burned through him. It was better this way, he realized, better to be in command, to accept responsibility for what was to happen. It had always been that way. At that moment he understood for the first time in his life that it always would.

The statue loomed directly before them, a massive chunk of stone that seemed to defy the light Walker had evoked to defuse the darkness. The thinker faced away from them, a gnarled and lumpish form, kneeling half-seated and half-slumped, one arm folded across his stomach, the second closed to a fist and cocked to brace his chin. It might have been intended that there be a cloak thrown about him or he might simply have been covered with hair; it was impossible to discern. There was no writing on the base he rested upon; indeed, it was a rather awkward pedestal that seemed to join the legs of the statue to the dome's floor as if the rock had simply melted away once upon a distant time.

They reached the statue and began to circle it. The face came slowly into view. It was a monster's face, ravaged and pocked, a mass of protuberances and knots, all misshapen in the manner of a sculpture partially formed and then abandoned. Eyes of stone stared blankly from beneath a glowering brow. There was horror written in the statue's features; there were demons captured in the shaping that could never be dislodged. Walker glanced away uneasily to search again the dome's shadows. The silence winked back at him.

Suddenly Quickening stopped, freezing in place like a startled deer. "Walker," she whispered, her voice a low hiss.

She was looking at the statue. Walker wheeled catlike to follow her gaze.

The eyes of the statue had shifted to fix on him.

He heard Morgan's blade clear its sheath in a rasp of metal.

The statue's misshapen head began moving, the stone grating eerily as it shifted, not breaking off or cracking, but rearranging somehow, as if become both solid and liquid. The grating echoed through the hollow shell of the dome like the shifting of massive mountain boulders in a slide. Arms moved and shoulders followed. The torso swiveled, the stone rubbing and grinding until the short hairs on Walker's neck were rigid.

Then it spoke, mouth opening, stone rubbing on stone.

—Who are you—

Walker did not reply, so astonished at what he was seeing that he could not manage to answer. He simply stood there, dumbfounded. The statue was alive, a thing of stone, frighteningly shaped by a madman's hand, lacking blood and flesh, yet somehow alive.

In the next instant he realized what he was seeing and even then he could not speak the creature's name. It was Quickening who spoke for him.

"Uhl Belk," she whispered.

—Who are you—

Quickening stepped forward, looking tiny and insignificant in the shadow of the Stone King, her silver hair swept back.

"I am called Quickening," she replied. Her voice, surprisingly strong and steady, reverberated through the stillness. "These are my companions, Walker Boh and Morgan Leah. We have come to Eldwist to ask you to return the Black Elfstone."

The head shifted slightly, stone crackling and grinding.

—The Black Elfstone belongs to me—

"No, Uhl Belk. It belongs to the Druids. You stole it from

them. You stole it from the Hall of Kings and brought it into Eldwist. Now you must give it back.''

There was a long pause before the Stone King spoke again.

—Who are you—

''I am no one.''

—Have you magic to use against me—

''No.''

—What of these others, do they have magic—

''Only a little. Morgan Leah once had use of a sword given him by the Druids which possessed the magic of the Hadeshorn. But it is broken now, the blade shattered, and its magic failed. Walker Boh once had the use of magic he inherited from his ancestors, from the Elven house of Shannara. But he lost the use of most of that magic when he suffered damage to his arm and his spirit. He has yet to gain it back. No, they have no magic that can harm you.''

Walker was so astonished he could barely credit what he was hearing. In a matter of seconds, Quickening had undone them completely. She had revealed not only what it was that they had come to find but also that they lacked any reasonable chance of gaining possession of it. She had admitted that they were virtually powerless against this spirit creature, that they were unable to force it to comply with their demands. She had removed even the possibility that they might run a bluff. What was she thinking?

Uhl Belk was apparently wondering the same thing.

—I am to give up the Black Elfstone simply because you ask me to do so, give it up to three mortals of finite lives, a girl with no magic, a one-armed man, and a swordsman with a broken blade—

''It is necessary, Uhl Belk.''

—I determine what is necessary in the Kingdom of Eldwist; I am the law and the power that enforces that law; there is no right but mine and therefore no necessity but mine; who would dare say no to me; not any of you; you are as insignificant as the dust that blows across the surface of my skin and washes into the sea—

He paused.

—The Black Elfstone is mine—

Quickening did not respond this time, but simply continued to stare into the Stone King's scarred eyes. Uhl Belk's massive body shifted again, moving as if mired in quicksand, the stone grinding resolutely, a wheel of time and certainty given the skin of substance.

—You—

He pointed to Walker, a finger straightening.

—The Asphinx claimed a part of you; I can sense its stink upon your body; yet somehow you still live; are you a Druid—

"No," Quickening answered instantly. "He is a messenger of the Druids, sent by them to recover the Black Elfstone. His Elven magic saved him from the poison of the Asphinx. His claim to the Black Elfstone is the rightful one, granted him by the Druids."

—The Druids are all dead—

Quickening said nothing, waiting for the Stone King, standing fearlessly beneath him. A sudden movement of one massive arm and she would be crushed. She seemed unconcerned. Walker glanced quickly at Morgan, but the Highlander's eyes were on the face of Uhl Belk, transfixed by the ugliness of it, hypnotized by the power he saw there. He wondered what he was expected to do. Anything? He wondered suddenly what he was doing there at all.

Then the Stone King spoke again, a slow rasping in the silence.

—I have been alive forever and I will live on long after you are dust; I was created by the Word and I have survived all that were given life with me save one and that one will soon be gone as well; I care nothing for the world in which I exist save for the preservation of that over which I was given dominion—eternal stone; it is stone that weathers all things, that is unchanging and fixed and therefore as close to perfection as life can achieve; I am the giver of stone to the world and the architect of what is to become; I use all necessary means to see that my purpose is fulfilled; therefore I took the Black Elfstone and made it mine—

The dome echoed with his words, and then the echoes died away into silence. The shadows were lengthening already as Walker's light began slowly to fail, the magic fading. Walker felt the futility of what they were about. Morgan's sword arm had lowered uselessly to his side; what purpose was there in trying to employ a weapon of iron against something as ancient and immutable as this? Only Quickening seemed to believe there was any hope.

—The Druids were as nothing compared to me; their precautions to hide and protect their magic were futile; I left the Asphinx to show my disdain for what they had attempted to do;

they were believers in the laws of nature and evolution, foolish purveyors of the creed of change; they died and left nothing; stone is the only element of the earth's body that endures, and I shall live in that stone forever—

"Constant," Quickening whispered.

—Yes—

"Eternal."

—Yes—

"But what of your trust, Uhl Belk? What of that? You have disdained to be that which you were created—a balancing force, a preservationist of the world as it was created to be." Her voice was low and compelling, a web weaving images that seemed to take form and shimmer in the dead air before her. "I was told your story. You were given life to preserve life; that was the trust given you by the Word. Stone preserves nothing of life. You were not instructed to transform, yet you have taken it upon yourself to subvert everything, to alter forever the composition of life upon the land, to change living matter to stone—all this to create an extension of who and what you are. And look what it has done to you."

She braced herself against the anger already forming on the Stone King's brow. "Give back the Black Elfstone, Uhl Belk. Let us help you become free again."

The massive stone creature shifted on his bed of rock, joints grating, the sounds cracking through the arena as if some invisible audience sought to respond. Uhl Belk spoke, and his voice had a new and frightening edge to it.

—You are more than you pretend to be; I am not deceived; yet it does not matter; I care nothing for who you are or what you want; I admitted you to me so that I might examine you; the magic with which you touched me caught my attention and made me curious as to who you might be; but I need nothing from you; I need nothing from any living thing; I am complete; think of me as the land on which you walk and you as the tiniest of fleas that live upon me; if you should become a bother I will eliminate you in an instant; if you should survive this day you will probably not survive another—

The great brow knitted, and the gnarled face re-formed its ridges and lines.

—What am I if not the whole of your existence; look about you and I am everything you see; look where you stand within Eldwist and I am everything you touch; I have made myself so;

I have made myself one with the land I create; I am free of all else and shall ever be—

Suddenly Walker Boh understood. Uhl Belk wasn't a living thing in the conventional sense of the words. He was a spirit in the same way as the King of the Silver River. He was more than the statue that crouched before them. He was everything they walked upon; he was the entire Kingdom of Eldwist. The stone was his skin, he had said—a part of his living self. He had found a way to infuse himself into everything he created, ensuring his permanency in a way that nothing else could.

But that meant he was a prisoner as well. That was why he didn't rise to greet them or come hunting for them or involve himself directly in any way in what they were about. That was why his legs were sunk down into the stone. Mobility was beyond him, an indulgence meant for lesser creatures. He had evolved into something greater; he had evolved into his own world. And it held him trapped.

"But you are not free, are you?" Quickening questioned boldly, as if reading Walker's thoughts. "If you were, you would give us the Black Elfstone, for you would have no real need of it." Her voice was hard and insistent. "But you cannot do that, can you, Uhl Belk? You need the Black Elfstone to stay alive. Without it, the Maw Grint would have you."

—No—

"Without it, the Maw Grint would destroy you."

—No—

"Without it . . ."

—No—

A stone fist crashed downward, barely missing the girl, shattering a portion of the ground next to her, sending jagged cracks along its surface for a hundred yards in every direction. The Stone King shuddered as if stricken.

"The Maw Grint is your child, Uhl Belk," Quickening continued, ramrod straight before him, as if it were she who had the size and the power and not the Stone King. "But your child does not obey you."

—You know nothing; the Maw Grint is an extension of me, as is everything in Eldwist an extension of me; it has no life except what I would give; it serves my purpose and no other, turning the lands adjoining and all that live within them to stone, the permanency of myself—

The girl's black eyes were bright and quick. "And the Black Elfstone?"

The Stone King's voice was resonant with some strange mix of emotions that refused to be identified.

—The Black Elfstone allows—

The jagged mouth ground closed and the Stone King hunched down into himself, limbs and body knotting together as though they might disappear into a single massive rock.

"Allows?" Quickening breathed softly.

The flat, empty eyes lifted.

—Watch—

The word reverberated like a splitting of the Stone King's soul. Rock grated and ground once more, and the wall of the dome behind them parted. Gray, hazy daylight spilled through as if to flee the steady curtain of rain that fell without. Clouds and mist drifted past, bending and twisting about the buildings that loomed beyond, cloaking them as if they were a gathering of frozen giants set patiently at watch. An eerie wail burst from the Stone King's mouth and it filled the emptiness of the city with a sound like a thin sheet of metal vibrating in the wind. It rose and died quickly, but its echo lingered as if it would last forever.

—Watch—

They heard the Maw Grint before they saw it, its approach signaled by a rumble deep beneath the city's streets that rose steadily as the creature neared, a low growl building to a roar that jolted everything and brought the three from Rampling Steep to their knees. The Maw Grint burst into view, shattering apart the stone that was Uhl Belk's skin, splitting it wide just beyond the wall of the dome, just without the opening through which they stared wide-eyed and helpless. They could see the Stone King flinch with pain. The Maw Grint rose and seemed to keep rising, a leviathan of impossible size that dwarfed even the buildings themselves, swaying like a snake, a loathsome cross between burrowing worm and serpent, as black as pitch with foul liquid oozing from a rock-encrusted body, eyeless, headless, its mouth a sucking hole that seemed intent on drinking first the rain and then the air itself. It shot into view with a suddenness that was terrifying and filled the void of the dome's opening like a wave of darkness that would collapse it completely.

Walker Boh went cold with disbelief and horror. The Maw Grint wasn't real; it was impossible even to imagine such a thing. For the first time in his life he wanted to run. He watched Morgan Leah stagger back and drop to his knees. He watched

Quickening freeze in place. He felt himself lose strength and only barely managed to keep from falling. The Maw Grint writhed against the skyline, a great spineless mass of black ooze that nothing could withstand.

Yet the Stone King did not waver. A thick, gnarled hand lifted, the one that had cradled his chin when they had thought him a statue, and the fingers slowly began to open. Light burst forth—yet it was light the like of which none of them had ever seen. It sprayed in all directions at first and did not illuminate in the manner of ordinary light but instead turned everything it touched dark.

This is not light, Walker Boh realized as he fought to hold back a flood of sensations that threatened to overwhelm him. *This is the absence of light!*

Then the fingers of the Stone King spread wide, and they could see what he held. It was a perfectly formed gemstone, its center as black and impenetrable as night. The stone glittered as it reflected the thin streamers of gray daylight and let not even the smallest trace pass within. It looked tiny cradled in Uhl Belk's massive stone palm, but the darkness it cast stretched away into the farthest corners of the dome, into the deepest recesses, seeking out and enveloping the whole of Walker's scattered luminescence so that in a matter of seconds the only light remaining came from the rent in the dome's stone skin.

Walker Boh felt his own magic stir within him in recognition.

They had found the Black Elfstone.

Uhl Belk cried out then, a thundering howl that rose above even the sounds of the Maw Grint's coming, of the wind and the rain and the sea far beyond, and he thrust the Black Elfstone before him. The blackness gathered and tightened into a single band that shot forward to strike the Maw Grint. The Maw Grint did not resist. Instead, it simply hung there, transfixed. It shuddered—pained and pleasured both somehow, wracked with feelings that the humans crouched before it could only imagine. It twisted, and the blackness twisted in response. The blackness spread, widening, flowing out, then back again, until the Stone King was enveloped as well. They could hear him groan, then sob, again with feelings that were mixed in some veiled way, not clearly defined and not meant to be. The Elfstone's magic joined them, father and son, monsters each, a substanceless lock that bound them as surely as iron chains.

What is happening? Walker Boh wondered. *What is the magic doing to them?*

Then the nonlight disappeared, a line of shadow fading, steadily dissipating like ink soaking into and through white netting, the air brightening until the daylight returned and the link between the Stone King and the Maw Grint had vanished. The Maw Grint sank from sight, oozing back into the earth. The hole that it had made closed after it, the stone knitting into place, as smooth and hard as before, leaving the street whole again, creating the illusion that nothing at all had happened. The rain washed away all traces of the creature's coming, streams of water loosening the greenish film of poison secreted from its body and carrying it from sight.

Uhl Belk's fingers closed once more about the Black Elfstone, his eyes lidded, his face transformed in a way that Walker could not describe, as if he had been made over somehow, created anew. Yet he was more frightening looking than ever, his features harsher, less human, and more a part of the rock that encased him. He withdrew the Elfstone, his hand clasping it tightly to his body. His voice rumbled.

—Do you see—

They did not, not even Quickening. The puzzlement in her dark eyes was evident. They stood mute before the Stone King, all three, feeling tiny and uncertain.

"What has happened to you, Uhl Belk?" the girl asked finally.

Rain hammered down, and the wind ripped through the dome's rent.

—Go—

The massive pitted head began to turn away, the stone grating ominously.

"You must give us the Black Elfstone!" Quickening shouted.

—The Black Elfstone is mine—

"The Shadowen will take it from you—just as you took it from the Druids!"

Uhl Belk's voice was weary, disinterested.

—The Shadowen are children; you are all children; you do not concern me; nothing that you do can harm or affect me; look at me; I am as old as the world and I shall last as long; you shall be gone in the blink of an eye; take yourselves out of my city; if you remain, if you come to me again, if I am disturbed by you in any way, I shall summon the Rake to dispose of you and you shall be swept away at once—

The floor rippled beneath them, a shudder that sent them tumbling backward toward the opening in the wall. The Stone

King had flinched the way an animal would in an effort to shed itself of some bothersome insect. Walker Boh rose, pulling Quickening back with him, beckoning to Morgan. There was nothing to be gained by staying. They would not have the Black Elfstone this day—if indeed ever. Uhl Belk was a creature evolved far beyond any other. He was right; what could they do that would harm or affect him?

Yet Quickening seemed unconvinced. "It is you who shall be swept away!" she shouted as they backed through the opening into the street. She was shaking. "Listen to me, Uhl Belk!"

The craggy face was turned again into shadow, the massive shoulders hunched down, the thinker's pose resumed. There was no response.

Standing outside in the rain they watched the wall seal over, the skin knit, the rent fade away as if it had never been. In moments the dome was an impenetrable shell once more.

Morgan moved to place his hands on Quickening's shoulders. The girl seemed unaware of him, a thing of stone herself. The Highlander leaned close and began whispering.

Walker Boh moved away from them. When he was alone, he turned once again to face Uhl Belk's haven. A fire consumed him and at the same time he felt detached. He was there and he was not. He realized that he no longer knew himself. He had become an enigma he could not solve. His thoughts tightened like a cinched cord. The Stone King was an enemy that none of them could defeat. He was not simply ruler of a city; he was the city itself. Uhl Belk had become Eldwist. He was a whole world, and no one could change an entire world. Not Allanon or Cogline or all of the Druids put together.

Rain streamed down his face. No one.

Yet he already knew that he was going to try.

XXVI

Pe Ell had changed his mind twice before finally settling the matter. Now he slipped down the darkening street and ducked into the doorway of the building in which the others had concealed themselves with his misgivings comfortably stowed. Rain dripped from his cloak, staining the stone of the stairs he followed, tracking his progress in a steady, meandering trail. He paused at the landing to listen, heard nothing, and went on. The others were probably out searching. There or not, it made no difference to him. Sooner or later, they would return. He could wait.

He passed down the hallway without bothering to conceal his approach and stalked through the doorway of their hiding place. At first glance the room appeared empty, but his instincts warned him instantly that he was being watched and he stopped a dozen feet through. Shadows dappled the room in strange patterns, clustered about haphazardly as if stray children chased inside by the weather. The patter of the rain sounded steadily in the silence as Pe Ell stood waiting.

Then Horner Dees appeared, slipping noiselessly from the shadows of a doorway to one side, moving with a grace and ease that belied his bulky frame. He was scratched and bruised and his clothing was torn. He looked as if some animal had gotten hold of him. He fixed Pe Ell with his grizzled look, as rough and suspicious as ever, an ageing bear come face-to-face with a familiar enemy.

"You constantly amaze me," Pe Ell said, meaning it, still curious about this troublesome old man.

Dees stopped, keeping his distance. "Thought we'd seen the last of you," he growled.

"Did you, now?" Pe Ell smiled disarmingly, then moved

across the room to where a collection of withered fruits sat drying in a makeshift bowl. He picked one up and took a bite. It was bitter tasting, but edible. "Where are the others?"

"Out and about," Dees answered. "What difference does it make to you?"

Pe Ell shed his damp cloak and seated himself. "None. What happened to you?"

"I fell down a hole. Now what do you want?"

Pe Ell's smile stayed in place. "A little help."

It was difficult to tell if Horner Dees was surprised or not; he managed to keep his face from showing anything but seemed at a momentary loss for a response. He hunched down a few inches, as if settling himself against an attack, studied Pe Ell wordlessly, then shook his head.

"I know you, Pe Ell," he declared softly. "I remember you from the old days, from the time you were just beginning. I was with the Federation then, a Tracker, and I knew you. Rimmer Dall had plans for me as well; but I decided not to go along with them. I saw you once or twice, saw you come and go, heard the rumors about you." He paused. "I just want you to know."

Pe Ell finished the fruit and tossed the pit aside. He wasn't sure how he felt about this unexpected revelation. He guessed it really didn't matter. At least now he had an inkling of what it was that bothered him so about Dees.

"I don't remember you," he said finally. "Not that it matters." The hatchet face inclined away from the light. "Just so we understand each other, Rimmer Dall's plans for me didn't work out quite as he expected either. I do what I choose. I always have."

Dees rugged face nodded. "You kill people."

Pe Ell shrugged. "Sometimes. Are you frightened?"

The other man shook his head. "Not of you."

"Good. Then if we've finished with that topic of conversation, let's move back to the other. I need a little help. Care to lend me some?"

Horner Dees stood mute a moment, then moved over to seat himself. He settled down with a grunt and stared at Pe Ell without speaking, apparently assessing the offer. That was fine with Pe Ell. He had thought the matter through carefully before coming back, weighing the pros and cons of abandoning his plan of entering the Rake's shelter alone, of seeking assistance in determining whether or not the Stone King hid within. He had nothing to hide, no intention to deceive. It was always best to take a straightforward approach when you could.

Dees stirred. "I don't trust you."

Pe Ell laughed tonelessly. "I once told the Highlander he was a fool if he did. I don't care if you trust me; I'm not asking for your trust. I'm asking for your help."

Dees was intrigued despite himself. "What sort of help?"

Pe Ell hid his satisfaction. "Last night I tracked the Rake to its lair. I watched it enter, saw where it hides. I believe it likely that where the Rake hides, the Stone King hides as well. When the Rake goes out tonight to patrol the streets of the city, I intend to go in for a look."

He shifted forward, bringing Dees into the circle of his confidence. "There is a catch that releases a door through which the Rake passes. If I trip it, I should be able to go in. The trouble is, what if the door closes behind me? How will I get out?"

Dees rubbed his bearded chin, digging at the thick whiskers as though they itched. "So you want someone to watch your back for you."

"It seems like a good idea. I had planned to go in alone, to confront the Stone King, kill him if need be, and take the Stone. That's still my plan, but I don't want to have to worry about the Rake crawling up my back when I'm not watching."

"So you want me to watch for you."

"Afraid?"

"You keep asking that. Fact is, I should be asking you. Why should you trust me? I don't like you, Pe Ell. I'd be just as happy if the Rake would get you. That makes me a poor choice for this job, don't you think?"

Pe Ell unfolded his legs and stretched his lean body back against the wall. "Not necessarily. You don't have to like me. I don't have to like you. And I don't. But we both want the same thing—the Black Elfstone. We want to help the girl. Doesn't seem likely either of us can do much alone—although I have a better chance than you do. The point is, if you give your word that you will keep watch for me, I think that's what you'll do. Because your word means something to you, doesn't it?"

Dees laughed dryly. "Don't tell me you're about to make a plea to my sense of honor. I don't think I could stomach that."

Pe Ell quit smiling. "I have my own code of honor, old man, and it means every bit as much to me as yours does to you. If I give my word, I keep it. That's more than most can say. I'm telling you I'll watch out for you if you watch out for me—just until this business is finished. After that, we each go back to watching out for ourselves." He cocked his head. "Time is slipping away. We have to be in place by sunset. Are you coming or not?"

Horner Dees took a long time to answer. Pe Ell would have been surprised and suspicious if he had not. Whatever else Dees was, he was an honest man, and Pe Ell was certain he would not enter into an arrangement he did not think he could abide by. Pe Ell trusted Dees; he wouldn't have asked the old man to watch his back if he didn't. Moreover, he thought Dees capable, the best choice of all, in some ways, not inexperienced like the Highlander or flighty like Carisman. Nor was he unpredictable like Walker Boh. Dees was nothing more nor less than what he appeared to be.

"I told the Highlander about you," Dees announced, watching. "He's told the others by now."

Pe Ell shrugged once more. "I don't care about that." And he didn't.

Dees hunched his heavy frame forward, squinting into the faint gray light. "If we get possession of the Stone, either of us, we bring it back to the girl. Your word."

Pe Ell smiled in spite of himself. "You would accept my word, old man?"

Dees' features were hard and certain. "If you try to break it, I'll find a way to make you sorry you did."

Pe Ell believed him. Horner Dees, for all of being old and used up, for the weathered look of him and the wear of the years, would be a dangerous adversary. A Tracker, a woodsman, and a hunter, Dees had kept himself alive for a long time. He might not be Pe Ell's equal in a face-to-face confrontation, but there were other ways to kill a man. Pe Ell smiled inwardly. Who should know better than he?

Pe Ell reached out his hand and waited for the old man to take it. "We have a bargain," he said. Their hands tightened, held momentarily and broke. Pe Ell came to his feet like a cat. "Now let's be off."

They went out the door of the room and down the stairs again, Pe Ell leading. The gloom without had thickened, the darkness growing steadily as nightfall approached. They hunched their cloaked shoulders against the rain and started away. Pe Ell's thoughts drifted to his bargain. It had been an easy one to make. He would return the Elfstone to the girl because not to do so would be to risk losing her completely and to face an eternity of being tracked by all of them.

Never leave your enemies alive to follow after you, he thought. Better to kill them when you had the chance.

Daylight was fading rapidly by the time Walker, Morgan, and Quickening approached the building Pe Ell and Horner Dees had vacated less than an hour earlier. The rain was falling steadily, a dark curtain that shaded the tall, somber buildings of the city, that masked away the skies and the mountains and the sea. Morgan walked with his arm protectively encircling the girl's shoulders, his head lowered to hers, two shadowed and hooded figures against the mist. Walker stayed apart, leaving them to each other. He saw how Quickening leaned into the Highlander. She seemed to welcome his embrace, an uncharacteristic response. Something had happened to her during the confrontation with the Stone King that he had missed, and he was only now beginning to make sense of what it was.

A thick stream of rainwater clogged the gutter ahead, blocking the walkway's end like a moat, and he was forced to move outside and around it. He was leading still, choosing their path, his cloaked form darkened by rain and gloom. A wraith, perhaps, he thought. A Grimpond, he corrected. He had not thought of the Grimpond for a long time, the memory too painful to retrieve from the corner of his mind to which he had confined it. It was the Grimpond with its twisted riddles who had led him to the Hall of Kings and his encounter with the Asphinx. It was the Grimpond who had cost him his arm, his spirit, and something of what he had been. Wounded in body and spirit—that was how he saw himself. It would make the Grimpond glad if it knew.

He lifted his face momentarily and let the rain wash over it, cooling his skin. He hadn't thought it possible to be so hot in such dank weather.

It was the Grimpond's visions, of course, that haunted him— the three dark and enigmatic glimpses of the future, not accurate necessarily, lies twisted into half-truths, truths shaded by lies, but real. The first had already come to pass; he had sworn he would cut off his hand before he would take up the Druid cause and that was exactly what he had done. Then he had taken up the cause anyway. Ironic, poetic, terrifying.

The second vision was of Quickening. The third . . .

His good hand clenched. The truth was, he never got beyond

thinking about the second. Quickening. In some way, he would fail her. She would reach out to him for help, he would have the chance to save her from falling, and he would let her die. He would stand there and watch her tumble away into some dark abyss. That was the Grimpond's vision. That was what would come to pass unless he could find a way to prevent it.

He had not, of course, been able to prevent the first.

Disgust filled him, and he banished his memory of the Grimpond back to the distant corner from which it had been set loose. The Grimpond, he reminded himself, was itself a lie. But, then, wasn't he a lie as well? Wasn't that what he had become, so determined to keep himself clear of Druid machinations, so ready to disdain all use of the magic except that which served to sustain his own narrow beliefs, and so certain that he could be master of his own destiny? He had lied to himself repeatedly, deceived himself knowingly, pretended all things, and made his life a travesty. He was mired in his misconceptions and pretenses. He was doing what he had sworn he would never do—the work of the Druids, the recovery of their magic, the undertaking of their will. Worse, he was committed to a course of action which could only result in his destruction—a confrontation with the Stone King to take back the Black Elfstone. Why? He was clinging to this course of action as if it were the only thing that would stop his drifting, as if it were all that was left that would keep him from drowning, the only choice that remained.

Surely it was not.

He peered through the damp at the city and realized again how much he missed the forestlands of Hearthstone. It was more than the city's stone, its harsh and oppressive feel, its constant mist and rain. There was no color in Eldwist, nothing to wash clean his sight, to brighten and warm his spirit. There were only shadings of gray, a blurring of shadows layered one upon another. He felt himself in some way a mirror of the city. Perhaps Uhl Belk was changing him just as he changed the land, draining off the colors of his life, reducing him to something as hard and lifeless as stone. How far could the Stone King reach? he wondered. How deep into your soul? Was there any limit? Could he stretch his arms out all the way to Darklin Reach and Hearthstone? Could he find a human heart? In time, probably. And time was nothing to a creature that had lived so long.

They crossed to the front entry of their after-dark refuge and began to climb the stairs. Because Walker led, he saw the stains of rainwater preceding him on the stone steps that his own trail-

ing dampness masked to those following. Someone had entered
and gone out again recently. Horner Dees? But Dees was supposedly already there and waiting for their return.

They moved down the maze of hallways to the room which
served as their base of operations. The room was empty. Walker's eyes swept the trail of dampness to the shadows of the doors
exiting through each wall; his ears probed the quiet. He crossed
to where someone had seated himself and eaten.

His instincts triggered unexpectedly.

He could almost smell Pe Ell.

"Horner? Where are you?" Morgan was peering into other
rooms and corridors, calling for the old Tracker. Walker met
Quickening's gaze and said nothing. The Highlander ducked out
momentarily, then back in again. "He said he would wait right
here. I don't understand."

"He must have changed his mind," Walker offered quietly.

Morgan looked unconvinced. "I think I'll take a look
around."

He went out the door they had come through, leaving the
Dark Uncle and the daughter of the King of the Silver River
staring at each other in the gloom.

"Pe Ell was here," she said, her black eyes locked on his.

He let the fire of her gaze warm him; he felt that familiar
sense of kinship, of shared magics. "I don't sense a struggle,"
he said. "There is no blood, no disruption."

Quickening nodded soberly and waited. When he didn't speak
further, she crossed to stand before him. "What are you thinking, Walker Boh?" she asked, discomfort in her eyes. "What
have you been thinking all the way back, so lost within
yourself?"

Her hands reached out to take his arm, to hold it tight. Her
face lifted and the silver hair tumbled back, bathed in the weak
gray light. "Tell me."

He felt himself laid bare, a thin, rumpled, battered life with
barely enough strength remaining to keep from crumbling entirely. The ache in him stretched from his severed limb to his
heart, physical and emotional both, an all-encompassing wave
that threatened to sweep him away.

"Quickening." He spoke her name softly, and the sound of
it seemed to steady him. "I was thinking you are more human
than you would admit."

Puzzlement flashed across her perfect features.

He smiled, sad, ironic. "I might be a poor judge of such

things, less responsive than I should be, a refugee from years of growing up a boy with no friends and few companions, of living alone too much. But I see something of myself in you. You are frightened by the feelings you have discovered in yourself. You admit to possessing the human emotions your father endowed you with when he created you, but you disdain to accept what you perceive to be their consequences. You love the High-lander—yet you try to mask it. You shut it away. You despise Pe Ell—yet you play with him as a lure would a fish. You grapple with your emotions, yet refuse to acknowledge them. You work so hard to hide from your feelings."

Her eyes searched his. "I am still learning."

"Reluctantly. When you confronted the Stone King, you were quick to state what had brought you. You told him everything; you hid nothing. There was no attempt at deception or ruse. Yet when Uhl Belk refused your demand—as you surely knew he would—you grew angry, almost . . ." He searched for the word. "Almost frantic," he finished. "It was the first time I can re-member when you allowed your feelings to surface openly, with-out concern for who might witness them."

He saw a flicker of understanding in her eyes. "Your anger was real, Quickening. It was a measure of your pain. I think you wanted Uhl Belk to give you the Black Elfstone because of something you believe will happen if he does not. Is that so?"

She hesitated, torn, then let her breath escape slowly, wearily. "Yes."

"You believe that we will gain the Elfstone. I know that you do. You believe it because your father told you it would be so."

"Yes."

"But you also believe, as he told you, that it will require the magics of those you brought with you to secure it. No amount of talking, no manner of persuasion, will convince Uhl Belk to give it up. Yet you felt you had to try."

Her eyes were stricken. "I am frightened . . ." Her voice caught.

He bent close. "Of what? Tell me."

Morgan Leah appeared in the doorway. He slowed, watched Walker Boh draw back from Quickening, and completed his entrance. "Nothing," he said. "No sign of Horner. It's dark out now; the Rake will be about. I'll have to postpone any search until tomorrow." He came up to them and stopped. "Is something wrong?" he asked quietly.

"No," said Quickening.

"Yes," said Walker.

Morgan stared. "Which is it?"

Walker Boh felt the shadows of the room close about, as if darkness had descended all at once, intending to trap them there. They stood facing one another across a void, the Highlander, the Dark Uncle, and the girl. There was a sense of having reached an expected crossroads, of now having to choose a path which offered no return, of having to make a decision from which there was no retreat.

"The Stone King . . ." Quickening began in a whisper.

"We're going back for the Black Elfstone," Walker Boh finished.

Barely a mile away, at a window two floors up in a building fronting the lair of the Rake, Pe Ell and Horner Dees waited for the Creeper to emerge. They had been in position for some time, settled carefully back in the shadows with the patience of experienced hunters. The rain had stopped finally, turned to mist as the air cooled and stilled. A thin vapor rose off the stone of the streets in wisps that curled upward like snakes. From somewhere deep underground came the faint rumble of the Maw Grint awakening.

Pe Ell was thinking of the men he had killed. It was strange, but he could no longer remember who they were. For a time he had kept count, first out of curiosity, later out of habit, but eventually the number had grown so large and the passing of time so great that he simply lost track. Faces that had been clear in the beginning began to merge and then to fade altogether. Now it seemed he could remember only the first and the last clearly.

The fact that his victims had lost all sense of identity was disconcerting. It suggested that he was losing the sharpness of mind that his work required. It suggested that he was losing interest.

He stared into the blackness of the night and felt an unfamiliar weariness engulf him.

He forced the weariness away irritably. It would be different, he promised himself, when he killed the girl. He might forget the faces of these others from Rampling Steep, the one-armed man, the Highlander, the tunesmith, and the old Tracker; after all, killing them was nothing more than a matter of necessity. But he would never forget Quickening. Killing her was a matter of pride. Even now he could visualize her as clearly as if she were seated next to him, the soft curve and sweep of the skin

over her bones, the tilting of her face when she spoke, the way
her eyes drew you in, the weave and sway of her hands when
they moved. Surely she was the most wondrous of creatures,
spellbinding in a way that defied explanation. Hers was the magic
of the King of the Silver River and therefore as old as the beginning of life. He wanted to drink in that magic when he killed
her; he believed he could. Once he had done so, she would be
a part of him, living inside, a presence stronger than even the
most indelible memory, stirring within him as nothing else
could.

Horner Dees shifted softly beside him, relieving cramped
muscles. Still wrapped in his private thoughts, Pe Ell did not
glance over. He kept his eyes fixed on the flat surface of the
hidden entry across the street. The shadows that cloaked it remained still and unmoving.

What would happen when he slid the blade of the Stiehl into
her body? he wondered. What would he see in those depthless
black eyes? What would he feel? The anticipation of the moment
burned through him like fire. He had not thought of killing her
for some time, waiting because he had no other choice if he
was to secure the Black Elfstone, letting events take matters
where they would. But the moment was close now, he believed. Once he had gained entry into the lair of the Rake,
once he had discovered the hiding place of the Stone King,
once he had secured possession of the Black Elfstone and
disposed of Horner Dees . . .

He jerked upright.

Despite his readiness he was startled when across the way the
stone panel lifted and the Rake emerged. He quickly dispensed
with all further thoughts of Quickening. The Creeper's dark body
glimmered where thin streamers of starlight managed to penetrate the blanket of clouds and reflect off the plates of armor.
The monster stepped through the entry, then paused momentarily as if something had alarmed it. Feelers lifted and probed
the air tentatively; the whiplike tail curled and snapped. The two
in hiding shrank lower into the shadows. The Creeper remained
motionless a moment longer, then, apparently satisfied, reached
back and triggered the release overhead. The stone panel slid
silently into place. The Rake turned and scuttled away into the
mist and gloom, its iron legs scraping the stone like trailing
chains.

Pe Ell waited until he was certain it was gone, then motioned
for Horner Dees to follow him. Together they slipped down to

the street, crossed, and stood before the Rake's lair. Dees produced the rope and grappling hook he was carrying and flung them toward a stone outcropping that projected above the secret entry. The grappling hook caught with a dull clank and held. Dees tested the rope, nodded, and passed the end to Pe Ell. Pe Ell climbed effortlessly, hand over hand, until he was level with the release. He triggered it, and the entry panel began to lift. Pe Ell dropped down quickly and with Horner Dees beside him, watched the black cave of the building's interior open into view.

Cautiously, they edged forward.

The entry ran back into deep shadow. Faint gray light slipped through the building's upper windows, seeped downward through gaps in the ruined floors, and illuminated small patches of the blackness. There was no sound from within. There was no movement.

Pe Ell turned to Dees. "Watch the street," he whispered. "Whistle if there's trouble."

He moved into the blackness, fading into it as comfortably as if he were one of its shadows. He was immediately at home, confident within its cloaking, his eyes and ears adjusting to its sweep. The walls of the building were bare and worn with age, damp in places where the rain had seeped through the mortar and run down the stone, tall and rigid against the faint light. Pe Ell slipped ahead, picking his way slowly, cautiously, waiting for something to show itself. He sensed nothing; the building seemed empty.

Something crunched underfoot, startling him. He peered down into the blackness. Bones littered the floor, hundreds of them, the remains of creatures the Rake had gathered in its nightly sweeps and carried back to its lair to consume.

The entry turned down a vast corridor to a larger hall and ended. No doors opened in, no passageways led out. The hall had once been an inner court and rose hundreds of feet through the building to a domed ceiling speckled with strange light patterns and the slow movement of shadows thrown by the clouds. The hall was silent. Pe Ell stared about in distress. He knew at once that there was nothing to discover—not the Stone King, not the Black Elfstone. He had guessed wrong. Anger and disappointment welled up within him, forcing him to continue his search even after he knew it was pointless. He started toward the far wall, scanning the mortared seams, the lines of floor and ceiling, desperate to find something.

Then Horner Dees whistled.

At almost the same moment Pe Ell heard the soft scrape of metal on stone.

He wheeled instantly and darted back through the darkened hall. The Rake had returned. There was no reason for it to have done so unless it had detected them. How? His mind raced, clawing back the layers of confusion. The Rake was blind, it relied on its other senses. It could not have seen them. Could it have smelled them? He had his answer instantly. Their scent about the doorway had alerted it; that was why it had paused. It had pretended to go out, waited, then circled back.

Pe Ell raged at his own stupidity. If he didn't get out of there at once, he would be trapped.

He burst into the darkened entry just in time to discover that he was too late. Through the raised door he caught a glimpse of the Rake rounding the corner of the building across the way, moving as fast as its metal legs would carry it toward its lair. The rope and Horner Dees were gone. Pe Ell melted into the darkest section of one wall, sliding forward soundlessly. He had to reach the entrance and get past the Creeper before it triggered the release. If he failed, he would be caught in the creature's lair. Even the Stiehl would not be enough to save him then.

The Rake rumbled up to the opening, iron claws rasping, and tentacles lashing out against the stone walls, beginning its probe within. Pe Ell slipped the Stiehl free of its sheath and crouched down against the dark. He would have to be quick. He was oddly calm, the way he was before a kill. He watched the monster fill the opening and start to move through.

At once he was up and running. The Rake sensed him instantly, its instincts even keener than Pe Ell's. A tentacle lashed out and caught him, inches from the door. The Stiehl whipped up, severing the limb, freeing the assassin once more. The Rake wheeled about, huffing. Pe Ell tried to run, but there were snaking arms everywhere.

Then the grappling hook shot out of the darkness behind the advancing Creeper, wrapping about its back legs. The rope securing it went taut, and the monster was jerked backward. Its limbs flailed, and its claws dug in. For a moment its attention was diverted. That moment was enough. Pe Ell was past it in a split second, racing into the street, darting to safety. Almost immediately Horner Dees was running beside him, his bearish form laboring from the strain. Behind them, they heard the rope snap and the Rake start after in pursuit.

"Here!" Dees yelled, pulling Pe Ell left into a gaping doorway.

They ran through an entry, up several flights of stairs, down a hall, and out onto a back ramp that crossed to another building. The Creeper lumbered behind, smashing everything that blocked its way. The men hastened into the building at the end of the ramp and down a second set of stairs to the street again. The sounds of pursuit were beginning to fade. They slowed, rounded a corner, peered cautiously down the empty street, then followed the walkway south several blocks to where a cluster of smaller buildings offered an impassable warren into which they quickly crept. Safe within, they slid down wearily, backs to the wall, side by side, breathing heavily in the stillness.

"I thought you'd run," Pe Ell said, gasping.

Dees grunted, shook his head. "I would have, but I gave my word. What do we do now?"

Pe Ell's body steamed with sweat, but deep inside a cold fury was building. He could still feel the Rake's tentacle wrapped about his body. He could still feel it beginning to squeeze. He experienced such revulsion that he could barely keep from screaming aloud.

Nothing had ever come so close to killing him.

He turned to Horner Dees, watched the rough, bearded face furrow, the eyes glitter. Pe Ell's voice was chilly with rage. "You can do what you wish, old man," he whispered. "But I'm going back and kill that thing."

XXVII

Morgan Leah was appalled. "What do you mean we're going back?" he demanded of Walker Boh. He was not just appalled; he was terrified. "Who gave you the right to decide anything, Walker? Quickening is leader of this company, not you!''

"Morgan," the girl said softly. She tried to take his hand, but he stepped quickly away.

"No. I want this settled. What's going on here? I leave the room for just a moment, just long enough to make sure Horner isn't . . . and when I come back I find you close enough to . . .'' He choked on the words, his brown face flushing as the impact of what he was saying caught up with him. "I . . .''

"Morgan, listen to me," Quickening finished. "We have to recover the Black Elfstone. We have to.''

The Highlander's fists clenched helplessly. He was aware of how foolish he looked, how young. He made a studied effort to control himself. "If we go back there, Quickening, we will be killed. We didn't know what we were up against before; now we do. Uhl Belk is too much for us. We all saw the same thing— a creature changed into something only vaguely human, armored in stone, and capable of brushing us aside like we were nothing. He's part of the land itself! How do we fight something like that? He'll swallow us whole before we have a chance even to get close!''

He forced his breathing to slow. "And that's only if he doesn't call the Maw Grint or the Rake first. We can't stand up to *them* let alone *him*. Think about it, will you? What if he chooses to use the Elfstone against us! Then what do we do—you without any magic at all that you can use, me with a broken sword that's lost most of its magic, and Walker with . . . I don't know, what? With what, Walker? What are you?''

The Dark Uncle was unfazed by the attack, his pale face expressionless, his eyes steady as they fixed on the Highlander. "I am what I always was, Morgan Leah.''

"Less an arm!'' Morgan snapped and regretted it immediately. "No, I'm sorry, I didn't mean that.''

"But it is true," the other replied quietly.

Morgan looked away awkwardly for a moment, then back again. "Look at us," he whispered. "We're barely alive. We've trekked all the way to the end of the world and it's just about finished us. Carisman's already dead. Maybe Horner Dees as well. We're beaten up. We look like scarecrows. We haven't had a bath in weeks, unless you want to count getting rained on. We're dressed in rags. We've been running and hiding so long we don't know how to fight anymore. We're caught in this gray, dismal world where all we see is stone and rain and mist. I hate

this place. I want to see trees and grass and living things again.
I don't want to die here. I especially don't want to die when
there is no reason for it! And that's exactly what will happen if
we go looking for the Stone King. Tell me, Walker, what chance
do we have?''

To his surprise, Walker Boh said, ''A better chance than you
think. Sit down a minute and listen.''

Morgan hesitated, suspicion mirrored in his eyes. Then slowly
he sat, his anger and frustration momentarily spent. He allowed
Quickening to move next to him again, to wrap her arms about
him. He let the heat of her body soak through him.

Walker Boh crossed his legs before him and pulled his dark
cloak close. ''It is true that we appear to be little more than
beggars off some Southland city street, that we have nothing
with which to threaten Uhl Belk, that we are as insignificant to
him as the smallest insects that crawl upon the land. But that
appearance may be an illusion we can use. It may give us the
chance we need to defeat him. He sees us as nothing. He does
not fear us. He disdains to worry about us at all. It is possible
that he has already forgotten us. He believes himself invulnerable. Perhaps we can use that against him.''

The dark eyes were intense. ''He is not what he believes,
Highlander. He has evolved beyond the spirit creature he was
born, beyond anything he was intended to be. I believe he has
evolved even beyond the King of the Silver River. But his evolution has not been a natural one. His evolution has been brought
about by his usage of the Black Elfstone. It is ironic, but the
Druids protected their magic better than Uhl Belk realizes. He
thinks that he stole it easily and uses it without consequence.
But he is wrong. Just by calling up the Elfstone's magic, he is
destroying himself.''

Morgan Leah stared. ''What are you talking about?''

''Listen to him, Morgan,'' Quickening cautioned, her soft
face bent close, her dark eyes expectant.

''I did not understand before today what it was that the Black
Elfstone was intended to do,'' Walker Boh continued, hurrying
now, anxious to complete his explanation. ''I was given the
Druid History by Cogline and told to read it. I learned that the
Black Elfstone existed and that its purpose was to release Paranor from its spell and return it to the world of men. I learned
from Quickening that the Black Elfstone's magic was conceived
to negate the effects of other magics—thus the magic that sealed
away Paranor could be dispelled. Such power, Highlander! How

could such power exist? I kept wondering if it was possible, and if possible, why the Druids—who were so careful in such matters—took no better precautions to protect against its misuse. After all, the Black Elfstone was the only magic that could restore their Keep, that could initiate the process that would restore them to power. Would they let that magic slip away so easily? Would they allow it to be utilized by others, even a creature as powerful as Uhl Belk?

"I knew, of course, that they would not. But how could they prevent it? Today I discovered the answer to that question. I watched the Stone King summon the Maw Grint; I watched what passed between father and son. Did you see it? When Uhl Belk invoked the power of the Stone, there was a binding of the two, a bringing together. The magic was a catalyst. But what did it do? I wondered. It seemed to give life to them both. It was clearly addictive; they reveled in its use. The magic of the Black Elfstone was stronger than their own in the moment of its release. It was so strong that they could not resist what it was doing to them; in fact, they welcomed its coming."

He paused, and his voice lowered to a guarded whisper. The room's shadows cloaked them like conspirators. "This is what I believe must happen when the magic is invoked. Yes, it negates whatever magic it is directed against, just as the Druid History suggests, just as Quickening was told by her father. It confronts and steals away that magic's power. But it must do more. It cannot simply cause the magic to disappear. It cannot take a magic and change it into air. Something must happen to that magic. The laws of nature require it. What it does, I believe, is to absorb and transfer the effects of that other magic to the user of the Stone. When Uhl Belk turns the Black Elfstone on the Maw Grint he takes his child's magic and makes it his own; he takes the poison that transforms the land and its creatures to stone and alters himself as well. That is why he has evolved as he has. And perhaps even more important than that, each time he siphons off a part of the Maw Grint's magic, Uhl Belk is brought close again for a few moments to the son he created. Using the Black Elfstone to share the Maw Grint's magic has given them a bond they could not otherwise enjoy. They hate and fear each other, but they need each other as well. They feed on each other, a giving and taking that only the Black Elfstone can facilitate. It is as close as they can come to a father/son relationship. It is the only bond they can share."

He hunched forward. "But it is killing Uhl Belk. It is chang-

ing him to stone entirely. In time, he will disappear into the
stone that encases him. He will become like any other statue—
inanimate. He is doing it to himself without even realizing it.
That is the way the Elfstone works; that is why he was able to
steal it so easily. The Druids didn't care. They knew that anyone
using it would suffer the consequences eventually. Magic cannot
be absorbed without consequence. Uhl Belk is addicted to that
magic. He needs the feeling of transformation, of adding to his
stone body, to his land, to his kingdom of self. He could not
stop now even if he tried.''

"But how does this help us?'' Morgan asked, impatient once
more. He hunched forward curiously, caught up in the possibilities that Walker's explanation offered. "Even if you're right,
what difference does it make? You're not suggesting that we
simply wait until Uhl Belk kills himself, are you?''

Walker Boh shook his head. "We haven't time enough for
that. The process may take years. But Uhl Belk is not as invulnerable as he believes. He has become largely dependent on the
Black Elfstone, cocooned within his stone keep, changed mostly
to stone himself, interested not so much in what is happening
about him as in the feeding he requires so that his mutation can
continue. He is largely stationary. Did you watch him when he
tried to move? He cannot change positions quickly; he is welded
to the rock of the floor. His magic is old and unused; most of
what he does relates to feeding himself through use of the Stone.
Fear of losing the Black Elfstone, of being deprived of his source
of feeding, and of being left to the questionable mercy of his
maddened child dominates his thinking. He has crippled himself
with his obsessions. That gives us a chance to defeat him.''

Morgan studied the other's face wordlessly for several long
moments, thinking the matter through in spite of his reluctance
to believe there was any possibility of succeeding, conscious of
Quickening's eyes on him as he did so. He had always believed
in Walker Boh's ability to reason matters through when others
could not. He was the one who had suggested Par and Coll
Ohmsford go to their uncle when they needed advice in dealing
with the dreams of Allanon. He was frightened by what the Dark
Uncle was suggesting, but not so big a fool as to discount it
entirely.

Finally he said, "Everything you say may be so, Walker, but
you have forgotten something. We still have to get inside the
dome to have any chance of overcoming Uhl Belk. And he's not
going to invite us in a second time. He's already made that clear.

Since we haven't been able to find a way in on our own, how are we supposed to get close enough to do anything?''

Walker folded his hands before him thoughtfully. ''Uhl Belk made a mistake when he admitted us to the dome. I was able to sense things that were hidden from me before, when I was forced to stand without. I was able to divine the nature of his fortress keep. He has settled himself above that cavern where the rats cornered us while we were searching the tunnels beneath the city. He places the Tiderace between himself and the Maw Grint's underground lair. But he miscalculated in doing so. The constant changing of the tide has worn and eroded portions of the stone on which he rests.''

The Dark Uncle's eyes narrowed. ''There is an opening that leads into the dome from beneath.''

Another pair of eyes narrowed as well, these in disbelief as Horner Dees weighed the implications of Pe Ell's words in the dark silence of the building in which the two men were crouched. ''Kill it?'' he questioned finally, unable to keep himself from repeating the other's words. ''Why would you want to do that?''

''Because it's out there!'' Pe Ell snapped impatiently, as if that explained everything.

His stare challenged the Tracker, daring him to object. When Dees did not respond, Pe Ell bent forward like a hawk at hunt. ''How long have we been in this city, old man—a week, two? I can't even remember anymore. It seems as if we've been here forever! One thing I do know. Ever since we arrived, that thing has been hunting us. Every night, everywhere we go! The Rake, sweeping up the streets, cleaning up the garbage. Well, I've had enough!''

He was stiff with rage, fighting back against the memory of that iron tentacle wrapped about him, struggling to control his revulsion. When he killed, it was quick and clean. Not a slow squeezing, not a death that choked and strangled. And nothing ever touched him. Nothing ever got close.

Not until now.

His failure to find the Stone King in the Rake's lair hadn't done anything to improve his disposition either. He had been certain that he would find Uhl Belk and the Black Elfstone. Instead, he had almost succeeded in getting himself killed.

His knife-blade face was set and raw with feeling. ''I won't be hunted anymore. A Creeper can die like anything else.'' He paused. ''Think about this. Once it's dead, maybe the Stone

King will show himself. Maybe he'll come out to see what killed his watchdog. Then we'll have him!''

Horner Dees did not look convinced. "You're not thinking straight."

Pe Ell flushed. "Are you frightened once more, old man?"

"Of course. But that doesn't have anything to do with the matter. The fact is, you're supposed to be a professional killer, an assassin. You don't kill without a reason and never without being sure that the odds are in your favor. I don't see any evidence of that here."

"Then you're not looking hard enough!" Pe Ell was furious. "You already have the reason! Haven't you been listening? It doesn't have to be money and it doesn't have to be someone else's idea! Do you want to find Uhl Belk or not? As for the odds, I'll find a way to change them!"

Pe Ell rose and wheeled away momentarily to face the dark. He shouldn't care one way or the other what this old man thought; it shouldn't matter in the least. But somehow, for some reason, it did, and he refused to give Dees the satisfaction of thinking he was somehow misguided. He hated to admit that Horner Dees might have saved his life, even that he might have helped him escape. The old man was a thorn in his side that needed removing. Dees had come out of his past like a ghost, come out of a time he had thought safely buried. No one alive should know who he was or what he had done save Rimmer Dall. No one should be able to talk about him.

He found suddenly that he wanted Horner Dees dead almost as much as he wanted to dispose of the Rake.

Except that the Rake was the more immediate problem.

He turned back to the old Tracker. "I've wasted enough time on you," he snapped. "Go back to the others. I don't need your help."

Horner Dees shrugged. "I wasn't offering it."

Pe Ell started for the door.

"Just out of curiosity," Dees called after him, rising now as well, "how do you plan to kill it?"

"What difference does it make to you?" Pe Ell called over his shoulder.

"You don't have a plan, do you?"

Pe Ell stopped dead in the doorway, seized by an almost overpowering urge to finish off the troublesome Dees here and now. After all, why wait any longer? The others would never know. His hand dropped through the crease in his pants to close about the Stiehl.

"Thing is," Horner Dees said suddenly, "you can't kill the Rake even if you manage to get close enough to use that blade of yours."

Pe Ell's fingers released. "What do you mean?"

"I mean that even if you lay in wait for the thing, say you drop on it from above or sneak up on it from underneath—not likely, but say that you do—you still can't kill it quick enough." The sharp eyes glittered. "Oh, you can cut off a tentacle or two, maybe sever a leg, or even put out an eye. But that won't kill it. Where do you stab it that will kill it, Pe Ell? Do you know? I don't. Before you've taken two cuts, the Rake will have you. Damage the thing? A Creeper builds itself right back again, finds spare pieces of metal and puts what it's lost back in place."

Pe Ell smiled—mean, sardonic, empty of warmth. "I'll find a way."

Dees nodded. "Sure you will." He paused deliberately, his bearish frame shifting, changing his weight from one foot to the other. In the near darkness, he seemed like a piece of the wall breaking loose. "But not without a plan."

Pe Ell looked away in disgust, shook his head, then looked back again. He'd spent too much time trudging about this dismal city, this tomb of stone and damp. He'd been fighting too long to keep from being swallowed up in its belly. That coupled with prolonged exposure to Quickening's magic had eroded his instincts, dulled the edge of his sharpness, and twisted the clearness of his thought. He was at a point where the only thing that mattered was getting back to where he had started from, to the world beyond Eldwist, and to the life that he had so fully controlled.

But not without the Black Elfstone. He would not give it up.

And not without Quickening's life. He would not give that up either.

Meanwhile, Horner Dees was trying to tell him something. It never hurt to listen. He made himself go very still inside—everything, right down to his thoughts. "You have a plan of your own, don't you?" he whispered.

"I might."

"I'm listening."

"Maybe there's something to what you say about killing the Rake. Maybe that will bring Belk out of hiding. Something has to be tried." The admission came grudgingly.

"I'm still listening."

"It'll take the two of us. Same agreement as before. We look out for each other until the matter's done. Then it's every man for himself. Your word."

"You have it."

Horner Dees shuffled forward until he was right in front of Pe Ell, much closer than Pe Ell wanted him, wheezing like he'd run a mile, grinning through his shaggy beard, big hands knotting into fists.

"What I think we ought to do," he said softly, "is drop the Rake down a deep hole."

Morgan Leah stared at Walker Boh wordlessly for a moment, then shook his head. He was surprised at how calm his voice sounded. "It won't work. You said yourself that the Stone King isn't just a moving statue; he's made himself a part of the land. He's everything in Eldwist. You saw what he did when he finally decided to let us into the dome and then after, when he summoned the Maw Grint. He just split the rock wall apart. His own skin, Walker. Don't you think he'll know if we try to climb through that same skin from beneath? Don't you think he'll be able to feel it? What do you think will happen to us then? Squish!"

Morgan made a grinding motion with his palms. A dark flush crept into his face; he found that he was shaking.

Walker's expression never changed. "What you suggest is possible, but unlikely. Uhl Belk may be the heart and soul of the land he has created, but he is also, like it, a thing of stone. Stone feels nothing, senses nothing. Uhl Belk would not have even discovered we were here if he had been forced to rely on his external senses. It was our use of magic that alerted him. There may remain enough of him that is human to detect intruders, but he relies principally on the Rake. If we can avoid using magic we can enter the dome before he knows what we are about."

Morgan started to object, then cut himself short. Quickening was clutching his arm so hard it hurt. "Morgan," she whispered urgently. "We can do it. Walker Boh is right. This is our chance."

"Our chance?" Morgan looked down at her, fighting to keep his balance as the black eyes threatened to drown him, finding her impossibly beautiful all over again. "Our chance to do what, Quickening?" He forced his gaze away from her, fixing on

Walker. "Suppose that you are right about all this, that we can get into the dome without Belk knowing it. What difference does it make? What are we supposed to do then? Use our broken magics, the three of us—a weaponless girl, a one-armed man, and a man with half a sword? Aren't we right back where we started with this conversation?"

He ignored Quickening's hands as they pulled at him. "I won't pretend with you, Walker. You can see what I'm thinking. You can with everyone. I'm terrified. I admit it. If I had the Sword of Leah whole again, I would stand a chance against something like Uhl Belk. But I don't. And I don't have any innate magic like you and Par. I just have myself. I've stayed alive this long by accepting my limitations. That's how I was able to fight the Federation officials who occupy my homeland; that's how I managed to survive against something far bigger and stronger. You have to pick and choose your battles. The Stone King is a monster with monsters to command, and I don't see how the three of us can do anything about him."

Quickening was shaking her head. "Morgan . . ."

"No," he interrupted quickly, unable to stop himself now. "Don't say anything. Just listen. I have done everything you asked. I have given up other responsibilities I should have fulfilled to come north with you in search of Eldwist and Uhl Belk. I have stayed with you to find the Black Elfstone. I want you to succeed in what your father has sent you to do. But I don't know how that can happen, Quickening. Do you? Can you tell me?"

She moved in front of him, her face lifting. "I can tell you that it will happen. My father has said it will be so."

"With my magic and Walker's and Pe Ell's. I know. Well, then, what of Pe Ell? Isn't he supposed to go with us? Don't we need him if we are to succeed?"

She hesitated before giving her answer. "No. Pe Ell's magic will be needed later."

"Later. And your own?"

"I have no magic until you recover the Elfstone."

"So it is left to Walker and me."

"Yes."

"Somehow."

"Yes."

Walker Boh stepped forward impatiently, his pale face hard. "Enough, Highlander. You make it sound as if this were some mystical process that required divine intervention or the wisdom of the dead. There is nothing difficult about what we are being asked to do. The Stone King holds the Black Elfstone; he must be made to give it up. We must sneak through the floor of the dome and surprise him. We must find a way to shock him, to stun him, to do something that will make him release his grip on the Stone, then snatch it from him. We don't have to stand against him in battle; we don't have to slay him. This isn't a contest of strength; it is a contest of will. And cleverness. We must be more clever than he.''

The Dark Uncle's eyes burned. ''We have not come all this way, Morgan Leah, just to turn around and go back again. We knew there were no answers to be given to our questions, that we would have to find a way to do everything that was required. We have done so. We need do so only one time more. If we don't, the Elfstone is lost to us. That means that the Four Lands are lost as well. The Shadowen have won. Cogline and Rumor died for nothing. Your friend Steff died for nothing. Is that what you wish? Is that your intent? Is it, Morgan Leah?''

Morgan pushed past Quickening and seized the front of the other's cloak. Walker seized his in turn. For an instant they braced each other without speaking, Morgan's face contorted with rage, Walker's smooth and intense.

''I am frightened, too, Highlander,'' Walker Boh said softly. ''I have fears that go far beyond what we are being asked to do here. I have been charged by the shade of Allanon with using the Black Elfstone to bring back Paranor and the Druids. If using the Elfstone on the Maw Grint turns Uhl Belk to stone, what will using it on disappeared Paranor do to me?''

There was a long, empty silence in which the question hung skeletal and forbidding against the dark of the room. Then Walker whispered, ''It doesn't matter, you see. I have to find out.''

Morgan let the other's cloak slip from his fingers. He took a slow step back. ''Why are we doing this?'' he whispered in reply. ''Why?''

Walker Boh almost smiled. ''You know why, Morgan Leah. Because there is no one else.''

Morgan laughed in spite of himself. ''Brave soldiers? Or fools?''

''Maybe both. And maybe we are just stubborn.''

''That sounds right.'' Morgan sighed wearily, pushing back the oppressiveness of the dark and damp, fighting through his sense of futility. ''I just think there should be more answers than there are.''

Walker nodded. "There should. Instead, there are only reasons and they will have to suffice."

Morgan's mind spun with memories of the past, of his friends missing and dead, of his struggle to stay alive, and of the myriad quests that had taken him from his home in the Highlands and brought him at last to this farthest corner of the world. So much had happened, most of it beyond his control. He felt small and helpless in the face of those events, a tiny bit of refuse afloat in the ocean, carried on tides and by whim. He was sick and worn; he wanted some form of resolution. Perhaps only death was resolution enough.

"Let me speak with him," he heard Quickening say.

Alone, they knelt at the center of the room in shadow, facing each other, their faces so close that Morgan could see his reflection in her dark eyes. Walker had disappeared. Quickening's hands reached out to him, and he let her fingers come to rest on his face, tracing the line of his bones.

"I am in love with you, Morgan Leah," she whispered. "I want you to know that. It sounds strange to me to say such a thing. I never thought I would be able to do so. I have fears of my own, different from yours and Walker Boh's. I am afraid of being too much alive."

She bent forward and kissed him. "Do you understand what I mean when I say that? An elemental gains life not out of the love of a man and a woman for each other but out of magic's need. I was created to serve a purpose, my father's purpose, and I was told to be wary of things that would distract me. What could distract me more, Morgan Leah, than the love I have for you? I cannot explain that love. I do not understand it. It comes from the part of me that is human and surfaces despite my efforts to deny it. What am I to do with this love? I tell myself I must disdain it. It is . . . dangerous. But I cannot give it up because the feeling of it gives me life. I become more than a thing of earth and water, more than a bit of clay made whole. I become real."

He kissed her back, hard and determined, frightened by what she was telling him, by the sound of the words, by the implications they carried. He did not want to hear more.

She broke away. "You must listen to me, Morgan. I had thought to keep to my father's path and not to stray. His advice seemed sound. But I find now that I cannot heed it. I must love you. It does not matter what is meant for either of us; we are not alive if we do not respond to our feelings. So it is that I will

love you in every way that I am able; I will not be frightened
any longer by what that means.''

"Quickening . . .''

"But," she said hurriedly, "the path remains clear before us
nevertheless and we must follow it, you and I. We have been
shown where it leads, and we must continue to its end. The
Stone King must be overcome. The Black Elfstone must be
recovered. You and I and Walker Boh must see that these things
are done. We must, Morgan. We must.''

He was nodding as she spoke, helpless in the face of her
persistence, his love for her so strong that he would have done
anything she asked despite the gravest reservations. The tears
started in his eyes, but he forced them back, burying his face in
her shoulder, hugging her close. He combed her silver hair with
his fingers; he stroked the curve of her back. He felt her slim
arms go around him, and her body tremble.

"I know," he answered softly.

He thought then of Steff, dying at the hands of the girl he had
loved, thinking her something she was not. Would it be so with
him? he wondered suddenly. He thought, too, of the promise he
had once made his friend, a promise they had all made, Par and
Coll and he, that if any of them found a magic that would help
free the Dwarves, they would do what they could to recover it
and see that it was used. Surely the Black Elfstone was such a
magic.

He felt a calm settle through him, dissipating the anger and
foreboding, the doubt and uncertainty. The path was indeed laid
out for him, and he had never had any choice but to follow it.

"We'll find a way," he whispered to her and felt her own
tears dampen his cheek.

Standing in the blackness of the room beyond, Walker Boh
looked back at the lovers as they embraced and felt the warmth
of their closeness reach out to him like a lost child's tiny hands.
He turned away. There could be no such love for him. He felt
an instant's remorse and brushed it hastily aside. His future was
a shining bit of certainty in the darkness of his present. Sometimes his prescience revealed a cutting edge.

He moved soundlessly through the building until he reached
an open window high above the street and looked down into the
roil of mist and gloom. The world of Eldwist was a maze of
stone obstructions and corridors that glared back at him through

a hard, wet sheen. It was harsh and certain and pointless and it reminded him of the direction of his life.

Yet now, at last, his life might become something more.

One puzzle remained. The Highlander had touched on it, brushed by it in his effort to understand how it was that they could stand against a being with the power of Uhl Belk. The puzzle had been with them since the beginning of their journey, a constant presence, and an enigma that refused to be revealed.

The puzzle was Quickening. The daughter of the King of the Silver River, created out of the elements of the Garden, given life out of magic—she was a riddle of words in another tongue. She had been sent to bring them all into Eldwist. But wouldn't a summons have done the job as well? Or even a dream? Instead the King of the Silver River had sent a living, breathing bit of wonder, a creature so beautiful she defied belief. Why? She was here for a reason, and it was a reason beyond that which she had revealed.

Walker Boh felt a dark place inside shiver with the possibilities.

What was it that Quickening had really been sent to do?

XXVIII

At dawn the three left their concealment and went down into the streets. The rain had ceased to fall, the clouds had lifted above the peaks of the buildings, and the light was gray and iron hard. Silence wrapped the bones of Eldwist like a shroud, the air windless, unmisted, and empty. Far distant, the ocean was a faint murmur. Their footfalls thudded dully and receded into echoes that seemed to hang like whispers against the skies. Unsuccessfully, they searched the city for life. There was no sign of either Horner Dees or Pe Ell. The Rake had retreated to its daylight lair. The Maw Grint slept within the earth. And in his domed fortress, Uhl Belk was a dark inevitability awaiting confrontation.

Yet Walker Boh was at peace.

He strode before Morgan and Quickening, surprised at the depth of his tranquility. He had given so much of himself to the struggle to understand and control the purpose of his life, battling with the twin specters of legacy and fate. Now all that was cast aside. Time and events had rushed him forward to this moment, an implacable whirlwind that would resolve the purpose of his life for him. His meeting with the Stone King would settle the matter of who and what he was. Either he merited the charge that the shade of Allanon had given him or he did not. Either he was meant to possess the Black Elfstone and bring back Paranor and the Druids or he was not. Either he would survive Uhl Belk or he would not. He no longer questioned that his doubt must give way to resolution; he did not choose to mire himself further in the "what ifs" that had plagued him for so long. Circumstance had placed him here, and that was enough. Whether he lived or died, he would finally be free of the past. Was the Shannara magic alive within him, strong beyond the loss of his arm to the poison of the Asphinx, powerful enough to withstand the fury of the Stone King? Was the trust Allanon had given to Brin Ohmsford meant for him? He would find out. Knowledge, he thought with an irony that he could not ignore, was always liberating.

Morgan Leah was less certain.

Half-a-dozen steps back, his hand clasped in Quickening's, the Highlander was a fragile shell through which fears and misgivings darted like trapped flies. In contrast to Walker Boh, he already knew far too much. He knew that Walker was not the Dark Uncle of old, that the myth of his invincibility had been shattered along with his arm, and that he was swept along on the same tide of prophecies and promises as the rest of them. He knew that he himself was even less able, a man without a whole weapon, bereft of the magic that had barely sustained him through previous encounters with far lesser beings. He knew that there were only the two of them, that Quickening could not intervene, that she might share their fate but could not affect it. He could say that he understood her need to gain possession of the Black Elfstone, her belief in her father's promises, and her confidence in them—he could speak the words. He could pray that they would find some way to survive what they were undertaking, that some miracle would save them. But the fears and

the misgivings would not be captured by words and prayers;
they would not be allayed by false hope. They darted within like
startled deer, and he could feel the beating of his heart in response to their flight.

What would he do, he wondered desperately, when the Stone
King turned those empty eyes on him? Where would he find his
strength?

He glanced covertly at Quickening, at the lines and shadows
of her face, and at the darkly reassuring glitter of her eyes.

But Quickening walked beside him without seeing.

They passed down the empty streets toward the heart of the
city, stalking like cats along the stone ribbon of the walkways,
their backs to the building walls. They could almost feel the
earth beneath them pulse with the Stone King's life; they could
almost hear the sound of his breathing through the hush. An old
god, a spirit, a thing of incomprehensible power—they could
feel his eyes upon them. The minutes slipped away, and the
streets and buildings came and went with a sameness that whispered of ages come and gone and lives before their own that had
passed this way without effect. An oppressive certainty settled
down about them, an unspoken voice, a barely remembered
face, a feathered touch, all designed to persuade them of the
futility of their effort. They felt its presence and reacted, each
differently, each calling up what defenses could be found. No
one turned back. No one gave way. Locked together by their
determination to make an end of this nightmare, they continued
on.

In the east, dawn's faint gray light brightened to a chilly silver
mist that mingled with the clouds and left the city crystallized.

They caught their first glimpse of the dome shortly after and
when Walker Boh, still leading, pressed them back into the shadows of the building they followed as if afraid the dome could
see. He took them back along the walkway and down a second-
ary street, then over and down another, winding this way and
that, twisting about through the maze. They slid along the dampness like a trail of water seeking its lowest level and never
slowed. Their path meandered, but the dome drew closer beyond the walls that concealed them.

Finally Walker stopped, head lifting within the cowl of his
dark cloak as if to sniff the air. He was lost within himself,
casting about in the darkness of his mind, the magic working to
lead him to where his eyes could not see. He started out again,
taking them across a street, down an alleyway and out again,

down another street to where a building entry opened onto a set of broad stairs. The stairs took them into the earth beneath the building, a dark and engulfing descent into a cavernous chamber where dozens of the ancient carriages of the old world sat resting on their stone tracks. Massive hulks, broken apart by time and age, the carriages gave the chamber the look of a boneyard. Light fell across the carcasses in narrow stripes, and dust motes decorated the air in a thin, choking haze.

The stairs went farther down, and the three continued their descent. They entered an anteroom with a circular portal set in the far wall, stepped through hesitantly, and found themselves back in the city's sewers. The sewers burrowed in three directions into the darkness, catacombs wrapped in silence and the smell of dead things. Walker's good hand lifted and silver light wrapped about it. He paused once more, as if testing the air. Then he took them left.

The tunnel swallowed them effortlessly, its stone walls massive and impenetrable, threatening to hold them fast forever. Silence was a stealthy, invisible watcher. They heard nothing of the Maw Grint—not a rumble, not even the tremor of its breathing. Eldwist had the feel of a tomb once more, deserted of life, a haven for the dead. They stretched ahead in a line, Walker leading, Quickening next, and Morgan last. No words were exchanged, no glances. They kept their eyes on the light that Walker held forth, on the rock of the tunnel floor they followed, and on the movement of the shadows they cast.

Walker slowed, then stopped. His lighted hand moved to one side, then the other. A faint glimmer caught the outline of a dark opening in the wall left and stairs beyond.

Once again they started down, following damp, slick, roughened steps through a wormhole in the earth. They began to smell the Tiderace, then to hear the faint roar of its waters against Eldwist's shore. They listened closely, guardedly for the squealing of the rats, but it did not come. When they reached the end of these stairs, Walker took them right into a narrow gap studded with stone projections honed razor-sharp by nature and time. They moved slowly, inching their way along, hunched up close to each other to keep within the circle of the light. The dampness spread up the walls before them, a dark stain. Things began moving in the light, skittering away. Morgan caught a glimpse of what they were. Sea life, he recognized in surprise. Tiny black crabs. Were they far enough down from Uhl Belk that such things could live? Were they close enough to the water?

Then they emerged once more into the subterranean cavern that lay beneath the city. Rock walls circled away from the ledge on which they stood and the ocean crashed wildly into the rocks below. Mist churned overhead, draping the cavern's farthest reaches with curtains of white. Daylight brightened the shadows where the rocks were cleft to form small, nearly colorless rainbows against the mist.

The ledge ran away to either side, dipping, climbing, jagged and uneven, disappearing into rock and shadow. Walker Boh cast both ways, feeling for the presence he knew he would find, sensing the pulse of its magic. His eyes lifted toward the unseen. Uhl Belk.

"This way," he said quietly, turning left.

Then the rumble of the Maw Grint's waking sounded, elevating from a stir to a roar, and the whole of Eldwist shook with fury.

The plan was simple, but then simple plans were the ones that usually worked best. The only trouble with this one, thought Pe Ell as he stood in the shadows of the building across from the Rake's lair, was that he was the one taking all the chances while Horner Dees remained safe and sound.

The plan, of course, had been the old man's.

Like Quickening, Walker, and Morgan Leah, they had gone out at dawn, slipping from their refuge back to the streets, greeting the cheerless gray light with squinted eyes and suspicious frowns. A brief exchange of glances and they had been off, going first to the Rake's lair, then tracing the route that Pe Ell would lure the Creeper down. When Dees had satisfied himself that Pe Ell had memorized it, they hooked the old man's harness in place, checked the leverage on the makeshift pulley, and parted company.

Pe Ell had backtracked to the Rake's lair, and now there he stood, waiting.

Stealth and speed were what he would need, first the one, then the other, and not too much of either—an assassin's tools.

He listened to the silence for a long time, judging the distance he must cover and measuring the retreat he would make. There would be no one to help him escape this time if things went wrong. His narrow face turned this way and that, lifted into the smell of the sea and the stone, knifed against the mist, sifted through the instincts that warned him the Creeper was still awake.

He smiled his cold, empty smile. The anger was gone. The anticipation of killing calmed him like Quickening's touch, soothed him, and gave him peace. He was still and settled within himself, everything ready, in place, as sharp as the edge of the Stiehl and as certain.

Noiselessly, he crossed the street to the door of the lair. He carried the grappling hook and rope firmly in hand. Standing before the door, he tossed the hook skyward to wrap about the same stone projection they had used the previous night. The grappling hook caught with a sharp clang and held. Pe Ell backed away, waiting. But the door remained closed. The Rake had either not heard or was preparing itself for whatever would happen next. Pe Ell had hoped that the noise of the hook would bring the beast out and save him the trouble of making the climb. But he knew that was asking too much.

He took a deep breath. This was where the plan became really dangerous.

He stepped forward, grasped the rope that dangled from the grappling hook, and began to climb. He went swiftly, hand over hand, strong enough that he did not require the use of his legs. Once up, he gripped the release that triggered the hidden entry to the lair, yanked violently on it, and immediately dropped away, skinning down the rope like a cat. The door was already coming up when he struck the ground. There was a whisper of sound from within, and he sprang back instantly. A tentacle barely missed catching him, whistling past his feet. The Rake was already moving, lumbering forward, a nest of tentacles outstretched and grasping.

In another instant the door to the lair was completely up. The Creeper rushed forth, skittering madly, wildly, heedless of the fact that it was no longer night. Enraged by Pe Ell's invasion, it gave immediate pursuit. The assassin raced away, darting just ahead of the maddened beast, racing into the shadows of the alleyway across the street. The Creeper followed, faster than Pe Ell had expected. For an instant he wondered if he had misjudged his chances. But there was no time to ponder the matter now, and the doubts evaporated in a surge of determination that propelled him forward.

Down the alleyway he ran and out into the adjoining street. He skidded to a halt. Careful of the traps, he thought. Careful you don't get caught in one yourself. That was what they had planned for the Rake, the old man and he—a long drop down a deep hole, a drop into the bowels of Eldwist. If he could stay alive that long.

The Creeper crashed through the entry of the building next to him, choosing its own route now, almost catching him by surprise. He barely eluded the closest tentacles, knife thin as he twisted away, gone almost before the beast could track him. He darted along the building's edge, the Rake in pursuit. The iron that armored the creature clanked and grated, thudded and scraped. He could feel the size of the thing looming over him, an avalanche waiting to fall. He went through one building, through a second, and emerged another street over. Close now, just two blocks more. But the beast? He turned, searching. He could hear it coming, but the sound seemed to project from everywhere at once. Where . . . ?

Out from the shadows of a darkly recessed entry the Creeper tore, iron arms slamming into the earth inches from Pe Ell as the assassin leaped free. Pe Ell howled in fury and dismay.

So quick!

He wanted to turn and fight, to see the monster react to the cold iron of the Stiehl as he slashed its body to ribbons. He wanted to *feel* the Creeper die. Instead he ran once more, racing along the stone paths of the city, down the streets, along the building walls, through shadows and gray light, a wisp of something darker than night. Tentacles rustled and slithered after him, catching at doors and windowframes, tearing them apart, leaving showers of stone dust scattered in their wake. The massive body hammered and careened, and the legs tore at the walk. The Rake seemed to pick up speed, coming faster still. If daylight bothered it, if blindness inhibited it, it showed nothing of it here. Pe Ell could feel its rage as if it were palpable.

The chase took them down another street and around a final corner. Pe Ell could sense that he was losing ground. Ahead, the street deadended at a stone park. A basin of steps led down to a statue of a winged figure with streamers and ribbons trailing from its body—and to a trap, the same trap that had snared the old man and the Highlander days before.

Horner Dees was waiting, secured in his harness, standing at the edge of the hidden door, bait for the trap. Pe Ell leaped sideways to a walkway and picked up speed as the Rake rounded the corner behind him, tentacles whipping. He went past Horner Dees on the fly, caught a glimpse of his rough face, pale beneath the heavy beard, and sprang onto the wall where the lines securing the harness were laid. He pulled them taut, hoisting Dees out over the hidden pit. He heard the Creeper rumble into the street, heard Horner Dees yell. The Rake became aware of the old man, deviated direction slightly, and charged. Dees tried to backpedal in spite of himself as the juggernaut bore down on him, metal parts shrieking.

Then the trapdoor dropped open, and the monster began to fall. It tumbled wildly down the stone ramp, its armored body rasping. It had been so eager to reach the Tracker that it had forgotten where it was. Now it was caught, sliding away, disappearing from view. Pe Ell howled with delight.

But suddenly the tentacles lashed out and began snaring stone projections—a corner of the basin stairs, a section of a crumbling wall, anything within reach. The sliding stopped. Dust rose into the air, obscuring everything. Pe Ell hesitated, forgetting momentarily to pull in on the harness that secured Dees. Then he heard the old man scream. Yanking frantically on the ropes, he found they would not move. Something was pulling from the other end, something far stronger than himself. He had waited too long. The Rake had Horner Dees.

Pe Ell never hesitated. He wasn't thinking of his promise; keeping his word had never much concerned him. He simply reacted. He dropped the ropes, leaped from the wall, and raced through the basin park into the street. He saw the old Tracker sliding across the stone toward the edge of the drop, hands grasping and feet kicking, a tentacle wrapped about his stout body. He caught up with Horner Dees just as the old man was about to be pulled from view. One slice of the Stiehl severed the tentacle that bound him; a second severed the ropes of the harness.

"Run!" he screamed, shoving the bulky form away.

A tentacle snaked about him, trying to pin his arms fast. He twisted, the Stiehl's blade glowing white with magic, and the tentacle dropped away. Pe Ell raced left, cutting at the tentacles that secured the Rake, severing its hold. There was dust everywhere, rising into the gray light, mingling with the mist until it was uncertain where anything lay. Pe Ell was moving on instinct. He darted and skipped through the tangle of arms, hacked at each, heard the scraping begin again, and the sliding resume.

Then there was a rush of metal and flailing arms and the Rake was gone. It dropped into the chute and fell, tumbling down into the chasm. Pe Ell smothered his elation, racing back the way he had come, searching for Dees. He found him crawling weakly along the basin stairs. "Get up!" he cried, hauling him to his feet in a frenzied lunge, propelling him ahead.

The earth behind them exploded, the street shattering apart, stone fragments flying everywhere. The two men stumbled and fell and turned to look.

The remaining pieces of Horner Dees' plan tumbled into place.

Out of the depths of Eldwist rose the Maw Grint, awakened by the impact of the Rake's fall, aroused and angered. The monster roared and shook itself as it lifted skyward, worm body glistening, all ridges and scales, so huge that it blocked even the faint gray daylight. The Rake dangled from its mouth, turning to stone as the poison coated it, its struggles beginning to lessen. The Maw Grint held it firm a moment, then tossed it as a dog might a rat. The Rake flew through the air and struck the side of a building. The wall collapsed with the impact, and the Rake shattered into pieces.

Back down into the tunnels slid the Maw Grint, its thunder already fading to silence. Clouds of dust settled in its wake, and the light brightened to slate.

Impulsively Pe Ell reached out and locked hands with Horner Dees. Their labored breathing was the only sound in the stillness that followed.

Underground, in the cavern beneath the Stone King's fortress dome, the rumble of the Maw Grint's waking disappeared into the pounding of the Tiderace against Eldwist's rocky shores. Morgan Leah's sun-browned face lifted to peer through the mists.

"What happened?" he whispered.

Walker Boh shook his head, unable to answer. He could still feel the tremors in the earth, lingering echoes of the monster's fury. Something had caused it to breach—something beyond normal waking. The creature's response had been different than when the Stone King had summoned it, more impatient, more intense.

"Is it sleeping again?" the Highlander pressed, anxious now, concerned with being trapped.

"Yes."

"And him?" Morgan pointed into the mists. "Does *he* know?"

Uhl Belk. Walker probed, reaching through the layers of rock in an effort to discover what might be happening. But he was too far away, the stone too secure to be penetrated by his magic.

Not unless he used his touch, and if he did that the Stone King would be warned.

"He rests still," Quickening answered unexpectedly. She came forward to stand next to him, her face smooth and calm, her eyes distant. The wind rushed into her silver hair and scattered it about her face. She braced against its thrust. "Be at ease, Morgan. He does not sense the change."

But Walker sensed it, whatever it was, just as the girl had. Barely perceptible yet, but the effects were beginning to reach and swell. It was something beyond the passing of time and the erosion of rock and earth. The wind whispered it, the ground echoed with it, and the air breathed it. Born of the magic, the daughter of the King of the Silver River and the Dark Uncle had both felt its ripple. Only the Highlander was left unaware.

Walker Boh felt a rough, unexpected urgency clutch at him. Time was slipping away.

"We have to hurry," he said at once, starting away again. "Quickly, now. Come."

He took them left down the rocky outcropping of the ledge, across its ragged, slippery surface. They inched along with their backs to the wall, the ledge no more than several feet wide in places, the ocean's spray redampening its surface with each newly broken wave. Beyond where they stood the cavern spread away like some vast hidden world, and it seemed as if they could feel the eyes of its invisible inhabitants peering out at them.

The ledge ended at a cave that burrowed into darkness. Walker Boh lifted the magic of his silver light to the black and a staircase appeared, winding away, circling upward into the rock.

With Quickening and Morgan following shadowlike, the Dark Uncle began to climb.

XXIX

When Morgan Leah was a boy he often played in the crystal-studded caves that lay east of the city. The caves had been formed centuries earlier, explored and forgotten by countless generations, their stone floors worn smooth by the passing of time and feet. They had survived the Great Wars, the Wars of the Races, the intrusions of living creatures of all forms, and even the earth fires that simmered just beneath their surface. The caves were pockets of bright luminescence, their ceilings thick with stalactites, floors dotted with pools of clear water and darkly shadowed sinkholes, and their chambers connected by a maze of narrow, twisting tunnels. It was dangerous to go into the caves; there was a very high risk of becoming lost. But for an adventure-seeking Highland boy like Morgan Leah, any prospect of risk was simply an attraction.

He found the caves when he was still very small, barely old enough to venture out on his own. There were a handful of boys with him when he discovered an entrance, but he was the only one brave enough to venture in. He went only a short distance that day, intimidated more than a little; it seemed a very real possibility that the caves ran to the very center of the earth. But the lure of that possibility was what called him back in the end, and before long he was venturing ever farther. He kept his exploits secret from his parents, as did all the boys; there were restrictions enough on their lives in those days. He played at being an explorer, at discovering whole worlds unknown to those he had left behind. His imagination would soar when he was inside the caves; he could become anyone and anything. Often he went into them alone, preferring the freedom he felt when the other boys were not about to constrict the range of his play-

acting, for their presence imposed limits he was not always prepared to accept. Alone, he could have things just as he wished.

It was while he was alone one day, just after the anniversary
of the first year of his marvelous discovery, that he became lost.
He was playing as he always played, oblivious of his progress,
confident in his ability to find his way back because he had done
so every time before, and all of a sudden he didn't know where
he was. The tunnel he followed did not appear familiar; the
caves he encountered had a different, foreign look; the atmo-
sphere became abruptly and chillingly unfriendly. It took him a
while to accept that he was really lost and not simply confused,
and then he simply stopped where he was and waited. He had
no idea what it was that he was waiting for at first, but after a
time it became clear. He was waiting to be swallowed. The
caves had come alive, a sleeping beast that had finally roused
itself long enough to put an end to the boy who thought to trifle
with it. Morgan would remember how he felt at that moment
for the rest of his life. He would remember his sense of despair
as the caves transformed from inanimate rock into a living,
breathing, seeing creature that wrapped all about him, snakelike, waiting to see which way he would try to run. Morgan did
not run. He braced himself against the beast, against the way it
hunched down about him. He drew the knife he carried and held
it before him, determined to sell his life dearly. Slowly, without
realizing what he was doing, he disappeared into the character
he had played at being for so many hours. He became someone
else. Somehow that saved him. The beast drew back. He walked
ahead challengingly, and as he did so the strangeness slowly
vanished. He began to recognize something of where he was, a
bit of crystallization here, a tunnel's mouth there, something
else, something more, and all of a sudden he knew where he
was again.

When he emerged from the caves it was night. He had been
lost for several hours—yet it seemed only moments. He went
home thinking that the caves had many disguises to put on, but
that if you looked hard enough you could always recognize the
face beneath.

He had been a boy then. Now he was a man and the beliefs
of boyhood had long since slipped away. He had seen too much
of the real world. He knew too many hard truths.

Yet as he climbed the stairs that curled upward through the
rock walls of the cavern beneath Eldwist he was struck by the
similarity of what he felt now and what he had felt then, trapped

both times in a stone maze from which escape was uncertain.
There was that sense of life in the rock, Uhl Belk's presence,
stirring like a pulse in the silence. There was that sense of being
spied upon, of a beast awakened and set at watch to see which
way he would try to run. The weight of the beast pressed down
upon him, a thing of such size that it could not be measured in
comprehensible terms. A peninsula, a city and beyond, an entire
world—Eldwist was all of these and Uhl Belk was Eldwist. Morgan Leah searched in vain for the disguise that had fooled him
as a boy, for the face that he had once believed hidden beneath.
If he did not find it, he feared, he would never get free.

They ascended in silence, those who had come from Rampling Steep, the only ones left who could face the Stone King.
Morgan was so cold he was shivering, and the cold he felt derived from far more than the chill of the cavern air. He could
feel the sweat bead along his back, and his mind raced with
thoughts of what he would do when the stairs finally came to an
end and they were inside the dome. Draw his sword, the one of
ordinary metal, yet whole? Attack a thing that was nearly im-
mortal with only that? Draw his shattered talisman, a stunted
blade? Attack with that? What? What was it that he was expected
to do?

He watched Quickening move ahead of him, small and delicate against Walker Boh's silver light, a frail bit of flesh and
blood that might in a single sweep of Uhl Belk's stone hand
scatter back into the elements that had formed it. Quickening
gone—he tried to picture it. Fears assailed him anew, darts that
pierced and burned. Why were they doing this? Why should
they even try?

Walker slipped on the mist-dampened steps and grunted in
pain as he struck his knee. They slowed while he righted himself, and Morgan waited for Uhl Belk to stir. Hunter and
hunted—but which was which? He wished he had Steff to stand
beside him. He wished for Par Ohmsford, for Padishar Creel.
He wished for any and all of them, for even some tiny part of
them to appear. But wishing was useless. None of them were
there; none of them would come. He was alone.

With this girl he loved, who could not help.

And with Walker Boh.

An unexpected spark of hope flashed inside the Highlander.
Walker Boh. He stared at the cloaked figure leading them, one-
armed, escaped from the Hall of Kings, risen from the ashes of
Hearthstone. A cat with many lives, he thought. The Dark Uncle

of old, evolved perhaps from the invincible figure of the legends, but a miracle nevertheless, able to defy Druids, spirits, and the Shadowen and live on. Come here to Eldwist, to fulfill a destiny promised by the shade of Allanon or to die—that was what Walker Boh had elected to do. Walker, who had survived everything until now, Morgan reminded himself, was not a man who could be killed easily.

So perhaps it was not intended that the Dark Uncle be killed this time either. And perhaps—just perhaps—some of that immortality might rub off on him.

Ahead, Walker slowed. A flick of his fingers and the silver light vanished. They stood silently in the dark, waiting, listening. The blackness lost its impenetrability as their eyes adjusted, and their surroundings slowly took shape—stairs, ceiling, and walls, and beyond, an opening.

They had reached the summit of their climb.

Still Walker kept them where they were, motionless. When Morgan thought he could stand it no longer, they started ahead once more, slowly, cautiously, one step at a time, shadows against the gloom. The steps ended and a corridor began. They passed down its length, invisible and silent save for their thoughts which seemed to Morgan Leah to hang naked and screaming and bathed in light.

When the corridor ended they stopped again, still concealed within its protective shadow. Morgan stepped forward for an anxious look.

The Stone King's dome opened before them, vast and hazy and as silent as a tomb. The stands that circled the arena stretched away in symmetrical, stair-step lines, a still life of shadows and half-light that lifted to the ceiling, its highest levels little more than a vague suggestion against the aged stone. Below, the arena was flat and hard and empty of movement. The giant form of Uhl Belk crouched at its center, turned away so that only a shading of the rough-hewn face was visible.

Morgan Leah held his breath. The silence of the dome seemed to whisper the warnings that screamed inside his head.

Walker Boh moved back to stand beside him, and the pale, hollowed face bent close so that the other's mouth was at his ear. "Circle left. I'll go right. When I strike him, be ready. I shall try to cause him to drop the Stone. Seize hold of it if he does. Then run. Don't look back. Don't hesitate. Don't stop for anything." The other's hand seized his wrist and held it. "Be swift, Highlander. Be quick."

Morgan nodded voicelessly. For an instant Quickening's black eyes met his own. He could not read what he saw there.

Then Walker was gone, slipping from the mouth of the corridor into the arena, moving to his right along the front wall of the stands into the gloom. Morgan followed, turning left. He pushed aside his dread and gave himself over to the Dark Uncle's command. He passed across the stone like a wraith, quick and certain, finding a surprising reassurance simply from being in motion. But his fear persisted, a cornered beast within his skin. Shadows seemed to circle about him as he went, and the dome's silence hissed at him in his mind, a voiceless snake. His eyes fixed on the bulky form at the arena's center; he found himself searching for even the smallest movement. There was none. Uhl Belk was carved stone against the gray, still and fixed. Quick, now, thought Morgan as he went. Quick as light. He saw Walker at the far side of the arena, a lean and furtive figure, nearly invisible in the gloom. Another few moments, he thought. And then . . .

Quickening.

He suddenly realized that in his haste to obey Walker he had forgotten about the girl. Where was she? He stopped abruptly, casting about for her without success, scanning the risers, the tunnels, the shadows that issued from everywhere. He felt something drop in his chest. Quickening!

Then he saw her—not safely concealed or well back from where they crept, but fully revealed, striding out from the corridor into the arena directly toward the massive figure of Uhl Belk. His breath caught sharply in his throat. What was she doing?

Quickening!

His cry was silent, but the Stone King seemed to hear, responding with an almost inaudible grunt, stirring to life, lifting away from his crouch, beginning to turn . . .

Brilliant white light flared across the canopy of the dome, so blinding that for an instant even Morgan had to look away. It was as if the sun had exploded through the clouds, the gray haze, the stone itself, to set fire to the air imprisoned there. Morgan saw Walker Boh with his single arm raised, thrust out from his dark robes, the magic bursting from his fingers. Uhl Belk howled in surprise, his massive body shuddering, arms raising to shield his eyes, his stone parts grinding with the effort.

Walker Boh leaped forward then, a shadow against the light, charging at the Stone King as the latter flailed ponderously at the painful brightness. Again his good arm raised, thrusting forth. An entire bag of Cogline's volatile black powder flew at Uhl Belk and exploded, hammering into the Stone King. Bits and pieces of the ragged body shattered into fragments. Fire burned along his arm to where his fist clenched the Black Elfstone.

But still he held the talisman fast.

And suddenly Morgan Leah found that he could not move. He was frozen where he stood. Just as had happened at the Jut when the Creeper had gained the heights under cover of darkness and the outlaws of the Movement had gone to meet its attack, he found himself paralyzed. All his fears and doubts, all his misgivings and terrors descended on him. They seized him with their clawed fingers and bound him up as surely as if he had been wrapped in chains. What could he do? How could he help? His magic was lost, his Sword blade shattered. He watched helplessly as Uhl Belk began to turn, to fight past Walker Boh's assault, and to brush back his magic. The Dark Uncle renewed his attack, but this time he struck without the element of surprise to aid him and the Stone King barely flinched. Already the brightness of Walker's false sun was beginning to fade and the gray of the dome's true light to return.

Walker Boh's words echoed tauntingly in Morgan's ears.

Be swift, Highlander. Be quick.

Morgan fought through his immobility and wrenched free from its scabbard the broadsword he wore strapped to his back. But his fingers refused to hold it; his hands would not obey. The broadsword slipped away, tumbling to the arena floor with a hollow clang.

The Stone King's breath hissed as one monstrous hand swept out to seize Walker Boh and crush the life from him. The Dark Uncle had gotten too close; there was no chance for him to escape. Then suddenly he was gone, reappearing first as two images, then four, and then countless more—Jair Ohmsford's favorite trick, three centuries ago. The Stone King grabbed at the images, and the images evaporated at his touch. The true Walker Boh sprang at the monster, scattered new fire into his face, and slid nimbly away.

The Stone King howled in rage, clawed at his face, and shook himself like an animal seeking to rid itself of flies. The whole of the arena shuddered in response. Fissures opened in jagged lines across the floor, the stands buckled and snapped, and a shower of dust and debris descended from the ceiling. Morgan lost his footing and fell, the impact of the stone jarring him to his teeth.

He felt pain, and with the coming of that pain the paralyzing chains fell away.

The Stone King's fist came up, and the fingers of his hand began to open. The nonlight of the Elfstone seeped through, devouring what remained of Walker Boh's fading magic. The Dark Uncle threw up a screen of fire to slow the magic's advance, but the nonlight enveloped it in a wave of blackness. Walker stumbled backward toward the shadows, chased by the nonlight, harried by the fissures and the cracking of stone.

Another few seconds and he would be trapped.

Then Quickening caught fire.

There was no other way to explain it. Morgan watched it happen and still couldn't believe what he was seeing. The daughter of the King of the Silver River, less than twenty feet away from Uhl Belk by now, standing exposed and unprotected beneath his shadow, elevated like a creature made of air, until she was level with the giant's head, then burst into flames. The fire was golden and pure, its blaze a cloaking of light, flaring all along her body and limbs, leaving her illuminated as if by the midday sun. She was, in that instant, more beautiful than Morgan had ever seen her, radiant and flawless and exquisite beyond belief. Her silver hair lifted away from her, feathering outward against the fire, and her eyes glistened black within the gold. She hung there revealed, all wondrous, impossible magic come to life.

She is trying to distract him, Morgan realized in disbelief. *She is giving herself away, revealing who she is, in an effort to distract him from us!*

The Stone King turned at the unexpected flaring of light, his already crumpled face twisting until his features virtually ceased to exist. The slash of his mouth gaped at the sight of her and his voice sounded in anguish.

—You—

Uhl Belk forgot about Walker Boh. He forgot about the Dark Uncle's magic. He forgot about everything but the burning girl. In a frenzy of grinding stone limbs and joints, he struggled to reach her, surging up against the stone floor that welded him fast, grappling futilely for her, then in desperation bringing the hand that cupped the Black Elfstone to bear against her. His voice was a terrifying moan become a frenzied roar. The earth shuddered with the urgency of his need.

Morgan acted then, finally, desperately, even hopelessly. Surging back to his feet, his eyes fastened on Quickening and on the monster who sought to destroy her, he attacked. He went without thought, without reason, driven by need and armored in determination he had not thought he could ever possess. He raced into the haze of dust and debris, leaping past the fissures and drops, speeding as if he were carried on the strong autumn winds of his homeland. One hand dropped to his waist, and he pulled forth the shattered blade of his ancestors, the jagged remnant of the Sword of Leah.

Though he was not aware of it, the Sword shone white with magic.

He screamed the battle cry of his homeland. "Leah! Leah!"

He reached the Stone King just as the other became aware of his presence and the hard, empty eyes began to turn. He sprang onto a massive bent leg, vaulted forward, seized the arm that extended the Black Elfstone, and drove the shattered blade of the Sword of Leah deep into its stone.

Uhl Belk screamed, not in surprise or anger this time, but in terrifying pain. White fire burst from the shattered blade into the Stone King's body, lines of flame that penetrated and seared. Morgan stabbed Uhl Belk again and yet again. The stone hands trembled and clutched, and the stricken monster shuddered.

The Black Elfstone tumbled from his fingers.

Instantly Morgan yanked free his Sword and scrambled down in an effort to retrieve it. But the Stone King's damaged arm blocked his way, swinging toward him like a hammer. He dodged wildly, desperate to escape its sweep, but it clipped him anyway and sent him tumbling back, arms and legs flying. He barely managed to keep hold of his weapon. He caught a brief glimpse of Quickening, an oddly clear vision, her face bright even though the magic of her fire had faded. He caught a snatch of dark motion as Walker Boh appeared next to her out of the shadows. Then he struck the wall, the force of the blow knocking the breath from him, jamming the joints of his body so that he thought he had broken everything. Even so, he refused to stay down. He staggered back to his feet, dazed and battered, determined to continue.

But there was nothing more to do. As quickly as that, the battle was ended. Walker Boh had gained possession of the fallen Elfstone. He braced the Stone King, the Druid talisman clutched menacingly in his raised hand. Quickening stood beside him, returned to herself, the magic she had summoned gone again.

As his vision slowly cleared, as his sense of balance restored itself, Morgan saw her again in his mind, all on fire. He was still astonished at what she had done. Despite her vow she had used the magic, revealed herself to Uhl Belk, and risked everything to give them a chance to survive.

The questions whispered at him then, insidious tricksters.

Had she known that he would come to save her?

Had she known what his Sword would do?

The gloom of the dome's interior returned again with the fading of the magic, cloaking Uhl Belk's massive form in shadow. The Stone King faced them from a cloud of swirling dust, his body sagging as if melted by the heat of his efforts to defend himself, still joined to the stone of Eldwist in the chaining that had undone him. Try as he might, he had not been able to rise and break free. By choosing to become the substance of his kingdom he had rendered himself virtually immobile. His face was twisted into something unrecognizable, and when he spoke there was horror and madness reflected in his voice.

—Give the Elfstone back to me—

They stared up at him, the three from Rampling Steep, and it seemed none of them could find words to speak.

"No, Uhl Belk," Walker Boh replied finally, his own voice strained from the effort of his battle. "The Elfstone was never yours in the first place. It shall not be given back to you now."

—I shall come for you then; I shall take it from you—

"You cannot move from where you stand. You have lost this battle and with it the Elfstone. Do not think to try and steal it back."

—It is mine—

The Dark Uncle did not waiver. "It belongs to the Druids."

Dust geysered from the ravaged face as the creature's breath exploded in a hiss of despair.

—There are no Druids—

The accusation died away in a grating echo. Walker Boh did not respond, his face chiseled with emotions that seemed to be tearing him apart from within. The Stone King's arms rose in a dramatic gesture.

—Give the Black Elfstone back to me, human, or I shall command Eldwist to crush the life from you; give the talisman back now or see yourself destroyed—

"Attack me or those with me," Walker Boh said, "and I shall turn the Elfstone's magic against this city! I shall summon power enough to shatter the stone casing that preserves it and

turn it and you to dust! Do not threaten further, Uhl Belk! The
power is no longer yours!''

The silence that followed was profound. The Stone King's
hand closed into a fist and the sound of grinding rose out of it.

—You cannot command me, human; no one can—

Walker's response was immediate. ''Release us, Uhl Belk.
The Black Elfstone is lost to you.''

The statue straightened with a groan, and the sound of its
voice was thick with weeping.

—It will come for me; the Maw Grint will come; my son, the
monster I have made will descend upon me, and I shall be forced
to destroy it; only the Black Elfstone kept it at bay; it will see
me old and wearied and believe me without strength to defend
against its hunger; it shall try to devour me—

Depthless hard eyes fixed on Quickening.

—Child of the King of the Silver River, daughter of he who
was my brother once, give thought to what you do; you threaten
to weaken me forever if you steal away the Stone; the Maw
Grint's life is no less dear to me than your own to your father;
without him there can be no expansion of my land, no fulfillment
of my trust; who are you that you should be so quick to take
what is mine; are you completely blind to what I have made;
there is in the stone of my land a changeless beauty that your
father's Gardens will never have; worlds may come and go but
Eldwist will remain; it would be better for all worlds to be so;
your father believes himself right in what he does, but his vision
of life is no clearer than my own; am I not entitled to do what I
see is right as the Word has given me to see right—

''You subvert what you touch, Uhl Belk,'' the girl whispered.

—And you do not; your father does not; all who live within
nature do not; can you pretend otherwise—

Quickening's frail form eased a step closer to the giant, and
the light that had radiated from her before flared anew.

''There is a difference between nurturing life and making it
over,'' she said. ''It was to nurture that you were charged when
given your trust. You have forgotten how to do so.''

The Stone King's hand brushed at the particles of light that
floated from her body, an unconscious effort to shield himself.
But then he drew his hand back sharply, the intake of his breath
harsh with pain.

—No—

The word was an anguished cry. He straightened, caught by
some invisible net that wrapped him and held him fast.

—Oh, child; I see you now; I thought that in the Maw Grint I had created a monster beyond all belief; but your father has done worse in you—

The rough voice gasped, choked as if it could not make the words come further.

—Child of change and evolution, you are the ceaseless, quick-silver motion of water itself; I see in truth what you have been sent to do; I have indeed been stone too long to have missed it; I should have realized when you came to me that you were madness; I am mired in the permanency I sought and have been as blind as those who serve me; the end of my life is written out before me by the scripting of my own hand—

"Uhl Belk." Quickening whispered the name as if it were a prayer.

—How can you give what has been asked after tasting so much—

Morgan did not understand what the Stone King was talking about. He glanced at Quickening and started in surprise. Her face was stricken with guilt, a mirror of the hidden secrets that he had always suspected but never wanted to believe she kept.

The Stone King's voice was a low hiss.

—Take yourself from me, child; go into the world again and do what you must to seal all our fates; your victory over me must seem hollow and bitter when the price demanded for it is made so dear—

Walker Boh was staring as well, his mouth shaped with a frown, his brow furrowed. He did not seem to understand what Uhl Belk was saying either. Morgan started to ask Quickening what was happening and hesitated, unsure of himself.

Then Uhl Belk's head jerked up with a sharp crack.

—Listen—

The earth began to shudder, a low rumbling that emanated from deep within, rising to the surface in gathering waves of sound. Morgan Leah had heard that rumble before.

—It comes—

The Maw Grint.

Walker began backing away, yelling at Morgan and Quickening to follow. He shouted at the Stone King, "Release us, Uhl Belk, if you would save yourself! Do so now! Quickly!"

Walker's arm lifted, threatening with the fist that held the Black Elfstone. Uhl Belk barely seemed to notice. His face had become more haggard, more collapsed than ever, a parody of human features, a monster's face grown hideous beyond thought.

The giant's voice hissed like a serpent's through the roar of the
Maw Grint's approach.

—Flee, fools—

There was no anger in the voice—only frustration and emptiness. And something more, Morgan Leah thought in amazement. There was hope, just a glimmer of it, a recognition beyond
the Highlander's understanding, a seeing of some possibility
that transcended all else.

A section of the dome's massive wall split apart directly
behind them, stone blocks grinding with the movement, gray
daylight spilling through.

—Flee—

Morgan Leah broke for the opening instantly, chased by demons he did not care to see. He felt, rather than saw, the Stone
King watch him go. Quickening and Walker followed. They
gained the opening in a rush and were through, running from
the fury of the Maw Grint's coming, racing away into the gloom.

XXX

I t appeared that the Maw Grint had gone mad.

Twice before the three who fled had observed the monster's coming, once when it had surfaced as they stood on
the overlook above the city and once when it had been summoned by Uhl Belk. There hadn't been a day since they had
arrived in Eldwist that they hadn't heard the creature moving
through the tunnels below them, astir at the coming of each
sunset to prowl with the dark. Each time its approach had been
prefaced with the same unmistakable deep, low rumbling of the
earth. Each time the city had trembled in response.

But there had never been anything like this.

The city of Eldwist was like a beast shaking itself awake from
a bad dream. Towers and spires rocked and trembled, shedding

bits and pieces of loose stone amid a shower of choking dust.
The streets threatened to buckle, stone cracking in jagged fissures, trapdoors dropping away as their catches released, supports and trestles snapping apart. Whole stairways leading downward to the tunnels crumbled and disappeared, and sky-bridges connecting one building to another collapsed. Against a screen of gray haze and clouds Eldwist shimmered like a vanishing mirage.

Racing to escape the Stone King's dome, Walker Boh barely gained the closest walkway before the tremors drove him to his knees. He pitched forward, his outstretched arm curling against his body to protect his hold on the Black Elfstone. He took the force of the fall on his shoulder, a sharp, jarring blow, and kept skidding. He struck the wall of the building ahead of him, and the breath left his body. For a moment he was stunned, bright pinpricks of light dancing before his eyes. When his vision cleared he saw Quickening and Morgan sprawled in the street behind him, knocked from their feet as well.

He rose with an effort and started away again, yelling for them to follow. As he watched them struggle up, his mind raced. He had threatened Uhl Belk with the Black Elfstone by saying that he would invoke its magic against the city if they were not released. The threat had been an idle one. He could not use the Elfstone that way without destroying himself. It was fortunate for them all that Uhl Belk still did not understand how the Druid magic worked. Even so they were not free yet. What would they do if the Maw Grint came after them? There was every reason to believe that it would. The magic of the Black Elfstone had provided a link between father and son, spirit lord and monster, that Walker Boh had broken. The Maw Grint already sensed that break; it had awakened in response. Once it discovered that the Elfstone was gone, that the Stone King no longer had possession of it, what was to prevent the beast from giving chase?

Walker Boh grimaced. There wasn't any question as to how such a chase would end. He couldn't use the Black Elfstone on the Maw Grint either.

A stone block large enough to bury him crashed into the street a dozen feet ahead, sending the Dark Uncle sprawling for the second time. Quickening darted past, her beautiful face oddly stricken, and raced away into the gloom. Morgan appeared, reached down as he caught up with Walker, and hauled him back to his feet. Together they ran on, sidestepping through the gathering debris, dodging the cracks and fissures.

"Where are we going?" the Highlander cried out, ducking his head against the dust and silt.

Walker gestured vaguely. "Out of the city, off the peninsula, back up on the heights!"

"What about Horner Dees?"

Walker had forgotten the Tracker. He shook his head. "If we can find him, we'll take him with us! But we can't stop to look! There isn't time!" He shoved the Elfstone into his tunic and reached out to grasp the other as they ran. "Highlander, stay close to Quickening. This matter is not yet resolved! She is in some danger!"

Morgan's eyes were white against his dust-streaked face. "What danger, Walker? Do you know something? What was Uhl Belk talking about back there when he spoke about her victory being hollow, about the price she was paying? What did he mean?"

Walker shook his head wordlessly. He didn't know—yet sensed at the same time that he should, that he was overlooking something obvious, forgetting something important. The street yawned open before them, a trapdoor sprung. He yanked the Highlander aside just in time, pulling him clear, propelling him back onto the walkway. The roaring of the Maw Grint was fading slightly now, falling back as the Stone King's fortressed dome receded into the distance.

"Catch up to her, Highlander!" Walker yelled, shoving him ahead. "Keep an eye out for Dees! We'll meet back at the building where we hid ourselves from the Rake!" He glanced over his shoulder and back again, shouting, "Careful, now! Watch yourself!"

But Morgan Leah was already gone.

Pe Ell and Horner Dees had only just reached the building to which the others now fled when the tremors began. Their battle with the Rake completed, they had come in search of the remainder of the company from Rampling Steep, each for his own reasons, neither sharing much of anything with the other. The truce they had called had ended with the destruction of the Rake, and they watched each other now with careful, suspicious eyes.

They whirled in surprise as the rumbling began to build, deeper and more pronounced than at any time before. The city shuddered in response.

"Something's happened," Horner Dees whispered, his bearded face lifting. "Something more."

"It's come awake again," Pe Ell cried with loathing. When they had left the Maw Grint it was sunk back down into the earth and gone still.

The street on which they faced shook with the impact of the creature's rising.

Pe Ell gestured. "Look upstairs. See if anyone is there."

Dees went without argument. Pe Ell stood rooted on the walk while the city's tremors washed over him. He was taut and hard within himself, the battle with the Rake still alive inside, driving through him like the rushing of his blood. Things were coming together now; he could sense the coalescing of events, the weaving of the threads of fate of the five from Rampling Steep. It would be over soon, he sensed. It would be finished.

Horner Dees reappeared at the building entry. "No one."

"Then wait here for their return," Pe Ell snapped, starting quickly away. "I'll look toward the center of the city."

"Pe Ell!"

The hatchet face turned. "Don't worry, old man. I'll be back." *Perhaps,* he added to himself.

He darted into the gloom, leaving the ageing Tracker to call uselessly after him. Enough of Horner Dees, he thought bitterly. He was still rankled by the fact that he had saved the bothersome Tracker from the Rake, that he had acted on instinct rather than using common sense, that he had risked his life to save a man he fully intended to kill anyway.

On the other hand his plans for Dees and the other fools who had come with Quickening were beginning to change. He could feel those plans settling comfortably into place even now. Everything always seemed much clearer when he was moving. It was all well and good to anticipate the event, but circumstances and needs evolved, and the event did not always turn out as expected, the coming about of it not always as foreseen. Pe Ell revised his earlier assessment of the necessity of killing his companions. Quickening, of course, would have to die. He had already promised Rimmer Dall that he would kill her. More important, he had promised himself. Quickening's fate was unalterable. But why bother with killing the others? Unless they got in his way by trying to interfere with his plans for the girl, why expend the effort? If he somehow managed to gain possession of the Black Elfstone there was no possible harm they could cause him. And even if he was forced to abandon that part of his plan—as it now appeared he would have to—the old Tracker, the one-armed man, the Highlander, and the tunesmith offered no threat to him. Even if they escaped Eldwist to follow him he had little to fear. How would they find him? And what would they do if they did?

No, he need not kill them—though he would, he added, almost as an afterthought, if the right opportunity presented itself.

The tremors continued, long and deep, the growl of the earth protesting the coming of the monster worm. Pe Ell darted this way and that along the empty walkways, down streets littered with debris and past buildings weakened by ragged, wicked cracks that scarred their smooth surface. His sharp eyes searched the shadows for movement, seeking those who had come with him or even perhaps some sign of the elusive Stone King. He hadn't given up completely on the Black Elfstone. There was still a chance, he told himself. Everything was coming together, caught in a whirlpool. He could feel it happening . . .

Out of the haze before him raced Quickening, silver hair flying as she ran, her reed-thin body a quicksilver shadow. Pe Ell moved to intercept her, catching her about the waist with one arm before she realized what was happening. She gasped in surprise, stiffened, and then clung to him.

"Pe Ell," she breathed.

There was something in the way she spoke his name that surprised him. It was a measure of fear mingled with relief, an odd combination of dismay and satisfaction. He tightened his grip instinctively, but she did not try to break away.

"Where are the others?" he asked.

"Coming after me, escaped from Uhl Belk and the Maw Grint." Her black eyes fixed on him. "It is time to leave Eldwist, Pe Ell. We found the Stone King and we took the Black Elfstone away from him—Morgan, Walker Boh, and I."

Pe Ell fought to stay calm. "Then we are indeed finished with this place." He glanced past her into the gloom. "Who has the Elfstone now?"

"Walker Boh," she replied.

Pe Ell's jaw tightened. It would have to be Walker Boh, of course. It would have to be him. How much easier things would be if the girl had the Stone. He could kill her now, take it from her, and be gone before any of them knew what had happened. The one-armed man seemed to stand in his way at every turn, a shadowy presence he could not quite escape. What would it take to be rid of him?

He knew, of course, what it would take. He felt his plans begin to shift back again.

"Quickening!" a voice called out.

It was the Highlander. Pe Ell hesitated, then made up his mind. He clamped his hand about Quickening's mouth and hauled her into the shadows. Surprisingly, the girl did not struggle. She was light and yielding, almost weightless in his arms. It was the first time he had held her since he had carried her from the Meade Gardens. The feelings she stirred within him were distractingly soft and pleasant, and he forced them roughly aside. Later for that, he thought, when he used the Stiehl . . .

Morgan Leah burst into view, pounding along the walkway, shouting for the girl, searching. Pe Ell held Quickening close and watched the Highlander run past. A moment later, he was gone.

Pe Ell released his hand from the girl's mouth, and she turned to face him. There was neither surprise nor fear in her eyes now; there was only resignation. "It is almost time for us, Pe Ell," she whispered.

A flicker of doubt tugged at his confidence. She was looking at him in that strange way she had, as if he were transparent to her, as if everything about him were known. But if everything were known, she would not be standing there so calmly. She would be attempting to flee, to call after the Highlander, or to do something to save herself.

The rumbling beneath the city increased, then faded slightly, a warning of the slow, inevitable avalanche bearing down on them.

"Time for us to do what?" he managed hesitantly, unable to break away from her gaze.

She did not answer. Instead she glanced past him, her black eyes searching. He turned to stare with her and watched the dark form of Walker Boh materialize from out of the haze of dust and gray light.

Unlike the Highlander, the Dark Uncle had seen them.

Pe Ell swung the girl in front of him and unsheathed the Stiehl from its hiding place, the blade gleaming bright with the magic. The one-armed man slowed perceptibly, then came on.

"Pe Ell," he whispered softly, as if the name itself were venomous.

"Stand back from me, Walker Boh," Pe Ell ordered. The other stopped. "We've seen enough of each other to know what we are capable of doing. No need to test it. Better that we part now and go our separate ways. But first give me the Stone."

The tall man stood without moving, seemingly without life,

eyes fixed on the assassin and his hostage. He appeared to be weighing something.

Pe Ell's smile was sardonic. "Don't be foolish enough to think you might be quicker than me."

"We might neither of us be quick enough to survive this day. The Maw Grint comes."

"It will find me gone when it does. Give me the Black Elf-stone."

"If I do so, will that be enough to satisfy you?" the other asked quietly, his gaze intense, as if trying to read Pe Ell's thoughts.

Like the girl, Pe Ell thought. Two of a kind. "Pass it to me," he commanded, ignoring the question.

"Release Quickening."

Pe Ell shook his head. "When I am safely away. Then I promise that I will set her free." *Free, forever.*

They stood staring at each other wordlessly for a moment, hard looks filled with unspoken promises, with visions of possibilities that were dark and forbidding. Then Walker Boh reached down into his tunic and brought forth the Stone. He held it out in his palm, dark and glistening. Pe Ell smiled faintly. The Elfstone was as black as midnight, opaque and depthless, seamless and unflawed. He had never seen anything like it before. He could almost feel the magic pulsing within.

"Give it to me," he repeated.

Walker Boh reached down to his belt and worked free a leather pouch marked with brilliant blue runes. Carefully he used the fingers of his solitary hand to maneuver the Stone into the pouch and pull the drawstrings tight. He looked at Pe Ell and said, "You cannot use the Black Elfstone, Pe Ell. If you try, the magic will destroy you."

"Life is filled with risks," Pe Ell replied. Dust churned in the air about them, sifted by a faint sea breeze. The stone of the city shimmered, swept up in the earth's distant rumble, wrapped in a gauze of mist and clouds. "Toss it to me," he ordered. "Gently."

He used the hand with the Stiehl to keep tight hold of Quickening. The girl did not stir. She waited passively, her slender body pressed against him, so compliant she might have been sleeping. Walker held out the pouch with the Black Elfstone and carefully lobbed it. Pe Ell caught it and shoved it into his belt, securing the strings to his buckle.

"Magic belongs to those who are not afraid to use it," he

offered, smiling, backing cautiously away. "And to those who can keep it."

Walker Boh stood rock-still against the roiling dust and tremors. "Beware, Pe Ell. You risk everything."

"Don't come after me, Walker Boh," Pe Ell warned darkly. "Better for you if you remain here and face the Maw Grint."

With Quickening securely in his grasp he continued to move away, following the line of the walkway until the other man vanished into the haze.

Walker Boh remained motionless, staring after the disappearing Pe Ell and Quickening. He was wondering why he had given up the Black Elfstone so easily. He had not wanted to, had resolved not to in fact, and had been prepared instead to attack Pe Ell, to go to the girl's rescue—until he looked into her eyes and saw something there that stopped him. Even now he wasn't sure what it was that he had seen. Determination, resignation, some private insight that transcended his own— something. Whatever it was, it had changed his mind as surely as if she had used her magic.

His head lowered and his dark eyes narrowed.

Had she, he wondered, used her magic?

He stood lost in thought. A light dusting of water sprinkled his face. It was beginning to rain again. He looked up, remembering where he was, what he was about, and hearing again the thunder caused by the movement of the Maw Grint beneath the city, feeling the vibration of its coming.

Cogline's voice was a whisper in his ear, reminding him gently to understand who he was. He had always wondered before. Now he thought he knew.

He summoned his magic, feeling it rise easily within him, strong again since his battle with the Stone King, as if that confrontation had freed him of constraints he had placed upon himself. It gathered at the center of his being, whirling like a great wind. The rune markings on the pouch in which the Black Elfstone rested would be its guide. With barely a lifting of his head he sent it winging forth in search of Pe Ell.

Then he followed after.

Pe Ell ran, dragging Quickening behind him. She came without resisting, moving obediently to keep pace, saying nothing, asking nothing, her eyes distant and calm. He glanced back at her only once and quickly turned away again. What he saw in those dark eyes bothered him. She was seeing something that he could not, something old and immutable, a part of her past or her future—he wasn't sure which. She was an enigma still, the one secret he had not yet been able to solve. But soon now he would, he promised himself. The Stiehl would give him an answer to what she hid. When her life was fading from her she would stand revealed. There would be no secrets then. The magic would not permit it. Just as it had been with all the others he had killed, there would be only truth.

He felt the first drops of rain strike his heated face.

He darted left along a cross street, angling away from the direction Morgan Leah had gone and Walker Boh would follow. There was no reason to give them any chance of finding him. He would slip quickly from the city onto the isthmus, cross to the stairs, gain the heights of the overlook, and then with time and privacy enough to take full advantage of the moment he would kill her. Anticipation washed through him. Quickening, the daughter of the King of the Silver River, the most wondrous magical creature of all, would be his forever.

Yet the flicker of doubt continued to burn within him. What was it that bothered him so? He searched for the answer, pausing briefly as he remembered what she had said about needing their magics, the magics of all three—the Highlander, Walker Boh, and himself. All three were required, the King of the Silver River had proclaimed. That was why she had recruited them, persuaded them to come, and kept them together through all the anger and mistrust. But it had been Walker Boh and the Highlander alone who had discovered the hiding place of Uhl Belk and secured the Black Elfstone. He had done nothing—except to destroy the Rake. Was that the use for which his magic had been intended? Was that the reason for his coming? It didn't seem enough somehow. It seemed there should be something more.

Pe Ell slid through the murk of Eldwist's deepening morning, holding the girl close to him as he went, thinking to himself that this whole journey had been a puzzle with too many missing pieces. They had come in search of the Stone King—yet the others, not Pe Ell, had found him. They had come to retrieve the Black Elfstone—yet the others, not Pe Ell, had done so. The magic of the Stiehl was the most deadly magic that any of them possessed—yet what purpose had it served?

Uneasiness stole through him like a thief, draining his elation at having both Quickening and the Stone.

Something was wrong and he didn't know what it was. He should feel in control of things and he did not.

They passed back onto a roadway leading south, winding their way down between the buildings, passing through the haze, two furtive shadows fleeing into light. Pe Ell slowed now, beginning to tire. He peered through the thin curtain of rain that hung before him, blinking uncertainly. Was this the way he had intended to come? Somehow, he didn't think so. He glanced right, then left. Wasn't this street the one he had been trying to avoid? Confusion filled him. He felt Quickening's eyes on him but would not allow himself to meet her gaze.

He steered them down another sidestreet and crossed to a broad plaza dominated by a tiered basin encircled by benches, some crumbling and split, and the remains of poles from which flags had once flown. He was working his way left toward an arched passageway between the buildings, intent on gaining the open street beyond, a street that would take him directly to the isthmus, when he heard his name called. He whirled, pulling the girl close, the blade of the Stiehl coming up to her throat.

Morgan Leah stood across the plaza from him, a lean and dangerous figure. Pe Ell stared. How had the Highlander found him? It was chance, he quickly decided. Nothing more. Dismay grappled with anger. Any misfortune that resulted from this encounter must not be his.

The Highlander did not appear to know what was happening. "What are you doing, Pe Ell?" he shouted through the forest of broken poles.

"What I wish!" Pe Ell responded, but there was a weariness in his voice that surprised him. "Get away, Highlander. I have no wish to hurt you. I have what I came for. Your one-armed friend has given me the Elfstone—here, in this pouch at my belt! I intend to keep it! If you wish the girl to go free, stand away!"

But Morgan Leah did not move. Haggard-looking and worn, just a boy really, he seemed both lost and unresolved. Yet he refused to give way. "Let her go, Pe Ell. Don't hurt her."

His plea was wasted, but Pe Ell managed a tired nod. "Go back, Highlander. Quickening comes with me."

Morgan Leah seemed to hesitate momentarily, then started forward. For the first time since he had seized her, Pe Ell felt Quickening tense. She was worried for the Highlander, he realized. Her concern enraged him. He pulled her back and brought the Stiehl against her throat, calling to the other man to stop.

And then suddenly Walker Boh appeared as well, materializing out of the gloom, close by Morgan Leah. He stepped forward unhurriedly and grasped the Highlander's arm, pulling him back. The Highlander struggled, but even with only one arm the other man was stronger.

"Think what you are doing, Pe Ell!" Walker Boh called out, and now there was anger in his voice.

How had the big man caught up to him so quickly? Pe Ell felt a twinge of uneasiness, a sense that for some unexplainable reason nothing was going right. He should have been clear of this madness by now, safely away. He should have had time to savor his victory, to speak with the girl before using the Stiehl, to see how much he could learn of her magic. Instead he was being harried unmercifully by the very men he had chosen to spare. Worse, he was in some danger of being trapped.

"Get away from me!" he shouted, his temper slipping, his control draining away. "You risk the girl's life by continuing this chase! Let me leave now or she dies!"

"Let her go!" the distraught Highlander screamed again. He had fallen to his knees, still firmly in the grip of the one-armed man.

Behind Pe Ell, still too far away to make any difference but closing on him steadily, came Horner Dees. The assassin was now ringed by his enemies. For the first time in his life he was trapped, and he sensed a hint of panic setting in. He jerked Quickening about to face the burly Tracker. "Out of my way, old man!" he bellowed.

But Horner Dees simply shook his head. "I don't think so, Pe Ell. I've backed away from you enough times. I've a stake in this business, too. I've given at least as much of myself as you. Besides, you've done nothing to earn what you claim. You simply seek to steal. We know who and what you are, all of us. Do as Morgan Leah says. Let the girl go."

Walker Boh's voice rose. "Pe Ell, if the Shadowen sent you to steal the Elfstone, take it and go. We won't stop you."

"The Shadowen!" Pe Ell laughed, fighting to contain his rage. "The Shadowen are nothing to me. I do for them what I wish and nothing more. Do you think I came all this way because of them? You are a fool!"

"Then take the Elfstone for yourself if you must."

The rage broke free. Caution disappeared in a red mist. "If I must! Of course, I must! But even the Elfstone isn't the real reason I came!"

"Then what is, Pe Ell?" Walker Boh asked tightly.

"She is!" Pe Ell yanked Quickening around once more, lifting her exquisite face above the point of his knife. "Look at her, Walker Boh, and tell me that you don't desire her! You cannot, can you? Your feelings, mine, the Highlander's—they're all the same! We came on this journey because of her, because of the way she looked at us and made us feel, because of the way she wove her magic all about us! Think of the secrets she hides! Think of the magic she conceals! I came on this journey to discover what she is, to claim her. She has belonged to me from the first moment of her life, and when I am finished here she shall belong to me always! Yes, the Shadowen sent me, but it was my choice to come—my choice when I saw what she could give me! Don't you see? I came to Eldwist to kill her!"

The air went still suddenly, the tremors and the thunder fading into a vague and distant moan, leaving the assassin's words sharp and clear against the silence. The stone of the city caught their sound and held the echo within its walls, a long, endless reverberation of dismay.

"I have to discover what she is," Pe Ell whispered, trying vainly to explain now, unable to think what else to do, stunned that he had been foolish enough to reveal so much, knowing they would never let him go now. How had he managed to lose control of matters so completely? "I have to kill her," he repeated, the words sounding harsh and bitter. "That is how the magic works. It reveals all truths. In taking life, it gives life. To me. Once the killing is done, Quickening shall be mine forever."

For an instant no one spoke, stunned by the assassin's revelation. Then Horner Dees said slowly, deliberately, "Don't be stupid, Pe Ell. You can't get away from all of us. Let her go."

It was uncertain then exactly what happened next. There was an explosion of shattered rock as the Maw Grint broke free of the tunnels and reared skyward against the buildings of the city somewhere close to where the Stone King hid within his fortressed dome. The monster rose like a bloated snake, swaying against the shroud of mist and damp, huffing as if to catch its breath, as if the air were being sucked from it. Pe Ell started, feeling the earth begin to shudder so violently that it seemed Eldwist would be shaken apart.

Then Quickening broke free, slipping from his grasp as if she were made of air. She turned to him, disdaining to run, standing right against him, her hands gripping the arm that held the Stiehl, her black eyes shackling him as surely as if he were chained. He could not move; he just stood there, frozen in place. He saw the symmetry of her face and body as if seeing it for the first time; he marveled at the perfection of her, at beauty that lay not just upon the surface of her wondrous form, but ran deep within. He felt her press forward—or did he? Which was it? He saw her mouth open with surprise and pain and relief.

He glanced down then and saw that the handle of the Stiehl was flush against her stomach, the blade buried in her body. He could not remember stabbing her, yet somehow he had. Confusion and disbelief surged through him. How had this happened? What of his plan to kill her where and when he chose? What of his intention to savor the moment of her dying? He looked quickly into her eyes, desperate to snare what was trapped there and about to be set free, anxious to capture her magic. He looked, and what he saw filled him with rage.

Pe Ell screamed. As if seeking to hide what he had discovered, he stabbed her again and again, and each time it was a frantic, futile attempt to deny what he was seeing. Quickening's body jerked in response, but her gaze remained steady, and the visions shimmering in her eyes remained fixed.

Pe Ell understood at last, and with understanding came a horror against which he had no defense. His thoughts collapsed, tumbling into a quagmire of despair. He shoved himself free of the girl and watched her slump to the street in a slow, agonizing fall, her black eyes never leaving him. He was aware of Morgan Leah crying out in fury, of Walker Boh racing forward, and of Horner Dees charging at him from the rear. They did not matter. Only the girl did. He stepped away, shaking with a cold that threatened to freeze him in place. Everything he had hoped for had been stolen from him. Everything he had wanted was lost.

What have I done?

He wheeled about and began to run. His cold turned abruptly to fire, but the words buzzed within his mind, a nest of hornets with sharp and anxious stingers.

What have I done?

He darted past Horner Dees with a quickness born of fear and despair, gone so fast that the old Tracker had no chance of stopping him. The stone street shuddered and quaked and was slick with rain, but nothing could slow his flight. Gloom shrouded him with its gray, friendless mantle, and he shrank to a tiny figure in the shadow of the city's ancient buildings, a speck of life caught up in a tangle of magic far older and harsher than his own. He saw Quickening's face before him. He felt her eyes watching as the Stiehl entered her body. He heard her sigh with relief.

Pe Ell fled through Eldwist as if possessed.

XXXI

Morgan Leah was the first to reach Quickening. He broke free of Walker with a strength that surprised the other, raced across the empty plaza as she tumbled to the stone, and caught her up almost before she was done falling. He knelt to hold her, turned her ashen face into his chest, and began whispering her name over and over again.

Walker Boh and Horner Dees hurried up from opposite sides, bent close momentarily, then exchanged a sober glance. The entire front of Quickening's shirt was soaked with her blood.

Walker straightened and peered through the gloom in the direction Pe Ell had gone. The assassin was already out of sight, gone into the maze of buildings and streets, fled back toward the isthmus and the cliffs beyond. Walker remembered the look he had seen on the other's face—a look filled with horror, disbelief, and rage. Killing Quickening clearly hadn't given him what he had been looking for.

"Walker!"

Morgan Leah's voice was a plea of desperation. Walker glanced down. "Help her! She's dying!"

Walker looked at the blood on her clothes, at the collapsed, broken body, at the face with its long hair spilled across the lovely features like a silver veil. *She's dying.* He whispered the words in the silence of his mind, marveling first that such a thing could be and second that he hadn't recognized much sooner its inevitability. He stared at the girl, as helpless and despairing as the Highlander, but beginning as well to catch a glimmer of understanding into the reason that it was happening.

"Walker, do something!" Morgan repeated, urgent, stricken.

"Highlander," Horner Dees said in response, taking hold of his shoulder gently. "What would you have him do?"

"What do you think I would have him do? Use his magic! Give her the same chance she gave him!"

Walker knelt. His voice was calm, low. "I can't, Morgan. I haven't the magic she needs." He reached out to touch the side of her throat, feeling for a pulse. It was there, faint, irregular. He could see her breathing. "She must do what she can to save herself."

Morgan stared at him momentarily, then began talking again to Quickening, urging her to wake, to speak to him. His words were jumbled, desperate, filled with need. The girl stirred sluggishly in response.

Walker looked again at Horner Dees. The old man shook his head slowly.

Then Quickening's eyes opened. They were clear and frightened, filled with pain. "Morgan," she whispered. "Pick me up. Carry me out of the city."

Morgan Leah, though he clearly thought to do otherwise, did not argue the matter. He lifted her effortlessly, carrying her as if she were weightless. He held her close against himself, infusing her with his warmth, whispering down to her as he went. Walker and Dees trailed after wordlessly. They moved across the plaza and into the street down which Pe Ell had fled.

"Stay back on the walkways," Walker cautioned hurriedly, and Morgan was quick to comply.

They had gone only a short distance when the earth began to rumble anew. All of Eldwist shook in response, the buildings cracking and splitting, shards of stone and clouds of dust tumbling down. Walker glanced back toward the heart of the city. The Maw Grint was moving again. Whatever the outcome of its confrontation with Uhl Belk, it had clearly decided on a new course of action. Perhaps it had put an end to its parent. Perhaps it had simply concluded that the Black Elfstone was more important. In any case, it was coming straight for them. Disdaining the use of its underground tunnels, it surged down the streets of Eldwist. Walls shattered and collapsed with its passing. The poison of its body spit wickedly. The air about it shimmered and steamed.

Those who remained of the company from Rampling Steep

began to run southward toward the isthmus, fighting to keep their balance as the earth beneath them shuddered and quaked. Trapdoors sprang open all about, jarred loose by the tremors, and the debris of the crumbling buildings littered the pathway at every turn. Behind them, the Maw Grint huffed and grunted with the urgency of its movements and came on. Despite having to carry Quickening, Morgan set an exhausting pace, and neither Walker nor Horner Dees could maintain it. The old Tracker had already fallen fifty paces back by the time they broke clear of the city, his breathing short and labored, his bulky form lurching as he struggled to keep up. Walker was between the two, his own chest constricting with pain, his legs heavy and weak. He yelled once at Morgan to slow him down, but the Highlander was deaf to him, the whole of his attention focused on the girl. Walker glanced back at Dees, at the trembling of the buildings where the Maw Grint passed, closer to them now than before, at the shadow the monster cast against the graying light. He did not think they would escape. He could not help reflecting on how ironic it was that they were going to be killed for something they no longer even had.

The moments lengthened impossibly as they fled, receding into the pounding of their boots on the stone. The waves crashed against the shores of the isthmus to either side, the spray washing across their heated faces. The rocks grew slippery, and they stumbled and tripped as they ran. The clouds darkened, and it began to rain again. Walker thought again of the look on Pe Ell's face when he had stabbed Quickening. He revised his earlier assessment. What he had seen there was surprise. Pe Ell hadn't been ready for her to die. Had he even wanted to use the Stiehl? There was something in the movements of the two immediately before the stabbing that was troubling. Why hadn't Quickening simply run? She had been free of him for an instant, yet had turned back. Into the blade? Deliberately? Walker shivered. Had she done more than stand there and wait? Had she actually shoved herself against Pe Ell?

His jumbled thoughts seemed to crystallize, freezing to ice. Shades! Was that why Pe Ell had been summoned? Pe Ell, the assassin with magic in his weapon, magic that nothing could withstand—was that why he was there?

Ahead of him, Morgan Leah reached the base of the cliffs and the pathway leading up from the isthmus. Without slowing, he began to climb.

Behind them, the Maw Grint appeared, its monstrous head

thrusting into view through the ruined buildings, lifting momentarily to test the air, then surging ahead. It oozed through the walls of the city like something without bones. It filled the whole of the isthmus with its bulk, hunching its way forward, a juggernaut of impossible size.

Walker scrambled up the pathway toward the summit of the cliffs, Horner Dees still lagging behind. He forced his thoughts of Quickening and Pe Ell aside. They made no sense. Why would Quickening want Pe Ell to kill her? Why would she want to die? There was no reason for any of it. He tried to concentrate on what he would do to slow the advance of the Maw Grint. He glanced back once more, watching the massive slug-thing work its way across the rock. Could he collapse the isthmus beneath it? No, the rock was too deep. The cliffs on top of it, then? No, again, it would simply tunnel its way free. Water would slow it, but all the water was behind them in the Tiderace. Nothing of Walker's magic or even Cogline's was strong enough to stop the Maw Grint. Running away was their only choice, and they could not run for long.

He reached the summit of the cliffs and found Morgan Leah waiting. The Highlander knelt gasping for breath on the ramp that overlooked the peninsula and Eldwist, his head lowered. Quickening was cradled in his arms, her eyes open and alert. Walker crossed to them and stopped. Quickening's face was chalk white.

Morgan Leah's eyes lifted. "She won't use her magic," he whispered in disbelief.

Walker knelt. "Save yourself, Quickening. You have the power."

She shook her head. Her black eyes glistened as they found Morgan's. "Listen to me," she said softly, her voice steady. "I love you. I will always love you and be with you. Remember that. Remember, too, that I would change things if I could. Now set me down and rise."

Morgan shook his head. "No, I want to stay with you . . ."

She touched him once on the cheek with her hand, and his voice trailed off, the sentence left hanging. Wordlessly, he laid her on the ground and backed away. There were tears running down his face.

"Take out your Sword, Morgan, and sheath it in the earth. Do so now."

Morgan drew out the Sword of Leah, gripped it in both hands, and jammed it into the rock. His hands remained tightly fixed about the hilt momentarily, then released.

He looked up slowly. "Don't die, Quickening," he said.

"Remember me," she whispered.

Horner Dees lumbered up beside Walker, panting. "What's going on?" he asked, bearded face close, rough voice hushed. "What's she doing?"

Walker shook his head. Her black eyes had shifted to find his. "Walker," she said, calling him.

He went to her, hearing the sounds of the Maw Grint advancing below, thinking they must run again, wondering like Dees what it was that she intended. He knelt beside her.

"Help me up," she said, her words quick and hurried, as if she sought to give voice to them while she still could. "Walk me to the edge of the cliffs."

Walker did not question what she asked. He put his arm about her waist and lifted her to her feet. She sagged against him weakly, her body shuddering. He heard Morgan cry out in protest, but a sudden glance from the girl silenced him. Walker held her up to keep her from falling as he maneuvered her slowly toward the drop. They reached the edge and stopped. Below, the Maw Grint hunched across the rock of the isthmus, an obscene cylinder of flesh, body rippling and poison oozing down. It was more than halfway to them now, its monstrous bulk steaming, the trail of its poison stretched back across the causeway to the city. Eldwist rose raggedly against the skyline, towers broken off, buildings split apart, walls crumbled and shattered. Dust and mist formed a screen against the dampness of the rain.

The dome where the Stone King made his lair stood intact.

Quickening turned and her face lifted. For an instant she was beautiful once more, as alive as she had been when she had brought Walker back from the dead, when she had restored his life and driven the poison of the Asphinx from his body. Walker caught his breath seeing her so, blinking against the momentary illusion. Her dark eyes fixed him.

"Dark Uncle," she whispered. "When you leave this place, when you go back into the world of the Four Lands, take with you the lessons you have learned here. Do not fight against yourself or what you might be. Simply consider your choices. Nothing is predetermined, Walker. We can always choose."

She reached up then and touched his face, her fingers cool against his cheek. Images flooded through him, her thoughts, her memories, and her knowledge. In an instant's time, she revealed herself completely, showing him the secrets she had kept hidden so carefully during the whole of their journey, the truth of who and what she was. He cried out as if he had been burned, staggered by what he saw. He clutched her tightly to him, and his pale face lowered into her hair in dismay.

Both Morgan and Horner Dees started forward, but Walker shouted for them to stand where they were. They stopped, hesitant, uncertain. Walker half-turned, still holding Quickening against him, his face an iron mask of concentration. He understood now; he understood everything.

"Walker." She spoke his name again. Her hand brushed him one final time, and a single image appeared.

It was the Grimpond's second vision.

Her eyes lifted to his. "Let me fall," she said softly.

He saw the vision clearly, himself standing at the summit of these cliffs with the Four Lands stretched out below and Quickening beside him, her black eyes beseeching as he shoved her away.

Here. Now. The vision come to pass.

He started to shake his head no, but her eyes stopped him, her gaze so intense it was threatening.

"Goodbye, Walker," she whispered.

He released her. He held her in the circle of his arm for just an instant more, then spun her away over the precipice. It was almost as if someone else was responsible, someone hidden inside himself, a being over which reason could not prevail. He heard Horner Dees gasp, horror-stricken. He heard Morgan scream out in disbelief. They rushed at him in a frenzy, grasped him roughly, and held him as Quickening tumbled away. They watched her fall, a small bundle of cloth with her silver hair streaming out behind her. They watched her shimmer.

Then, incredibly, she began to disintegrate. She came apart at the edges first, like fraying cloth, bits and pieces scattering away. Mute, awestruck, the three at the edge of the precipice stared downward as she disappeared. In seconds she was no more, her body turned to a dust that sparkled and shone as it was caught by the wind.

Below, the Maw Grint ceased its advance, its head lifting. Perhaps it knew what was about to happen; perhaps it even understood. It made no effort to escape, waiting patiently as the dust that had been Quickening settled over it. It shuddered then, cried out once, and began to shrink. It withered rapidly, its bulk shriveling away, disappearing back into the earth until nothing remained.

The dust blanketed the isthmus next and the rock began to change, turning green with grass and moss. Shoots sprang to life, vibrant and bright. The dust swept on, reaching the peninsula and Eldwist, and the transformation continued. Centuries of Uhl Belk's dark repression were undone in moments. The stone of the city crumbled—walls, towers, streets, and tunnels all collapsing. Everything gave way before the power of Quickening's magic, just as it had at the Meade Gardens in Culhaven. All that had existed before the Stone King had worked his change was brought to life again. Rocks shifted and reformed. Trees sprang up, gnarled limbs filled with summer leaves that shone against the gray skies and water. Patches of wildflowers bloomed, not in abundance as in Culhaven, for this had always been a rugged and unsettled place, but in isolated pockets, vibrant and rich. Sea grasses and scrub swept over the broken rock, changing the face of the land back into a coastal plain. The air came alive again, filled with the smell of growing things. The deadness of the land's stone armor faded into memory. Slowly, grudgingly, Eldwist sank from view, swallowed back into the earth, gone into the past that had given it birth.

When the transformation was complete, all that remained of Eldwist was the dome in which the Stone King had entombed himself—a solitary gray island amid the green of the land.

''There was nothing we could do to save her, Morgan,'' Walker Boh explained softly, bent close to the devastated Highlander to make certain he could hear. ''Quickening came to Eldwist to die.''

They were crouched down together at the edge of the cliffs, Horner Dees with them, speaking in hushed voices, as if the silence that had settled over the land in the aftermath of Quickening's transformation was glass that might shatter. Far distant, the roar of the Tiderace breaking against the shoreline and the cries of seabirds on the wing were faint and momentary. The magic had worked its way up the cliffs now and gone past them, cleansing the rock of the Maw Grint's poison, giving life back again to the land. Island breezes gusted at the clouds, forming breaks, and sunshine peeked through guardedly.

Morgan nodded wordlessly, his head purposefully lowered, his face taut.

Walker glanced at Horner Dees, who nodded encouragingly.

"She let me see everything, Highlander, just before she died. She wanted me to know, so that I could tell you. She touched me on the cheek as we stood together looking down at Eldwist, and everything was revealed. All the secrets she kept hidden from us. All of her carefully guarded mysteries."

He shifted a few inches closer. "Her father created her to counteract the magic of Uhl Belk. He made her from the elements of the Gardens where he lived, from the strongest of his magic. He sent her to Eldwist to die. In a sense, he sent a part of himself. He really had no other choice. Nothing less would be sufficient to overcome the Stone King in his own domain. And Uhl Belk had to be overcome there because he would never leave Eldwist—could not leave, in fact, although he didn't know it. He was already a prisoner of his own magic. The Maw Grint had become Uhl Belk's surrogate, dispatched in his stead to turn the rest of the Four Lands to stone. But if the King of the Silver River waited for the monster to get close enough to confront, it would have grown too huge to stop."

His hand came up to rest on Morgan's shoulder. He felt the other flinch. "She selected each of us for a purpose, Highlander—just as she said. You and I were chosen to regain possession of the Black Elfstone, stolen by Belk from the Hall of Kings. The problem Quickening faced, of course, was that her magic would not work while Uhl Belk controlled the Elfstone. As long as he could wield the Druid magic, he could siphon off her own magic and prevent the necessary transformation from taking place. He would have done so instantly if he had discovered who she was. He would have turned her to stone. That was why she couldn't use her magic until the very last."

"But she changed the Meade Gardens simply by touching the earth!" Morgan protested, his voice angry, defiant.

"The Meade Gardens, yes. But Eldwist was far too monstrous to change so easily. She could not have done so with a simple touching. She needed to infuse herself into the rock, to make herself a part of the land." Walker sighed. "That was why she chose Pe Ell. The King of the Silver River must have known or at least sensed that the Shadowen would send someone to try to stop Quickening. It was no secret who she was or how she could change things. She was a very real threat. She had to be eliminated. A Shadowen, it appears now, would lack the necessary means. So Pe Ell was sent instead. Pe Ell believed that his purpose was a secret, that killing Quickening was his own idea. It wasn't. Not ever. It was hers, right from the beginning. It was the reason she sought him out, because her father had told her to do so, to take with her to Eldwist the man and the weapon that could penetrate the armor of her magic and allow her to transform."

"Why couldn't she simply change by willing it?"

"She was alive, Morgan—as human as you and I. She was an elemental, but an elemental in human guise. I don't think she could be anything else in life. It was necessary for her to die before she could work her magic on Eldwist. No ordinary weapon could kill her; her body would protect her against common metals. It required magic equal to her own, the magic of a weapon like the Stiehl—and the hands and mind of an assassin like Pe Ell."

Walker's smile was brief, tight. "She summoned us to help her—because she was told to and because we were needed to serve a purpose, yes—but because she believed in us, too. If we had failed her, any of us, even Pe Ell, if we had not done what she knew we could do, Uhl Belk would have won. There would have been no transformation of the land. The Maw Grint would have continued its advance and Uhl Belk's kingdom would have continued to expand. Combined with the onslaught of the Shadowen, everything would have been lost."

Morgan straightened perceptibly, and his eyes finally lifted. "She should have told us, Walker. She should have let us know what she had planned."

Walker shook his head gently. "No, Morgan. That was exactly what she couldn't do. We would not have acted as we did had we known the truth. Tell me. Wouldn't you have stopped her? You were in love with her, Highlander. She knew what that meant."

Morgan stared at him tight-lipped for a moment, then nodded reluctantly. "You're right. She knew."

"There wasn't any other way. She had to keep her purpose in coming here a secret."

"I know. I know." Morgan's breathing was ragged, strained. "But it hurts anyway. I can almost believe she isn't gone, that she will find a way to come back somehow." He took a deep breath. "I need her to come back."

They were silent then, staring off in separate directions, remembering. Walker wondered momentarily if he should tell the other of the Grimpond's vision, of how he had spoken of that vision with Quickening yet she had brought him anyway, of how she must have known from the first how it would end yet had come nevertheless so that her father's purpose in creating her could be fulfilled. He decided against it. The Highlander had heard enough of secrets and hidden plans. There was nothing to be gained by telling him any more.

"What's become of Belk, do you think?" Horner Dees' rough voice broke the silence. "Is he still down there in that dome? Still alive?"

They looked as one over the cliff edge to where the last vestige of Eldwist sat amid the newborn green of the peninsula, closed about and secretive.

"I think a fairy creature like Uhl Belk does not die easily," Walker answered, his voice soft, introspective. "But Quickening holds him fast, a prisoner within a shell, and the land will not be changed to his liking again any time soon." He paused. "I think Uhl Belk might go mad when he understands that."

Morgan reached down tentatively and touched a patch of grass as if searching for something. His fingers brushed the blades gently. Walker watched him for a moment, then rose. His body ached, and his spirits were dark and mean. He was starved for real food, and his thirst seemed unquenchable. His own odyssey was just beginning, a trek back through the Four Lands in search of Pe Ell and the stolen Black Elfstone, a second confrontation to discover who should possess it, and if he survived all that, a journey to recover disappeared Paranor and the Druids . . .

His thoughts threatened to overwhelm him, to drain the last of his strength, and he shoved them away.

"Come, Highlander," Horner Dees urged, reaching down to take Morgan's shoulders. "She's gone. Be glad we had her for as long as we did. She was never meant to live in this world. She was meant for a better use. Take comfort in the fact that she loved you. That's no small thing."

The big hands gripped tight, and Morgan allowed himself to be pulled to his feet. He nodded without looking at the other. When his eyes finally lifted, they were hard and fixed. "I'm going after Pe Ell."

Horner Dees spat. "We're all going after him, Morgan Leah. All of us. He won't get away."

They took one final look down from the heights, then turned and began walking toward the defile that led back into the mountains. They had gone only a few steps when Morgan stopped suddenly, remembering, and looked over to where he had left the Sword of Leah. The Sword was still jammed into the rocks, its shattered blade buried from sight. Morgan hesitated a moment, almost as if thinking to leave the weapon where it was, to abandon it once and for all. Then he stepped over and fastened his hands on the hilt. Slowly, he began to pull. And kept pulling, far longer than he should have needed to.

The blade slid free. Morgan Leah stared. The Sword of Leah was no longer broken. It was as perfect as it had been on the day it had been given to him by his father.

"Highlander!" Horner Dees breathed in astonishment.

"She spoke the truth," Morgan whispered, letting his fingers slide along the blade's gleaming surface. He looked at Walker, incredulous. "How?"

"Her magic," Walker answered, smiling at the look on the other's face. "She became again the elements of the earth that were used by her father to create her, among them the metals that forged the blade of the Sword of Leah. She remade your talisman in the same way she remade this land. It was her final act, Highlander. An act of love."

Morgan's gray eyes burned fiercely. "In a sense then, she's still with me, isn't she? And she'll stay with me as long as I keep possession of the Sword." He took a deep breath. "Do you think the Sword has its magic back again, Walker?"

"I think that the magic comes from you. I think it always has."

Morgan studied him wordlessly for a moment, then nodded slowly. He sheathed his weapon carefully in his belt. "I have my Sword back, but there is still the matter of your arm. What of that? She said that you, like the blade, would be made whole again."

Walker thought carefully a moment, then pursed his lips. "Indeed." With his good hand, he turned Morgan gently toward the defile. "I am beginning to think, Highlander," he said softly, "that when she spoke of becoming whole, she was not referring to my arm, but to something else altogether."

Behind them, sunlight spilled down across the Tiderace.

Her eyes!

They stared down at Pe Ell from the empty windows of the buildings of Eldwist, and when he was free of the city they peered up from the fissures and clefts of the isthmus rock, and when he was to the cliffs they peeked out from behind the misted boulders of the trail leading up. Everywhere he ran, the eyes followed.

What have I done?

He was consumed with despair. He had killed the girl, just as he had intended; he had gained possession of the Black Elf-stone. Everything had gone exactly as planned. Except for the fact that the plan had never been his at all—it had been hers from the beginning. That was what he had seen in her eyes, the truth of why he was here and what he had been summoned to do. She had brought him to Eldwist not to face the Stone King and re-trieve the Black Elfstone as he had believed; she had brought him to kill her.

Shades, to kill her!

He ran blindly, stumbling, sprawling, clawing his way back to his feet, torn by the realization of how she had used him.

He had never been in control. He had merely deluded himself into thinking he was. All of his efforts had been wasted. She had manipulated him from the first—seeking him out in Cul-haven knowing who and what he was, persuading him to come with them while letting him think that he was coming because it was his choice, and keeping him carefully away from the others, turning him this way and that as her dictates required, using him! Why? Why had she done it? The question seared like fire. Why had she wanted to die?

The fire gave way to cold as he saw the eyes wink at him from left and right and all about. Had it even been his choice at the end to stab her? He couldn't remember making a conscious decision to do so. It had almost seemed as if she had impaled herself—or made his hand move forward those few necessary inches. Pe Ell had been a puppet for the daughter of the King of the Silver River all along; perhaps she had pulled the strings that moved him one final time—and then opened her eyes to him so that all her secrets could be his.

He tumbled to the ground when he reached the head of the cliff path, flinging himself into a cleft between the rocks, hud-dling down, burying his gaunt, ravaged face in his arms, wishing he could hide, could disappear. He clenched his teeth in fury. He hoped she was dead! He hoped they were all dead! Tears streaked his face, the anger and despair working through him, twisting him inside out. No one had ever done this to him. He could not stand what he was feeling! He could not tolerate it!

He looked up again, moments later, longer perhaps, aware suddenly that he was in danger, that the others would be coming in pursuit. Let them come! he thought savagely. But no, he was not ready to face them now. He could barely think. He needed time to recover himself.

He forced himself back to his feet. All he could think to do was run and keep running.

He reached the defile leading back through the cliffs, away from the ramp and any view of that hated city. He could feel tremors rock the earth and hear the rumble of the Maw Grint. Rain washed over him, and gray mist descended until it seemed the clouds were resting atop the land. Pe Ell clutched the leather bag with its rune markings and its precious contents close against his chest. The Stiehl rested once again in its sheath on his hip. He could feel the magic burning into his hands, against his thigh, hotter than he had ever felt it, fire that might never be quenched. What had the girl done to him? What had she done?

He fell, and for a moment was unable to rise. All the strength had left him. He looked down at his hands, seeing the blood that streaked them. Her blood.

Her face flashed before him out of the gloom, bright and vibrant, her silver hair flung back, her black eyes . . .

Quickening!

He managed to scramble back to his feet and ran faster still, slipping wildly, trying to fight against the visions, to regain his composure, his self-control. But nothing would settle into place, everything was jumbled and thrown about, madness loosed within him like a guard dog set free. He had killed her, yes. But she had made him do it, made him! All those feelings for her, false from the start, her creations, her twisting of him!

Bone Hollow opened before him, filled with rocks and emptiness. He did not slow. He ran on.

Something was happening behind him. He could feel a shifting of the tremors, a changing of the winds. He could feel something cold settling deep within. *Magic!* A voice whispered, teasing, insidious. *Quickening comes for you!* But Quickening was dead! He howled out loud, pursued by demons that all bore her face.

He stumbled and fell amid a scattering of bleached bones, shoved himself back to his knees, and realized suddenly where he was.

Time froze for Pe Ell, and a frightening moment of insight blossomed within.

The Koden!

Then, abruptly, it had him, its shaggy limbs enfolding him, its body smelling of age and decay. He could hear the whistle of its breath in his ear and could feel the heat of it on his face. The closeness of the beast was suffocating. He struggled to catch a glimpse of it and found he could not. It was there, and at the same time it wasn't. Had it somehow become invisible? He tried to reach for the handle of the Stiehl, but his fingers would not respond.

How could this be happening?

He knew suddenly that he was not going to escape. He was only mildly surprised to discover that he no longer cared.

An instant later, he was dead.

XXXII

L ess than an hour later the last three survivors of the company from Rampling Steep made their way into Bone Hollow and found Pe Ell's body. It lay midway through, sprawled loose and uncaring upon the earth, lifeless gaze fixed upon the distant sky. One hand clutched the rune-marked leather bag that contained the Black Elfstone. The Stiehl was still in its sheath.

Walker Boh glanced about curiously. Quickening's magic had worked its way through Bone Hollow, changing it so that it was no longer recognizable. Saw grass and jump weed grew everywhere in tufts that shaded and softened the hard surface of the rock. Patches of yellow and purple wildflowers bent to find the sun, and the bones of the dead had faded back into the earth. Nothing remained of what had been.

"Not a mark on him," Horner Dees muttered, his rough face creased further by the frown that bent his mouth, his voice wondering. He moved forward, bent down to take a close look, then straightened. "Neck might be broke. Ribs crushed. Something like that. But nothing that I can see. A little blood on his hands, but that belongs to the girl. And look. Koden tracks all around, everywhere. It had to have caught him. Yet there's not a mark on his body. How do you like that?''

There was no sign of the Koden. It was gone, disappeared as if it had never been. Walker tested the air, probed the silence, closed his eyes to see if he could find the Koden in his mind. No. Quickening's magic had set it free. As soon as the chains that bound it were broken, it had gone back into its old world, become itself again, a bear only, the memories of what had been done to it already fading. Walker felt a deep sense of satisfaction settle through him. He had managed to keep his promise after all.

"Look at his eyes, will you?'' Horner Dees was saying. "Look at the fear in them. He didn't die a happy man, whatever it was that killed him. He died scared.''

"It must have been the Koden,'' Morgan Leah insisted. He hung back from the body, unwilling to approach it.

Dees glanced pointedly at him. "You think so? How, then? What did it do, hug him to death? Must have done it pretty quick if it did. That knife of his isn't even out of its case. Take a look, Highlander. What do you see?''

Morgan stepped up hesitantly and stared down. "Nothing,'' he admitted.

"Just as I said.'' Dees sniffed. "You want me to turn him over, look there?''

Morgan shook his head. "No.'' He studied Pe Ell's face a moment without speaking. "It doesn't matter.'' Then his eyes lifted to find Walker's. "I don't know what to feel. Isn't that odd? I wanted him dead, but I wanted to be the one who killed him. I know it doesn't matter who did it or how it happened, but I feel cheated somehow. As if the chance to even things up had been taken away from me.''

"I don't think that's the case, Morgan,'' the Dark Uncle replied softly. "I don't think the chance was ever yours in the first place.''

The Highlander and the old Tracker stared at him in surprise. "What are you saying?'' Dees snapped.

Walker shrugged. "If I were the King of the Silver River and it was necessary for me to sacrifice the life of my child to an assassin's blade, I would make certain her killer did not escape.'' He shifted his gaze from one face to the other and back again. "Perhaps the magic that Quickening carried in her body was meant to serve more than one purpose. Perhaps it did.''

There was a long silence as the three contemplated the prospect. "The blood on his hands, you think?" Horner Dees said finally. "Like a poison?" He shook his head. "Makes as much sense as anything else."

Walker Boh reached down and carefully freed the bag with the Black Elfstone from Pe Ell's rigid fingers. He wiped it clean, then held it in his open palm for a moment, thinking to himself how ironic it was that the Elfstone would have been useless to the assassin. So much effort expended to gain possession of its magic and all for nothing. Quickening had known. The King of the Silver River had known. If Pe Ell had known as well, he would have killed the girl instantly and been done with the matter. Or would he have remained anyway, so captivated by her that even then he would not have been able to escape? Walker Boh wondered.

"What about this?" Horner Dees reached down and unstrapped the Stiehl from around Pe Ell's thigh. "What do we do with it?"

"Throw it into the ocean," Morgan said at once. "Or drop it into the deepest hole you can find."

It seemed to Walker that he could hear someone else speaking, that the words were unpleasantly familiar ones. Then he realized he was thinking of himself, remembering what he had said when Cogline had brought him the Druid History out of lost Paranor. Another time, another magic, he thought, but the dangers were always the same.

"Morgan," he said, and the other turned. "If we throw it away, we risk the possibility that it will be found again—perhaps by someone as twisted and evil as Pe Ell. Perhaps by someone worse. The blade needs to be locked away where no one can ever reach it again." He turned to Horner Dees. "If you give it to me, I will see that it is."

They stood there for a moment without moving, three worn and ragged figures in a field of broken stone and new green, measuring one another. Dees glanced once at Morgan, then handed the blade to Walker. "I guess we can trust you to keep your word as well as anyone," he offered.

Walker shoved the Stiehl and the Elfstone into the deep pockets of his cloak and hoped it was so.

They walked south the remainder of the day and spent their first night free of Eldwist on a barren, scrub-grown plain. A day earlier, the plain had been a part of Uhl Belk's kingdom, infected by the poison of the Maw Grint, a broken carpet of stone. Even with nothing more than the scrub to brighten its expanse, it felt lush and comforting after the deadness of the city. There was little to eat yet, a few roots and wild vegetables, but there was fresh water again, the skies were star filled, and the air was clean and new. They made a fire and sat up late, talking in low voices of what they were feeling, remembering in the long silences what had been.

When morning came they awoke with the sun on their faces, grateful simply to be alive.

They traveled down again through the high forests and crossed into the Charnals. Horner Dees took them a different way this time, carefully avoiding dead Carisman's tribe of Urdas, journeying east of the Spikes. The weather stayed mild, even in the mountains, and there were no storms or avalanches to cause them further grief. Food was plentiful again, and they began to regain their strength. A sense of well-being returned, and the harshest of their memories softened and faded.

Morgan Leah spoke often of Quickening. It seemed to help him to speak of her, and both Walker and Horner Dees encouraged him to do so. Sometimes the Highlander talked as if she were still alive, touching the Sword he carried, and gesturing back to the country they were leaving behind. She was there, he insisted, and better that she were there than gone completely. He could sense her presence at times; he was certain of it. He smiled and joked and slowly began to return to himself.

Horner Dees became his old self almost as quickly, the haunted look fading from his eyes, the tension disappearing from his face. The gruffness in his voice lost its edge, and for the first time in weeks the love he bore for his mountains began to work its way back into his conversation.

Walker Boh recovered more slowly. He was encased in an iron shell of fatalistic resignation that had stripped his feelings nearly bare. He had lost his arm in the Hall of Kings. He had lost Cogline and Rumor at Hearthstone. He had nearly lost his life any number of times. Carisman was dead. Quickening was dead. His vow to refuse the charge that Allanon had given him was dead. Quickening had been right. There were always choices. But sometimes the choices were made for you, whether you wanted it so or not. He might have thought not to be ensnared by Druid machinations, to turn his life away from Brin Ohmsford and her legacy of magic. But circumstances and conscience made that all but impossible. His was a destiny woven by threads that stretched back in time hundreds, perhaps thousands, of years, and he could not be free of them, not entirely, at least. He had thought the matter through since that night in Eldwist when he had agreed to return with Quickening to the lair of the Stone King in an effort to recover the Black Elfstone. He knew that by going he was agreeing that if they were successful he would carry the talisman back into the Four Lands and attempt to restore Paranor and the Druids—just as Allanon had charged him.

He knew without having to speak the words what that meant.

Make whatever choice you will, Quickening had advised.

But what choices were left to him? He had determined long ago to search out the Black Elfstone—perhaps from the moment he had first discovered its existence while reading the Druid History; certainly from the time of the death of Cogline. He had determined as well to discover what its magic would do—and that meant testing Allanon's charge that Paranor and the Druids could be restored. He might argue that he had been considering the matter right up until the moment Eldwist had met its end. But he knew the truth was otherwise. He knew as well that if the magic of the Black Elfstone was everything that had been promised, if it worked as he believed, then Paranor would be restored. And if that happened, then the Druids would come back into the Four Lands.

Through him.

Beginning with him.

And that reality provided the only choice left to him, the one he believed Quickening had wanted him to make—the choice of who he would be. If it was true that Paranor could be restored and that he must become the first of the Druids who would keep it, then he must make certain he did not lose himself in the process. He must make certain that Walker Boh survived—his heart, his ideas, his convictions, his misgivings—everything he was and believed. He must not evolve into the very thing he had struggled so hard to escape. He must not, in other words, turn into Allanon. He must not become like the Druids of old— manipulators, exploiters, dark and secretive conjurers, and hiders of truths. If the Druids must return in order to preserve the Races, in order to ensure their survival against the dark things of the world, Shadowen or whatever, then he must make them as they should be—a better order of Men, of teachers, and of givers of the power of magic.

That was the choice he could still make—a choice he must make if he were to keep his sanity.

It took them almost two weeks to reach Rampling Steep, choosing the longer, safer routes, skirting any possibility of danger, sheltering when it was dark, and emerging to travel on when it was light. They came on the mountainside town toward midday, the skies washed with a gray, cloudy haze left by a summer shower that suggested spun cotton pulled apart by too-anxious hands. The day was warm and humid, and the buildings of the town glistened like damp, squat toads hunched down against the rocks. The three travelers approached as strangers, seeing the town anew, the first since Eldwist. They slowed as one as they entered the solitary street that navigated the gathering of taverns, stables, and trading stores to either side, pausing to look back into the mountains they had descended, watching momentarily as the runoff from the storm churned down out of the cliffs into gullies and streams, the sound a distant rush.

"Time to say goodbye," Horner Dees announced without preliminaries and stuck out his hand to Morgan.

Morgan stared. There had been no talk of his leaving until now. "You're not coming on with us?"

The old Tracker snorted. "I'm lucky to be alive, Highlander. Now you want me to come south? How far do you expect me to push things?"

Morgan stammered. "I didn't mean . . ."

"Fact is, I shouldn't have gone with you the first time." The other cut him short with a wave of one big hand. "It was the girl who talked me into it. Couldn't say no to her. And maybe it was the sense of having left something behind when I fled the Stone King and his monsters ten years ago. I had to go back to find it again. So here I am, the only man to have escaped Eldwist and Uhl Belk twice. Seems to me that's enough for one old man."

"You would be welcome to come with us, Horner Dees," Walker Boh assured him, taking Morgan's part. "You're not as old as you pretend and twice as able. The Highlander and his friends can use your experience."

"Yes, Horner," Morgan agreed hurriedly. "What about the Shadowen? We need you to help fight them. Come with us."

But the old Tracker shook his bearish head stubbornly. "Highlander, I'll miss you. I owe you my life. I look at you and see the son I might have had under other circumstances. Now isn't that something to admit? But I've had enough excitement in my life and I'm not anxious for any more. I need the dark quiet of the ale houses. I need the comforts of my own place."

He stuck out his hand once again. "Who's to say that won't change though? So. Some other time, maybe?"

Morgan clasped the hand in his own. "Any time, Horner." Then, forsaking the hand, he embraced the old man. Horner Dees hugged him back.

The journey went swiftly after that, time slipping away almost magically, the days and nights passing like quicksilver. Walker and Morgan came down out of the Charnals into the foothills south and turned west along their threshold toward the Rabb. They forded the north branch of the river and the land opened into grasslands that stretched away toward the distant peaks of the Dragon's Teeth. The days were long and hot, the sun burning out of cloudless skies as the intemperate weather of the mountains was left behind. Sunrise came early, and daylight stayed late, and even the nights were warm and bright. The pair encountered few travelers and no Federation patrols. The land grew increasingly infected by the Shadowen sickness, dark patches that hinted at the spread of the disease, but there was no sign of the carriers.

At week's end, the Dark Uncle and the Highlander reached the south entrance to the Jannisson Pass. It was nearing noon, and the pass stretched away through the juncture of the cliffs of the Dragon's Teeth and the Charnals, a broad empty corridor leading north to the Streleheim. It was here that Padishar Creel had hoped to rally the forces of the Southland Movement, the Dwarf Resistance, and the Trolls of Axhind and his Kelktic Rock in an effort to confront and destroy the armies of the Federation. The wind blew gently across the flats and down through the pass, and no one stirred.

Morgan Leah cast about wearily, a resigned look on his face. Walker stood silently beside him for a moment, then put his hand on the other's shoulder. "Where to now, Highlander?" he asked softly.

Morgan shrugged and smiled bravely. "South, I suppose, to Varfleet. I'll try to make contact with Padishar, hope that he's found Par and Coll. If that fails, I'll go looking for the Valemen on my own." He paused, studying the other's hard, pale face. "I guess I know where you're going."

Walker nodded. "To find Paranor."

Morgan took a deep breath. "I know this isn't what you wanted, Walker."

"No, it isn't."

"I could come with you, if you'd like."

"No, Highlander, you've done enough for others. It is time to do something for yourself."

Morgan nodded. "Well, I'm not afraid, if that's what you're thinking. I have the magic of the Sword of Leah again. I might be of some use."

Walker's fingers tightened on the other's shoulder and then dropped away. "I don't think anyone can help me where I'm going. I think I have to help myself as best I can. The Elfstone will likely be my best protection." He sighed. "Strange how things work out. If not for Quickening, neither of us would be doing what he is or even be who he is, would he? She's given us both a new purpose, a new face, maybe even a new strength. Don't forget what she gave up for you, Morgan. She loved you. I think that in whatever way she is able she always will."

"I know."

"Horner Dees said you saved his life. You saved my life as well. If you hadn't used the Sword, even broken as it was, Uhl Belk would have killed me. I think Par and Coll Ohmsford could ask for no better protector. Go after them. See that they are well. Help them in any way you can."

"I will."

They clasped hands and held tight for a moment, eyes locked.

"Be careful, Walker," Morgan said.

Walker's smile was faint and ironic. "Until we meet again, Morgan Leah."

Then Walker turned and walked into the pass, angling through sunlight into shadow as the rocks closed about. He did not look back.

For the remainder of that day and the whole of the one following Walker Boh traveled west across the Streleheim, skirting the dark, ancient forests that lay south, cradled by the peaks of the Dragon's Teeth. On the third day he turned down, moving into the shadowed woods, leaving the plains and the sunshine behind. The trees were massive, towering sentinels set at watch like soldiers waiting to be sent forth into battle, thick trunks grown close in camaraderie, and limbs canopied against the light. These were the forests that for centuries past had sheltered the Druid's Keep against the world beyond. In the time of Shea Ohmsford there had been wolves set at watch. Even after, there had been a wall of thorns that none could penetrate but Allanon himself. The wolves were gone now, the wall of thorns as well, and even the Keep itself. Only the trees remained, wrapped in a deep, pervasive silence.

Walker navigated the trails as if he were a shadow, passing soundlessly through the sea of trunks, across the carpet of dead needles, lost in the roil of his increasing indecision. His thoughts of what he was about to do were jumbled and rough-edged, and whispers of uncertainty that he had thought safely put to rest had risen to haunt him once again. All his life he had fought to escape Brin Ohmsford's legacy; now he was rushing willingly to embrace it. His decision to do so had been long in coming and repeatedly questioned. It had resulted from an odd mix of circumstance, conscience, and deliberation. He had given it as much thought as he was capable of giving and he was convinced that he had chosen right. But the prospect of its consequences was terrifying nevertheless, and the closer he came to discovering them, the deeper grew his misgivings.

By the time he arrived at the heart of the forests and the bluff on which Paranor had once rested, he was in utter turmoil. He stood for a long time staring upward at the few stone blocks that remained of what had once been the outbuildings, at the streaking of red light across the bluff's crest where the sunset cast its heated, withering glow. In the shimmer of the dying light he could imagine it was possible to see Paranor rise up against the coming night, its parapets sharply defined and its towers piercing the sky's azure crown like spears. He could feel the immensity of the Keep's presence, the sullen bulk of its stone. He could touch the life of its magic, waiting to be reborn.

He built a fire and sat before it, awaiting the descent of night. When it was fully dark, he rose and walked again to the bluff's edge. The stars were pinpricks of brightness overhead, and the woods about him were anxious with night sounds. He felt foreign and alone. He stared upward once more at the crest of the rise, probing from within with his magic for some sign of what waited. Nothing revealed itself. Yet the Keep was there; he could sense its presence in a way that defied explanation. The fact that his magic failed to substantiate what he already knew made him even more uneasy. Bring back lost Paranor and the Druids, Allanon had said. What would it take to do so? What beyond possession of the Black Elfstone? There would be more, he knew. There would have to be.

He slept for a few hours, though sleep did not come easily, a frail need against the whisper of his fears. He lay awake at first, his resolve slipping away, eroded and breached. The trappings of a lifetime's mistrust ensnared him, working free of the restraints under which he had placed them, threatening to take control of him once again. He forced himself to think of Quickening. What must it have been like for her, knowing what she was expected to do? How frightened she must have been! Yet she had sacrificed herself because that was what was needed to give life back to the land. He took strength in remembering her courage, and after a time the whispers receded again, and he fell asleep.

It was already daybreak when he awoke, and he washed and ate quickly, woodenly, anxious in the shadow of what waited. When he was done he walked again to the base of the bluff and stared upward. The sun was behind him, and its light spilled down upon the bluff's barren summit. Nothing had changed. No hint of what had been or what might be revealed itself. Paranor remained lost in time and space and legend.

Walker stepped away, returning to the edge of the trees, safely back from the bluff. He reached into the deep pockets of his cloak and lifted free the pouch that contained the Black Elfstone. He stared blankly at it, feeling the weight of its power press against him. His body was stiff and sore; his missing arm ached. His throat was as dry as autumn leaves. He felt the insecurities, doubts, and fears begin to rise within him, massing in a wave that threatened to wash him away.

Quickly, he dumped the Elfstone into his open palm.

He closed his hand instantly, frightened to look into its dark light. His mind raced. One Stone, one for all, one for heart, mind, and body—made that way, he believed, because it was the antithesis of all the other Elfstones created by the creatures of the old world of faerie, a magic that devoured rather than expended, one that absorbed rather than released. The Elfstones that Allanon had given to Shea Ohmsford were a talisman to defend their holder against whatever dark magic threatened. But the Black Elfstone was created for another reason entirely—not to defend, but to enable. It was conceived for a single purpose— to counteract the magic that had been called forth to spirit away the Druid's Keep, to bring lost Paranor out of limbo again. It would do so by consuming that magic—and transferring it into the body of the Stone's holder—himself. What that would do to him, Walker could only imagine. He knew that the Stone's protection against misuse lay in the fact that it would work the same way no matter who wielded it and for what purpose. That was what had destroyed Uhl Belk. His absorption of the Maw Grint's

magic had turned him to stone. Walker's own fate might be
similar, he believed—yet it would also be more complex. But
how? If use of the Black Elfstone restored Paranor, then what
would be the consequence of transference to himself of the magic
that bound the Keep?

*Whosoever shall have cause and right shall wield it to its
proper end.*

Himself. Yet why? Because Allanon had decreed that it must
be so? Had Allanon told the truth? Or simply a part of the truth?
Or was he gamesplaying once more? What could Walker Boh
believe?

He stood there, solitary, filled with indecision and dread,
wondering what it was that had brought him to this end. He saw
his hand begin to shake.

Then suddenly, unexpectedly, the whispers broke through his
defenses in a torrent and turned to screams.

No!

He brought the Black Elfstone up almost without thinking,
opened his hand, and thrust the dark gem forth.

Instantly the Elfstone flared to life, its magic a sharp tingling
against his skin. Black light—the nonlight, the engulfing darkness. *Whosoever.* He watched the light gather before him, building on itself. *Shall have cause and right.* The backlash of the
magic rushed through him, shredding doubt and fear, silencing
whispers and screams, filling him with unimaginable power.
Shall wield it to its proper end.

Now!

He sent the black light hurtling forth, a huge tunnel burrowing through the air, swallowing everything in its path, engulfing
substance and space and time. It exploded against the crest of
the empty bluff, and Walker was hammered back as if struck a
blow by an invisible fist. Yet he did not fall. The magic rushed
through him, bracing him, wrapping him in armor. The black
light spread like ink against the sky, rising, broadening, angling
first this way, then that, channeling itself as if there were runnels
to be followed, gutters down which it must flow. It began to
shape. Walker gasped. The light of the Black Elfstone was etch-
ing out the lines of a massive fortress, its parapets and battlements, and its towers and steeples. Walls rose and gates
appeared. The light spread higher against the skies, and the
sunlight was blocked away. Shadows cast down by the castle
enveloped Walker Boh, and he felt himself disappear into them.

Something inside him began to change. He was draining away.

No, rather he was filling up! Something, the magic, was washing through. *The other*, he thought, weak before its onslaught, helpless and suddenly terrified. It was the magic that encased lost Paranor being drawn down into the Elfstone!

And into him.

His jaw clenched, and his body went rigid. *I will not give way!*

The black light flooded the empty spaces of the image atop the bluff, coloring it, giving it first substance and then life—Paranor, the Druid's Keep, come back into the world of men, returned from the dark half-space that had concealed it all these years. It rose up against the sky, huge and forbidding. The Black Elfstone dimmed in Walker's hand; the nonlight softened and then disappeared.

Walker's hoarse cry ended in a groan. He fell to his knees, wracked with sensations he could not define and riddled with the magic he had absorbed, feeling it course through him as if it were his blood. His eyes closed and then slowly opened. He saw himself shimmering in a haze that stole away the definition of his features. He looked down in disbelief, then felt himself go cold. He wasn't really there anymore! He had become a wraith!

He forced his terror aside and climbed back to his feet, the Black Elfstone still clutched in his hand. He watched himself move as if he were someone else, watched the shimmer of his limbs and body and the shadings that overlapped and gave him the appearance of being fragmented. *Shades, what has been done to me!* He stumbled forward, scrambling to gain the bluff, to reach its crest, not knowing what else to do. He must gain Paranor, he sensed. He must get inside.

The climb was long and rugged, and he was gasping for breath by the time he reached the Keep's iron gates. His body reflected in a multitude of images, each a little outside of the others. But he could breathe and move as a normal man; he could feel as he had before. He took heart from that, and hastened to reach Paranor's gates. The stone of the Keep was real enough, hard and rough to his touch—yet forbidding, too, in a way he could not immediately identify. The gates opened when he leaned into them, as if he had the strength of a thousand men and could force anything that stood before him.

He entered cautiously. Shadows enfolded him. He stood in a well of darkness, and there was a whisper of death all about.

Then something moved within the gloom, detached, and took

shape—a four-legged apparition, hulking and ominous. It was a moor cat, black as pitch with luminous gold eyes, there and not there, like Walker himself.

Walker froze. The moor cat looked exactly like . . .

Behind the cat, a man appeared, old and stooped, a translucent ghost, shimmering. As the man drew near, his features became recognizable.

"At last you've come, Walker," he whispered in an anxious, hollow voice.

The Dark Uncle felt the last vestiges of his resolve fade away. The man was Cogline.

XXXIII

*T*he King of the Silver River sat in the Gardens that were his sanctuary and watched the sun melt into the western horizon. A stream of clear water trickled across the rocks at his feet and emptied into a pond from which a unicorn drank, and a breeze blew softly through the maidenhair, carrying the scent of lilacs and jonquils. The trees rustled, their leaves a shimmer of green, and birds sang contented day-end songs as they settled into place in preparation for the coming of night.

Beyond, in the world of Men, the heat was sullen and unyielding against the fall of darkness, and a pall of weariness draped the lives of the people of the Four Lands.

So must it be for now.

The eyes that could see everything had seen the death of his child and the transformation of the land of the Stone King. The Maw Grint was no more. The city of Eldwist had gone back into the earth, returned to the elements that had created it, and the land was green and fertile again. The magic of his child was rooted deep, a river that flowed invisibly about the solitary dome in which Uhl Belk was imprisoned. It would be long before his brother could emerge into the light again.

Iridescent dragonflies buzzed past him without slowing and disappeared into the twilight's glow.

Elsewhere, the battle against the Shadowen went on. Walker Boh had invoked the magic of the Black Elfstone, as Allanon had charged him, and the Druid's Keep had been summoned out of the mists that had hidden it for three centuries. What would the Dark Uncle make, the King of the Silver River wondered, of what he found there? West, where the Elves had once lived, Wren Ohmsford continued her search to discover what had become of them—and, more important, though she did not yet realize it, what would become of herself. North, the brothers Par and Coll Ohmsford struggled toward each other and the secrets of the Sword of Shannara and the Shadowen magic. There were those who would help and those who would betray, and all of the wheels of chance that Allanon had set in motion could yet be stopped.

The King of the Silver River rose and slipped into the waters of the pond momentarily, reveling in the cool wetness, letting himself become one with the flow. Then he emerged and passed down the Garden pathways, through stands of juniper and hemlock onto a hillock of centauries and bluebells that reflected gold about the edges of their petals with the day's fading light. He paused there, staring out again into the world beyond.

His daughter had done well, he reflected.

But the thought was strangely bleak and empty. He had created an elemental out of the life of his Gardens and sent that elemental forth to serve his needs. She had been nothing to him—a daughter in name only, a child merely by designation. She had been only a momentary reality, and he had never intended that she be anything more.

Yet he missed her. Shaping her as he did, breathing his life into her, he had brought himself too close. The human feelings they had shared would not dissolve as easily as their human forms. She should have meant nothing to him, now that she was gone. Instead, her absence formed a void he could not seem to fill.

Quickening.

A child of the elements and his magic, he repeated. He would do the same again—yet perhaps not so readily. There was something in the ways of the creatures of the mortal Races that endured beyond the leaving of the flesh. There was a residue of their emotions that lingered. He could still hear her voice, see her face, and feel the touch of her fingers against him. She was gone from him, yet remained.

Why should it be so?

He sat there as darkness cloaked the land and wondered at himself.

Here ends Book Two of *The Heritage of Shannara*. Book Three, *The Elf Queen of Shannara*, will reveal more of the mystery of Cogline and Paranor and chronicle the efforts of Wren Ohmsford to discover what has become of the missing Westland Elves.

Don't miss one exciting installment of the
Magic Kingdom of Landover series!

Find out which Terry Brooks
novel you need...

MAGIC KINGDOM
FOR SALE—SOLD!

Landover was a genuine magic kingdom, with
fairy folk and wizardry, just as the advertise-
ment had promised. But after he purchased
it, Ben Holiday learned that there were a few
details left out.

The kingdom was in ruin. The Barons
refused to recognize a king, and the peasants
were without hope. A dragon was laying
waste the countryside while an evil witch
plotted to destroy everything.

The task of proving his right to be King
seemed hopeless. But Ben Holiday was not
about to give up...

MAGIC KINGDOM FOR SALE—SOLD!
Book One of *The Magic Kingdom of Landover*
by Terry Brooks
Published by Del Rey® Books.
Available in your local bookstore.

THE BLACK
UNICORN

A year had passed since Ben Holiday had
bought the Magic Kingdom from the wizard
Meeks, who had set a series of pitfalls against
him. Troubled by dreams of disaster to his
former partner, Miles Bennett, Ben had
traveled to Earth. But unknown to Ben, the
dreams had been a trap set by Meeks, who
then returned to the Magic Kingdom as a tiny
insect hidden in Ben's clothing and cast a spell
to switch appearances with him. Soon Ben
became an outcast, no longer recognized by
any friend. Of course, there was the prism
cat, whatever that was… And where was
Willow—and the mysterious black unicorn
she had set out to find?

THE BLACK UNICORN
Book Two of *The Magic Kingdom of Landover*
by Terry Brooks
Published by Del Rey® Books.
Available in your local bookstore.

WIZARD AT LARGE

It all began when the half-able wizard Questor Thews announced that, finally, he could restore the Court Scribe Abernathy to human form. It was his spell that had turned Abernathy into a Wheaten Terrier—though with hands and the ability to talk.

All went well—until the wizard breathed in the magic dust of his spell and suddenly sneezed. Then, where Abernathy stood, there was only a bottle containing a particularly evil imp.

High Lord Ben Holiday set forth for Earth, but without the soil of Landover in which to root as a tree at times, Willow could not long survive.

That left it up to Questor Thews to save them. And to make matters worse, the imp had escaped…

WIZARD AT LARGE
Book Three of *The Magic Kingdom of Landover*
by Terry Brooks
Published by Del Rey® Books.
Available in your local bookstore.

THE TANGLE
BOX

Everything should have been quiet and
pleasant for Ben Holiday, former Chicago
lawyer become sovereign of the Magic
Kingdom of Landover. But it wasn't.

Horris Kew, conjurer, confidence man, and
trickster, had returned to Landover from Ben's
own world, sent by the Gorse, a sorcerer of
great evil, whom Horris had unwittingly freed
from the magic Tangle Box. Now it had
returned to enslave those who had once
dared condemn it. But first it would rid
Landover of all who could stand in its way...

THE TANGLE BOX
Book Four of *The Magic Kingdom of Landover*
by Terry Brooks
Published by Del Rey® Books.
Available in your local bookstore.

WITCHES' BREW

Former Chicago lawyer Ben Holiday was proud and happy. And why not? The Magic Kingdom of Landover, which he ruled as High Lord, was finally at peace, and he and his wife, the sylph Willow, could watch their daughter Mistaya grow.

Ben's idyll was interrupted when Rydall, a king of lands beyond the fairy mist, threatened to invade unless Ben met his challenge. But Ben could not refuse, for Mistaya had been snatched from her guardians by foul magic. And Rydall held the key to her fate…

WITCHES' BREW
Book Five of *The Magic Kingdom of Landover*
by Terry Brooks
Published by Del Rey® Books.
Available in your local bookstore.